Someone To Love

Book 1 of the Lost Girls Trilogy

CHERYL HOLT

Praise for *New York Times* Bestselling Author
CHERYL HOLT

BOOKS BY CHERYL HOLT

Cover Design: Angela Waters
Paperback Design & eBook Formatting: Dayna Linton • Day Agency • www.dayagency.com

Someone
To Love

Prologue

"Oh, my. Would you look at that?"

Libby cowered in the traveling trunk where she'd been hiding, determined to make herself as small as possible. She'd shut her eyes, yearning to be invisible, but it hadn't worked. The man who was looming over her could definitely see her.

He was wearing a uniform, so he appeared very large and very important. There were gold buttons on the front of his blue coat, and he had a belt with a big knife dangling on one hip and a big gun dangling on the other.

"Out with you now," he said, but she simply stared up at him, wondering if she could jump out and escape.

In the time she'd been living on the deserted island, the few adults who'd been stranded with her had constantly advised her to watch out for bad men, but how was she supposed to know if he was bad or not? How was she supposed to know if she could trust him?

The adults had all passed away, so she had no one to answer those questions. She was only five, and it was frightening to have to decide so many issues on her own.

She peeked over the edge of the trunk, wishing Caroline and Joanna would be standing there. When the man's ship had dropped anchor out in the bay, when the sailors had rowed to shore in their longboat, the sight had been so alarming that her two friends had run into the jungle.

Libby was smarter than Caroline and Joanna, so she'd assumed the traveling trunk was a better spot to hide. She'd been wrong though. The man had entered their dilapidated hut and opened it almost immediately.

What should she do? She was tired and hungry and anxious for him to help them. Tears welled into her eyes, which she hated. She wasn't a baby, and she'd been told repeatedly that she had to stop acting like one.

"Let's go, you adorable moppet," the man said, and when she didn't move, he reached down and lifted her out.

The instant her feet touched the ground, she tried to bolt out the door to freedom, but he was too quick for her. He grabbed her arm, and though she wrestled and kicked, she couldn't get away.

"Hold on, missy, just hold on."

He continued to talk, offering calming words until she was too fatigued to keep fighting him. Once her skirmishing ceased, he knelt down and asked, "What's your name?"

She scowled forever, debating whether to admit it. Her mother had warned her over and over that she should never confess it to anyone. It was a powerful secret, and if wicked people learned who she was, they'd take her away. Even though her mother had to be dead, the admonition still resonated.

The man recognized her consternation. "You can tell me what it is. Don't be afraid."

She debated a bit more, then said, "It's Libby."

"Libby . . . what?"

"Libby Carstairs."

"Hello, Miss Libby. I'm Captain Ralston. Is your mother or father with you?"

"No."

"Where are they?"

"I don't know."

"Do you have any idea what happened to them?"

"I think they drowned."

"Were you on a ship? Did it sink?"

"Yes. In a storm."

"I'm betting that was scary. Did you swim to shore?"

"I don't remember."

She thought she'd swum though. She had terrifying dreams of huge waves, dark water, angry clouds, and wind. For ages afterward, the palms of her hands had been sore and blistered, and she recalled gripping a piece of wood, loud voices shouting at her not to let go of it, and she hadn't.

The Captain glanced around the hut, assessing the crude beds, the ramshackle construction. They'd carried on the best they could with what they'd had, but it hadn't been much.

"Are there any adults with you?"

"No."

"Were there some in the beginning?"

"Yes."

"How many?"

"There were six, but they died."

"How?"

"They were hurt."

"When the ship sank?"

"Yes. Then they got sick."

"How long have you been here?"

She leaned in so they were nose to nose. "For a really, really long time."

She didn't have a number to explain how many days it had been. At first, Joanna's mother had survived with them, and she'd counted to eighty-five, but after she'd cut her leg on a tree stump and had passed away, they'd lost track.

"Gad, but aren't you pretty?" he murmured. "You'll break some hearts when you grow up."

"That's what my papa always said."

"Your papa was right."

He stood and patted the top of her head, and the gesture made her feel safer. She didn't think he was a bad man, so he might agree to fix what was wrong.

"What was your papa's name, peanut?" he asked her.

"Papa?"

He snorted at that. "What about your mother?"

"Mama?" She frowned and posed a question that had been vexing her. "Could you find them for me? If they didn't drown, I'm worried they might be searching for me, but they don't know where I am."

"I will assist you as much as I can, but you shouldn't hope we'll locate your parents. I'm sorry, but I doubt you'll see them ever again."

"Maybe in Heaven someday?"

"Maybe in Heaven."

He sighed, and from outside, a sailor called, "Captain, would you come out? I have a surprise to show you."

On being summoned, he walked out, but he kept a hand on Libby's shoulder so she couldn't flee, but she'd decided she wouldn't. He appeared incredibly commanding to her, so he'd be able to tell her what should occur next.

Perhaps she could go home to England. She'd been happy there. At least she *thought* she'd been happy. She seemed to recollect a large mansion, a kind nanny, and a pony.

The sailor had stumbled on Caroline and Joanna where they'd been crouched in the foliage. Caroline shrugged at Libby, as if to admit their plan to hide in the jungle had been stupid.

Libby supposed they were a fearsome sight. Their hair was long and tangled, bleached blond from the hot sun, their dresses bleached too, the fabric worn thin and faded to white. They were barefoot, their skin bronzed, their condition bedraggled.

"Look what I found," the sailor said to the Captain. He indicated Caroline and Joanna. "They're all alone, and apparently, they've been living like a pack of wild animals."

"No, we haven't!" Libby furiously insisted. "We have a hut and everything."

The sailor ignored her and addressed the Captain. "They're like a trio of abandoned wolf pups."

"We had mothers!" Libby huffed. "It's not our fault that they died."

But she was ignored again.

"Are there any others?" the Captain asked the sailor.

"Not that we saw."

The Captain peered down at her. "Is it just the three of you? And don't lie to me. This is important."

"There's just us three," Libby said.

"Lord almighty," he muttered as he led Libby over to Caroline and Joanna. "Will you introduce me to your companions?"

"This is Caroline"—Libby pointed to her—"and this is Joanna."

"Are you sisters?" he asked.

"No."

"None of you?"

"No. We're like sisters though," Libby told him. "We're closer than sisters."

"I'm sure you are."

The Captain studied their surroundings. The sky was so blue, the ocean a brilliant turquoise color, the sand blazing under the sun's unrelenting rays. The palm trees swayed but provided no real shade.

"What shall we do with them, Captain?" the sailor inquired.

The Captain grimaced with disgust. "It's beyond me. We'll convey them to the nearest port, and the authorities can figure it out."

"Shouldn't I stay here?" Libby asked. "What if my parents come for me?"

The Captain and the sailor exchanged a tormented glance, then the Captain said, "Trust me, Miss Libby, they won't come. Now then, are there any items you'd like to take with you? Have you any dolls or clothes or other mementoes you'd like to bring?"

"No, I don't have anything," Libby said.

"That's the saddest comment I ever heard." He spun to Caroline and Joanna. "How about you two girls? Are there things you'd like to take?"

They shook their heads, not keen to talk to him. It seemed like a dream, as if they would eventually wake up and the day would glide along as all the other days had glided along since they'd arrived.

"There's no reason to linger then," the Captain said, and he motioned to the longboat. "Let's get you out to the ship."

Libby blanched with dismay. "I won't go on a ship! None of us will go on a ship ever again!"

"It's all right," the Captain said. "Mine won't sink."

"It's what Mother claimed about the last one, but it wasn't true."

"I'll make it true," the Captain firmly stated, "and you have to be very brave, so Caroline and Joanna will watch you and realize how to be very brave too. Can you do that for me?"

"I guess," she grudgingly replied.

He picked her up and balanced her on his hip. She couldn't remember an adult picking her up before. And she was five, so she wasn't exactly tiny. For once in her short life, she felt protected.

"I'll climb onto a boat for you," she said, "but only if you promise I'll be safe."

"You'll be safe. I promise."

Libby rested her head on his shoulder and told herself to believe him. What other choice did she have?

Chapter

1

Twenty years later . . .

LIBBY CARSTAIRS STROLLED THROUGH the dark garden, following the
path to the river. Colored lanterns lighted the way. With each step she
took, the sounds of celebration faded behind her, which was a relief.

The mansion was packed to the rafters, with guests jostling elbow
to elbow, and she was never comfortable in tight spaces. She'd been
desperate to get outside into the fresh air.

The farther she walked from the house, the quieter it became. She
arrived at the dock, delighted to find a bench perfectly positioned for
ideal viewing.

She plopped down and gazed out at the black water. It was a beautiful July evening, the sky clear so she could see the stars overhead. Boats
bobbed in the channel, their lamps swinging with the current.

Usually, she loved being in the middle of a crowd, but recently,
she'd been growing weary of the attention that was regularly showered
on her. Nightmares had been plaguing her, and her nerves flared at the

oddest moments. Discomfort was a constant companion. It was like an old friend that visited occasionally.

The foundation of her world had collapsed without warning, so who wouldn't be a tad disturbed? She had too much on her mind, too many decisions to make, too many options to consider.

"You stupid fool," she muttered, addressing her deceased Uncle Harry. "How could you leave me to fend for myself?"

She sent the words winging upward—on the off chance that he was in Heaven. He'd been a charming cad and charlatan though, so it was very likely he was residing in a spot quite a bit lower and quite a bit hotter.

From the day she'd been delivered back to England as a little girl and he'd blustered forward to claim her, he'd been the center of her universe. He'd declared himself her uncle, and the authorities who'd been searching for her relatives had allowed him to traipse off with her.

He *wasn't* her uncle though. Not that she'd apprised anyone. She'd discovered the shocking news by accident, while riffling in his papers after he'd died, and she was still flummoxed by it.

He'd fed and clothed her, had trained and nurtured her. He'd turned her into a celebrity who could dazzle with her sad songs and stories, but he'd used her too: to earn money, to keep a roof over his head, to support his mistresses and dissolute friends.

She'd been a gorgeous, talented child who—with her curly blond hair, big blue eyes, and waiflike expression—had brought audiences to tears. She'd seduced them with her singing, dancing, and emotional tales about her puzzling childhood, a few of them true, most of them not.

Harry had had a vivid imagination, and he'd written a history for her that people never tired of hearing. Who had her parents been? How had she ended up alone on a deserted island in the Caribbean? The fascination never waned, and even though she wasn't proud of it, she'd dutifully played her part in his schemes.

She was a very aged twenty-five, and she'd nearly left him a thousand times, but she never had. He'd been her family. He'd replaced the father she'd believed lost in the shipwreck, had filled the role of kin she'd been anxious to have. He'd understood humans, and it was why he'd been able to trick, plunder, and swindle with such relish.

He'd understood her too, had understood her yearning to belong, to be accepted and wanted. He'd supplied just enough attention and flattery to keep her by his side, and now—now!—when the pathetic idiot had gotten himself shot dead by a jealous husband, she was devastated.

How could he abandon her?

Her mother had been his acquaintance, a fact he'd hidden—due to Libby's past supposedly being a mystery—and he'd slyly recognized profitable traits in Libby. He'd tutored her in how to be magnificent, then he'd pushed her out into the world where she'd become irresistible.

She reveled in the applause and fame—she couldn't deny it—but when Harry wasn't there to revel in it too, it all seemed pointless.

Grief was a heavy load to carry, and she would eventually shuck it off, but with his only being deceased for three months, she was still mourning and having trouble balancing the load he'd dumped on her slender shoulders.

Suddenly, she smelled smoke from a cheroot, and she glanced down the dock, irked to see a man standing there. He was being so quiet that she hadn't noticed him.

He was thirty or so, casually leaned against the wooden railing and watching her intently, as if debating whether to make his presence known.

"Hello," she said. "Are you having a private moment? I hope I haven't interrupted."

"You haven't interrupted."

His voice was a deep, soothing baritone that tickled her innards, and she tamped down a scoff of exasperation. Men never enticed her in a feminine fashion. She was much too smart to ever be bowled over.

Because she worked in the theater, she was constantly surrounded by scoundrels. They doted on her and plied her with gifts, but she was never interested in any of them in a romantic way. They couldn't tempt her. They couldn't woo her.

She'd witnessed too much of their bad behavior. Harry's wealthy friends had all been married, but they'd had mistresses and second families. They'd gambled, cheated on their wives, and squandered their fortunes on vice and debauchery.

She'd never met an affluent fellow who wasn't an absolute beast in his personal habits. Harry had taught her how to finagle and tease so they would shower her with presents, but also how to put her foot down too to prevent any mischief from occurring.

Her aloof attitude merely drove her admirers to paroxysms of purpose, where they swore they would soften her heart and win her for their very own—by which they meant they expected she'd agree to be a mistress. She'd never be considered as a wife, a situation that should have been insulting, but she didn't exactly view matrimony as an attractive choice.

She would never enter into a relationship where a husband would have the right to boss her or fritter away her hard-earned money. She was too independent and wasn't adept at following orders. Any dolt who thought he could control her was sorely mistaken. She never listened, as her poor Uncle Harry had learned over and over.

If she'd deemed it possible—and she didn't—she'd have been delighted to wed the man of her dreams and live happily ever after, but her past was a weighty ball and chain. There was no chance of Prince Charming riding up to declare himself.

"Would you like me to leave?" she asked him. "I don't have to tarry."

"I don't mind you being here."

"Thank you. It's so crowded inside. I can't bear to return to the party just yet."

"I feel the same."

For several minutes, they were silent. He puffed on his cheroot to the very end, then he dropped it into the water, the tip hissing as the flame sizzled out.

"When you first sat down," he said, "who were you talking to? It sounded as if you were scolding someone."

"It was my uncle. He passed away a few months ago, in a very stupid manner, and in case he can hear me, I continue to chastise him for being such a fool."

He was polite enough not to question her about Harry's demise, and she would have been too embarrassed to explain it, so she was grateful for the courtesy.

"May I join you on the bench?" he asked.

"Of course."

She patted the empty spot next to her, and he walked over. It was a dark night, but a lantern hung from a nearby post, so there was sufficient light for a clear assessment. He moved with the grace of a dancer or an athlete, looking completely comfortable in his skin.

He was enormously handsome, with black hair and sparking eyes that she predicted would be very blue. He was tall, six feet at least, so if she'd been standing, he'd have towered over her, and she'd always loved a tall man.

She was short, just five-foot-four in her slippers and still very thin. After suffering her ordeal when she was tiny, her frame had never filled out as a normal girl's might have. She was willowy and exotic, and she wondered if he liked to dance. On the dance floor, they would be a striking couple.

He had a classic aristocratic face—high cheekbones, strong nose, firm chin—and she was curious as to who he was. She'd been in London for weeks, with her cousin, Simon. He was Harry's bastard son, and he was trolling salons and soirees to drum up a gaggle of devoted swains.

Harry had been a veritable master at keeping her admirers panting after her, at wrangling gifts from them that he would promptly sell.

Simon possessed Harry's worst tendencies, and with Harry's death, he was proving himself adept at placing her in the right circumstances. He was cajoling the cads she beguiled to help him book performances for her, usually at gatherings arranged by the premier hostesses in the city. She was also doing a regular stint at a theater, in the coveted spot after the first intermission.

Theater-goers flocked to see her, so she'd met all the appropriate people in the gilded salons about town. But she hadn't met *him*.

Her seamstress and companion, Edwina Fishburn—called Fish by everyone—had taught her about clothes and fashion, so she had a keen eye for style, and he didn't disappoint.

He was dressed in a formal black evening suit, sewn from expensive material and perfectly tailored to enhance his male physique. His cravat was stitched from the finest Belgian lace and tied in an intricate knot.

Manly odors swirled—tobacco, horses, cologne—but there was another, more subtle scent too, and it tantalized her on an elemental level she didn't understand. It made her eager to rub herself against him like a contented cat.

It was obvious he was rich, and she always liked to befriend a rich man. As Harry had constantly insisted, *rich* men were the only ones who had money to toss around.

"Will you faint if I introduce myself?" he asked.

"I'm not the fainting type."

"Praise be, but how about if I use my Christian name? Will I shock you by being too familiar?"

"I'm *un*shockable too."

"Good. I never could abide a trembling ninny."

"Then you'll absolutely love me. I don't have a weak bone in my body."

He turned slightly, so she turned too. It was a small bench, so they were sitting very close, their arms and thighs crushed together all the way down.

"I'm Lucas, but you can call me Luke."

She noticed that he didn't provide a surname, didn't add a grand title to awe and astound. Briefly, she wondered why not, but she didn't suppose it mattered. He wanted to be cordial, and she was a very cordial person.

"Libby," she said, not offering a surname either, and it was refreshing to keep it to herself.

Whenever her identity was revealed, she was peppered with questions about her past, but she barely recollected that terrible time. Most of the information she furnished to others had been invented by her Uncle Harry so she'd seem more tragic and interesting.

"Have we met?" he asked.

"No, I'm sure we haven't."

"You look as if I should know you from somewhere."

She was definitely recognizable. There were often sketches of her on playbills, but she was recognized by her stage name too: *Little Libby Carstairs . . . Mystery Girl of the Caribbean!*

"I have a good memory," she said, "and I'm positive I'd remember *you*."

"Why is that?"

"You're a handsome devil who's probably a great rogue and breaker of hearts."

"Me? A breaker of hearts?" He laughed. "I can categorically state that I have never broken a single heart." He paused, then scowled. "Well, there was a neighbor when I was twelve who was sweet on me, but I can't be held responsible for any amorous misadventures I committed as a boy."

"You're correct, and I won't demand you share the gory details."

"I didn't even kiss her. I wasn't yet intrigued by girls, and I thought the entire episode was silly. I might have given her a rose from the garden though."

"It would have created exactly the wrong impression, so she's likely still pining away."

"If she is, then I will confess to breaking that *one* heart, but just that one."

He realized how they'd leaned toward each other, as if their bodies couldn't resist, and he drew away, but there wasn't any space to maneuver.

"What brought you to the party?" she asked.

"I was bored, and a friend insisted I'd enjoy myself."

"Are you?"

"Not really. Why do you imagine I'm lurking out here in the dark?"

She chuckled. "You poor thing. You're more of a recluse than I am."

"What about you? What spurred you to attend?"

"My cousin dragged me to it. He's a social climber who likes to see and be seen. If it had been left up to me, I'd have stayed at home and drunk a whiskey by the fire."

He raised a brow. "You—a female—would have been drinking a whiskey? What a scandalous admission."

"I'm full of outrageous behavior."

"I'll bet you are." He snorted at that, then he sighed, sounding as if he had the weight of the world on his shoulders. "It's odd for me to be in London."

"It's the center of the universe. Why would you declare it to be odd? I've always deemed it to be thrilling."

Most of her life, she, Harry, and Simon had journeyed around the country with a traveling troupe. She'd performed at fairs and on stages in village greens. She'd charmed audiences with her poignant accounts of the shipwreck and her rescue.

It was only recently that she was wallowing in London. There was more money to be made in the city, and she was able to glom onto a richer class of acquaintances.

"I've been away in the navy," he said.

"You're a sailor?"

"Yes."

"For how many years?"

"Too many."

She chuckled again. "Your tale of woe is more depressing by the moment."

He scoffed with disgust. "Don't listen to me. I'm in a foul mood. It's why I'm on this dock. I was glowering at the guests inside—as if I'd never previously been to a ball. My friend claimed I was scaring people."

"Were you?"

"Probably."

"I think we're destined to be great chums."

"I'm flattered," he said, "but why have you decided so hastily? What if I turn out to be a grouch and a complainer?"

"I have a special affection for members of the British navy."

"Why is that?"

The instant she uttered the remark, she mentally kicked herself. She'd been hoping to have a pleasant chat where *Little Lost Libby* wasn't mentioned once. She wasn't about to clarify the reason she was fond of the navy, but she still dreamed about that large, imposing captain who'd found her hiding in that trunk.

She'd only been on his vessel for a few days before he'd handed her over to British authorities, then she never saw him again. Dear Captain Miles Ralston. For years, she'd pretended he was her father, that he was searching for her so he could whisk her off to be his pampered daughter.

"My father and uncles were sailors," she breezily lied. She was adept at lying; she'd spent her life doing it.

"Tell me their names. Perhaps I know some of them."

"I'm sure not," she swiftly said. "From the cut of your evening suit, I'm certain you were quite a bit higher in rank than any of them."

"From the cut of *my* clothes? What about your own? You're not exactly dressed like a pauper yourself."

She was wearing a red velvet gown, with cap sleeves and an obscenely low neckline. Her corset was laced so tight she could barely inhale, so she was displaying a shocking amount of bosom. Her throat, ears, wrists, and fingers were dripping with red jewelry that matched her gown. The stones were fake, but they looked real.

Fish had styled her hair in an elaborate concoction of curls and braids, with flowers and feathers woven in the soft strands. She appeared rich and glamorous.

"Was that a compliment?" she asked.

"Gad, it was, wasn't it? I'll have to guard my wayward tongue or you'll assume I'm flirting."

"Heaven forbid."

"You don't like flirting?"

"I can't abide it."

"What a peculiar female you are. I thought every woman enjoyed flirting."

"Not me. I never learned how, so I'm not good at it, and it seems to be rife with pitfalls."

"So you've never wed?" he asked.

"No. How about you?"

"No."

"We're a miserable pair, aren't we? But then, who would want us?"

He snorted again. "If a dashing prince rushed up and proposed, would you accept? Or are you completely averse to the entire notion of matrimony?"

"If a prince rode up, I might consider it, but otherwise, I'm content to remain a spinster."

"That's the strangest comment I've ever heard. What female wouldn't like to wed? You grow more abnormal by the second."

"It's what I've always been told: I'm abnormal. What about you? How old are you?"

"I'm thirty this year. And you?"

"Twenty-five. Will you ever break down and permit some debutante to attach a leg-shackle?"

He gave a mock shudder. "I suppose I'll have to eventually."

"Your opinion about matrimony is worse than mine."

"Can you imagine me fettered to a debutante? The very idea leaves me nauseous."

"You're a pathetic character, aren't you? Every fellow like you marries sooner or later, and thirty is on the edge of decrepit."

"I know."

"Do you always feel this sorry for yourself?"

"Only since I arrived back from the navy."

"Have you resigned your commission? Or are you on furlough?"

"I've resigned."

"You're at loose ends."

"Yes, my brother died, so I have to take over at home, and it means I'm about to become a gentleman farmer. That prospect leaves me nauseous too."

"Oh, you are such a baby!" she scolded. "You've had an exciting career in the navy, and now, you have a country property to inherit. In my view, your life is perfect. Stop whining."

"I sound like an ingrate, don't I?"

"Yes, and ungrateful people annoy me."

"Then I shall try to mind my manners. We should talk about something more interesting. You, for instance. Tell me more about yourself."

"I'm so boring that any details would put you to sleep. I find *you* to be incredibly entertaining though. Let's stick with you."

She flashed the smile for which she was renowned. It was a special smile—one Harry had her practice in the mirror—that riveted those who observed it. It made her appear young and vulnerable, and of course, she was very beautiful. It wasn't vanity to admit it.

She had long, curly, golden-blond hair and big, expressive blue eyes. When she'd been a girl, Harry had dressed her like a homeless waif, as if she was still lost and alone and being forced to beg for alms.

Men were swept up by her mesmerizing allure, and she used it to captivate and enchant. If she chose to flaunt herself, she had a stunning effect, and Luke's reaction was typical.

They stared forever, and it was very thrilling to endure his potent assessment. He had a powerful focus that tantalized her, that had her wishing he'd never look away, and the result he produced was unsettling.

She wasn't an innocent miss. Over the years, she'd been kissed occasionally by tedious, vain oafs, so she recognized passion when it was stirring, and it was definitely stirring. She'd never felt anything like it. It seemed as if their bodies were generating sparks, as if the air around them was crackling with energy.

Fish, who'd disgraced herself in numerous torrid flings, swore that human desire could sizzle hot enough to burn a female to ash, but Libby hadn't believed her. The men in her world were too dreary to ever create any ardent stimulation, so Luke's attention had her flummoxed.

His gaze dipped to her mouth, and it was obvious he was thinking about kissing her which, on one level, was extremely hilarious. They were strangers, and he hadn't bothered to supply his surname. Wasn't it exactly like a man to immediately ponder amour?

Yet on another level, she would deem it perfectly appropriate to be kissed by him. While they'd just crossed paths, there was a delicious perception of lengthy acquaintance. Why shouldn't he kiss her?

But that sort of rumination was dangerous and absurd.

She knew his kind of gentleman, knew what they expected from a woman like her. There could never be a benefit for her in getting closer.

She'd suffered too many losses in her life, and she was a very gentle soul who bonded with a desperate determination. When a relationship ended—as they always did—she mourned for ages, so she'd built high walls to guard her tender heart, and she never let them be breached.

"Are you sure we haven't met?" he asked.

"I'm positive."

"I'm gaping to the point of rudeness."

"I'm very arrogant," she said, "so I enjoy your gaping."

"You look like someone I know, but I can't figure out who it is."

"Don't all British women look alike? Don't we all have blond hair and blue eyes? Perhaps you're confusing me with every other female in the kingdom."

"You haven't confused me. In fact, I'm betting there's no other woman quite like you out there in the whole world."

"My goodness. If you keep complimenting me like that, I won't be able to walk back into the house. My head won't fit through the door."

He chuckled, his cheeks heating with chagrin. "You've driven me to an embarrassing ledge where I'm nearly spouting poetry about you, and I have no idea why."

She jokingly batted her lashes. "I have that effect on men."

"On *me* especially."

He pressed her into the bench, and she was convinced yet again that he would kiss her. If he tried, she'd decided to allow it. She suspected it would be shockingly pleasant.

But he eased away and asked, "How do you occupy yourself in the day?"

"I suppose like every young lady. I eat, read, shop, and write letters."

"Do you ride?"

"Doesn't everyone?"

She was actually a very nimble equestrian. During lean times, mostly when Harry had been hiding from creditors or the law, they'd traveled with circuses where she'd learned all sorts of tricks and acrobatics.

She could *ride* better than any man she'd ever met, and she could even accomplish it hanging upside down!

"Will you ride with me tomorrow?" he asked. "Where are you staying? I'll fetch you at two. How does that sound?"

He rested a hand on her waist, his dazzling eyes searching hers, as if he could dig out the secrets buried there. She was enthralled by that hand, and she held herself very still, reveling in a pretty picture of the liaison they could pursue. They'd socialize in the afternoons and dance at balls in the evenings. They'd chat and dine and grow very close. It would be precious and delightful, and she'd fall madly in love with him. Then . . .

He'd propose an illicit alliance, and she'd refuse. He'd start nagging and pressuring her, and her refusals would be more strident. Eventually, they'd quarrel, and he'd leave in a huff. She'd never see him again, and the loss would spur her to pine and regret for months afterward.

Or, more likely, she'd begin to see him at various soirees, and he'd have a beautiful woman on his arm, one who'd been decadent enough to latch onto him when he'd suggested his indecent association.

She'd be crushed by waves of jealousy, would pine and regret for months afterward over that ending too. So, no, an affair was impossible.

"I'm sorry, but I'm busy tomorrow," she told him.

"How about the next day? Or will you always be busy?"

"It's not in the cards for us to be friends."

"Are you sure about that? It seems to me that there's a remarkable attraction stirring between us."

"I won't deny that there's a powerful impulse swirling, but if I jumped into a relationship with you, there's only one role that could open up for me. And it's not a role I would ever play."

"It's merely a ride in the park."

She tsked with exasperation. "It would turn out to be much more than that."

He pondered, then nodded. "You're probably right. I haven't offended you, have I?"

"Not in the slightest."

"I'm not usually so inept in my banter."

"You've been stuck on a navy ship for years," she said, "so you've been surrounded by men. You're finding your land legs and having to mingle with females again. You'll get your conversations up to speed in no time at all."

"I'm completely bowled over by you, but I can't figure out why. I'm behaving like an idiot."

"I think you're very sweet."

"Sweet! Gad. I really must be out of practice with my seduction skills."

She reached out and laid a palm on his cheek. It was a brazen, shameless gesture, but she was anxious to touch him just once. By declining his invitation, she was suffering from the oddest perception that she was making a huge mistake.

If Harry could speak from the grave, he'd tell her to leap in with both feet. He'd tell her Luke was precisely the kind of man to bring her whatever she required, but she and Harry had never shared the same view about romance. She simply wasn't the person Harry had always hoped, just as she couldn't be the person Luke would ultimately demand she be.

"Are your eyes blue?" she asked.

"Yes. Are yours?"

"Yes." She pulled away and stood. "Are you ready to head back to the party? Will you walk with me?"

"Would you be terribly upset if I admit I can't return just yet? I'd like to tarry a while longer. I feel better when I can look out at the water."

"You sailor, you." She smiled, an enormous wave of affection rocking her. "Nothing much ever upsets me, and I'm not a trembling girl in need of an escort. I'm totally capable of walking to the house on my own."

"Do you imagine we'll ever see each other again?"

"It's entirely possible—if you keep attending these over-crowded, tedious parties."

She nearly invited him to her performance at the theater the following night, but she managed to bite her tongue. If she encouraged him in the least, he'd badger her about an illicit liaison. It was madness to contemplate it for a single second.

He was still seated on the bench, not rising as was appropriate after she'd stood. He clasped her hand and linked their fingers as if they were adolescent sweethearts.

"I'll miss you after you leave," he absurdly said.

"I will convince myself that's true."

"I don't suppose you'd tell me where you live."

"It's not a good idea."

"Why must we have *good* ideas? I find them dreadfully boring myself."

"I don't."

"Then how about if you give me some hint of how to contact you?"

"It's not a good idea either."

"I've stated my opinion about *good* ideas. Let's do something wild."

"My whole life has been wild, so I make it a specific point to never have any out-of-the-ordinary events happen. I seek tedium at all costs."

His torrid gaze swept down her torso. "I don't believe you."

She drew away, realizing if she didn't extricate herself, she'd never escape. He certainly wasn't about to end the encounter.

"I'll be in London for the next week," he said.

"You mention it like a threat."

"I'll be watching for you everywhere. You could have mercy on me and simply tell me where you'll be tomorrow evening. That way, I wouldn't have to wade through every soiree in the city in order to stumble on you."

"I don't go out much in the evenings." If she was out after dark, it was because she was working. "Tonight was an exception."

He studied her, then scoffed. "You're lying about so many topics. Why?"

"Why would you think I'm lying?"

"You have the most expressive face I've ever seen. I can read every emotion that's written there."

"Your comment alarms me. I constantly cultivate an air of mystery, and I deem myself to be completely enigmatic."

"You have no secrets from me."

"Then I will have to create some."

She winked and sauntered away, figuring he'd jump up and escort her after all, but he wasn't the type to chase after any woman. The more likely scenario was that women chased *him* and probably always had.

He was handsome, landed, and maybe even titled, so he'd expect to be fawned over as his absolute due. She'd never been a sycophant though, so clearly, she was wrong for him in every way.

She'd enjoyed meeting him though, and she'd spend weeks, replaying every word they'd spoken so she could consider what might have been. She lived every moment, wondering what *might* have been.

What if her mother hadn't been deranged? What if she hadn't sailed for the Caribbean with Libby? What if she hadn't drowned in that violent storm? What if Libby hadn't been rescued on that deserted island? What if Harry hadn't claimed her when she'd been brought back to London? What if he hadn't taught her to sing, dance, and spew sad stories?

What sort of woman might she have become instead?

Luke was one more intriguing character, added to a long list of them, who'd drifted by. She was adept at reflecting on the roads that could have been taken, but it never changed anything.

Chapter

⟨decorative divider⟩

2

"I've agreed to one more week."

"Why just one? Isn't he happy with me?"

Libby scowled at her cousin, Simon Carstairs, who used the stage name of Simon Falcon.

He was Harry's bastard son and looked exactly like him: blond hair, blue eyes, handsome, slender, and fit. He was flamboyant like Harry, smart like Harry, cunning like Harry. He'd just turned twenty, but he could read people and situations better than anyone.

He had Harry's knack for feigned empathy and insincere flattery, but for chicanery and vice too. He could talk to a person for a minute, and he'd have deduced all sorts of secrets he oughtn't to have discovered. Because he had no scruples and possessed convoluted morals, others befriended him at their peril.

"He's very happy," Simon said, "and with you on the poster out front, the house is filling up every night, but he's not willing to shell out what it's worth to have you here."

They were discussing the theater manager. He was a wily cretin she couldn't abide.

"It won't kill me to accept a bit less," she said.

"It might kill me," Simon retorted. "I won't let him take advantage of you. He's a brute who doesn't deserve to have you gracing his establishment."

"It's kind of you to put your foot down, but we have to pay our bills."

"We're paying them."

They were in a changing room at the rear of the theater. She was seated at the dressing table, and he leaned over and dropped a bag of coins onto it. He'd negotiated a deal whereby she could keep half the coins tossed to her by the crowd during her act, and she had no idea how he'd arranged it.

The actors didn't usually get to keep any of the money thrown at them, but then, they didn't ever generate the level of applause or weeping Libby induced.

"It was a grand night," Simon said, and he kissed her on the cheek. "You were particularly sorrowful."

She snorted with amusement. "I try my best."

"Even the men were bawling into their sleeves."

"What if they tire of me someday? They've been listening to my pathetic narrative for twenty years. What if some other unlucky female suffers a tragedy, then bursts forward and steals my thunder?"

"I would never allow that to happen."

She hoped he wouldn't.

She supported him and Fish. It was her talent and drive that kept them clothed, housed, and fed. If she somehow lost her ability to tantalize, she couldn't imagine what would become of them. Simon would probably join a circus and perform dazzling magic tricks. Fish was a skilled seamstress and costumer, and she could work at a theater until her fingers and eyes gave out.

But what would Libby do?

"Besides," he added, "who could be as mesmerizing as you? No one can spin a yarn like you."

Harry had crafted hundreds of vignettes where she wove story and song to entice spectators with her baffling history. All these years later, the tale still riveted.

Little Lost Libby . . . Mystery Girl of the Caribbean!

Who was she? Who had her parents been? How and why had her ship sunk? How had she reached the deserted island where she'd been found? How long had she been stranded? How had she and her two companions survived?

She had few answers to any of those questions. Her memories were sparse and sprinkled with tidbits Harry had wedged into her mind, so she wasn't clear on what was true and what was fiction. When she was younger, she'd had vivid recollections of her mother, but those had faded with time until she recalled nothing that she would consider valid.

Harry had been adamant that her parents were Kit and Maude Carstairs. Kit Carstairs was his brother, and they'd been missionaries, sailing to Jamaica to settle and preach. Libby had swallowed that lie for two decades. It was only recently, after Harry had died, that she'd stumbled on a box of old letters that he'd hidden from her. With his being dead, she couldn't ask him why he'd deceived her.

She, Caroline, and Joanna had created an enormous stir when they'd first arrived back in England. They'd scarcely known their names and could furnish no details about their families. An article, along with a drawing of the three of them, had been printed in the newspapers, and Libby still had a tattered copy of it. Occasionally—when she was feeling lonely or nostalgic—she'd pull it out and study it.

On the island, they'd been living like feral wolf pups, and the authorities had been determined to reunite them with responsible kin. Numerous people had stepped forward, and they'd been swiftly separated and whisked off to different destinations without being given a chance to say goodbye to each other.

She remained haunted by that separation. Who had claimed Caroline and Joanna? Where had they gone? Harry had always insisted he had no information and couldn't find out, but as with so much of what Harry had shared, she was certain it was false.

She had thrived in the world Harry had handed to her. What about them?

It was the twentieth anniversary of their being rescued, and she caught herself thinking about them constantly. Could she locate them? Might someone at the navy be able to help her? Should she purchase an advertisement in the newspaper? Might it be that easy?

Unfortunately, any publicity would fuel the flames of speculation. A reporter was already sniffing around, anxious to interview her for a retrospective, but she'd been avoiding him. What purpose would be served by dragging it all up again?

She thought there might be dangerous secrets lurking beneath the surface. Whenever she was distressed, they tried to break out, but she kept them tamped down. With her having read Harry's letters and discovering her real father's identity—it definitely hadn't been Kit Carstairs—she couldn't bear to look too closely at the past.

She needed more time to decide how to proceed. She needed more time to figure out the best path.

Fish was with them, in the adjoining closet where she was fussing with Libby's costume for the following evening. She peeked out and asked, "If Libby only performs for another week, what will we do after she's finished?"

"We've been invited to a house party," Simon told her.

"In the country?" Fish asked.

"No, in the middle of the ocean," Simon facetiously replied. "Of course it's in the country."

Fish glanced at Libby. "What is your opinion? Would you enjoy it? Or would you rather stay in town?"

Libby shrugged. She loved loafing in fancy houses, being waited on hand and foot and treated like a princess. She was so comfortable in posh surroundings that she'd always assumed, and Harry had always teased, that she must have had many gallons of blue blood running in her veins.

She asked Simon, "Where's the party?"

"It's at Lord Roland's estate. Roland Manor?"

Libby could barely keep from sucking in a sharp breath, but she managed to refrain. She'd been desperately plotting to devise a reason to visit Roland. Was this Fate providing a sign? Or was Fate tricking her? If she forged ahead, would it all collapse in a huge morass?

"He's showing off his daughter," Simon said. "The mansion will be open, the liquor will flow, and the guests will be elegant and wealthy. In other words, Libby, it will be right up your alley."

Fish scoffed and said to Simon, "How on earth have you wrangled an invitation from Charles Pendleton?"

"Who is Charles Pendleton?"

"Lord Roland," Fish said, and when Libby and Simon glared at her, demanding she clarify her familiarity, she explained, "He and I are old friends, and he'd never welcome a measly crew like us, so please tell me how you finagled this."

"I met a Pendleton cousin."

"Gambling?"

"Yes, and he absolutely adores Libby," Simon said. "He thinks I'm a grand fellow too."

"Then he's obviously an idiot."

Fish rolled her eyes and whipped into the closet.

Simon was a magician who was adept at slight-of-hand. If he was gambling, he was cheating. Libby and Fish were terrified—if his nefarious tendencies were ever unmasked—he'd get himself killed.

"Shall I accept or not?" Simon asked Libby.

Libby called to Fish, "What's your preference, Fish? Shall we spend a week at an ostentatious mansion and let ourselves be spoiled rotten? Or would you like to dawdle in town and trudge along in the rut where we're currently stuck?"

Fish called back, "I guess we can go. It'll be a nice change."

"We heartily agree," Libby said to Simon.

He grinned and strutted out. He was as proficient at manipulating them as Harry had been, and they always wound up following his suggestions. The fact that he usually had ulterior motives never seemed to prevent them from latching onto any proposal.

Once the door shut behind him, Fish emerged. She was forty, a short, plump, pretty woman with auburn hair and emerald eyes who'd never wed. Instead, she'd wasted her life trailing after charismatic, debauched men like Harry. She liked the freedom of the theater and traveling troupes, and she had a stellar reputation as a seamstress and costumer.

She'd been Harry's mistress off and on for years and was a kind of substitute mother to Libby. Or maybe an older sister with loose morals and a pragmatic view of the world. She never lectured or scolded, and she felt that females labored under too many unfair restrictions.

She constantly advised Libby to shuck off her prim inclinations and enjoy herself a bit more, but Libby had had all the excitement she could abide by staggering after Harry for two decades.

"Will we really go to Roland?" Fish asked.

"Yes."

"Then I declare that it will be very fun, and who can predict what might happen? Perhaps we'll both meet handsome scoundrels and make fools of ourselves over them."

"You are the consummate optimist, Fish."

"Someone should be. If you grew anymore dour, your face would crack from all your frowning."

"I miss Harry," Libby said. "I didn't think I would, but I do. Don't you miss him too?"

"I miss him, but I'm not surprised by how he left us. He was destined for a bad end. If he could have picked his own conclusion, he'd have relished the chance to be shot climbing out a paramour's window. It was precisely the type of mischief I'd have expected to lay him low."

"You were sort of his wife. Didn't his philandering upset you?"

"There's a reason I never married him, Libby. The moment I was introduced to him, I recognized all his sordid proclivities. Before involving myself, I weighed his various traits, and I decided I could tolerate the horrid ones. Don't rewrite my history with him; it wasn't exactly a love match." She went to the door. "I want to watch the final act of the play. Will you watch with me?"

"I'd rather wash and relax in private. Fetch me when the curtain falls. We'll walk home together."

"Simon might have arranged a party for you to attend."

"He'll have to go without me. I'm fatigued tonight."

"I'll see you in a bit then," Fish said.

"If my gushing admirers inquire about me, tell them I've already departed."

"I shall be a veritable castle wall that succeeds in keeping them away."

Fish marched out, and Libby chuckled, listening as her strides faded, then it was very quiet. She could hear the hum of actors' voices in the front of the building, but she was very much alone, which she never liked.

From the day Harry had claimed her, her life had been filled with people and activity. She carried on in a very public way, on stages scattered throughout the kingdom. She hadn't had much practice at being by herself.

She stared into the mirror, wondering what path she'd wind up traveling next. She always felt as if she was on a raft and rushing down a raging river, powerless to control the route or the speed. With Harry deceased, the sense of floating free had increased in intensity.

"I'm going to Roland!" she murmured to her reflection. "Fancy that!"

During her performances, she wore her hair in a simple style, tied back with a ribbon. She yanked it away so the curly locks swirled around her shoulders, then she headed into the closet to get dressed. Fish had removed her costume, so she was attired in just chemise and drawers, a silky robe over top.

As she reached for her gown, the door in the outer room opened and shut.

"Fish," she said, "is that you? Will you help me with my corset?"

There was no answer, and she peeked out, curious as to who had arrived, and she hoped it wasn't a man from the audience. Usually, they were courteous enough to wait until the show was over, and by then—if she wasn't in the mood for socializing—she'd have sneaked off.

To her astonishment and delight, Luke was standing there, and she suffered a trill of pleasure. How had he found her? What could he want?

Since they'd parted the prior evening, she'd been mooning over him every minute. It was a disgusting admission, but apparently, she'd been totally bowled over for once.

A peculiar spark had flared between them, and she'd been eager to linger in order to see how hot it might burn. She was never stupid about men though, so she'd forced herself to depart, but she couldn't deny that she'd been yearning to meet him again.

He was more handsome than she recalled, wearing another black formal suit, an exquisite cravat knotted at his throat. He was displaying quite a bit of jewelry, and it glittered in the lamplight. She suspected the stones—as opposed to her fake ones—were real diamonds.

His torrid gaze landed on her, and he grinned a devil's grin that—if she'd been a fragile type of female—might have left her weak in the knees.

"My goodness!" he said like a complaint. "If it isn't Little Libby Carstairs, Mystery Girl of the Caribbean!"

"Hello, Lucas/Luke."

"When we chatted last night, you might have warned me that you are a celebrity who's taken London by storm. I would have been much more impressed. I was incredibly overwhelmed when I simply deemed you to be exquisite. I didn't realize you would turn out to be so vastly extraordinary."

"I'm not a celebrity," she felt compelled to state, "and I have never *stormed* anywhere."

"I beg to disagree. People in the seats around me couldn't stop raving about you."

"Were you in the theater just now?"

"Yes."

"So you saw my performance."

"Yes," he said again.

She hadn't noticed him and was glad she hadn't. She wouldn't have been able to focus on her lyrics and lines.

"What did you think?" she asked.

"It was a tad maudlin for my tastes."

"Then you probably shouldn't watch me in the future. I have hundreds of vignettes just like it. They scarcely vary from night to night."

"Such a tragic story!" There was a teasing glint in his eye. "Such a tale of woe! I was extremely moved by it."

"Liar."

"Do you make a good living from telling strangers about your disastrous past?"

"I make a fair living."

She didn't add that it fluctuated widely, by season and town and area of the country. It depended on the kind of group they'd joined, the reputation of the troupe, the split of the money paid to the actors. It hadn't always been posh theaters and high-born audiences.

She was often weary, but she was never bored, and she'd never been hungry.

He was staring at her as if he'd like to gobble her up, and the air was charged with the perception that any wild behavior might be allowed.

She nervously clutched the lapels of her robe, the instinctive gesture reminding her that she wasn't dressed. She'd grown up on the stage, so she wasn't squeamish about being viewed in her current condition, but she'd never previously permitted herself to be caught in such a scandalous situation.

She only greeted admirers when she was fully styled and coifed for maximum effect. It was all part of her act to keep men besotted and wondering what chance they might ultimately have with her. The answer had always been, *no chance at all*, but they never believed that.

He started toward her, and she commanded, "Stay where you are, you bounder!"

"I don't think I will."

She dashed into the closet, but there was no rear exit, so she had nowhere to go. He scooped her to his chest and wedged her against a dresser, then he kissed her as if they'd been lovers for years, as if he had every right.

He might have been possessed. His hands were in her hair, his tongue in her mouth, and his palms roamed over her torso. His masculine frame was crushed to her more feminine one. His belly was flat, his thighs hard and muscled. As she snuggled with him, she felt petite and vulnerable, as if she'd been in dire need of his help and was finally about to receive it.

She wrapped her arms around him and pulled him closer. She was no trembling ninny, and she knew how to kiss a man. He was quite adept at it too, and it occurred to her that the fellows who'd dared to proceed in the past had been tepid and cautious.

He was fierce, blatant, and brazen, and she was quickly overwhelmed.

She'd been told blunt secrets about private conduct. Fish had never thought a girl should be kept in the dark about sexual matters, so she'd been very candid as to what was expected in the bedchamber. Libby had learned all sorts of things she shouldn't, and with Luke proving himself to be very skilled at seduction, she was suddenly considering dissipation she had no business considering.

With her clothes off and her wearing just her robe, chemise, and drawers, it seemed as if she was naked. It had her wishing she was wanton, that she'd paid more attention when Fish had been clarifying the woman's role in a tryst.

Down below, there was obvious carnal evidence of how she'd enticed him, how his body was inflamed by their proximity. He was pressing his loins into hers in a delicious rhythm that stunned and thrilled her. Her anatomy recognized the road he was determined to walk and joined in with incredible vigor.

She couldn't guess how long they continued. Nor could she predict what might have happened, but he was better at controlling himself than she was. If it had been left up to her, there was no telling what wickedness she might have pursued.

He slowed and drew away, and he peered down at her with such affection that she was exceedingly flummoxed. Because of her odd upbringing, she'd convinced herself that she understood how affairs commenced and flared, but clearly, she'd had no genuine idea of the furious passion that could be immediately generated.

How was she to handle all the sensation he'd ignited? How would she ever revert to being the woman she'd been before he'd started in on her?

He smirked with manly arrogance. "I've been dying to do that ever since I first laid eyes on you. I've been thinking about you all day."

"How utterly marvelous to hear it."

"I had decided, once I crossed paths with you again, and I refused to suppose I wouldn't, that I would put myself out of my misery by kissing you—whether you were amenable or not."

She chuckled. "I might have been a tad amenable."

"It hasn't calmed me down though. Not in the slightest. I want to do it again. I want to do it forever and never stop."

"You're dangerous."

"Not usually, but you've stirred a beast inside me."

"Should I be flattered or terrified?"

"You should be both."

He leaned in and nibbled a trail down her neck to her nape, and he took bites on her skin, at the spot where her neck met her shoulder. Goose bumps slithered down her arms.

"I like the way you smell," he said. "It drives me wild."

"I can tell."

"What are your plans for the rest of the evening?"

"I'm going home."

"No, you're not. You're coming with me."

"To where?"

"I haven't figured out the location yet, but it will be somewhere quiet where I can have you all to myself for hours and hours."

"I'm sorry to report that you have completely misconstrued the kind of woman I am."

He frowned. "Meaning what?"

"Meaning I'm a singer and performer, so you're assuming I'm loose."

"Aren't you?"

"No. I'm actually very boring and moralistic."

His lazy gaze wandered down her torso, his ferocious regard lingering on all her aroused female areas.

He scoffed. "I don't believe you."

"It's true."

His frown deepened. "Are you playing a vixen's game with me? Is that it? Are you hoping I'll offer you money to socialize with me?"

"Don't be ridiculous."

"If that's your ploy, you should be aware that I never pay for companionship."

"As if I would agree to such a sordid arrangement."

She must have looked sufficiently offended because he studied her, then said, "I've insulted you."

"Of course you have. In my line of work, I receive many, many suggestive proposals, but I never accept any of them." She motioned to the door. "Would you leave?"

"No."

"Please?"

"No. What are you doing tomorrow?"

"I have a show."

"At night?"

"Yes."

"How about in the afternoon?"

He delivered another thrilling kiss that went on and on. It lowered her defenses and shot down any walls she'd erected to keep him at bay.

"Two o'clock," he said. "We'll go for a ride."

"Fine," she grumbled, and she kicked herself for capitulating so easily.

"I'll pick you up at your home. Where do you live?"

"I'm not about to tell you."

"Then I'll meet you here at the theater, out on the front walk."

"All right."

"Wear your most scandalous gown so I'll be absolutely tantalized."

"What is your favorite color?" she asked.

"Red."

"I have several red ones. I'll select the most alluring one for you, but I can't imagine why I'm being so accommodating."

"I always get my way. You're simply learning fast." He stole a final kiss. "If you think you can avoid me, if you're not here at two, I'll come to the theater tomorrow night. During the middle of your performance, I will march onto the stage and carry you off while everyone is watching."

"You probably would, wouldn't you?" She bristled with disgust. "What type of *ride* are you planning? Are we taking a carriage or will horses be involved? Should I don a riding habit rather than a dress? What sort of promenade are you envisioning?"

"I'll bring a carriage so I can lock you inside and have you all to myself."

"I must be mad to have consented to this," she said.

"If you weren't mad before, you will be after I'm finished with you. Don't disappoint me, Libby."

"I wouldn't dream of it."

He turned to start out, and to Libby's dismay, Fish was standing there, a stunned expression on her face. Libby never entertained gentlemen in her dressing room unless she was fully clothed *and* there was a chaperone lurking to prevent any untoward advances, so Luke's presence was strange and wildly out of character.

"May I help you?" Fish asked him.

"No," he cockily replied. "Libby has provided all the assistance I require for one evening."

He nodded imperiously at Fish, winked at Libby, then strolled out.

She and Fish were frozen in their spots, listening as his footsteps faded down the hall.

"Who on earth was that?" Fish inquired when it was quiet again.

"I have no idea."

"What's his name?"

"Lucas. Luke."

"Lucas what?"

"I have no idea about that either."

"Are you all right?"

"Yes—just a bit bewildered."

"What did he want?" Fish asked.

"Nothing good."

"I wouldn't be too sure about that."

"I'm riding with him tomorrow at two."

Fish raised a brow. "Really?"

"He demands I wear red. It's his favorite color."

Fish snorted with what sounded like excitement or maybe glee. "I already know which gown it will have to be."

Chapter

3

"Who shall I tell her is calling?"

"Luke. I'd provide my surname, but she's never learned what it is, so it won't help to put me in her good graces."

The footman who'd answered the door pulled it wide, and Luke entered the foyer of Libby's small home. He glanced around, being incredibly curious as to what sort of abode would house such an odd creature.

He'd always heard that actors skated on the edge of poverty, that they hid from debt collectors and snuck out of town in the middle of the night to avoid paying their bills. Her prosperous condition obliterated that notion. Gad, she employed a footman! It was a peculiar fact that was completely unanticipated.

The dwelling was two stories high, constructed of red brick with white trim and black shutters. Flower boxes hung under the windows, and fragrant rose bushes hugged the walk. The property was located in the theater district, so her neighbors were artists, dancers, and musicians.

The front parlor was spacious and comfortable. There was scant evidence of female fussing and hobbies though. He saw no knitted shawls on the backs of the chairs, no embroidered doilies under the lamps. Then again, she wasn't the type to sit by the fire with her knitting needles clicking.

He wasn't certain what he was doing, but he felt halfway bewitched by her. Although he was a sailor, he wasn't superstitious. He didn't worry about spells or signs, didn't believe a fellow could be ensnared by magic, but it seemed as if that was what had happened.

He was a rich, titled gentleman, a decorated navy hero, and beautiful women threw themselves at his feet. They always had, so in stumbling on her, it wasn't as if he'd never trifled with a gorgeous woman before. Yet he'd seen her, and he'd had to have her. An impulse of jealous possession had taken root, and he couldn't free himself from it.

These days, he was the most boring man in the world. After his deceased older brother, Bertie, had ruined the family's reputation with vice and dissipation, Luke had made a pact with himself that he would never cause a scene or rock a boat. He was determined to prove that he was stable, solid, and dependable—and nothing like his dead wastrel brother.

He intended to settle down, marry appropriately and quickly to a wealthy debutante with perfect bloodlines, and live—if not *happily* ever after—then contentedly ever after.

So why was he in Libby Carstairs's parlor? He had no idea.

"Miss Carstairs is preparing to go out," the footman said.

"Yes, she's planning to meet *me* at the theater, but I decided to pick her up instead."

"Might you give me your last name anyway? Just so I can introduce you properly?"

"Tell her it's Lucas Watson, Lord Barrett."

The footman had to be new at his job. He blanched when he wasn't supposed to ever display a reaction to any comment. Apparently, they weren't expecting an aristocrat to arrive.

It was his own fault for being so furtive. He'd been too busy mooning over her to bother with the formalities, and he was humored to discover that she still didn't know who he was. What would she think when his identity was revealed? He doubted she'd be impressed.

"Would you like a brandy, Lord Barrett?"

"I would love one."

The footman gestured to the sofa. "Will you sit?"

"No. I'll stand. I'm eager to snoop." The poor boy's brows rose to his hairline, and Luke asked, "How long has Miss Carstairs resided here?"

"I'm not sure, my lord, but it hasn't been very long. I've only been working for her for two weeks myself."

Luke's brandy was poured and handed over, and he shooed the footman out to fetch her.

It hadn't been difficult to find out where she was staying. He'd simply bribed an actor at the theater. If he'd had any sense, he would have met her there as arranged, but he'd been convinced she wouldn't appear. If she hadn't, he'd have been extremely annoyed, so he'd intervened to prevent any mischief on her part.

He'd been to the theater on dozens of occasions in his life, but he'd never encountered a performer who could mesmerize an audience like Libby. When they'd chatted on that dock bench, he'd wondered who she was and how he might cross paths with her in the future, but when she'd strolled out from behind the curtain to begin her monologue, he'd almost fainted with astonishment.

He'd been seated in a box with acquaintances, and they'd all known her and had greeted her with rousing applause. Once she'd been announced, he'd realized *he* knew her too. Who hadn't heard of the little *lost* girls who'd been rescued in the Caribbean?

They'd been too young to provide much information about themselves. They couldn't explain how long they'd been stranded or how they'd survived. They only remembered that their ship had sunk. It was like a plot out of an adventure novel.

It had been British sailors who'd chanced upon them, and with him being a sailor himself, it was a story told too many times to count. After they'd been brought home, it had created a huge uproar in London that had never completely faded.

On stage, she'd been a dazzling vision, wearing a diaphanous white gown so she might have been an angel or a fairy. She'd sung a trio of haunting ballads, and interspersed between the songs, there were several narratives about her being on the island, she and her two tiny friends huddled together at night in the sand and staring up at the stars.

The spectators had been transfixed, and more than one person had dabbed at tears with a kerchief. Not *him* of course. He was much too manly to exhibit such a maudlin response, but he'd been as spellbound as everyone else.

Footsteps sounded on the stairs, and she waltzed in, looking stunning and splendid and exasperated. At the sight of her, his bones seemed to melt, and his breath hitched in his lungs. He felt overwhelmed as an adolescent boy with his first girl. How did she have such a dramatic effect? What was causing it?

She sauntered over to where he was dawdling by the window and sipping the brandy her footman had dispensed. She grabbed the glass, downed the contents and, with a great deal of irritation, smacked it down on a nearby table.

"*Lord* Barrett?" she said as if in accusation. "Are you joking?"

"It's the newly-minted *Earl* of Barrett." He grinned. "Have I surprised you?"

"No. You are a pompous bully, so I deem it to be absolutely typical that you would turn out to be an aristocrat."

"I'm not a bully," he insisted.

"Whether a man is a bully or not is in the eye of the individual being bullied. That would be *me*. What are you thinking? I could have sworn we were meeting at the theater."

"I was positive you wouldn't oblige me, so I bribed an actor to tattle about you."

"You are totally absurd. Or perhaps you're simply deranged."

His grin widened. "Tell me the truth. If I hadn't shown up here, would you have shown up there?"

"Yes, I'd have arrived—for I understood that you are an arrogant fiend who can't bear to have his wishes ignored. If I hadn't come, you'd have tracked me to the ends of the Earth to find out why, and then, you'd have nagged until I obeyed."

"You know me so well."

His approving male gaze roamed down her torso. She was slender, willowy, and petite, but curved in all the right spots. She'd gone to an enormous amount of trouble with her appearance, so evidently, she had planned to attend him.

"You wore red as I requested," he said.

"I had to. You're like a force of nature. Who can resist you?"

"You're learning fast."

He made a twirling motion with his finger, indicating she should spin and let him view the entire ensemble.

Her gown was bright red—his favorite shade—with black piping along the sleeves and waist. It was cut low in the front, her corset laced so tight that she was practically falling out of the bodice, and he just adored a woman who was brave enough to display so much bosom.

Her glorious blond hair was curled and braided, with black feathers woven into the pretty strands. She was chic and elegant and much too fascinating for him. Normally, he was a very vain fellow, but he couldn't imagine how he'd ever match her in style and sophistication.

He was as British as the next man, and he comprehended that blood determined a person's lot in life. Who could have sired such a magnificent specimen?

In his memories about her return to England, she'd been referred to as an unnamed orphan. Had her family ever been found? He didn't recall how it had ended, but who might her father have been? She had to have an elevated lineage. How else could her stellar traits be explained?

"Are you ready to depart?" he asked her. "Or will I have to cool my heels for an hour or two while you finish primping and preening?"

"I'm ready, you wretch, but it would be nice if you'd told me where we're going. I hope I'm dressed appropriately."

"I originally claimed it would be a carriage ride, but I've changed my mind. We're having a picnic."

"A picnic? Will I have to sit in the grass and pick leaves out of my hair?"

"I'd never make you suffer through such a repugnant episode."

"Thank goodness. May I inquire as to where this picnic will be held?"

"No, you may not."

"That sounds dangerous, and just so you know, I always carry a small pistol."

He frowned. "A pistol? Why?"

"Why do you think? It's so I can shoot any fellow who acts like an idiot."

It was the wildest comment any woman had ever uttered in his presence, and he was completely enchanted, but he had no idea why. If he'd been pressed to state an opinion, he'd have declared himself to prefer modest, demur females who guarded their tongues, exhibited perfect manners in all situations, and went to church on Sundays.

Apparently, there was a hidden side to him that liked sass, brazen attitude, and cocky temperament. It vividly occurred to him that his brother, Bertie, had constantly chased doxies, so perhaps Luke was more like Bertie than he'd ever care to admit.

Another woman entered the room. She'd been in the dressing room at the theater as he'd strolled out. She delivered items to Libby—a black lace shawl, a reticule, and fan—and Libby retrieved them and draped the shawl over her shoulders.

Every detail of her outfit had been meticulously selected for maximum effect, and as she spun toward him again, with her fan flicked open and seductively cooling her face, he realized he was gaping. She was an actress, singer, and avid storyteller, but she was also very likely a confidence artist.

How had she learned to conduct herself in such a devastatingly superior way?

She addressed the other woman. "Fish, this is Lord Barrett."

"My, my," Fish said a tad snottily. "Aren't we stepping into high company all of a sudden? How did this happen?"

She didn't curtsy or provide any sign that she was in awe of Luke or that she should show him any deference.

"Luke . . ." Libby stopped and scowled. "May I still call you Luke? Or now that you've revealed your true status, must I call you Lord Barrett?"

"We can stick with Luke. I'm fine with that."

"This is my dear friend, Miss Edwina Fishburn. Fish? This is Lucas Watson, Lord Barrett."

"Hello, Miss Fishburn."

"It's Fish, my lord," she responded, "and hello to you too."

"Will you be joining us?" he asked.

"Gad, no. Libby doesn't need me telling her how to behave. Even if I tried, she wouldn't listen."

His raised a brow at Libby. "You don't travel with a chaperone?"

"No, but then, I don't require one. I have my pistol, remember?"

"I stand warned."

He extended his arm, and she clasped hold. Sparks ignited as they always did when she was in close proximity. The air was charged with so much energy that he was dizzy from wading through it.

"She has to perform tonight," Fish told him. "Please don't make her late where we'd have to rush to get her prepared."

"I won't let her be late," Luke said.

Libby smirked. "If you expect me to dawdle with you for hours, you'll have to entertain me, and I'm easily bored. Will you be able to amuse me for more than a few minutes at a time?"

He scoffed. "You'll be so thoroughly diverted that you'll be begging me not to bring you back."

"Keep hope alive, Lord Barrett," she saucily retorted, and she sauntered off.

He followed like a puppet on a string.

They walked out to his carriage. His driver and outriders snapped to attention, and as he helped her in and climbed in behind her, they all furtively watched her, their gazes warm with male appreciation.

What would it be like to be bound to such a magnetic woman? Any fellow who tried would likely turn into a jealous, vigilant fool who would exhaust himself by chasing off admirers. There'd be no way to stay sane.

He settled on the seat, and when she moved to the seat across, he yanked on her wrist and snuggled her onto his lap. He urged her forward and kissed her as he'd been dying to do since they'd parted the night before.

As she pulled away, they both sighed with pleasure, and she remained right where she was, a pert breast crushed to his chest. She studied him meticulously, as if hunting for clues that would clarify what was happening, and the explanation was simple.

They were one of those lucky couples who enjoyed a strident, uncontrollable attraction. There were frequent stories about the sort of passion they stirred, and poets wrote sonnets about it, but he'd never believed it was real.

"Who is Fish to you?" he asked.

"She sews my clothes and tends my wardrobe."

"She's magnificent at her job. You're so glamorous."

"Thank you."

"I have to admit that I'm surprised by your home."

"Why? Had you predicted I would be camping in the woods with a wagon of gypsies?"

"Yes. I'm a terrible snob, and I possess every low opinion about actors. I had no idea what I'd find, but your residence is so . . . *normal.*"

She chuckled. "And *I* am so abnormal."

"You live with Fish?"

"Yes, and my cousin, Simon. He's twenty."

On hearing a cousin mentioned, he scowled. "Simon Carstairs?"

"Yes, but he typically uses the stage name of Simon Falcon."

"I met him at a gambling club. He's a flamboyant devil, so it's not odd that he would be related to you."

"We haven't been in London very long, so he's been out making friends and opening doors for me." She wrinkled up her nose. "May I tell you a secret about him?"

"You should tell me all yours secrets."

"Don't gamble with him."

"He cheats?"

She clucked her tongue. "I would never accuse him of cheating. I will just say that he's worked in circuses and carnivals, and his fingers are quick and sly."

"You are surrounded by an interesting group of people."

"I've had an interesting life."

"You certainly have. Were you born fascinating? Or have you grown to be enthralling through years of practice?"

"I think some of it is innate, but it's mostly practice. My Uncle Harry is responsible for much of my appeal. From the start, he was determined to earn money off my tragedy."

"That's sounds horrific. Greedy too."

She shrugged. "It was all right. I had natural talent, so it was a good path for me. I doubt I'd have thrived in the kind of dreary existence most girls are forced to endure."

"I doubt it too. So you had family to claim you back then? I've been trying to remember how your story ended."

"Harry Carstairs claimed me and raised me."

"He is your uncle?"

"He announced to the world that he was, and everyone believed him. Recently however, I found out he was an acquaintance of my mother's and no kin to me at all. But would you keep that information to yourself? I haven't told anyone. I'm still a tad disturbed by it."

At the news, he was aghast. "I'm disturbed too. The authorities handed you over to him?"

"You had to be there to understand how it was. Harry was a very convincing fraud who could persuade others to participate in any deranged scheme."

"He didn't ... didn't ... abuse you, did he? He didn't mistreat you?"

"No. He was generally a grand fellow, and he gave me a grand future. Look at me!" She waved over her torso. "I wouldn't have become the person I am without him."

They were nose to nose, and he dipped in and kissed her again, but his mind was awhirl with questions.

Apparently, the tales she shared on stage were only part of her depressing history. The more she talked, the more he realized she was a damsel in distress. What gallant swain wouldn't be anxious to rescue her?

It occurred to him that he needed to tread cautiously. If he wasn't wary, he might wind up offering boons he should never extend.

"Where is Harry?" he asked. "Is he the uncle who passed on? Is he the one you were privately scolding on the dock for dying in a stupid way?"

"Yes, that's him. It's why I'm in London. He always booked my appearances, but Simon has started to manage it. We've had to restructure how we carry on."

"You support Simon and Fish?"

"Yes, I always have. I supported Uncle Harry too."

"Since you were a little girl?"

"Yes."

She admitted it as if it was customary for a child to support her family, and he wondered what it would be like to sing for your supper, to never know what sort of income would be generated from night to night. The weight of it had to have been enormous.

You could support her . . .

The dangerous prospect whispered through his head, and suddenly, it was on the tip of his tongue to propose an indecent arrangement. His brother, Bertie, had been a gambler and spendthrift who'd bankrupted the estate, but Luke had his own funds due to an inheritance from his maternal grandfather.

He would wed shortly. Now that he was the earl he had to, and his bride would be an appropriate aristocrat's daughter with a fine dowry. He would use her fortune to rebuild the property, but *his* money was his own. He was completely entitled to fritter it away on nefarious amusements such as a mistress.

Why not engage in a torrid fling before he wed? For the moment, he was a bachelor. He'd settle into matrimony and monogamy soon enough. In the meantime, why shouldn't he enjoy a salacious adventure?

Libby Carstairs would deliver months—perhaps years—of delicious entertainment, and the notion was too thrilling to ignore. But would he really toss his money away in such an illicit manner? Despite how he pretended otherwise, was he that corrupt deep down? He was growing terribly afraid he might be.

The carriage rattled to a stop, and she slid off his lap and glanced out the window.

"Where are we?" she asked. "I thought you were taking me on a picnic, but I could swear we're still in the middle of the city."

"This is my town house. We'll eat in the rear garden."

She scowled ferociously. "You brought me to your home? If I didn't know better, I'd suspect you have devious intentions."

"I might, and I'm interested to learn how many of them will be realized."

She opened her reticule so he could peek in it. To his great surprise, she truly was concealing a pistol. It was tiny and silver, but probably very lethal when shot at close range.

"I wasn't joking about being armed," she said, "and as you are about to discover, I am very modest and reserved, so whatever plot you're hatching, you will be sorely disappointed. I never misbehave."

"There's a first time for everything." He drew her in for another kiss. "It's just a picnic."

"So you say."

"I'll have a gaggle of footmen standing guard to protect your virtue." He snorted with a bit of derision. "Does it need protecting? Have you any *virtue* left?"

"I'm chaste as the day is long," she insisted, "and don't be so rude."

"That was rude, wasn't it? I apologize."

"Apology accepted, and could you promise we won't quarrel? Once you recognize that I'm not the woman you're hoping, please don't shout and throw objects at me."

"I've never shouted at a woman in my life. And there's no female alive who could make me angry enough to throw something. I find displays of temper to be incredibly exhausting."

"Well, yes, but then, I have driven many men to new heights of fury and outrage."

"Of that fact, Miss Carstairs, I have no doubt at all."

A footman yanked on the door, and Luke climbed out. Libby hesitated, staring at him, staring at the house.

"You're pressuring me horridly," she complained.

"Yes. Is it working?"

"I have no idea why I put up with you."

"You're mad for me. Admit it."

"I'm mad for some reason, but I'm not sure it's your fault."

"Come." He extended his hand to her. "Let's get you inside, so I can attempt to have my wicked way with you. I'm anxious to see if I'll have any luck."

"You are so obnoxiously arrogant."

"I might be, but I'm predicting I'm also exactly the man you need."

Ultimately, she grabbed hold and climbed out too.

"You better not make me regret this," she said.

"You never will."

"I think I regret it already."

"I'll change your mind. I guarantee it."

Chapter

4

"It's pretty here. You're lucky."

"I am lucky. I can't deny it."

Libby smiled at Luke, studying his handsome face and broad shoulders. They were seated under a tree at a small table in the garden behind his house. It was a warm afternoon, so he'd shed his coat and rolled back his sleeves.

She was particularly mesmerized by his hands. They were a man's hands, the palms wide and calloused from his years in the navy. Obviously, he hadn't spent his time loafing at a desk.

She couldn't stop assessing how the fabric of his shirt shifted across his chest whenever he moved. The sight had a strange effect on her feminine sensibilities, and she didn't understand why.

He simply generated the most exciting impulses, and they had a stirring effect on her moral inhibitions. She'd spent her life watching Harry and his friends misbehave, and she knew right from wrong, having witnessed too many accounts of *wrong*.

But for once, she was seriously considering the benefits of committing a few sins. What could it hurt? Who would care?

It wasn't as if she was saving herself for marriage. Nor did she have a doting parent who would be horrified at the notion of misconduct. She could carry on however she liked, but she always picked the straight and narrow path.

Had she changed her mind about that? If she let Luke Watson lure her into indecency, where would she be when it was over?

Nowhere she wanted to be. She was certain of that one pertinent fact.

"I wasn't sure of your preferences," he said, "so I had my chef prepare a little of everything."

"Well, I like everything, so you made a wise choice."

There was a second table set up next to them, and it was covered with pans of hot food. A half-dozen footmen stood at attention, eager to be helpful.

He gestured to the food. "I thought we'd dine buffet style and serve ourselves."

"That will be perfect."

"Can I chase the footmen away? I'd like to have you all to myself without them hovering."

"I guess you can chase them away. I can't imagine you'd ravish me in your garden."

"You might be surprised by what I'd attempt with you." He waved toward the trees. "There's a bench over there. We could commit all sorts of wicked acts on it, if I could lure you over there."

"If that's the case, I can guarantee I shall remain right where I am."

He nodded to the footmen, and they trudged off, hating to depart. No doubt they were anxious to eavesdrop so they could gossip later in the kitchen. She and Luke were silent until they disappeared inside, but one of them was a sentinel at a window, ready to rush back if Luke motioned for assistance.

It would be lovely to be rich and pampered. Did he realize how fortunate he was? Probably not. In her experience, wealthy men took their affluence for granted. The more elevated the bloodline, the more convinced they were that they deserved every boon with which they'd been showered.

"Shall I fill a plate for you?" he asked. "Or will you join me to evaluate our options?"

"I believe I'd like you to wait on me hand and foot."

He grinned a grin she felt clear down to her toes.

"If I spoil you rotten, will I win a prize?"

"Don't be greedy."

He went over to the buffet and snooped under the lids, then he peered over his shoulder. "They've brought enough to provision an army."

"Then I shall be a disappointing guest. When I have to perform at night, I never eat much in the day. It makes me tired."

"I'll serve you tiny portions. What would you like? There are slices of beef and some fish in a white sauce. I see various steamed vegetables, a pudding, and two kinds of pie."

"Let me sample all of it. We'll decide if your chef is earning his wages."

"I must admit I don't really know. I've only just arrived in London myself. I've been off in the navy, remember? I haven't had much of a chance to appraise any of my properties or servants."

She noticed that he'd said *properties,* as in plural. Again, she thought it would be lovely to be rich. She wasted so much energy worrying about money, trying to hoard it, trying to accumulate a sufficient amount so she didn't have to fret.

Her current situation was typical. She'd rented her house for three months, not being able to ever plan farther ahead than that. She liked the city and hoped she'd book plenty of work so they could stay where they were. If not, they might have to sign on with a traveling troupe where they'd journey around England, having to hunker down during the winter months and praying their funds lasted until spring.

She was never overly concerned about herself, but she had Simon and Fish to consider. She would never permit them to suffer. She would never leave them behind.

Luke carried over several plates, the food piled high and nearly falling off the edges. He placed two of them in front of her and two in front of his own chair, then he sat across from her and whipped out his napkin, laying it on his lap.

She was completely fixated on him, and she distracted herself by pouring them both a glass of wine. He lifted his and toasted her with it.

"Here's to us," he said.

She blanched. "Us? There is no *us*."

"I'm declaring there is, and I always get my way."

"Fine, you bully. Here's to us."

They clinked the rims together.

"And here's to our new friendship," he added.

"Are we friends?"

"Yes, and we're going to become more than friends."

"What would that indicate?" she asked. "I'm not marriageable material for you, so where would I fit in your life?"

"You could be my mistress," he blithely announced.

"In some foreign world where corrupt people reside, that might happen. But in the world where I reside, it's not in the cards."

"We'll see what you wind up giving me in the end."

She snorted with amusement. "You're so vain. Should I tell you how many men over the years have voiced a comment like that to me? It's why I made you promise we wouldn't quarrel when you can't persuade me."

"I don't care how many there have been in the past. You didn't like any of them as much as you like me. I might be worth it."

The cocky statement had her laughing. "You are so full of yourself."

"Yes, I always have been."

He dug in ravenously, as if he'd been starving in a famine, and she was fascinated by every little detail: how he held his utensils, how he stuck his fork in his mouth, how he chewed.

She'd never dined intimately with a handsome gentleman before. Generally, she avoided this sort of encounter, and she still couldn't deduce why she agreed to participate in this one. Pathetic as it was to admit, she simply liked him much more than she should.

Finally, he noticed she wasn't eating, and he halted, his fork dangling in mid-air.

"Don't you like the food?" he asked.

"It's delicious," she said, even though she hadn't tried a single morsel.

"What's wrong then?"

"All of this is too odd for me." She gestured around the garden. "You, this mansion, this picnic. I'm overwhelmed."

"You are not. If I had to describe your condition, I'd say you're totally in your element. This kind of garden and house are exactly where you belong. I wouldn't deem it unusual to learn you were reared in a palace."

"I like fine things. It would be futile to deny it."

"You mentioned your Uncle Harry wasn't your uncle after all. Were you ever able to determine who your parents were? You're so magnificent. If you confess that your father was a king, I will absolutely believe it."

She smirked. "My father wasn't a king."

Luke raised a brow. "You found out who he is then?"

"Yes, recently—after Harry passed away."

She was stunned to find herself blabbing portions of her secret to him. She hadn't even told Fish or Simon, but he simply encouraged candor. Tidbits were begging to leak out, and she couldn't shut up.

"Tell me about your father," he said. "Is he noble? Is he British? Might I be acquainted with him?"

A myriad of replies flitted about in her head. She sifted through them, struggling to figure out the best response.

After she'd realized the import of Harry's old letters, she'd been dying to apprise someone of the discovery. She'd tamped down the urge though, having convinced herself to tread cautiously, to ponder the angles and ramifications. She had a very tender heart. If she stepped forward and was denounced as a liar—which was very likely—she'd be crushed.

Her greatest wish was to fit in somewhere, to have a family—a *real* family—where she was a cherished member. She now knew where she'd originally come from, but she couldn't fathom how to barge back to that spot and demand she be accepted. Her story was—like the monologues she performed on stage—too fantastical to be true.

"I'm certain you've never heard of him," she said, and he scoffed with disgust.

"You're lying to me again. Why? Is he a criminal? Is he a notorious scoundrel? What?"

She tsked with exasperation. "I might confide in you—someday. And why are you always so sure you can perceive when I'm lying."

"Your face is an open book to me. We shouldn't ever gamble."

"Trust me. We won't."

He pointed to the food, and she pretended to swallow small bites. Mostly, she pushed it around with her fork while they talked about everything and nothing. They finished by sharing a piece of pie, with him feeding her from his own slice. It seemed terribly intimate, and she hadn't understood that sharing a meal could be so personal.

Ultimately, he declared himself stuffed, and he shoved their plates aside and leaned toward her. He studied her in that severe manner he had, his fabulous blue eyes digging deep.

"What should I do with you?" he murmured.

"What a silly question."

"How shall we carry on? I'm interested in your opinion."

"I will be happy to dine with you or to join you on a carriage ride whenever you choose to invite me. I'd love to see some of your horses too. We could take a fast canter together."

She'd already decided that she'd have to devise ways to avoid him. He was entirely too enthralled, and she was beginning to worry that she was too, but she wouldn't lead him on and have him assume they could have more than a casual meeting.

"I don't suppose you'd ever agree to a night out at the theater," he said.

She chuckled. "Since I've spent my life on stages, it's not much of an enticement."

"If I could walk in with you on my arm, all the other men would be green with envy."

"I'm afraid it's an experience you will just have to miss."

He downed the last of his wine, then he patted his thigh. "Come here."

"Why?"

"I intend to kiss you senseless. We had pie to conclude the meal, but *you* are the real dessert."

"I don't like the gleam in your eye. It's obvious you're planning mischief."

"I won't do anything you don't want me to do."

"I don't believe you."

"You are so stubborn."

"So are you."

He rose and stepped around the table, and he lifted her and slid onto her chair, then he snuggled her onto his lap. She could have protested or leapt up and escaped, but the sad fact was that she'd wound up precisely where she'd been desperate to be.

"There's a potent attraction sizzling between us," he said.

"No, there isn't. I constantly suffer through flirtations like this."

"This isn't a mere flirtation. How shall we proceed?"

"I'm not the woman you imagine, and I'm definitely not the woman you seem to be seeking. I'm acquainted with dozens of trollops who would be delighted to have an affair with you. If you're looking for carnal companionship, I can introduce you to some of them."

He snorted at that. "I'm not looking just for carnal companionship, and with you voicing a word like *carnal,* I'm convinced you're not quite as innocent as you claim to be. It makes me want to try harder to wear you down."

"We're not at the spot where you'll get grouchy, are we?"

"No. You could never upset me."

"Even if I'm not loose with my favors?" she asked.

"Even then, but I think you're lying about it. I think you're reeling me in like a fish on a hook. Are you hoping to stir me to an insane level of infatuation in order to drive up your price?"

"You are being absurd, and I have no *price.*" She rolled her eyes with annoyance. "You've insulted me, and I'd like to leave. Will you take me? Or will you force me to find my own way home?"

"If that's how you presume I'd act, you're the one who's being absurd."

She struggled to scoot away, but he gripped her waist and wouldn't let her go.

"I'm sorry," he said. "I'm being an ass."

"Yes, you are, and if you're not careful, you'll spoil a perfectly lovely picnic."

"You simply tempt me as I've never previously been tempted."

"I wish I could prevent it, but I can't fathom how I would."

"I blame it on Fate," he bizarrely said. "The gods are pushing us together."

"Why would they?"

"Perhaps they want to see what sort of collision will occur."

"Perhaps."

He started kissing her then, and she heartily joined in. From the moment he'd strutted into her parlor, the air had been charged with yearning. It was probably best to dispel some of it before she departed, for of a certainty, she would have to hide from him in the future.

He wouldn't like it, but she was only scheduled to perform at the theater for another week, then she'd agreed to attend the house party Simon had arranged. After that, she couldn't predict where she'd be.

For the next few days, she would have to enlist Fish and the theater manager to keep him out of the dressing rooms. If he became particularly recalcitrant, she would vanish from London until his ardor cooled.

She prayed it wouldn't end like that. Once he realized she wouldn't succumb to his advances, he'd likely lose interest very quickly.

As always happened with them, their embrace heated up, and they continued forever. He simply kissed her, then kissed her some more. He didn't attempt any genuine mischief, didn't begin grabbing for buttons or laces. He did yank the combs from her hair though, so the lengthy locks floated over her shoulders and he could riffle his fingers through the soft strands.

Eventually, they slowed, then stopped. She rested against his chest, her face buried at his nape as he caressed a lazy hand up and down her back.

"Would you come up to my bedchamber?"

She laughed, but miserably. "I can't."

"I'd ask if you're sure, but I suspect you are."

She drew away and studied him, committing every detail to memory. She reached out and traced a finger over his nose, cheeks, and lips. He had such a luscious mouth. It was absolutely made for kissing.

"I'm heading to the country tomorrow," he abruptly announced. "Will you miss me?"

At the news, she was swamped by an enormous wave of disappointment, but she concealed it and grinned instead. "I would never admit that I might miss you. You're already much too vain, so I wouldn't dare stroke your massive ego. It doesn't need stroking."

"Tell me you'll miss me," he insisted. "Say it."

"All right, you rat. I'll miss you."

"That's more like it."

"How long will you be away?"

"Almost three weeks. I wish I didn't have to go, but the plans have been in place for ages. I can't skip out on any of them."

She was saddened to hear about his trip, but relieved too. It solved numerous problems with regard to him.

After she concluded her limited run at the theater, she'd leave London too, for the house party. Then she would order Simon not to seek further engagements in town for a while. She'd sneak off to a spot where Luke would never search for her.

Not that she expected he'd search. His attention span for a doxy—as he definitely deemed her to be—would be very short. As the old adage went, *out of sight, out of mind*. He'd forget all about her.

"What will occupy you for three whole weeks?" she asked.

"I have pressing business at my estate. My deceased brother left a terrible financial mess for me to clean up. I have many issues to deal with there."

"Will you return to town after you're finished?"

"Yes. Will you be impatiently waiting for me to arrive?"

"I'll be here," she fibbed, "but whether I'll be waiting for you is another matter entirely."

"I'll call on you the minute I'm back."

At the notion, her pulse raced, proving that she liked him much more than was wise and she'd allowed the situation to spiral out of control.

She sighed. "To what end, Luke? There's no reason for us to socialize."

"It makes me happy, which seems like a very good reason."

"Yes, I suppose it is."

He brushed a kiss across her lips. "We'll figure it out. Don't fuss over it."

"I won't."

"It would be wrong to simply walk away from you."

"It would be wrong, wouldn't it?" she said. "We've hardly started."

"Yes, and it will be thrilling to see where this wild ride takes us. I can't imagine what direction we'll ultimately travel."

She could imagine it quite clearly. He'd dote on her until he grew bored, then out of the blue, he'd declare himself to be over her. They'd part, and he'd never ponder her again.

She, on the other hand, would suffer the loss forever. On top of the emotional calamity, she might wind up with a bastard baby thrown into the mix. Then what? She'd have to beg him for assistance, hoping he'd toss her a few coins to help her support her child.

She wouldn't live that way. She couldn't.

For him, an amorous fling was all tantalizing sport that was practically expected from a man of his station. For her, it was nothing but peril and disaster. He'd mentioned that Fate must have pushed them together, and she suspected that might be true, but so what?

In a different world, if her young mother hadn't been insane, Libby might have been the precise girl Luke required. But in her current pathetic condition, she could never be his.

"Now then," she said, "I've had a wonderful afternoon, but I have to be going. I have preparations to complete before my show."

"I guess I can let you leave."

She slid off his lap, and she leaned down and picked up the combs he'd plucked from her hair. When she straightened, he was still on the chair, his mood visibly glum.

"Don't be so morose," she said. "You'll see me in three weeks."

"It's an eternity, and I'm humiliated to admit that I am devastated by the prospect of our pending separation."

"It will pass like that." She snapped her fingers to indicate the brevity.

"I could stop by the theater tonight. We could have supper afterward."

Her pulse raced again as she imagined the future trysts they could have. She'd never met a man like him, and she didn't know how to fend off the attraction he stirred. The only method she could concoct was to stay away from him, then vanish when he wasn't looking.

"I'm sorry," she lied, "but I have other plans."

"Cancel them."

"I have a performance at a private event later on. I'm contracted, so I can't cancel it."

He appeared petulant and aggrieved, providing ample evidence that no one ever told him *no*. The poor boy. He was so spoiled, and it was another sign that they could never have any kind of relationship. She was spoiled too, and she had a nasty habit of ignoring bossy men. If she ever relented and they commenced a liaison, they'd drive each other mad in just a few hours.

"Come," she said. "I have to get home."

He rose to his feet without further complaint. They had a delay as his carriage was harnessed, but it was a companionable delay. They chatted in the driveway, and he stood very close, whispering naughty suggestions in her ear and teasing her with compliments that made her laugh.

Once they were in the vehicle, they kissed all the way to her house, so that, by the time her footman helped her out, she was quite overcome.

He tried to climb out too, but she insisted he remain where he was. If he escorted her to the door, she'd invite him in, then would find every excuse to prolong their parting. But it would be ridiculous to prolong it.

She reached up to him where he was lounged on the seat like a lazy king, and he clasped her hand and kissed it.

"I'll miss you every second while I'm gone," he said.

"I'll miss you too."

"Be safe, will you? Take care of yourself."

"I'm always safe," she said, "and I always take care of myself."

"I doubt that's true, and I'll worry."

"I don't believe anyone's ever worried about me before."

"Then I shall be the first. I'll fret constantly until I can be with you again."

They shared a poignant gaze, where she catalogued his features. He was departing, but he didn't understand that it was farewell. They were smitten beyond reason, and she had to be sensible for both of them. She was better at saying goodbye than any woman in the kingdom; she'd had plenty of practice.

"Thank you for this afternoon," she told him.

"We'll have many more—as soon as I'm back."

"I can't wait."

She pulled away and motioned to the driver that they were finished. His outriders jumped aboard, and with a crack of the whip, they lumbered off. She dawdled in the street, her last glimpse of him the smile he flashed out the window.

After he rounded the corner, she spun and went inside. Fish had been watching for her, and she bounded down the stairs.

"Well?" she asked as she slid into the foyer. "Did anything interesting happen?"

"No. We simply ate a delicious picnic under a pretty tree."

"Your hair is down."

"I was kissed with a reckless abandon."

"Are you wild for him? Is he wild for you?"

"Yes, so we'll flee London for a bit."

Fish's shoulders slumped. "But we just got here! And I like this house."

"I realize that, but we're not the type to put down roots."

"Yes, but I'd like to think—at my age—we can manage to stay in one place for a month or two."

"We have to book a different engagement—and it has to be far from London."

"Lord Barrett must be incredibly besotted."

"He might be," Libby admitted.

"How about you? Are you besotted?"

"If I am or if I'm not, it can't ever matter."

"A girl can earn a ton of benefits by allying herself with such a wealthy man."

"A *girl* might be able to, but you know my opinion about that sort of illicit bargain."

"Yes, and you know mine. You're entirely too morally inclined. It's a mystery to me how I could have shaped your attitudes for most of a decade, only to have you make such peculiar choices."

"In most people's view, Fish, moral conduct is expected and admired."

"It never took me anywhere, and I don't see that it's done much for you either."

"That doesn't mean I shouldn't try to be a decent person."

Fish might have pursued the argument, but Libby held up a palm to prevent it.

"Let it go, Fish. I'm weary, and I need to prepare for tonight."

Fish scowled. "Is your heart broken? Is that the problem?"

"It's not broken yet, but if I continue on with him, it definitely will be. So could we please stop talking about him?"

She whirled away and climbed the stairs to her room, determined to act as if all was fine—and it would be shortly.

She had a show to perform, then she had to move and find a new situation. All of it would keep her busy, and she'd forget about Lucas Watson—as she was sure he would forget about her.

She would arrive at that ending. She would save Luke from himself, and in the process, she'd save herself too. She was certain she could accomplish it. In fact, she was already halfway there.

Chapter 5

"Tell me again. How many people have you invited?"

"Honestly, Father, you should pay attention to me once in a while."

Charles Pendleton, Lord Roland, dragged his gaze away from the morning newspaper and focused it on his daughter, Penelope, whom they called Penny. He was having breakfast in the small dining room, and she'd surprised him when she'd deigned to stagger down just past nine.

She'd never been a morning person, and after she'd proclaimed herself to be an adult and no longer a child, she'd declared that she could sleep the day away if she chose. It was odd to see her up and about before noon.

"I always pay attention to you," he lied, "but how many guests is it again?"

"A few dozen will be housed in the manor—as I've been explaining for weeks."

"And what about the various dances and suppers you've scheduled every evening? Will we host the neighbors over and over?"

"Yes, along with the tenant farmers and prominent merchants."

"What about the ball on the final Saturday night. How many have been invited to that?"

"It's quite a large group. Aunt Millicent can give you the exact number."

"For those staying in the manor, I suppose this will include their servants, luggage, horses, and carriages."

Penny gaped at him as if he was dim-witted. "Of course it will include all of those. The most important visitors are coming from London. We can't expect them to walk from town and not bring their bags or servants."

"No, I don't expect we can."

He sighed, wishing he could turn back the clock and rescind his offer to host a betrothal party for her.

She was eighteen, so she was barely out of the schoolroom, but even though she was much too young to be a bride, he'd succumbed to her nagging and had agreed to find her a husband. His search had been quick and successful, and they were already marching toward a wedding he wasn't convinced he should have encouraged.

Many of her friends were marrying that summer, and she was suffering from the feeling that she'd be left behind if she didn't marry too. He hadn't been able to persuade her that it would be better to wait, and he'd quit trying.

His own nuptial debacle, perpetrated when he'd been twenty, had taught him many hard lessons, the main one being that a man's spouse would ultimately furnish all of his happiness or misery. Before jumping into matrimony with both feet, an enormous amount of energy should be expended in pondering the consequences.

She was a female though and incredibly spoiled. She had to have her way in every situation, and again—because of his marital calamity at age twenty—he never had the heart to tell her *no*.

She was about to engage herself to the premier bachelor in the kingdom, and she'd culminated that coup by goading Charles into funding one of the most extravagant weddings High Society had ever witnessed.

She was adamant that her event be bigger and grander than any of those being planned by other brides, so he was facing a summer of balls and banquets, none of which he actually wanted to pay for and none of which he actually wanted to attend.

The current occasion was typical of how he was being swept along by Penny's whims. Her decisions were being validated by her Aunt Millicent who'd never seen a farthing she didn't spend.

Initially, Charles had intended a quiet weekend to ease everyone into the betrothal announcement. He'd envisioned a modest gathering of some cousins, and the engagement becoming official after several days of tepid entertaining.

Instead, Charles had wound up with a two-week ostentatious bash, where he'd have a packed home, overrun parlors, empty liquor decanters, and strangers strolling down the halls.

He'd been determined that the party be comfortable for Penny's pending fiancé, Luke Watson, who was the guest of honor. Penny had been acquainted with Luke since she was a baby, but he'd been in the navy for the prior fourteen years and mostly out of the country, leaving when she was just four.

She'd only socialized with him a few times, and though she was excited that Charles had picked such a handsome candidate for her, she didn't know the first thing about Luke. And Luke didn't know anything about her. Their sole common denominator was the fact that Charles and Luke owned neighboring estates and the families had a fond connection.

Luke was thirty, so he was twelve years older than she was, and Charles viewed it as a blessing and a problem. Penny required the stable influence a more mature husband would provide, but Luke had traveled the globe and fought dangerous battles in the navy. Penny—with her incessant babbling and her focus on clothes and frivolous hobbies—would likely drive him mad.

They needed an interval at Roland to amuse themselves at the pursuits betrothed couples normally enjoyed—chats by the fire, private picnics, walks in the garden—but with Penny being so set on herself, Charles's idea for a simple event had been smothered by her exaggerated arrangements.

The cost would be staggering, and the stress and strain on the servants would be overwhelming. Throughout the festivities, Penny would be surrounded by admirers, and Millicent had scheduled non-stop activities to keep their visitors busy. At the conclusion, poor Luke would return home no closer to Penny than he'd been when he arrived.

Yet maybe it was for the best that he didn't learn too much about her. He might realize how flighty and fickle she was. He might skitter back to the navy, never to be seen in England again.

"Have you invited anyone I know?" he asked Penny. "Or will it be all young people? Please tell me there will be some acquaintances of mine too."

"Well, Luke will be here."

"He's not exactly a friend of mine." Charles was forty-six, and he'd been cordial with Luke's father, not Luke or his deceased brother, Bertie. "When will he join us?"

"Tomorrow afternoon, and if you inquire again, I won't respond. I shouldn't have to repeat myself on every little detail. From how distracted you are, you're giving me the distinct impression that you don't care about any of this."

"I care," he said. "I just can't figure out how the numbers swelled from a handful of cousins to a hoard of strangers."

"You can't expect me to march toward my wedding as if I'm an *ordinary* girl, can you? I'm the only daughter of the Earl of Roland. It's proper that you make a fuss."

He could have corrected her that she wasn't his *only* daughter, but they were adept at pretending she was. He'd had another daughter once, but he didn't ever like to drag up that prior scandal. He never liked to remind himself—or others—how gullible he'd been.

Penny liked to think she and her brother, Warwick, were his only children, even though they understood they weren't. There had been a wife before their mother, and a daughter before them too, but they ignored those dark days from his past.

He was happy to let Penny and Warwick assume they were the center of his world, and it was reprehensible for him to act as if the first girl, Little Henrietta, had never existed, but years earlier, he'd accepted that she was dead. The courts had declared it too.

His wife, Amanda, had run off with her lover to Italy, and she'd taken Henrietta with her. Her lover had died in an accident in Rome, and after he'd perished, there had never been a single clue as to what had happened to Amanda and Henrietta. Charles had searched for an entire decade.

Amanda had been a flamboyant attention seeker, and she wouldn't have hidden herself away, but she and Henrietta had vanished off the face of the Earth. He'd spent a fortune, having investigators scour every corner of Europe, but there had never been any sign of them after they'd been in Rome.

He hadn't wanted Amanda back. Her actions during their brief marriage had forced him to admit that she'd probably belonged in an asylum. But he'd been terrified for Henrietta, so he'd searched for *her*.

Amanda had had no maternal tendencies and—after she'd left him—she'd had no money either, so her rash deed had meant Henrietta was gravely imperiled. It was ancient history now, and with Penny about to wed, he wasn't inclined to fret over the sordid incident. What was the point?

He'd ponder it later, when he was alone and kicking himself for the mistakes he'd pursued when he'd been young and stupid.

Penny was pretty: blond, blue-eyed, short, and plump. Her mother, his second wife, Florence, had been plain, dour, and gloomy, so Penny had turned out to be more fetching than he might have predicted. She'd gotten all of his handsome Pendleton features and very little of her unattractive mother's.

For a moment, he wondered—if Henrietta had had a chance to grow up—would she and Penny have looked alike? Henrietta would have been twenty-five that year, and if she waltzed in, would she and Penny appear to be sisters? Would there be a resemblance? Or had their mothers' bloodlines been too different?

Amanda had been gorgeous and glamorous, which was why he'd become so foolishly besotted. He'd had to have her despite the costs. Henrietta had burst from the womb as a precocious, charming vixen. The last time he'd seen her, she'd been two, and she'd already been exhibiting her mother's traits for dramatic posturing. She'd developed a knack for goading people into watching her.

No doubt she'd have been a stunning, elegant woman. Penny was likely a tepid, lesser version of what her half-sister would have been like and, if they'd ever stood side by side, would have paled in comparison.

He stopped his woolgathering and responded to Penny's comment.

"Yes, Penny, it's important that I fuss over you, and you are my only daughter. I intend to send you off to your husband as if you're a princess. I hope every minute of your party will be smashingly fun."

"Of course it will be. I'm Penny Pendleton. How could it not be perfect?"

She flounced out, and he sighed again.

He simply wished it wouldn't be horrid. He wished the gaggle of youthful guests wouldn't constantly annoy him. He wished Luke would find reasons to like Penny, reasons to proceed with the wedding and not change his mind. The contracts hadn't been signed yet, so he could walk away without consequence.

Penny's saving grace was that she had a fat dowry, and Luke's brother had bankrupted Barrett. That fact ought to keep him focused on what mattered. Penny might be immature and inexperienced, but she was a great heiress. If Luke started to waver in his interest, Charles would succinctly mention the fortune that hung in the balance.

Luke could be persnickety and stubborn, but he wasn't an idiot. Money always made a girl more beautiful, and he'd recognize the value Penny's wealth could deliver. Charles wouldn't consider any other conclusion.

⁙

"I have a question, Aunt Millicent."

"Please be brief. I have a thousand chores today."

Millicent Pendleton was seated at a table in her sitting room, enjoying a cup of morning chocolate. It was just after nine, and she wasn't dressed, but was snuggled in her favorite robe. Penny had blustered in without knocking. Despite how often Millicent counseled restraint, Penny never approached in a calm, ladylike manner.

She and her brother, Warwick, had been spoiled and coddled, and though Millicent had worked to rein in their worst habits, she'd had scant success. Charles was too lenient with them, and whenever she'd tried to put her foot down, the wily pair would rush to him, and he'd countermand any edict Millicent leveled.

He still felt guilty over what had happened when he'd wed that slattern, Amanda. He viewed himself as having been a negligent father who hadn't protected his tiny daughter, Little Henrietta. He'd let crazed Amanda abscond with her, and he blamed himself for not being more vigilant. The end result had been that he indulged Penny and Warwick, the children he'd sired during his second marriage.

He couldn't bear to tell them *no* on any subject.

Luckily, Warwick had joined the army and was stationed in Brussels, so for the foreseeable future, she didn't have to tolerate him. There was just Penny, and she'd be a bride soon and would live at Barrett with Luke. Millicent would finally have Charles all to herself.

"You're still wearing your robe," Penny said as she slid into the chair across, "so how can you be busy?"

"I will be dressed shortly, and as I've frequently pointed out, my schedule and plans are none of your business."

"I'm making them my business. The guests will begin arriving tomorrow, and it doesn't seem like we're ready."

"Don't fret. The staff has been in a frenzy for weeks, cleaning and preparing the house. The bedchambers are spotless, the menus picked, the musicians hired, the food ordered. I guarantee no crisis will arise, so what is your question? Ask it, then leave me be."

"There's a trio of guests coming at the last minute."

"They weren't on the list, and they're coming anyway?"

"Cousin Stewart asked them, and they accepted. We can hardly send a note and *un*-invite them, can we?"

"I would have no problem writing that letter. We'll be packed to the rafters, and this will mean we have to rearrange the bedchambers. Will they all need rooms? We don't have three rooms."

"They just need one. Two of them are servants, so they can bunk down in the attic."

"This is outrageous," Millicent fumed.

"Yes, yes, I figured you'd think so." Penny waved a hand, as if incorrigible manners were of no account. "I want them here."

"Why?"

"The woman is famous on the stage in London."

Millicent was surprised she didn't faint. "You expect me to play hostess to an actress?"

"She's not an actress. She's a performer."

"It's the same thing."

"No, it's not."

"What's her name?" Millicent inquired.

"She's one of the Lost Girls of the Caribbean. Libby Carstairs?"

"I haven't heard of her in years. I can't believe she's still alive."

"She's such a celebrity!" Penny gushed. "If she attends, people will be agog, and they'll talk about my party for ages."

"It would have been a success whether she was included or not."

"I was wondering this," Penny said. "Would it be uncouth of me to ask her to perform for us? And how many times could I ask? Since she's barging in, it's only fair that she entertain us. Or would she feel as if she has to sing for her supper?"

"I'll have to reflect on this. She might love to show off for us or she might consider that we're forcing her to work. We'll have to wait until we meet her. Once we have a notion of the sort of person she is, we can decide the best course."

"That sounds like a good plan."

Penny jumped up and headed to the door, and Millicent attempted to command her. "Find Mrs. Skaggs, would you?" Skaggs was the housekeeper. "Tell her we have to change the bedchamber assignments so we can make room for Miss Carstairs."

"You tell her," Penny snottily replied. "I'm just as busy as you are. I have a full plate today."

Then she was gone, and Millicent yearned to chase after her, to scold her and warn her to guard her impertinent tongue. But from long, exhausting experience, she'd learned that it was futile to reprimand Penny on any topic.

She and Penny had never bonded, and Penny had never recognized her as the mother she was anxious to be. She had limited maternal tendencies, and Penny had never acknowledged her as having any authority.

Millicent's sister, Florence, had been Charles's second wife. They were all cousins, and he'd married Florence after Amanda had vanished with Henrietta.

As a young man, he'd been betrothed to Florence, but he'd been swept off his feet by Amanda who'd been a cunning, seductive siren. They'd eloped without Charles first breaking it off with Florence, apprising his father, or garnering the man's permission. The shock of it had ultimately killed the poor fellow who'd suffered an abrupt apoplexy and died shortly after.

It was another layer of guilt under which Charles still labored.

After Amanda had run off with her lover, he'd promptly divorced her. He'd settled down, regrouped, and walked the path he'd been destined to walk from the start. He'd trudged to Florence and had begged her to wed him. He was an earl, so she'd relented without much argument or dithering. She'd never forgiven him though, and she'd never recovered from the shame of having a divorced man as her spouse.

She'd locked herself away in the country, never having guests or socializing. She'd been determined to never face anyone who knew of the scandal, but just about everyone knew.

She'd quickly birthed Warwick and Penny, then she'd perished when they were two and four years old. Millicent had been eager to take her place. She'd always loved Charles and had felt Florence didn't deserve him. Florence had been plain, boring, and miserable, while Millicent—with her lush brown hair, big brown eyes, and slender physique—was pretty and could be vivacious when the situation called for amusement.

She'd moved in when Penny and Warwick were toddlers, and she'd never left. She'd been certain that Charles—as a grieving widower—would be so happy to have her loyal assistance that he would finally notice her in an amorous way. But he never had.

Despite how helpful she'd been, how proficiently she'd managed his home and cared for his children, he remained blind to her keen interest in being his third wife.

She'd arrived when she was nineteen, and she was thirty-five now, an aging spinster who had nothing to show for her fond devotion. Charles didn't seem any closer than he'd ever been to picking another bride. He was content with Penny and Warwick and wasn't inclined to sire more children.

As to herself, her other romantic chances had passed her by. She didn't have any money of her own, and her brother had married a harpy who hated Millicent and would never let her move back to the family estate. She was stuck at Roland, a sort of glorified housekeeper and unnecessary nanny.

One of Charles's two children, Warwick, had fled. The other was about to, and Millicent had to hope—once Penny departed—Charles would realize that Millicent had been waiting for him to step up.

Penny would leave for Barrett with Luke, and Millicent's sole regret was that Barrett was just a few miles away. If Millicent had been allowed to choose Penny's husband, she'd have selected someone whose residence was up on the moon, but she couldn't ever mention that aloud.

She could simply smile and carry on in her role as Charles's dedicated sister-in-law. She intended to push the wedding along and get it accomplished as rapidly as she could. After Penny was gone for good, Charles would have to notice her then.

Wouldn't he? He'd have to see that his next wife was standing by his side, and it was time to claim her.

She refused to accept any other conclusion.

⌒⌒⌒

LUKE WAS IN HIS library at Barrett, and he stared out the window at the park, wishing he could think of a reason to tarry. It was a pleasant summer day, the sky blue, the sun shining brightly, the roads clear, so he had no excuse to postpone his appearance at Roland.

As the crow flew, he could practically throw a rock and hit the fence where his land adjoined Charles's. It took quite a bit longer to travel to Roland Manor by carriage, and he was expected that afternoon. He always behaved as was expected.

In that, he'd resolved to be the exact opposite of his brother, Bertie, who'd been extravagant and wild. He'd killed himself during a drunken horse race with a royal cousin. The cousin had been gravely injured in the process, so the name *Watson* was being disparaged throughout the kingdom. Until the Prince Regent stopped fuming over the debacle, Luke and the Barrett title were in disgrace in the highest circles.

Because of the predicament, he couldn't figure out why Charles had suggested the betrothal to Penny. It was likely because Charles—after his antics as a young man—was as averse to scandal as Luke declared himself to be.

When Charles had approached him about an engagement, they'd had a lengthy discussion about moral rectitude and public reputation. They'd heartily concurred that their families had had enough ignominy and dishonor. Charles had been adamant that he would only consent to the marriage if Luke could swear there would be no fast living or improprieties.

Luke had vowed that he would never commit a contemptable act, would never shame himself or Penny.

In the past, he'd never exhibited a single wicked proclivity. Up until he'd met Libby Carstairs, he hadn't assumed he possessed any. A man was judged by his relatives though, and after Bertie's many misadventures, he had a lot of cleaning up to do.

He wasn't firmly obligated to the engagement yet. He could back out if, after further reflection, he didn't like Penny, but short of her turning out to be deranged, he couldn't imagine reneging. She was the precise girl an aristocrat of his station hoped to locate: pretty, rich, educated, and trained to her duties so she'd be a stellar countess.

In picking a wife, he couldn't ask for more than that.

She was awfully young though, and he had no idea what type of life she envisioned for them. Would she want to spend their time in town attending soirees and balls? Was that what she planned? He probably ought to get his sorry behind over to Roland and find out—but he couldn't force himself to go.

His carriage was harnessed out in the drive, his bags loaded, the driver ready to depart. He could have ridden to Roland on horseback, but he was staying the entire two weeks, so he was arriving with luggage. If an emergency arose, he could rush home, but he intended to tarry at Roland and prove to Charles—and himself—that he was the perfect choice to be the man's son-in-law.

His own parents had been deceased since he was a boy, so he didn't have them to guide him in the important matter of selecting a bride. He was letting Charles steer him in the proper direction. He trusted Charles, but what if Charles had made the wrong decision? What then?

His collar suddenly felt much too tight.

His qualms were all Libby's fault. He understood that fact. He'd been fully prepared to shackle himself to Penny, and her Aunt Millicent had requested a September wedding. He'd been amenable to the quick schedule, having convinced himself that it was best not to dither.

But now, Libby had lodged herself into his head, and he simply wished he'd never agreed to the stupid party. He yearned to be in London with her instead. How could he wed Penny in ten weeks when he was so besotted with Libby that he couldn't think straight?

Footsteps sounded in the hall, and his butler, Mr. Hobbs, entered.

"Your driver is waiting, my lord. I thought I should remind you."

"I'm being a sluggard. I can't seem to get moving."

"It's not every day a bachelor goes off to engage himself. Are you having a few jitters?"

"I guess I am," Luke said.

Hobbs had worked at Barrett all of Luke's life, so he was in a position to offer a personal comment. "Lord Roland is a fine man, and Lady Penny is pretty as a picture. Your parents would be delighted with this match."

Luke smirked. "I'll keep telling myself exactly that, and I suppose I'd better be off."

"Have a grand time, Master Luke." It was the affectionate term Hobbs had always used when Luke was a boy. "I shall cross my fingers that, when you return, you will be well on your way to being a husband."

"I can't determine if that's a worthy goal or not. Does Lady Penny deserve the curse of having me as her spouse? If that's to be her fate, I pity the poor girl."

"She'll be lucky to have you," Hobbs loyally stated.

Luke snorted at that and trudged out to his carriage. He was the guest of honor at his apparent betrothal party, and it was being held just down the road.

Chapter

6

"OH, NO."

Luke glanced out the window of his carriage, and at the sight he observed, he moaned with frustration. They were rumbling up the driveway to Roland Manor, and it seemed as if the entire household was present to greet him. It meant there would be a big fuss, which he would hate.

He'd been earl for the prior year, having learned of Bertie's death when he was off on his navy ship. He'd come home as quickly as he could manage, and he'd slid into his higher role as quietly as possible.

He hadn't hosted any celebrations, hadn't printed announcements in the newspapers. He wasn't the type to tout his elevated situation. But once he departed Roland in two weeks, he'd likely be Penny's fiancé, so the grand welcome was probably just what he should have anticipated.

Charles was at the front, Penny on one side and her Aunt Millicent on the other. Millicent was practically snuggled to Charles, as if they were married, but as far as Luke was aware, no romance was blossoming.

Behind the three main characters, there was an array of the senior servants, elderly aunties, and Pendleton cousins. There were also many people who appeared to be Penny's age. He supposed they were her friends, and they looked so accursedly young. Like children really, with whom he'd have nothing in common.

He tamped down a sigh of aggravation. What would he talk about with any of them?

Charles had recommended the party as a way to mingle with the significant family members. He'd suggested too that Luke view the event as a sort of test for Penny where he could evaluate her attributes as she played hostess.

Luke had agreed to the plan, so it was a little late to complain about the size or the number of guests. Obviously, they didn't know what kind of man he was or what kind of entertainment he enjoyed. With any luck, after they trudged through the morass, they'd all end up with a better understanding of each other.

His coach lurched to a stop, and he dawdled as a footman walked over and opened the door. He climbed out to a few cheers and a bit of applause that was humorous and bizarre. He reminded himself that it was an indication that the Pendletons were excited about the match and wanted to lead things off on a positive note.

He went over and made his helloes, and Penny said, "I hope we didn't scare you with this large reception."

"Just a tad," he admitted. "I was expecting a small family gathering."

"That's how we initially started, but we constantly remembered relatives we'd like you to meet, and the list grew and grew."

Charles explained, "We weren't specifically watching for you. For the past hour or two, people continued to arrive, and the crowd expanded on its own. We simply haven't gone inside because one carriage, then another, rattled up the drive. We're curious as to who will roll in next."

"I'm delighted to hear it wasn't all for me," Luke said. "It will put me in my place and keep me from getting a big head."

"We have a secret guest coming too," Charles said. "We're mostly waiting for her."

"Is she more important than me?" Luke teased.

"Yes, sorry," Charles teased back. "Apparently, you quite pale in comparison."

"Who is it?" Luke asked.

"We'll let it be a surprise," Charles told him.

Luke didn't like surprises, and he prayed it wasn't anyone from the royal family. He was still in the doghouse with the Prince Regent, due to Bertie's misadventure, and Luke couldn't abide an awkward moment that would embarrass him and detract from his need to focus on Penny.

She knew why he was there. Luke had insisted Charles tell her they'd been discussing an engagement, and he had a very low bar with regard to his opinion about her. He was already certain he'd wind up proceeding, and he couldn't fathom why he wouldn't.

But he had to recollect that, while he was assessing her, she was also assessing him. It would be the ultimate irony if—at the conclusion of the party—she didn't care to wed him. He was always assuming that the entire choice lay on *his* shoulders, but she would be allowed to have a choice too, and if she spurned him, it would serve him right for being such a conceited ass.

While they'd been chatting, a small carriage had turned up the lane. It was noticeable because it was painted pink, and he'd never seen a pink carriage before. There were no outriders in livery and no crest on the door to supply a hint as to the identity of the occupants, but there were streamers of ribbon attached to the corners and back.

The spectacle made him think of a princess in a fairytale or perhaps Cinderella on her way to the ball.

He gestured to it, saying to Penny, "You have more guests arriving."

"It's been hectic like this all afternoon," she said.

"It's probably for the best. You'll have the greetings done at once, and you can progress to the socializing."

"I have people showing up tomorrow too, so we won't be finished today. And of course, the neighbors will join us tonight for dancing. I don't know when we'll finally have everyone accounted for."

At the news, he could barely hide a grimace. He'd spent too many years in the navy, surrounded by tough, brave men. He'd never been much of a reveler, but he had to muster the energy to play the part she was clearly expecting him to play.

He kept peeking at her, trying to imagine what it would be like to have her as his wife. She was quite fetching as British girls usually were: blond, blue-eyed, and brimming with good health.

She was a petite female, so he towered over her, and she was very young. He couldn't move beyond that pertinent observation, but it was commonly accepted that a man was wise to marry a younger bride. He could train her to her carnal duties before she developed more independent traits, but the whole notion of *training* a bride was exhausting.

He was especially disturbed by the prospect of fornicating with her. He simply couldn't envision crawling into a bed and touching her in intimate ways.

"Penny," Charles said, "I realize you love loitering in the driveway to discover who will appear next, but after this carriage, let's begin escorting people inside. The servants need to get bags unpacked and bedchambers assigned."

"Oh, Father," she fondly replied, "you always want every process to run in a perfectly normal manner. You're determined to ruin my fun."

"I am not. I dote on you, and don't you dare pretend in front of Luke that you aren't spoiled rotten."

She grinned up at Luke. "I can't deny it, Luke. I am spoiled rotten, but it's Father's fault. He permits me to behave however I like."

As she stared at him, he was taken aback. For an instant, she'd looked just like Libby. The slant of her eyes and the curve of her lips resembled Libby exactly. The sight was odd and unnerving, and he didn't suppose he had any business pondering Libby and Penny in the same breath.

In any assessment, Penny would come up short.

Penny was pretty, but Libby was gorgeous. Penny was plump, but Libby was curvaceous. Penny was friendly, but Libby was magnetic. Penny was ordinary, but Libby was extraordinary.

The carriage rolled to a stop, and people were craning their necks, curious as to who would emerge. What sort of person gadded about in a pink carriage? Luke wasn't the only one who deemed it peculiar.

A footman marched over and opened the door, saying, "Welcome to Roland."

A blond man leapt out first—with the grace and flair of an acrobat. Luke couldn't see his face, but he was flamboyantly dressed in flowing silk trousers, a white shirt, with an embroidered vest over top. He was exotic and foreign, as if he was a circus barker or maybe a servant in a sultan's harem.

His hair was a striking gold color, worn long and curling over his shoulders. He had rings on his fingers and an earring in his ear, which wasn't that strange to Luke. As a sailor, he'd encountered many men—generally natives—who had piercings, but it wasn't an adornment often witnessed in rural England.

Luke was incredibly intrigued, and when the man finally spun toward him, Luke was totally bewildered. It seemed to be Libby's cousin, Simon Falcon, but that wasn't possible. Why would Falcon be standing in Charles's driveway?

To his great astonishment, Miss Fishburn climbed out next. He scowled, his mind frantically trying to figure out why she would be there too. As with Mr. Falcon, there was no discernible reason for her to be present.

Then Falcon reached into the carriage and guided Libby out. If an angel from Heaven had suddenly flown down to join them, he couldn't have been more stunned. He was being pelted by numerous emotions: shock, amazement, aggravation, confusion, joy, alarm.

Why was she at Roland? She was supposed to be in London, performing at the theater and impatiently waiting for him to return from the country.

Was she an invited guest? Was she staying for the whole two weeks? If she was, how would he explain that the party was being held for *him* because he was contemplating marriage to Penny Pendleton?

He felt as if he was wading in a bog, and there were a thousand huge pits in front of him. He couldn't walk in any direction without falling into one of them.

Clearly, when Millicent had sent a note, asking if he'd like to review the guest list, he should have paid more attention. He'd simply sent a note back claiming that Penny's choices were fine with him. It had never occurred to him that Libby might be a Pendleton acquaintance.

This was a disaster!

She was attired like the vixen she was, wearing a vibrant pink gown that was the same shade as her carriage. Her outfit was embellished with matching shawl, slippers, parasol, and fan. Her hair was intricately styled, with pink feathers woven in the strands.

She was glamorous and magnificent, like a goddess eager to tempt mortal men. The other males were shifting in their shoes, anxious to get a better look at her.

Mr. Falcon whipped off his cap and made a sweeping gesture with it as he announced, "Ladies and gentleman, Miss Libby Carstairs, Mystery Girl of the Caribbean!"

There were gasps of surprise and wild applause from the spectators.

"Penny! You scamp," one girl murmured. "Why didn't you tell us?"

Another added, "How could you keep it a secret? You must have been dying with anticipation."

Libby gave an imperious toss of her blond curls, her lazy, dynamic gaze roaming over the crowd. It passed over Luke, landing on him like a hard jolt of lightning, but she furnished no sign that she recognized him.

Appearing majestic and grand, she sauntered over to Charles, and he was mesmerized by her. *She* should have been introduced to him, but he took the lead, seeming overwhelmed as a green boy.

"Miss Carstairs!" he gushed. "How lovely to have you grace our humble home. I am Charles Pendleton, Lord Roland."

"I'm very pleased to meet you, Lord Roland." Her voice was husky, sensual, and it floated out and caressed all of them. "And it is *I* who am honored to have been invited."

She executed the merest curtsy to Charles, then she motioned to her companions. "May I present my cousin, Simon Falcon? And this is my devoted advisor, Miss Fishburn."

Charles's jaw dropped, and he actually blanched. "Fish? Is it really you?"

"Yes, hello, Charles. I'm delighted to learn that you remember me."

With Fish blatantly using Charles's Christian name, everyone was a tad startled. Agitated utterances raced by. Apparently, Libby would deliver a ton of intrigue and drama. Millicent didn't care for the notion though. She frowned defensively, and she sidled a little closer to Charles—as if he was hers and she wasn't sharing.

Libby's regal focus slid to Fish. "You know Lord Roland, Fish? You didn't tell me. Shame on you."

"I did tell you. Have you forgotten? The Earl and I are old friends."

Fish imbued the word *old* with such innuendo that it induced numerous snickers, but they were hastily tamped down.

Charles's cheeks reddened, but he didn't elaborate on his connection to Fish. He turned to Millicent and introduced her. "This is my sister-in-law and cousin, Miss Millicent Pendleton. She runs my home and manages my family for me."

Libby nodded distractedly, as if Millicent was beneath her notice. "Hello, Miss Pendleton."

"Miss Carstairs." Millicent nodded too, briskly, indicating that there would be no love lost between them.

Charles continued. "This is my daughter, Lady Penelope. We call her Penny. It's her party. I'm just the father who's paying for it."

"I'm sure she's lucky to have you." Libby studied Penny, her expression cool and unreadable.

"Thank you for coming, Miss Carstairs!" Penny said. "After I was notified that my cousin had asked you, I was quite giddy with excitement."

"I'm thrilled to hear it," Libby replied. "We were included at the last minute. You must allay my worries and swear we haven't inconvenienced you."

"Not at all, and might I request—while you're here—that you entertain us with some of your stories and ballads? I've been hoping you'd agree!"

"I would be happy to perform for you," Libby said. "I'm enormously flattered that you'd like me to."

Luke was next in line, and he couldn't deduce how she might greet him. He didn't think she'd offer a humiliating remark, but it would likely depend on how he was described.

He might have seized the initiative and blundered forward on his own, but he couldn't shake off his perplexity at observing her precisely where she never should have been. But he was also completely puzzled by how much she and Penny resembled each other.

When he'd first arrived at Roland, he'd thought Penny looked a bit like Libby, but with their being side by side, the similarities were disconcerting.

With their blond hair and blue eyes, their comparable height and facial features, they were enough alike to be sisters, with one of them glamorous and chic and the other more common and provincial. It was like contrasting a queen and a dairymaid.

Libby looked like Charles too—the same nose, the same blue eyes, the same tilt of her head. Charles had once had blond hair, but with his being forty-six, it had faded to silver. He was thin and dapper, was handsome and distinguished, and he could have been related to her.

Was Luke the only one who'd perceived it? He could hardly survey the crowd to ask if anyone shared his opinion, but was it possible Libby had a Pendleton in her family tree?

Penny yanked him out of his tormented reverie. "Miss Carstairs, may I present my dear friend and neighbor, Lucas Watson, Lord Barrett?"

"Your *dear* friend?" Libby inquired. "Are you betrothed and I wasn't informed? Is this an engagement party? Are congratulations in order?"

"Well ... ah ... ah ..."

Penny was caught off guard by Libby's query. His arrangement with Penny wasn't official yet, so there was no appropriate answer, and Libby realized it. She didn't push for a response. Instead, she spun toward Luke in a slow motion that was nearly terrifying.

She cast a bored gaze over his person. "Haven't we met, Lord Barrett? I believe we might have crossed paths in London."

Her comment goaded him into a reply. "You're correct. I'm an ardent admirer. We met at the theater, after one of your shows."

"How nice."

There was a hint of disdain in her tone so the assembled group would suspect she hadn't been impressed.

An awkward pause ensued, and Millicent smoothed it over by stepping into the breach. "How about if we get you inside, Miss Carstairs? How about if we get everyone in? We've been loitering in the driveway, and the servants are irked that we haven't let them tend all of you."

Millicent started shooing people in. Libby was in the center of the crowd and whisked along. Penny strolled with her, agog and in awe as she babbled platitudes in a manner Libby probably hated. Libby was polite and attentive though, and she smiled and nodded to all those who talked to her.

Charles and Luke were bringing up the rear, and he frowned at Luke and whispered, "My goodness, but isn't she something?"

"She definitely is."

"When Penny told me she was coming, I wasn't sure what to think, but she's stunning. You've seen her on the stage?"

"Yes. She's indescribable."

"I imagine so." Charles chuckled. "She reminds me of someone, but I can't place who it is. Did she look familiar to you?"

Luke didn't dare voice his opinion: that she looked like Charles and Penny.

"No," he fibbed. "She's so magnetic though. She practically sucks the air out of the sky."

"Doesn't she just?" Charles smirked. "This bloody party just got quite a bit more interesting."

He sauntered off, not aware that Luke hadn't accompanied him. The servants and guests went in too, all of them enchanted by Libby. He didn't know how she pulled it off, but she simply exuded an aura that made others yearn to linger by her side.

That aura had certainly enveloped him with no difficulty at all. From the minute he'd first laid eyes on her, he'd been completely ensnared.

He stood alone on the gravel, watching as Libby's driver maneuvered her carriage to the barn.

"A *pink* carriage?" he muttered to no one in particular because there was no one left to hear.

The color offended him, which was stupid. Who cared what color she'd painted her carriage?

The woman was striking and absurd and totally fascinating, and now, she was at Roland and being led into the manor. She'd be given the fanciest bedchamber and would settle in as a prized visitor.

Though he hadn't been named as Penny's fiancé, Libby would discover the truth very soon. How would she react? No doubt she'd never speak to him again.

In London, he'd accused her of being loose with her favors, but he was an excellent judge of character, and he was beginning to suppose that she didn't have low morals.

She wouldn't pursue an affair with a man who was about to become engaged. Not only was the engagement imminent, but if he broke down and proposed to Penny, the wedding would be held in September.

Whatever scheme he'd hoped to implement with Libby, whatever torrid fling he'd envisioned, it would never transpire. The next fourteen days stretched ahead like the road to Hades. Every time he entered a parlor, she'd be standing there, taunting him with what he couldn't have. How would he survive the torture she'd inflict?

He couldn't see her without wanting her, and his blatant attraction couldn't be concealed. If Penny didn't notice it herself, cruel gossip traveled fast, so she would quickly have it pointed out to her. What if she accosted him and demanded an explanation? What could he say that wouldn't sound hideous?

He could have followed Libby's adoring mob into the manor, but he didn't. He turned instead and proceeded to the park behind the house. If he took a long, slow walk, perhaps he'd calm down enough to figure out how to stagger through the debacle.

For just that moment, he hadn't a clue as to how he'd manage.

Chapter

7

"How do you know Lord Roland?"

"How do you suppose? He and I had a torrid affair."

Libby glared at Fish and said, "You might have warned me."

"Why would I warn you? It's not as if it happened yesterday. It's ancient history and has no bearing on anything."

"This entire party will be awkward enough. I don't need to have you stirring extra drama."

"Why would I stir drama?" Fish looked innocent as a nun. "He and I have both lived a thousand lifetimes since then."

"He's still a handsome devil."

"I agree. He's definitely aging well."

"How old is he?"

"I believe he's forty-six."

"And you're forty."

"Yes, so? If you're worried our romance will heat up again, you're mad. I'm not interested in a quick fling, and his type likes his paramours to be quite a bit younger than me."

"His *type*?"

"He's an aristocrat, and there is always a line of women out the door, hoping to snag one of them. They grow prettier, younger, and more debauched every year."

"Where do you fit in that scenario?"

"I was desperately in love with him, but he would never have married me. I walked away so it wouldn't become horrid. I left him before he could leave me."

"So you hooked your wagon to Uncle Harry instead?"

"Harry and I had a satisfying decade together. With him, what you saw was what you got. I never deceived myself into thinking I could have a happy ending with him. I had no misconceptions about what was possible."

"Please don't seduce Lord Roland."

"I doubt there's any chance of it," Fish said. "That shrew, Millicent Pendleton, seems to have dug her claws into him, but why would you care if he sets his sights on me?"

"We shouldn't stay here, so I don't want you to start any mischief that would delay our departure."

They were in the bedchamber provided to Libby, and she'd been hiding so it was evening already, supper over and the festivities beginning in earnest.

Hers was a charming suite, with bright yellow wallpaper and big windows that offered a view of the park. It came complete with a sitting room, bedroom, and dressing room behind. She was being treated like a princess, but so far, the visit had been much more stressful than she'd anticipated.

She'd presumed she could arrive with her usual aplomb, but the whole episode was extremely taxing. She hadn't thought she'd meet Lord Roland immediately, and she'd expected to have more time to prepare for the encounter. Nor had she realized she and his daughter would look so much alike. The discovery was disturbing in a myriad of ways she hadn't considered before deciding to attend.

Now that she was ensconced in a bedchamber, she was kicking herself for her lack of planning, and she was trying to figure out how she could slip away without it being noticed. But that probably wasn't feasible. She'd deliberately shown up in grand style, so people were watching her every move.

"Why wouldn't we stay?" Fish asked. "And why are you so despondent? Is it that bounder, Lord Barrett? Don't permit him to chase us away."

"He's about to betroth himself to Lady Penny!"

"So? He's thirty. Of course he's about to become engaged. I can't fathom why he hasn't been wed for years."

"Last week in London, he was begging me to be his mistress! He's a cad and a cheat, and I'm so disappointed."

"Why are you surprised to learn this about him? You've frittered away plenty of hours where rich scoundrels doted on you. You're aware of what they're like. Don't pretend to be shocked."

"I liked him. I thought he liked me too."

"I'm sure he's wild for you, but you can't be so naïve that you assumed it mattered. Don't tell me you were silly about him. I'm the woman who taught you about men and their motives, so I know you were repeatedly cautioned."

"He claimed he had problems to deal with at his estate, but he conveniently neglected to mention that he would actually be at Roland, getting himself engaged."

Fish shrugged. "Why would he have admitted it to you? He wouldn't deem it to be any of your business. Besides, aren't you over him? Haven't we fled London because of him? You gave up your booking at the theater so you wouldn't be there when he returned to town."

"Yes, but I didn't intend to run into him in Lord Roland's driveway!" Libby threw up her hands in frustration. "This is a disaster!"

"Only if you let it be. I think it will be harder on him than on you. *He* is the one who's about to marry. He's the one who's in an awkward situation. Not you. If I were you—"

"Well, you're not me," Libby caustically interrupted.

Fish ignored her. "—I'd flaunt myself every second. I'd wear my most stunning gowns, and I'd preen and flirt with all the gentlemen to make him jealous. By the time we depart, his calm façade will be totally shattered."

"I just craved a quiet sojourn in the country."

"There's no chance of that. Not with him lurking and glowering. Would you stop feeling sorry for yourself? It's exhausting."

Fish strolled to the door, and Libby asked, "Where are you going?"

"I'm going down to dance and socialize. You can hide in your room if you like, but I traveled to Roland to have some fun. It's why we're here, isn't it?"

"I suppose," Libby grumbled.

"If you don't come with me, everyone will wonder about you."

"I don't care. Tell them I'm indisposed."

"I won't tell them that. I'll say I have no idea what's wrong, and they can gossip over whether you're snubbing them."

"Would you find Simon for me? Send him up. He and I need to confer about the best locations for a show away from London."

"The last I knew, he was in the card room, waiting for the games to start."

"Could you drag him out? Inform him that I forbid him to gamble."

"You might as well order the sun not to streak across the sky."

Fish walked out and left Libby alone with her morbid rumination.

It had been incredibly difficult to greet Lord Roland and his daughter, but she could have managed it without much effort if Luke hadn't been standing at Penny's side, looking very much as if he belonged in that very spot and nowhere else.

Fish was correct that Libby would vanish until his interest waned. If he was off courting an heiress, what was it to Libby?

But she wasn't leaving London just because Luke was fascinated. She was also leaving because *she* was smitten to a dangerous degree. If she'd continued to dally with him, she was terribly afraid that, for once, she would have misbehaved in a manner she'd regret, and she absolutely refused to have him break her heart.

Since their catastrophic meeting out in the driveway, she hadn't seen him again, but she kept pondering their next encounter. What would he say? How would she reply?

He'd be determined to *explain* himself, but she'd rather jump off a cliff than listen to any of his excuses. He'd proved himself a liar and a libertine, which placed him in a wretched pot with every despicable cad of her acquaintance, and she was inordinately crushed by the discovery.

It didn't matter how Fish nagged, didn't matter how much Simon wanted to gamble. It didn't even matter that she would give up the opportunity to befriend Lord Roland. They weren't staying and that was that!

The door opened, and she glanced over, expecting it to be Fish, having forgotten something, or Simon obeying her summons. It was neither of them though, and when she realized the identity of her visitor, she was so incensed she was amazed she didn't explode into tiny pieces.

"Get out of here! Right now!"

"No," Luke said. "I thought we should talk."

"There isn't a single topic we need to discuss, *Lord* Barrett." She imbued the word *lord* with a hefty amount of venom.

The brazen oaf shut the door and spun the key, then he stuck it in his pocket so she couldn't escape until he deigned to release her.

"Are you insane?" she hissed. "You can't be in here with me! We most especially can't be locked in! Have you any notion of the trouble we'll stir if we're caught?"

"No one saw me," he ludicrously stated.

"You can't be sure of that."

She marched over and yanked on the knob, hoping against hope that the key hadn't worked, but she was trapped with him.

Fish had stripped her out of her traveling costume and removed her corset, so she was attired in her chemise and petticoat, a robe over the top. It was the second time he'd observed her in such a scandalous condition, and she wouldn't faint merely because he'd barged in when she wasn't dressed. But without corset and gown, she'd shed some of the armor required to keep him at bay.

She whipped around and said, "Give me the key."

"No. Now listen . . ."

"Listen to you? Are you deranged?"

"Yes, I very much believe I might be, but *you* have driven me to this ledge of lunacy."

"Your fiancée is downstairs!"

"She's not my fiancée yet," he had the audacity to claim.

"That's your defense? You haven't proposed *yet*, so it's all right for you to be in my bedchamber?"

He grinned. "I continue to stumble on you without your clothes, and I'm taking it as a positive sign."

"What is there about any of this you deem to be positive?"

"I have previously suggested this solution, but you've chided me for it, and I'm suggesting it again. We should have an affair."

Of all the comments he could have voiced, it was the one most guaranteed to fuel her rage.

"We are in your betrothed's home and you have the gall to proposition me?"

"If I decide to wed Penny, which I definitely haven't, I won't be married for ages. There's no reason we can't pursue an amour."

"There's every reason!" she irately said.

"Name one."

"I would never hurt Lady Penny in the way you're requesting. You don't seem to care about how she would view a liaison between us, but I certainly do."

"I don't intend to tell her about it."

"Of course you don't. You'll simply skulk around behind her back. Perhaps bad luck would strike, and you would plant a babe in my womb just before your wedding. Wouldn't that be a lovely gift for your bride as you begin your life together?"

"What would you advise then? For the next two weeks, will we ignore each other?"

"It's my goal for this evening, but as of tomorrow, I will no longer have to fret about you."

"Really? Why is that?"

"I'm leaving."

"Leaving for where?"

"That, Lord Barrett, is none of your business."

"You're not leaving." He scoffed as if the notion was ridiculous.

"You are not my husband or my father, so you possess no authority to boss me."

"I suppose you think you'll vanish on me, and when I finally return to London, you'll be gone."

"You're about to become engaged!"

"And I told you the wedding is months away—if at all!"

She felt as if she was speaking in a foreign language he didn't comprehend. How could they assess the quagmire so differently? It made her realize that they hadn't been as intimately attuned as she'd assumed.

She stormed away from the door. The manor was packed with guests, and any of them could walk by and hear them arguing. She would not humiliate herself by having people discover she had a man in her room.

He didn't have the grace to slink out like the cur he was. He followed her into the bedchamber. She closed the door, isolating them further, but hopefully, tamping down any sounds that might waft into the hall.

She was about to scold him but, as if she were invisible, he sauntered over to a chair in the corner and plopped down. There was a decanter of wine on a table next to him, and he poured himself a glass.

She stomped over and snatched it away. "You're not loafing and drinking in my bedroom."

"Why don't you drink it then? You should calm down. Wine might help to soothe your dour mood."

"I don't need wine to maneuver through this debacle."

She was perched in front of him, but far enough away that he couldn't reach for her. He studied her, liking her state of dishabille, how the robe was loosely belted. She was sufficiently concealed by fabric that it wasn't exactly risqué, but then, it was extremely risqué too.

"I don't understand why you're so angry," he said.

"You wouldn't. You're rich and spoiled, so you presume you can wallow in any sort of wicked behavior."

"I'm merely attending a house party—as are you."

"When we parted in London, you told me you had business in the country."

"I did. I do."

"You told me you were having problems at your estate."

"I *am* having problems there, and I've been dealing with them."

"And now, you're here at Roland and about to get engaged."

He frowned. "Could we stop talking about it?"

"No. Tell me why you picked her. I'm disgustingly curious. She's so much younger than you are. What could you possibly have in common?"

He hemmed and hawed, nearly refused to clarify his motives, then he said, "Her father approached me about it. My property adjoins his.

She has a fine dowry, and I've known Lord Roland all my life. It's a good match for me."

"What's in her dowry? Will she bring you large tracts of land? Will she deliver money too? A lot of money?"

"Ah . . . yes."

His cheeks flushed—as if with chagrin—so apparently he was capable of some shame.

"If I hadn't stumbled on you," Libby said, "would you ever have confided in me about your betrothal?"

He shrugged. "Probably not."

"You'd have let me read about it in the newspapers?"

"I hadn't thought that far ahead."

"With you likely to wed Lady Penny, what was it you envisioned happening between us?"

"Don't refer to it in the past tense. We should have a long, satisfying affair, and I fail to see why my pondering matrimony has to change that situation. My relationship with you would be completely separate from my relationship with Penny."

She scoffed with fury. "That just might be the most cold-blooded comment ever uttered in my presence."

"It's the reality that's vexing me."

"If I jumped into an amour with you, then you wed Lady Penny, you'd be committing adultery."

He sighed. "Yes, I guess I would be."

"Have you the slightest notion how awful that sounds to me?"

"Well, what do *you* envision happening between us? You couldn't have believed we would wind up married. You're not a foolish, starry-eyed girl, so you're aware of how the world works. A man of my station never marries a woman of yours."

It was a true statement, but a callous one that wounded her.

She could have argued with him, could have insisted she was precisely the female he needed as his wife. Yes, Penelope Pendleton could bring him money and land, but Libby could have brought other things: joy, excitement, friendship. Even love eventually.

Yet as she tabulated the mental list, she chided herself for being ridiculous. She didn't want to ever be a bride, didn't want to be *his* bride. So why was she so upset? It made no sense.

"You're correct," she agreed. "A man of your station always selects a candidate who is much richer and grander than me."

"Don't denigrate yourself. I think you're magnificent, but there are only certain ways you and I can be together. I've told you what they are. I'm bound to wed as high as I'm able, and I fully intend to do that. But in the meantime, why shouldn't we be happy?"

"You would be happy in such a sordid arrangement, but I never could be."

"You haven't considered the benefits an affair could deliver."

"There could be no benefit," she vehemently said.

"Are you sure about that? Wouldn't you like to be happy too?"

At the question, she was taken aback, and her initial reaction was to proclaim that she'd always been plenty happy, but that was a lie.

From the period when she was tiny and had suffered her string of tragedies, there had been a huge cloud of despondency hanging over her. With what she'd endured as a small child, then with conniving Uncle Harry glomming onto her, there'd been no chance for her to grow up perky and vivacious.

She was charismatic and flamboyant, but she practiced constantly to exhibit those traits, and she couldn't honestly state that she'd ever been happy. She wasn't about to debate the point with him though.

"Give me the key to the door," she said.

"No. We're not done discussing this."

"Yes, we are. I've probed your opinion about Lady Penny, matrimony, and adultery. Much to my dismay, you are not faithful or loyal, and it indicates you're not a person I could ever respect or esteem."

She wasn't behaving as he'd expected, and he was becoming annoyed. "You're not listening to me."

"I'm listening, and I've heard every word. You're about to betroth yourself to Lady Penny. If you ultimately decide not to proceed, you'll pick someone else just like her. You'll be engaged very soon."

"I suppose I will be," he bluntly said. "I'm thirty this year. I have to get on with it."

"But *I* don't have to watch."

Events at Roland were occurring at lightning speed, and she couldn't keep up. If he wed Lady Penny, it would kill her with regret and remorse. She didn't usually rue the past. She couldn't alter or fix it, but why should Penelope Pendleton be allowed to marry him, but not Libby?

Why had Fate pushed Libby so far out of the proper path that she could never be an appropriate bride for a man like him?

He scowled quite violently. "Why are you being so aggravating? You're acting as if I made promises and broke them. We've merely shared a few torrid kisses, and I'd like to share a few more. I've explained the circumstances by which it can happen."

"I'm asking myself the very same question: Why am I so aggravated? I have no idea, and I concur. We shared a few delicious kisses, but it could never have been more than that."

"I'm sorry I've upset you."

"No, you're not. If I had to assess your condition, I'd say you're irked to have been caught. Now we're finished talking about this, and you have to leave."

His scowl deepened, his mind frantically whirring as he sifted through possibilities that would placate her, but she couldn't imagine how he could persuade her to relent.

"What if ... if ..." He cut off, his bewilderment clear. Then he tried again. "What if I ... ah ... pass on the betrothal to Penny? What if I speak to Lord Roland and tell him I need more time to think about it?"

"How long would you claim to need?" She didn't care about any delay and wouldn't encourage one, but she was curious about what number he'd select.

"How about a year? I'll declare that I'm too busy at the moment, what with straightening out the financial mess my brother left me. I could insist I'm not ready."

"You'd force Penny to wait a whole year? Are you that sure of her devotion?"

"No, but I'm willing to risk it—for you. During that interval, I wouldn't pursue an engagement with her or anyone, and I'll focus all my attention on you. Would that bring you down off your moral high horse?"

She sighed—with amusement and disgust. "I would never consent to that. As you mentioned, you're thirty. You're an aristocrat, with a title and an estate to protect. You have to get your future in order. You have to choose a bride and marry her, and I refuse to be an impediment to that swift conclusion."

His face was so expressive, his emotions plainly visible. "So just like that, it's over?"

"We never really started, so how could it be over?"

"If you never saw me again, you'd be fine with that ending?"

"I'd miss you," she admitted, "but I've had a life of goodbyes. They're not that difficult for me."

He stood and stepped over to where she was hovering by the bed. She was still holding the glass of wine he'd poured when he'd first sat down. He yanked it away and gulped the contents, then smacked it onto a nearby table so hard the stem snapped off.

"Have I told you, Libby Carstairs," he said, "that you are the most absurd female I've ever met?"

"I don't recall that exact insult, but if you've leveled it, I'm not surprised. You're a spoiled bully, and you're anxious to pressure me into an affair, but you can't."

"You're not absurd because you won't obey me," he ludicrously said. "You're absurd because your thought processes are absolutely convoluted."

Before she knew what he intended, he grabbed her by the waist and tumbled them onto the bed. They landed in a tangle of legs and petticoat, and he rolled them so they were stretched out with him on top and her on the bottom. His much larger male body crushed her much smaller female one into the mattress.

She'd never found herself in such a scandalous position, but she wasn't alarmed as a less worldly young lady might have been. He wouldn't hurt or ravish her. No, he'd expect he could use seduction to erode her defenses so, eventually, she gave him what he wanted.

The pathetic problem with that scenario was that he was probably correct.

He glared down at her and decreed, "We're not parting, and you're not leaving Roland, so toss those insane notions out of your head."

"You're mad, Lucas Watson."

"Yes, I am, and I believe I've clarified that it's all your fault. *You* have driven me to lunacy. Will you *please* stop complaining? I can't listen to another word from you."

With that, he began kissing her, his lips capturing hers in a wild, reckless way. It seemed as if he was drinking her in, gobbling her up. He'd been wandering in the desert, and she was the oasis he'd been struggling to find.

His tongue was in her mouth, his fingers in her hair, and he was touching her all over, his hands roaming everywhere, learning her shape and size.

She'd meant to lie stiff as a board and pretend she wasn't enjoying herself, but just as he was totally obsessed with her, she was totally obsessed with him. The fact that he was out of reach and could never bind himself didn't deter her in the least. She yearned to *try* to make him her very own. She yearned to keep him forever.

She jumped into the embrace with a great deal of enthusiasm, her hands busy too. Depending on where she caressed him, he would tense or purr or sigh, and as always when they were together, the tryst quickly spiraled out of control. They couldn't get close enough, couldn't hold each other tightly enough. They wrestled, scratched, and bit, going at each other like two cats trapped in a sack.

Who kissed like this? Who carried on with such feral abandon? It felt as if they'd tumbled off a cliff, and they were falling down and down and down. Where would they be when they hit bottom?

A rhythmic noise intruded. At first, she assumed it was the frantic beating of her heart, but as it grew more incessant, it dawned on her that someone was out in the hall and knocking on the door.

She jerked away, and he frowned, confused over why they'd halted. He would have asked what was wrong, but she pressed an angry finger to her lips, warning him to silence. Then she dug into his pocket and retrieved the key.

She slid out from under him and hurried to the sitting room, calling, "Yes? It's Miss Carstairs. May I help you?"

"Miss Carstairs! I'm so glad you answered me! It's Lady Penny."

Libby swallowed a gasp, and she peered over her shoulder at Luke, her eyes wide and furious, eager for him to see how irate she was that his irresponsible conduct had placed her in such an untenable predicament.

She shut the bedroom door so he wouldn't be observed loafing exactly where he never should have been, then she rushed over and jammed the key in the lock. She peeked out to find Lady Penny with two maids flanking her, both of them prepared to spring into whatever action was required.

Penny was attired for the gala that was occurring in the lower parlors, wearing an exquisite blue gown that enhanced the color of her hair and eyes. She looked like the pretty, rich heiress she was. She'd adorned her outfit with tasteful jewelry. A fan dangled from her wrist, and her curls were highlighted by a slim tiara that twinkled when she moved.

It was clear she'd planned to bluster inside, so Libby blocked any entrance with her body, letting the younger girl glimpse her robe and petticoat. Hopefully, good manners would prevent her from pushing her way in.

"Lady Penny?" Libby said. "I must admit I'm surprised to have you visit. Is there a problem down at the party?"

"The better question is: Are *you* all right? I spoke to Miss Fishburn, and she advised me that you were indisposed. I simply had to check on you."

Libby forced a smile. "That's very sweet. Thank you."

"You're not under the weather, are you? Or weary from your trip from town? Please tell me you're not. Please tell me you'll come downstairs. The guests are excited for you to join us, and I am too. It won't be the same without you."

Libby stifled a moan. "I am fatigued tonight. I had thought I might rest, then take part in the fun tomorrow."

Lady Penny, for all her being rich and spoiled, really was charming. "May I be frank, Miss Carstairs?"

"Certainly."

"I'm thrilled you're here, and I'd like us to be friends. There's something about you that makes me feel it's our destiny to be cordial. I sensed it the moment you climbed out of your carriage."

Libby could have validated Lady Penny's sentiment. She was aware of what was causing it to flare, but she wouldn't walk down that road. Probably not ever.

"I'd like us to be friends too."

"Won't you come down to the party with me?" Lady Penny said. "Say *yes!* Say you will."

Libby was usually very stern in sticking up for herself, but from the minute she'd arrived at Roland, she'd been distraught. What sort of trembling ninny would she be when the visit was over?

"When you've asked so kindly," Libby said, "I can't bear to disappoint you. Of course I'll come down."

Proving her youth, Penny clapped with glee. "I knew you'd agree. I brought my personal maids to help you dress. Will you let them? They can have you ready in an instant."

A thousand visions of disaster darted through Libby's mind. Luke was a few feet away and stretched out on her bed. There was no rear exit, so he couldn't sneak out.

"I'm flattered that they would volunteer," Libby said, "but Miss Fishburn handles my clothes. She's covetous of her spot by my side, and she'd be incensed if I allowed anyone else to assist me."

"I understand."

"Could you send her up? Would it be too much of a bother?"

"I'll locate her immediately and tell her you need her."

"I appreciate it, and I'll see you soon."

"You're serious, aren't you? You'll be down right away?"

"I'll be there before Miss Fish can button the last button."

"Wonderful!" Lady Penny gushed. "I'm so glad."

She spun away and glided off, her two maids trailing in her wake. Libby dawdled until they rounded the corner, then she shut the door and locked it again.

She marched to the bedroom where Luke had slithered off the mattress. He was over in the chair where he'd initially been sitting. He'd poured himself another glass of wine, and he sipped it casually, as if he didn't have a care in the world.

"I take it your presence is demanded downstairs," he said.

"Yes, and you have to leave."

"I suppose I should. Apparently, I've tempted catastrophe as much as I dare for one evening."

He rose and went over to her. He pulled her to him so their torsos were pressed together all the way down. Sparks ignited, and she was practically weak in the knees from feeling how luscious it was to be so close to him.

"Lady Penny seems to like you," he said.

"I have no idea why."

"You fascinate her."

"I'll try my best not to. Once I depart Roland, it's my specific intent that she never think about me again."

He kissed her, and she struggled to not kiss him back, but she couldn't keep from participating. He had that effect on her. Fate had shoved her into his path for a frightening purpose she couldn't yet identify, and she wouldn't be able to flee until that purpose was realized.

"You're not heading to London in the morning," he said, and it sounded like a command.

"I should," she half-heartedly responded.

"Yes, you probably should, but you are *not* going. You're staying here."

"Why, Lucas Watson? What can you hope to achieve with this torment?"

He grinned. "It amuses me, and we have to let it play out. For now, I can't agree to part from you."

He stared at her, his stunning blue eyes taunting her with the recognition that he had a hold over her she couldn't deflect. Ropes of connection were wrapping around her ankles, tethering her to his side, and she didn't have a knife sharp enough to cut the cord.

"I might return to London," she stupidly insisted. "You couldn't stop me."

"*If* you decide to be that ridiculous, I'll chase after you."

She smirked with exasperation. "You would, wouldn't you?"

"I am mad for you, Libby Carstairs, and until we figure out how to maneuver through this quagmire you've stirred, you're not sneaking off. I can read your mind, remember? You plan to flit off to town and disappear while I'm not there."

"I wasn't planning to disappear."

"Liar. How could you imagine you'd succeed? You are the *Mystery Girl* of the Caribbean. You're too notorious to hide."

"Perhaps I couldn't hide from you, but if I avoid you, your interest will wane. I'm sure of it."

He laughed a tad cruelly. "My interest isn't about to wane, so there's no point in vanishing. It would simply stoke my obsession."

He took another kiss, then walked to the door. She followed him and stuck the key in the lock. Then she peered out to be certain no one was strolling down the hall.

"Go," she mouthed.

"I will—for the moment," he whispered. "But I'll be back. I guarantee it."

He strutted out, not concerned if he was seen. When he reached the stairs, he glanced at her over his shoulder, shooting her a look of such passion and desire she was surprised it didn't knock her over.

She staggered to the nearest chair and eased into it.

"What now?" she asked the empty room, but the room had no answer.

She would wait for Fish so she could dress in her most stylish gown, then she'd waltz down to socialize with Lady Penny. Luke would be lurking in the corners, watching her, wanting her. She'd be watching and wanting him too. Would they light the house on fire with their strident attraction?

Any terrible detonation seemed likely.

Chapter
8

"FISH! THERE YOU ARE! I've been looking everywhere."

Fish braced, then relaxed. She smiled at Charles, her dear Lord Roland. He'd briskly approached, his hands outstretched, as if he'd pull her into a hug, and she shifted to the side, preventing an awkward embrace.

He scowled, but didn't comment.

She was standing on the verandah, leaned on the balustrade in a shadowed corner where she was mostly invisible. She could stare into the parlors and enjoy the festivities without having to actually be part of them.

She liked to watch the dancers twirl by, liked to watch the men gamble in the card room. She liked to keep an eye on Simon and Libby too, always suffering from the oddest perception that they might vanish if she wasn't paying attention.

She'd just turned forty, and for much of her life, she'd glommed onto corrupt cads, and thus had been supported by them through their dubious schemes and swindles. Harry Carstairs had been typical. He'd been a handsome scalawag with a felonious heart, and he'd had a sly way of accumulating money from people who shouldn't have trusted him.

Harry was dead, and it wasn't likely she'd persuade another rascal to let her attach herself. She'd grown more dependent on Libby and Simon, needing them for financial security, but needing them emotionally too.

They were her family, a mix-mash of disconnected orphans who'd bonded as if they were relatives. If she'd had any maternal tendencies, she'd have viewed them as her children, but she didn't have them, so perhaps she was more like a cordial aunt or a much older big sister. They would keep her company in her old age, and they were both loyal in their own way, but if she could find another paramour to take Harry's place, she wouldn't necessarily complain.

She liked to have a man around, but she liked being a spinster too. She was too independent, too stubborn and impatient. The notion of having a husband was like a tough piece of meat she'd never been inclined to chew.

"Hello, Charles," she said to him.

"Why are you lurking by yourself in the dark?"

"It was hot and crowded in the house. I was desperate for some fresh air. How about you? What dragged you out?"

"I told you. I've been searching for you."

From the moment he'd recognized her in the driveway, she'd figured he'd want to get her alone so they could talk. At least she'd been hoping he'd want that. It was the main reason she'd been hiding. She hadn't decided how she felt about bumping into him again.

When Simon had wrangled the invitation to Roland, she hadn't known what to expect, and she hated to be disappointed. It had been twenty years since she'd last seen Charles, so it hadn't seemed probable that he'd remember her. Their fling had occurred during a period when they'd been young and stupid and had thought they could break all the rules.

Back then, he'd had a passion for actresses and other loose strumpets. His debacle with his first wife, Amanda, hadn't cured him of it. Fish had been an actress herself, but without the talent to succeed at center stage. Eventually, she'd been forced to accept a different role, working behind the curtain to design costumes for glamorous vixens like Libby who had the special allure that captivated audiences.

Charles had been scandalously divorced by then and far down the road toward wedding his plain, dour cousin, Florence, as he should have done from the very start. Florence had been the bride initially selected for him by his father, but he'd met Amanda and had eloped with her instead.

By trudging forward with Florence, he'd convinced himself that his raucous proclivities were vanquished and that he could be happy with the small, ordinary existence she would provide. But in the interval Fish had consorted with him, his debauched appetites hadn't been vanquished in the slightest. He'd been an ardent beau who'd tantalized her with possibilities.

He'd been a wounded soul too, mourning his failed marriage and the loss of his daughter, Little Henrietta. He'd been a tormented man that any woman would have loved to save.

He'd temporarily flirted with the idea of spurning Florence a second time, of running off with Fish, but a friend had yanked him to his senses, which had been the only logical ending.

They'd parted on sweet terms, with him offering her money and jewelry as a goodbye gift. She'd been offended by the gesture and had refused them, but with how her fortunes had plummeted afterward, she shouldn't have been so proud. She'd been glad they'd dallied, and she'd been glad too over how completely he'd broken her heart.

It had galvanized her opinions about men. She'd come out of it smarter and much less gullible. After him, when she'd jumped into new affairs, she'd picked scoundrels from her same class, oafs like Harry who never surprised her and never made promises.

"What brought you to Roland?" he asked, pulling her out of her dreary reverie.

"I go where Libby goes."

"Are you her . . . mother?"

"No. Just her friend and costumer."

"You always had an aptitude for fashion."

"She's so gorgeous, and I'm lucky that she wears my clothes."

He snorted at that. "How long have you worked for her?"

"Too long probably, but I like helping her. It suits me."

She didn't really *work* for Libby though. She'd been Harry's paramour off and on for almost ten years, so she'd lived with them occasionally, but she'd never had any authority over Libby. She'd never supplied anything Libby had truly needed except for the fabulous outfits she sewed.

She didn't want to talk about any of that though. It would mean discussing her bad choices in life, such as hooking her wagon to a charlatan like Harry Carstairs. After falling for rich, titled, Charles Pendleton, Harry had been quite a step down.

"How have you been?" he absurdly asked.

"I haven't seen you in twenty years. What portion of that period would you like me to describe?"

"That was a stupid question, wasn't it?"

"Yes, but then, I always deemed you to be very silly."

"I remember that about you. You were never impressed by me."

"Well, you rarely displayed behavior that was impressive."

He laughed fondly. "You look good."

"Thank you. So do you, but then, you always were a handsome devil."

"And you were always a beautiful woman."

He was tall and slender, dapper and fit. He still had all his hair, but the blond color had faded to silver, so he appeared very distinguished, and no doubt, he'd grow more handsome as the decades passed.

Being forty, she was still plenty attractive too. At five-foot-five in her slippers, she was enticingly curvaceous. Her green eyes were merry, her auburn hair lush and curly as ever, but there were a few hints of gray woven into the strands.

In a world where nearly every female was blond and blue-eyed, she was incredibly unique, so she and Charles had been an arresting couple. They'd caused bystanders to stop and watch them when they'd walked down the street together. She missed those days when people had stared and wondered if she was someone important.

"If we keep tossing compliments at each other," she said, "the air will become so sickly sweet we won't be able to breathe."

"I'm just so delighted to see you. I can't guard my flattering tongue."

"I enjoy a bit of flattery so feel free to shower me with it."

"I've thought about you so many times," he ludicrously said.

She'd obsessed over him too. Not that she'd admit it. What was the point?

For years, she'd peeked out at audiences, checking the dandies up in the box seats, wishing he'd be there, but once he'd retired to the country to wed Florence, he'd never returned to town. Or if he had, she hadn't crossed paths with him.

She'd taken to reading the newspaper in the hopes that his name would be printed there, but after his debacle with Amanda, he'd sworn to never engage in any conduct that would put him back in the public eye, so there'd never been any articles.

Florence's obituary had been reported when the unlikable shrew had died, and with his being a widower, Fish had toyed with the idea of traveling to Roland to ask if he'd needed comforting. But in the end, she hadn't committed the idiotic act.

"You haven't thought about me," she told him. "Don't tell lies or my head will swell due to my assuming you're sincere."

"I'm not lying. I have often pondered you."

"Have you been fixated on what *might* have been for us?" She scoffed. "Nothing sensible could have transpired. At this late date, please don't rewrite our history."

"Haven't you ever imagined a different conclusion?"

"Since *I* was the one who would have been happy to stick around, and *you* were the one who scurried home to wed your cousin, I don't believe I should have to answer you."

"*Touché*, Fish. You always were pithy in your assessment of any situation."

"How was your marriage to Florence?" she brazenly inquired. It was a rude query, but she posed it anyway. "Was it as horrid as I predicted it would be?"

"I shouldn't speak ill of the dead."

She snorted with amusement. "Don't hold back on my account."

"I will confess—only to you—that it was very dreary, but in light of my first disastrous leap into matrimony, I was desperate for *dreary*. I was determined to never suffer a minute of excitement ever again."

"Did she ever forgive you for your elopement? I warned you that she wouldn't."

"No, she never forgave me, and she constantly apprised me—in quiet ways—that she was angry, but I fully deserved her ire."

He'd been betrothed to Florence when he was a boy. She'd been raised, expecting to be his countess, but he'd run off with Amanda instead. Amanda had been a singer who'd burst onto the London stage where she'd tantalized all the eminent men of his generation. He'd been anxious to claim her before anyone else could.

She'd been deranged though. She'd possessed none of the skills required to succeed as a wife or a countess, and she'd had wild tendencies that had grown more pronounced after she'd birthed Little Henrietta.

They'd fought relentlessly, and she'd finally left him, after accusing him of being an abusive ogre. From Fish's own experiences with him, she knew he wasn't violent or abusive, but Amanda had been a lunatic who could have driven even the most docile spouse to lash out.

"Florence birthed you two children," Fish said. "You must take some satisfaction from that."

"Yes, a boy and a girl. My son, Warwick, is in the army at my request. He was exhibiting some of the traits I displayed when I was twenty."

"Meaning what? He was consorting with actresses and other trollops?"

"Yes, but I shipped him off to a regiment so he couldn't become completely debauched."

"Lady Penny seems to have turned out all right."

"So far, I haven't noticed a single bad attribute in her. She's been the easiest daughter any father could ever have sired."

"I'm glad for you."

"Tell me about your life," he said. "Where have you been living? How have you been living. Did you ever wed? Before you respond, I must categorically state that I will be insanely jealous to hear that you did."

She chuckled. "I never married."

"May I hope—after falling in love with me—that no other fellow matched up?"

"No, you may not hope that. It was more along the lines of me learning how painful a broken heart could be and my vowing never to suffer one again."

"I broke your heart? Really?"

"Yes, you arrogant oaf, and you know it too. Don't pretend."

"I'm enjoying this conversation more and more. Admit it. You've been pining away all these years."

She rolled her eyes. "You are so full of yourself, and I don't want to talk about me."

"Why not?"

"Since we parted, nothing interesting ever happened. I realized I would never move into lead roles at the theater, so I reined in my dreams and built a place for myself behind the curtain."

"Sewing for people like Miss Carstairs? Was it a good choice?"

She shrugged. "It was good enough."

"Was there ever a beau who tickled your fancy after me?"

She could have told the truth and said *no*, but she wouldn't stroke his ego, so she claimed, "I work in the theater, Charles, around actors and rich dandies. I had dozens of affairs after the one I had with you."

He studied her, then scoffed. "You did not. Your face is still an open book to me. There haven't been any."

"There have been a few, and that's all you need to know about it. And we're finished discussing me."

"For now," he said like a threat. "I intend to dig out every detail of what's occurred since I last saw you."

"I already mentioned what they are: I stopped acting and became a costumer. I journey across the country, tagging after Libby and dressing her for her shows. That's it."

"You're much too fascinating for that to be the whole story."

He looked as if he'd start spewing a myriad of questions she'd refuse to answer. She didn't like to focus on herself, on the paths that had never opened, on the men who were never worth it. She was forty and a spinster and that was the total sum of her biography.

She had Simon and Libby to care for, and she was relieved to have them, but as she took stock of where she currently stood, it didn't seem like she'd come very far.

"We should talk about you," she said. "It's the topic you always relished the most."

"I'm still the vain brute you frequently accused me of being. I can't deny it."

"Was there ever any news of Little Henrietta?"

"No, never a word."

"Are you still searching for her?"

"Not anymore. I have acquaintances who travel in Europe, and they watch for Amanda, but there's never been a sighting. She was such a flamboyant character; I'm sure she'd have popped up on a stage somewhere."

"I'm sure too."

"She never could have hidden herself away," he said, "so I've had to accept that she and Henrietta met with a bad end."

"They died?"

"I'm certain of it."

"What a morbid comment. It proves you've spent too much time wallowing in the country with dullards like Florence. It makes me want to tarry so I can fill your head with positive thoughts."

"I like the sound of that." Suddenly, his gaze grew a tad more wolfish. "How long can you stay?"

"I'm here for two weeks—if Libby remains for the entire party."

"She might leave?"

"Yes." Lord Barrett's presence at Roland was irritating Libby, so Fish couldn't predict what she'd decide. "She's been offered a lucrative contract in London," Fish lied, "so we might have to return earlier than we planned."

"I'll have to convince her to delay. You only just arrived, and I'm not about to have you flit off immediately."

"I probably shouldn't have come."

He stepped in so he was much closer than he should be. She put a palm on his chest to push him back, but he didn't move.

"Why are you really at Roland?" he asked. "Please tell me it was because you were anxious to see me again."

"It wasn't that. I didn't actually think you'd remember me."

"Not remember you? Are you daft?"

"It would have been a huge blow to my ego, but I'd been bracing for that result."

"Would you walk in the garden with me?" he inquired out of the blue.

"Why?"

"Why would you suppose? I'd like to get you alone and take advantage of you."

"I'm forty."

"Yes, and I'm forty-six, but we're not dead."

"Not yet anyway."

"Let's go. Let's find a dark spot and misbehave. You can't have forgotten how."

He clasped her hand, ready to march off and expecting her to blithely follow him.

Men were such peculiar creatures. She hadn't spoken to him in almost twenty years. They'd chatted for a few minutes, and he was prepared to philander. Why would he instantly figure she'd be interested?

She glanced out into the garden, and she had to admit his suggestion was tempting. She was one of those odd women who relished a man's physical attentions, and in the past, he'd been remarkably adept at passionate sport. He probably still was.

Why not oblige him? Why not?

As the prospect raced through her head, she reminded herself why not: She had a tender heart that was easily broken. She'd learned to set her sights on cads like Harry, men who were born to be disappointments so—when they fled—nobody missed them, most especially herself.

If she dashed off to frolic with Charles, she'd be dragged right back into his life, and she couldn't let it happen.

"Answer one question for me," she said.

"If I can."

"Are you intimately attached to your sister-in-law?"

He was aghast. "To Millicent? Gad, no. She simply lives with us. She came to us after Florence died, to help out. Her brother married and started a family, so she stayed on because she has nowhere else to go."

"She has designs on you. Haven't you noticed?"

"Don't be absurd."

"It's plainly visible, but you're a man so it wouldn't have occurred to you."

"She's not sweet on me. She's cared for the children and run the house. It kept me from having to wed for a third time. She's glad to assist me."

"Is she?" Fish smirked. "I doubt she'd like to discover that we'd snuck off to dally on a park bench."

"It wouldn't be any of her business."

"If that's what you think, then you're still a fool." She drew her hand from his and stepped away. "I better get inside. Libby will be looking for me."

"Don't abandon me. Not yet."

"I'm sorry, but I have to."

He smiled a delicious smile, and she was terrified he was about to beg her. She wasn't sure she'd decline twice. She spun and hurried inside—before she could behave precisely as she shouldn't.

PENNY DAWDLED ON THE edge of the crowd surrounding Simon Falcon. He was performing magic tricks with a coin that had people gasping. He was so flamboyantly charming that it was difficult to *not* watch him.

He was slender and willowy, his body imbued with the grace of a dancer or an athlete, and he was incredibly handsome. His hair was blond, and his eyes blue, so he had the traits common to most any Englishman, but his hair was a golden blond, his eyes a dazzling blue. On him, the common traits were much more striking.

His hands were the most intriguing, moving with a casual air that was hypnotic. He talked constantly too, having an innate ability to keep the spectators laughing and listening.

She thought he was her same age of eighteen or perhaps he was a bit older than that, but he had a flair and confidence she would never have dared exhibit. She didn't realize there were men who carried on so flagrantly, and his antics had her wishing she could carry on flagrantly too.

He'd been twirling a coin, then it vanished, and he held up his palms to prove it wasn't there.

"Where is it?" he asked, then he turned to Penny and said, "Oh! I believe I see it!"

He walked over to her and brushed his fingers under her hair to caress her ear. The bold advance was audacious, and she should have been incensed that he'd touched her, but when he pulled his hand away, the coin had reappeared.

"Lady Penny!" he said. "You're such a scamp. Why were you hiding it from us?"

He displayed it for everyone, and the observers clapped and patted him on the back. Several of them patted Penny on the back too, as if she'd been his assistant. He winked at her, and for just an instant, it seemed as if Time stood still. Sounds faded away, and there was only dashing, brazen Simon Falcon.

"More! More!" the crowd urged. "Show us another!"

He shrugged them off, but in an affable way. "I can't show you all my tricks at once. You'll stop thinking I'm interesting."

People chuckled at that, and he sauntered away. She tried to ignore him as he left the room, but she couldn't conceal her piqued attention. But then, all the young ladies were furtively peeking at him.

She tarried where she was until she felt she could wander off without others assuming she was following him, but she definitely was. When she finally found him, he was in a different parlor and over by the doors that led onto the verandah. He was posed there, as if he'd been waiting for her.

He noted her immediately, and he nodded pompously, as if she'd behaved exactly as he'd been expecting.

He grabbed a glass of champagne from a passing waiter, then went outside, providing a clear invitation that she should accompany him. She hesitated for a minute, then a minute more, and she couldn't resist any longer than that.

Initially, she couldn't see him anywhere. She rushed over to the balustrade, and he was out in the grass, standing under a lantern, and he motioned for her to come down.

She recognized that she was perched on the edge of a significant ethical cliff. It would be wrong to go to him. He would escort her farther into the garden. They would find a secluded spot and . . . what?

Probably kiss, but she was so naïve that she couldn't guess with any certainty if that was what he planned.

At school, she and her classmates had spent untold hours, fantasizing about the husbands they would eventually have. They'd been determined to be swept off their feet by Prince Charming. In reality, they'd all been highborn heiresses who were destined to wed whomever their fathers picked. The man could be old or fat or horrid, and they'd have no say in the matter.

Their marriages would be contracted to make their fathers and husbands richer, to spur the united families to new heights of power and influence. Passion and love were irrelevant, but frivolous girls could always dream.

Her father was hosting her party for Luke, in the hopes that—at the conclusion—Luke would be so enamored of Penny that he would propose. Luke wasn't the worst choice. He was handsome in a dark, severe manner, and he was calm and courteous. With his wealth and title, he was the biggest catch in the Marriage Market.

For the next two weeks, if Penny acted like the appealing, pretty girl she was, she could win him with very little effort. But did she really want him?

He was so old—twelve years older than she was!—and almost as old as her father. He was very much like her father too: stern in his attitudes, strict in his habits, and morally inclined in every situation.

Because his deceased brother had been a wastrel, he shared her father's same zeal for quiet living and modest conduct. He wasn't the type who would entertain a rapt crowd with his exploits. He would never deliberately make himself the center of attention.

Mr. Falcon gestured again, and he raised a brow in question. Was she coming or not?

He was able to read her mind, was able to understand how conflicted she was. If she took a step into the garden, she'd be crossing a line she shouldn't cross. Then he smiled, sending her the distinct message that she'd be glad afterward.

She glanced over her shoulder, but no one was watching, and she practically ran to him. He extended his hand and clasped hold of hers. They dashed off together, heading deeper into the shadows, and they were laughing like naughty schoolchildren who'd gotten away with mischief.

They kept on until the noise from the manor faded behind them, then he guided her off the path and led her into the trees. Without asking, without furnishing her with a chance to decide what she'd like to have happen, he dipped down and kissed her. She was so astonished that, without hesitating, she kissed him back.

It was her very first kiss, but it wasn't awkward or strange. She joined in with incredible relish, and it seemed as if she had quite a knack for it. Or perhaps he was simply so good at it that he made it easy for her to participate.

The embrace went on forever, with neither of them disposed to call a halt. How long had she stolen away? Would she have been missed? By her Aunt Millicent most likely. If her aunt interrogated her about her absence, what excuse could she give?

Finally, he was the one to end it. He drew away and gazed down at her, his expression tender and intense. She'd never had a man look at her as he was looking, as if she was amazing and he couldn't live without her.

Luke—her possible fiancé—had definitely never looked at her like that. In fact, he barely noticed her at all. Whenever he deigned to speak to her, he was unfailingly polite to the point of dullness. So far, he hadn't evinced by the slightest word or deed that he found her to be exceptional. She definitely couldn't picture him dragging her into the garden for a torrid kiss.

They were mostly strangers, and it would never have occurred to him that she might like him to exhibit a bit of passionate interest. She, herself, hadn't realized she'd been hoping for it, and now that she'd dallied with Mr. Falcon, how would she ever view Luke as she had previously?

Her father had insisted Luke would be the perfect husband for her, and she hadn't doubted him. She'd accepted his opinion, as she accepted all of them. On a topic as important as matrimony, surely he knew best.

A match between them would be about land and money, but clearly, there were facets to a male-female relationship that she hadn't considered. She felt as if Mr. Falcon had opened a door that only adults could peer through, and suddenly, she was asking herself this question: Why would she settle for a boring, aristocratic marriage?

She was shocked to have asked it. How could a few desperate kisses have rattled her thought processes to such a stunning degree?

"You're the most beautiful girl I've ever seen," he murmured.

She was used to those sorts of compliments. "Thank you."

"I was positive you'd follow me out here."

"How could you have been? I wasn't certain myself."

"Sparks fly when you're near, so it indicates that the universe approves."

"Approves of what?"

"Of our being together, silly. I want to spend all my time with you. When can you get away?"

"To do what?"

He grinned a cocky grin. "I'll show you once we're alone."

"You're too vain by half."

"Yes, I always have been." He delivered another rousing kiss. "Where is your bedchamber located? I could sneak in later."

She gasped. "What?"

"Does your maid sleep with you? Or will you be by yourself?"

"I'll be by myself, but it's awfully brash of you to suppose you'd be welcome. What kind of girl do you think I am?"

"I think you're the kind who will fall in love with me."

She frowned. "This is my engagement party. You're aware of that. I'm about to be betrothed to Lord Barrett."

"Are you really? Can you actually picture yourself wed to him?"

"Well . . . yes. I imagine I can."

He vehemently shook his head. "He's all wrong for you, and you'd never be happy. He's so old and dreary. Is that the type of husband you seek?"

He'd uttered so many wild statements that she felt dizzy.

"My father picked him for me," she said.

"Just because your father picked him, that doesn't mean it was a good choice. Your father might like him very much, but your father isn't the one who has to climb into the marital bed with him. You need a husband who is young and exciting and who will make you smile constantly."

"Someone like you, for instance?" she warily asked.

"Yes, someone exactly like me." He leaned in and whispered, "Where is your bedroom? I'll meet you there after the house has quieted down for the night."

The prospect sent a shiver of exhilaration through her innards. Did men and women behave so scandalously? Was it common? Did they regularly sneak away to romp in bedrooms?

If she went to her bedchamber with him, she had no idea what would happen there. She'd heard plenty of rumors at school, but her fellow classmates had been as naïve as she was. They'd been guessing, sharing gossip. There was physical conduct involved. There was occasional nudity too. Depending on a male's amorous skills, the event could be thrilling and wonderful or embarrassing, painful, and unpleasant.

She suspected though, with Simon Falcon, it would be on the thrilling end of the scale.

Her curiosity was inflamed, and she almost agreed, but at the last second, better sense prevailed. He was cunning and seductive, and if he visited her, she had no doubt he could spur her to commit acts she shouldn't. It would imperil her future, so . . .

She had to ponder carefully. What were the benefits of a liaison? What were the risks? Was there a way to proceed, but without any genuine damage occurring?

Mr. Falcon would be at Roland for two weeks, and she couldn't bear to *not* be alone with him again. Already, she felt closer to him than she'd ever been to anyone. He'd stirred the sort of avid passion every girl yearned to experience, but it had pushed her to the verge of reckless decisions, so she had to think wisely and clearly.

"You can't come to my bedchamber," she told him.

"Are you sure?"

"Yes, I'm sure."

"I have to see you though—as often as we can manage it. Tell me you want that too."

The moon shone down, bathing him in a silver halo of light so he looked magical and mysterious. If she was shrewd, if she was clever, might she be able to keep him for her very own? Or perhaps, could she have him for a while? If she had some fun before she became engaged, how could it hurt? Who would ever know?

"I want to be with you again," she firmly declared. Of that fact, she wasn't confused at all.

He shuddered with relief. "If you'd refused, I can't predict what I'd have done."

"We'll have to be cautious."

"Of course we will be."

"No one can ever discover that we're flirting."

"It's more than flirting," he insisted.

"Maybe."

"The more we dally, the more you'll understand."

"Tomorrow," she said. "We'll find an excuse to sneak off."

"I will absolutely die a little bit until then."

She chuckled and shook a finger in his face. "Mind your manners, Mr. Falcon, and guard your wicked tongue."

"I never mind my manners. Haven't you figured that out?"

He pulled her in so the front of her body was crushed to his. He kissed her hard, kissed her fiercely, then said, "You're mine now. I can't allow Lord Barrett to have you."

"My father might have something to say about that."

"Bugger your father," he crudely muttered. "If he would select such an unsuitable candidate, why would you listen to him on any topic?"

"Why indeed?" she mused.

She was anxious to escape, and she stepped away, but he tightened his grip on her hand. He was that determined to keep her with him.

"You can't go," he said. "Not yet."

"I have to. My aunt will have been searching for me."

"Let her search. I don't care if she worries."

"I do." She stared at him forever, then sighed with gladness. "I'll see you tomorrow."

"You better mean it."

"I mean it," she responded.

She whipped away and ran to the manor, recognizing—if she didn't force herself to part from him—she'd have tarried all night. She continued to run until the lights from the windows illuminated the garden and she could have been observed racing toward the verandah.

She slowed and walked up the stairs and, because she couldn't resist, she stopped and glanced back. As she'd hoped, Mr. Falcon had followed her to be certain she arrived safe and sound. He was down in the grass, watching from the shadows, his focus intense and riveting.

His expression was smug, as if telling her she'd wind up giving him whatever he sought in the end. The notion was terrifying and thrilling.

She flashed a smug expression of her own, informing him he might have met his match. Then she spun and sauntered inside, positive he would remain transfixed until she vanished in the crowd.

Chapter

9

"Fish tells me you're sweet on Lord Barrett."

Libby glared at Simon. "Maybe Fish should mind her own business."

"Are you sweet on him? More importantly, is he sweet on you?"

They were trotting down a country lane, just the two of them having taken a pair of Lord Roland's horses for a ride. They'd grown up around horses, but their situation was never sufficiently stable that they kept their own animals. It was always delightful to have someone open his barn and allow them to entertain themselves in a way they relished.

"It doesn't matter if Lord Barrett and I enjoy a heightened affection," she said. "The only role I could possibly play for him is that of mistress, and you're aware of my feelings about that sort of relationship."

"And you're aware of mine," Simon cockily retorted. "If a rich idiot wants to toss his money at you, why not let him?"

"You sound too much like Harry for my liking."

Simon snorted. "My dear old father was a fool about many things, but he was never wrong about the advantages that could accrue from hitching your star to the right wagon."

"Where did it get him in the end?" Libby asked. "He died poor and disgraced, having been ignominiously shot by a jealous husband."

"No, he died happy, living an exciting life in which he reveled to excess."

Libby rolled her eyes. "You have his peculiar view of the world. It's clear Fish and I have had no influence in molding your character."

"I have plenty of character, and I'm smart enough not to waste my energy on ridiculous pursuits. I shrewdly expend it on vital amusements."

"Such as gambling and womanizing?"

"Yes, and you haven't answered my question. Are you sweet on Lord Barrett?"

Libby shrugged. "I suppose I am, and it's exhausting to bump into him at Roland. I wish we could have peeked at the guest list before we agreed to attend."

"Is he the reason you were so eager to scurry out of London?"

She'd been offered a contract for another three months at the theater where she'd been performing, but she'd had Simon decline it. They both knew that paying jobs were difficult to find, and he was irked at what he'd deemed a reckless decision.

"I need Lord Barrett's interest to wane," she said, "and I was certain if I disappeared while he was away from London, he'd forget about me. Now I show up in the country, and he's here too. He and I are disgustingly besotted, and I'm afraid people will notice our attraction. I'd hate to hurt Lady Penny over it. She seems to admire me, and I won't dampen her enthusiasm."

"Would you like Lord Barrett to reconsider his engagement to her?"

"What do you mean?"

"I could probably throw a wrench in that arrangement—if you'd like me to."

"I repeat: Meaning what? What are you talking about?"

"I'm becoming friendly with Lady Penny. In a few more days, I'm betting she won't be all that sure Lord Barrett is the husband for her."

At the comment, Libby's pulse pounded with dread. Simon was an incredibly handsome confidence artist. He'd grown up in circuses and with traveling troupes where he'd acquired all kinds of intriguing talents. He could ride like the wind, execute magic tricks like a god, and mesmerize audiences with his looks and seductive voice.

He'd been tutored by her Uncle Harry and other devious charlatans who'd helped him hone his flair for deception. He was particularly adept at charming young ladies and convincing them to give him boons they should never relinquish.

If he'd set his sights on Penelope Pendleton, it could never be for an honorable purpose, and the gullible girl would be harmed in the end.

Usually, Libby ignored his schemes and pretended they weren't happening, but she had a special affection for Lady Penny. She wouldn't stand idly by and permit Simon to coerce Penny into a predicament she'd always regret.

"Leave Lady Penny alone," Libby scolded.

"I don't want to." He grinned his lazy grin, the one that made every female who saw it fall in love.

"If you can't promise to behave, we'll pack up and depart tomorrow. At dawn."

"*You* can depart with your tail between your legs. I'd like to tarry for a bit. I can join you later after I'm finished here."

"I could speak to her father about you. He could run you off without much effort."

Simon scoffed. "You won't speak to him about me. Don't act as if you've suddenly developed a conscience."

He was correct that she wouldn't tattle. It was a trait hammered into them by Uncle Harry. There had constantly been a lot on the line with Harry, and at an early age, they'd learned to never trust outsiders and to keep their mouths shut.

"I like it at Roland," she said instead, "and I refuse to have my visit wrecked because you can't control your worst impulses. If you continue on with her, I can guarantee it will blow up into a big ruckus."

"Maybe I like Lady Penny," he ludicrously stated. "Maybe I'm absolutely enchanted."

It was Libby's turn to scoff. "I know you too well. If you're flirting with her, you have an ulterior motive."

"Perhaps I'm doing it for *you*, so she'll reject Lord Barrett. Is that so hard to believe?"

Libby oozed sarcasm. "For me? Really?"

"Yes. If she spurns him, her rebuff will sour him on matrimony for a while. He'll be free and available for romance. You could step into the void created by her snubbing him."

"Would you get it through your thick head? He only wants one thing from me, and he can't have it."

"What are you saving yourself for?" he asked. "Marriage? Why would you? It's not as if you have a dozen beaux eager to wed you. Why not sell that precious chastity of yours to Lord Barrett? I could negotiate a good agreement. You could walk away financially set for life."

"Please be silent. With every word you utter, I'm more certain we should flee Roland immediately."

His smile was very sly. "I already told you: If you slink off, I won't be accompanying you. I'm having a grand time, and I'm positive Lady Penny, our beautiful hostess, would be devastated if I vanished."

Libby grumbled with frustration and spurred her horse into a gallop, abruptly deciding she should have ridden out with a groom rather than him. He could be so annoying, and like Harry, he was always sure the cards would fall in his favor so there would be no downside to his mischief.

Since he rarely suffered any consequences, it was difficult to persuade him that she was right and he was wrong. She'd had enough of his arrogant posturing, and she didn't have the mental energy to spar with him. She was exasperated over her tryst with Luke the prior evening, disgusted that he'd brazenly blustered into her room, disgusted she'd been too weak to kick him out.

She'd let him needle and cajole about their affair until she'd promised she wouldn't sneak away, and wasn't that the most dangerous conclusion she could have engineered?

She approached a gate, and normally, she would have raced on by, but it was obviously a portal to a large estate. There was a fancy sign marking the entrance, the name, *BARRETT*, carved into the stone. She reined in, and Simon reined in too.

"I didn't realize Barrett was so close to Roland," he said.

"Lord Barrett mentioned it was. Their boundaries adjoin."

"Ooh, Lord Barrett chatted about all that, did he? You two definitely sound like chums." He nodded down the lane. "Let's meander down and catch a glimpse of the manor."

"Let's not. What if Lord Barrett saw us? Or what if a servant observed us and told him we'd stopped by? I have no desire to explain why I was spying."

"Come on! I'm determined that you understand how rich he is."

"I understand. I don't need his wealth thrown in my face."

"Yes, you do. You don't seem to grasp the benefits you could amass from an association with him."

"I grasp them. I'm just not interested in glomming onto any of them."

"Coward!" he taunted, recognizing it was the best way to coerce her.

She wasn't afraid of anything and never had been.

He yanked on his reins and trotted through the gate, and she followed him, being forced to admit that she was inordinately curious about Barrett. She couldn't deny it.

They traveled for some distance in orchards that didn't look all that healthy to her. She wasn't a country girl and didn't know any details about farming, but the trees hadn't been trimmed, and many of them appeared to be ill, with no leaves or fruit, as if they were on their last legs.

She recalled Luke's comments about his elder brother who'd died, how he'd neglected the property so it was in bad shape, and here were visible indications of it. It made her feel sorry for him, made her comprehend why he'd be anxious to marry Penny Pendleton for her dowry. The money would repair what his brother had ruined.

Once the house was up ahead, they stopped and stared. It was a splendid mansion, three stories high and constructed from a peach colored stone. There were hundreds of windows gleaming in the bright sun. A majestic staircase rose to ornate double doors so the building was very imposing, very regal.

One end sported turrets, as if the section was older and had originally been a castle. It provided evidence of the Watson family's permanence, their staking a claim that had endured for generations. For a female who had always yearned to belong somewhere, the prospect left her extremely jealous.

"It's awfully fancy," Simon murmured. "Could you picture yourself living there as Lord Barrett's countess?"

She laughed. "Don't be ridiculous. I'm not cut out to be anybody's countess. Especially Luke Watson's."

"I think you're quite as posh as they come," he loyally declared. "Why couldn't you be exactly who he needs? Don't sell yourself short. I never will."

His remarks sent a surge of vanity sweeping through her. Why couldn't she be Luke's bride?

She'd never previously considered marriage to a man like him, but why couldn't she have a home like this? She'd constantly felt as if she should have owned just this sort of place, and she suffered a wave of resentment and a heavy sense of loss over all that Fate had taken from her.

It had her reflecting on the dreadful year she'd experienced after being rescued by the navy on her deserted island. She'd been returned to England where strangers had bickered over what should be done with her. She'd been terrified every second, with no ease arriving until Harry had waltzed in and whisked her away.

With few questions asked, he'd been allowed to traipse off with her, which had stirred a whole new pot of problems. Why let Simon blather on until she dredged it all up? Why ponder any of it?

"I'm not discussing Lord Barrett with you ever again," she said, "and it's recently occurred to me that you are spending too much time with your nose poked into the middle of my private affairs."

"I'm simply trying to help, Cousin. I'm trying to guarantee you wind up precisely where you're supposed to be."

"And where is that?"

"Why, at Lord Barrett's side of course. Glued there by matrimony— if at all possible."

"You grow more absurd by the day."

She pulled her horse around and kicked it into a canter. She didn't glance back to see if he followed, for she couldn't bear to see his pompous grin.

***

LUKE DAWDLED AT THE back of the music salon at Roland. Supper was over, and there was an evening musicale in progress before the dancing began. Several guests had volunteered to sing or play the pianoforte, but Libby was to provide the finale.

There was a small stage so the audience would have a good view of the show. It was standing room only, and he was supposed to be sitting in the front row with Penny and Charles, but he hadn't dared join them while Libby performed her scene. He'd have been drooling over her, his obsession so blatant that he wouldn't have been able to conceal it.

After having convinced Libby to participate, Penny had been nervously touting the recital all day, anxious to be sure there were no empty seats, but she hadn't needed to publicize Libby's involvement. People were agog over her, and even those who'd seen her monologues in the past were excited to see her again.

He was Charles's neighbor, and they'd always been friendly. He would never deliberately provoke a conflict with him, would never insult his daughter by misbehaving with another woman—right under Charles's roof. Especially with one who was so inappropriate to his station in life.

Libby was the female a man picked to be his glamorous mistress. She was the one selected to waltz about on a fellow's arm when he was attending a decadent soiree. She wasn't the sort to be flaunted at a respectable venue, so what was he thinking?

His infatuation was almost scary in its intensity, and his inability to leave her alone was disgusting.

She'd vanished all day, and he'd been so afraid she might have fled Roland—even though she'd sworn she wouldn't—that he'd actually crept into her bedchamber and had checked that her clothes were still there.

He was dangerously curious about where she'd been for so many hours, and he'd tortured himself, speculating as to whether she might have spent the afternoon with someone else.

He truly did not know how he could continue on in such an agitated state. His possessive attitude was so out of character that he couldn't figure out what was occurring. He had to calm down before he completely disgraced himself.

The candles were blown out, the room growing dark except for a circle of light in the middle of the stage. Libby stepped into it, and she was attired like an orphaned waif in a thin white shift, her feet bare, her glorious hair curling around her shoulders.

She looked nothing like the seductive siren who was driving him insane. Instead, she looked like a young child who was lost, and her skill at repurposing herself attested to her prowess as an actress.

When he'd watched her at the theater in London, she'd told a tale about sleeping under the stars, snuggled like puppies with the other two girls who'd been marooned with her. This time, she told about being on a deserted beach, searching for an adult who would tell her how to carry on, but she was stranded and on her own.

She sang a bit and danced a bit, and in the shadows, it appeared that her cousin, Simon Falcon, was accompanying her on the harpsichord. They were an excellent team that held spectators rapt.

She interspersed the musical numbers with a running description of her woebegone plight. It was all terribly melodramatic, and he should have been bored silly, but she was so mesmerizing that it was impossible not to be swept up in her narrative.

She wound to the end, and there was a moment of delicious silence where no one moved, then wild clapping echoed out. The crowd jumped to its feet, and shouts of *bravo!* bounced off the ceiling.

She took many gracious bows, then dashed away. A door behind the stage opened and closed so, evidently, she'd tiptoed out rather than stay and mingle. Her admirers didn't seem to mind. They were chattering animatedly, discussing every aspect of the recital as if they'd just witnessed a Shakespearean drama.

How did she do it? Why was she so tantalizing? The shipwreck had happened twenty year earlier, but people never wearied of her retelling of the event. He ought to have been happy that she'd turned the tragedy into a career that supported her in quite a grand style, but he was pathetically jealous to have so many men avidly ogling her.

The servants were lighting the candles, and he hurried out before he could be waylaid and required to gush over her. He wondered where she was and decided she'd have hastened up to her bedchamber to change her clothes. He wandered down several halls until he arrived at a rear staircase. He hesitated forever, debating his choices, then he mumbled, "Why not?"

Why not debase himself yet again? Why not compound his ludicrous condition with more inexplicable acts?

He climbed to her suite, and when he reached it, he didn't bother knocking. He simply spun the knob and slipped inside. The sitting room was empty, the bedroom too, but he could hear her talking to Fish in the dressing room.

It dawned on him that he was behaving exactly like the dandies at the theater who swarmed around the prettiest actresses and opera dancers. He'd always derided those idiots, aggravated over how they'd been driven to such levels of stupidity. Now he knew. It merely took a vixen like Libby Carstairs to goad a man to recklessness.

What might he do for her? If she was shrewd enough to solicit boons, he might proffer any gift if it would garner him extended time in her exotic presence.

He didn't try for stealth, but simply marched forward. As he approached, she asked, "Simon, is that you?"

"It's not Simon," he replied as he appeared in the doorway.

For once, she was dressed, so he didn't catch her in her petticoat. Her hair was pinned up in a haphazard way that should have looked messy, but it only added to her allure. She was wearing the bright red gown he liked, her corset laced tight, so she was displaying plenty of bosom.

She was fabulous, a siren to tempt men to their doom. How could he be expected to resist her?

She sighed with resignation, and Fish glowered like a fussy nanny.

"Miss Carstairs doesn't receive callers after a performance," Fish scolded, "and you, Lord Barrett, are presuming on her good nature. You have to head downstairs. Immediately."

"I don't believe Miss Carstairs would like me to depart."

He stared at Libby, his hot regard enveloping her like a cloud. She was as enticed as he was, and she tsked with annoyance.

"It's all right, Fish," she said. "He can stay."

"You're courting trouble," Fish warned, and she scowled. "*Both* of you are courting trouble. What if Lord Roland discovers you were in here, Lord Barrett? You might be safe if you were dallying in your own home, but *his* servants have no duty to keep this kind of secret for you."

"Don't worry," he told her. "No one saw me sneak in."

Fish scoffed. "Spoken like a true cad."

"Don't nag, Fish," Libby said. "We're not children. Lord Barrett and I know what we're doing."

Fish chuckled, but nastily. "I'll be sure to jot that down in my journal: *Lord Barrett and Libby know what they're doing.*" She gestured over Libby's person. "Are you ready to go down? Do you need anything else from me?"

"I'm fine."

"Don't dawdle with him. I refuse to have Lady Penny badgering me as to your whereabouts."

"We won't dawdle," Libby said, but Luke had no comment.

He glared at Fish to inform her that she should leave. She stomped out, muttering, "Don't come crying to me if you're caught together. I will not defend either of you."

Luke listened until the door shut behind her, then he fell on Libby like a feral animal. It seemed as if they'd been parted for decades.

His hands were in her hair, his tongue in her mouth. He couldn't get close enough to her, couldn't hold her tightly enough, so he pushed her against the wall and lifted her, wrapping her legs around his waist so he could lean in and crush his loins to hers.

They scratched and bit, wrestled and groaned and grappled for purchase. It was debauched and wild, and he'd never experienced a similar episode with any woman.

He yanked her away from the wall and carried her into the bedroom. He dropped her onto the bed and tumbled down after her so she was stretched out beneath him. The entire time, he hadn't stopped kissing her. He couldn't stop.

He had no idea how long they continued, but gradually, they ran out of steam, the embrace cooling to something that was tender and sweet.

"I think you missed me today," she murmured when they finally came up for air.

"I feel as if I haven't seen you in years."

"I will confess to feeling the same."

"Where were you? I searched for you all afternoon."

"I went for a ride."

A dozen jealous images flew through his mind as he pictured every handsome man at the party.

"With who?" His tone was sullen and morose. "You'd best hurry and tell me you were alone."

"I was with my cousin, Simon."

"You were gone for hours," he petulantly said.

"You're irked that I was, so you're frowning and pouting. Why? Were you envisioning me enjoying a torrid tryst with someone other than you?"

"If I was pondering an incident that ridiculous, I would never admit it."

She smirked. "You are deranged. Have I mentioned that you are?"

"Yes, I believe you might have."

"If I had remained in the manor, I couldn't have fraternized with you."

"We could have tarried in the same rooms," he ludicrously said. "I could have glanced at you whenever I was in the mood."

"We're not destined to socialize in Lord Roland's parlors. We could never conceal our infatuation."

He blew out a heavy breath and slid off her. He rolled onto his back and stared at the ceiling. She was snuggled next to him, and she fit against him perfectly, as if she'd been created for that specific purpose and no other.

"I visited Barrett," she said after a bit.

"You did? Why?"

"Simon and I were sightseeing in the neighborhood. We passed the gate, and once I realized where we were, we snuck down the lane to gape at your house."

"I wish I'd been there. I'd have loved to welcome you inside."

"It's beautiful. I'm incredibly envious that you own such a place."

"I guess it's beautiful—if you're partial to rundown, decrepit mansions."

"You're lucky to have it. Don't be snotty about it or you'll annoy me."

"All right. I won't be snotty. I shall fib and state that it's a grand residence."

"That's better." She snorted with amusement.

"Your scolding is giving me a headache."

"I have that effect on men."

"No, you don't. You turn them into blithering idiots. I've watched you. It's absolutely diabolical how effortlessly you charm them."

"Have I charmed *you*? Are you wrapped around my little finger?"

"Maybe."

"How about your fiancée? Are you wrapped around her little finger too?"

"First off, I haven't decided whether I'm marrying Penny or not."

"Liar. You'll proceed with her. I have no doubt at all."

She was probably correct, but he wouldn't debate the issue. "And second, I'm *not* discussing Penny with you. Not while we're nestled together on your bed. We have so few chances to dally. Don't waste them by irritating me."

"Your fit of pique reminds me that I'm mad to have loafed up here with you. Penny will be looking for me. I'm surprised she hasn't already blustered in to check on me."

Just as Libby voiced the remark, the door from the hall opened, and they blanched with alarm. When Fish had stormed out, Luke had forgotten to lock the door after her. Why hadn't he? His only excuse was that Libby completely overwhelmed him.

He was a navy commander who barked orders and had them instantly obeyed. He was so used to being in charge that he frequently felt like a god who could control his destiny. Would it all crash down? Would his foolishness destroy his friendship with the Pendleton family? Was Libby Carstairs worth that type of upheaval?

He wasn't sure yet, but he was beginning to suspect he'd pay any price to have her.

"Libby, where are you hiding?" her cousin, Simon Falcon, called from the sitting room.

There was no opportunity to jump off the bed or pretend they hadn't been misbehaving, and for a brief moment, Luke couldn't deduce if he was relieved or not to have it be Mr. Falcon rather than someone else. But was his *arrival* preplanned? Would he express umbrage and demand Luke fork over damages for Libby's ruination?

Falcon appeared in the doorway, and if he was astonished to observe Libby stretched out on the mattress with Luke, he gave no sign. His lack of a reaction definitely made Luke wonder about what sort of life she'd led. He was convinced she wasn't nearly as innocent as she liked to claim.

"There you are," Falcon said to Libby. "You delivered a stellar performance, and people are dying to chat with you. Lord Roland is especially delighted. Fish sent me to drag you downstairs." Then he focused his caustic gaze on Luke. "And Lord Barrett, I won't say I'm shocked to stumble on you, but for pity's sake, if you intend to trifle with my cousin—and right under your fiancée's nose too—you really ought to spin the key in the lock before you start in."

Libby was nonchalant about being discovered. She slid off the bed and glared at Falcon. "Why are you pestering me, Simon?"

"I told you. Fish sent me to fetch you. I figure she knew what I'd find. I'm glad you're still dressed. Otherwise, I might have been struck blind."

"Go down without me," she said. "I'll be there in a minute."

"Apparently, that's what you insisted to Fish when you chased her off. I'm not as gullible as she is, and I have to inject some sanity into this situation or it will become totally untenable. What if Lady Penny had been with me? What then?"

Luke slid off the bed too, and he ignored Falcon and spoke to Libby. "Let's take a ride in the morning."

"You and I are not socializing," she responded. "How often must I explain this to you?"

"We can leave the manor at different times. We can meet out on the road."

"No!" she firmly stated.

Falcon tsked with aggravation. "Will you come with me, Lord Barrett? I'll escort you down to the gentlemen's card room."

"You should listen to Simon," she said to Luke. "We've been up here much too long. I'll follow in a bit."

"You'd better," Falcon said. "I'm tired of having to justify your absences."

"Yes, Simon, yes," she complained. "I heard you, and I'll be right down."

"Don't you dare avoid me tomorrow," Luke said to her. "Don't make me spend all day searching again."

Falcon raised a brow. "You spent the day searching for her? My, my, but you and I need to have a long, frank talk."

"No, you don't," Libby said to Falcon. "I won't have the two of you palavering over me like a pair of fishwives at the market."

She clasped Luke's hand and squeezed tight, silently telling him goodbye. They sighed, sounding like adolescent sweethearts who couldn't bear to part.

Falcon scoffed. "If you lunatics grow anymore infatuated, syrup will be dripping from the walls."

He stepped in and physically separated them. He pushed Libby toward the dressing room. She winked at Luke and sauntered off. He watched her go, his attention riveted on how her hips swished under the fabric of her skirt.

Falcon smirked. "You are in deep trouble, Lord Barrett."

"I know," he could only reply.

"We should tarry in a quiet spot and have a brandy. We have to wipe that besotted look off your face before anyone sees it."

"I'm fine."

"No, you're not, and I can guarantee your obsession will just get worse. This kind of attraction has bubbled up with her on a thousand occasions in the past, but it never leads anywhere. We have to nip it in the bud or you'll simply wind up angry and disappointed."

"I don't want to do any nipping."

"I have to persuade you then, and I shall demand you listen to me."

Falcon was a sly character. He had Luke out the door and down the hall before Luke realized they'd left Libby's bedchamber.

They headed down the stairs, and when they would have turned toward the party, they walked in the other direction, ultimately shutting themselves in a deserted parlor where there was a fully-stocked liquor tray. Falcon poured them both a tall brandy, and they clinked the rims together.

"To Libby," Falcon said, "and to you for being smart enough to capture her notice."

"I wouldn't call it smart. I'd call it deranged."

"I'm serious. Men constantly fall in love with her, but she never reciprocates their interest."

"Why not?"

Falcon shrugged. "She thinks they're fools, cheats, and wastrels."

"She's generally correct."

"Which type are you?"

"I'm not a wastrel, but with how I've been ensnared, I suppose I'm a fool."

"And you're a cheat too, aren't you?"

Luke scowled. "Why would you assume that?"

"You're here to propose to Lady Penny, but I just caught you rolling around on a mattress with my cousin. That seems a tad duplicitous to me."

Luke's cheeks flushed with chagrin. "As I've explained to Libby, over and over again, I'm not engaged *yet*. I'm a bachelor who is capable of choosing my companions and how I carry on with them."

"Would you like to keep Libby for your very own?"

Luke had just taken a swallow of his liquor, and it went down wrong. He coughed and pounded a fist on his chest. He'd never had such a blunt question posed, and Falcon was so young. It was disconcerting to have him mention such a salacious topic.

"Meaning what?" Luke asked. "I'm not about to marry her—if that's what you're hoping. I don't care if you stumbled on us in a compromising situation. Matrimony is not in the cards, so don't presume you can coerce me into that conclusion."

"I am her only male relative, and I have to protect her."

"Is this where you solicit money from me?" Luke shook his head with disgust. "I've been wondering if you two had a scheme brewing."

"Libby wouldn't pursue dishonorable conduct, but I would."

"Why am I not surprised?"

"You'd like her to be your mistress, yes?"

"Well . . . yes. I would like that, and I've already suggested it."

"I'm betting she was vehemently opposed to the idea."

"Yes, she was."

"I could change her mind." Falcon sounded as if he was boasting.

"How?"

"We're close, and she heeds my advice. I could convince her."

"I doubt it."

"I could have Fish work on her too. We could claim that an affair with you is exactly what she needs to truly be happy."

Luke studied him keenly, his skepticism intense. "What would you get out of it? I'm certain you don't have a benevolent bone in your body. There must be something you'd want in return."

"I agree that you'd have to make it worth my while, but I haven't decided on what my price might be. How about if I reflect on it for a few days? Once the party ends, we'll come to terms."

Luke snorted with annoyance. "I don't trust you, Falcon, and I have no desire to come to *terms* with you about Libby or any other subject."

The arrogant oaf grinned. "If you don't enlist my help, how will you win her?"

"It's entirely possible that you have overstated my level of fascination. Perhaps I'm not as desperate as you imagine."

"Aren't you?" Falcon laughed, then strolled out.

Luke downed the rest of his liquor, feeling dazed and bewildered.

What was he doing? What was he thinking?

He was as British as the next man, and he understood that blood dictated character. The bluer the blood, the more stellar the character. What were Libby's antecedents? She refused to confess them, but she'd been raised by her Uncle Harry who'd imprinted his own dubious traits.

It was obvious she was a bad risk. He only had to consider Mr. Falcon to realize it, so why tumble into an affair with her? Why squander a single farthing on her? There were such dangers involved in a risqué liaison. Why imperil himself and his reputation?

But what if he was mistaken and it all worked out perfectly? What if Falcon could persuade her to give Luke what he sought? Why not shoot for that outcome? Why not plan on it?

What if he could spend years with Libby Carstairs snuggled by his side? What sort of person would he be when she was through with him?

A much better one; he was sure of it.

In the meantime, he had a probable fiancée in the front parlor whom he had to assess and charm. He poured another brandy and drank it down, requiring some liquid courage in order to face Penny and her father, but needing it too in order to face Libby when he bumped into her in the crowd of guests.

Simon Falcon would be hovering too, observing Luke and snickering gleefully in the corners. He'd be aware that Luke was in abject misery—with Libby so close, yet so far away.

It was going to be a very long night.

Chapter

10

"I wasn't impressed."

"Why not?"

"It was too melodramatic for me."

Charles frowned at Millicent. They were in the front parlor, the festivities winding down. The younger people would likely revel until dawn, but he was exhausted and had had all the socializing he could stand for one evening.

"I found her to be incredibly mesmerizing," Charles said.

"I didn't," Millicent countered. They were discussing Libby Carstairs's monologue, presented a few hours earlier. Millicent leaned nearer and murmured, "Penny is quite taken with her. You might chat with her about it. *I* would warn her to be more circumspect, but it would only incense her. You know how mulish she can be these days."

"Is she being mulish? I hadn't noticed."

"Since she's about to become betrothed, she deems herself to be an adult. She no longer feels she should have to listen to me."

Penny had *never* felt much of an inclination to listen to Millicent. It was hardly a new phenomenon, but he didn't mention that fact. It was an old argument over which they'd regularly squabbled.

"There's no harm in her being friendly with Miss Carstairs," he said. "She's a celebrity. Why shouldn't Penny have a chance to gush and fawn?"

Millicent's lips were tight with disapproval. "Miss Carstairs is an actress or have you conveniently forgotten that pesky detail?"

"I haven't forgotten."

"I would think—with your history—you'd be a tad more concerned about the influence such a disreputable charlatan can exert on a gullible girl like Penny."

He breathed out a heavy sigh. "Let it go, Millicent. As far as I've observed, Miss Carstairs has exhibited the highest moral character while she's been in residence. She performed for us—once—at Penny's specific request, and her story was very moving."

"You can't have been tricked into believing her drivel. I'm not convinced she's one of those *lost* girls. It's been two decades since they were rescued. Who can be certain? She's probably an imposter, and her pathetic narratives are a charade to captivate audiences. How can we guess if any of her ridiculous tales are true? I wouldn't be surprised to learn that she made the whole thing up."

"I thought it was enormously stirring."

"You would."

Miss Carstairs's cousin, Mr. Falcon, sauntered by. Penny was walking with him, grinning at him in a flirtatious way. A slew of females tagged after them, all of them gazing at him with stars in their eyes. Obviously, Penny wasn't the only one who was enthralled by the boy's handsome looks and showy demeanor.

Penny was eighteen, and Charles had been that same age when he'd traipsed off to London and had landed himself in so much trouble. He'd swiftly stumbled into the decadence of gambling, vice, and debauched opera dancers, and he'd had no parents around to urge caution.

Penny was much more immature than he'd been back then. It was difficult to accept that she was old enough to engage in the antics that had once tantalized him so completely.

For a moment, he struggled to remember that passionate interlude, where every facet of his life had been so vital, but all of it seemed so bizarre now, as if it had happened in a dream or perhaps that it had happened to some other unfortunate dolt.

"That Mr. Falcon is a piece of work, isn't he?" Millicent sounded as if she was fuming.

"What's wrong with him?"

"He's so...so...attractive." She spat the word *attractive* as if it were an epithet. "The female guests are falling all over themselves, trying to get him to notice them."

"Is that type of conduct forbidden these days? I didn't realize it was a crime to be young and good looking."

"You're aware, better than anyone, that flash and dazzle can lead an unsuspecting person to ruin. I'm stunned that you're not more worried about him. If it was up to me, I'd quietly ask him to pack his bags and return to London."

"It's Penny's party, Millicent," he said. "She's happy to have him here, just as she's happy with Miss Carstairs. They'll depart soon, and we'll never see them again. You shouldn't fret over it, and it's absurd to be so riled."

"Don't tell me I'm over-reacting!" she curtly retorted, proving his point.

"I didn't say that." Charles never argued, and he especially wouldn't argue with her. "I merely think we're both tired, and I'm about to head to my bed."

"Yes, by all means, go to bed. Abandon me to play the chaperone by myself."

"There are plenty of other people to serve that role, and no one in this crowd needs a nanny. You're even more fatigued than I am—and a bit grouchy. You should head upstairs too."

"Grouchy!" she huffed.

"Yes, grouchy, and it's silly for you to tarry. Don't be a martyr. Besides, with how you're glowering, you'll spoil the fun."

"It's evident you don't appreciate all I do for you."

"I appreciate it, but I'm worn out, and it's too late to bicker. Even if it wasn't late, I wouldn't quarrel with you. As you know, I never quarrel over any issue, so why are you picking a fight with me?"

Unable to conceal his irritation, he glared at her, and she instantly smoothed her features, her fit of pique neatly tucked away.

"Maybe I am grouchy." It was her attempt at waving an olive branch. "It's been a long day, and it's stressful to entertain so many guests."

"Yes, it is, and you don't have to dawdle in this parlor. In fact, I would suggest you don't. Goodnight."

He hurried away, not inclined to let her waylay him further. She constantly reminded him of how lucky he was that she'd come to Roland after Florence died, and he couldn't figure out what was bothering her. She was always so eager to be sure *he* was content, but occasionally, he wondered how she was faring.

She'd hitched her star to his wagon when she was much too young to decide on that path, and she'd never left Roland, so she'd passed up any opportunity she might have had to marry and have a home of her own. Over the years, he'd frequently encouraged her to move on and build a life for herself that was separate from him, but she ceaselessly claimed that she'd rather remain at Roland.

Now she was a very aged thirty-five, so she was a confirmed spinster. Her wastrel brother had emptied the family's coffers, so even if she hadn't been quite so old, she didn't have a dowry. Was she starting to grasp that it had been a bad choice to stay at Roland? Was she wishing she hadn't stayed?

He recalled Fish's comment that Millicent was in love with him. The prospect hadn't previously occurred to him. After Florence's demise, he'd been very clear with everyone that he never planned to wed again. Two wives had been more than enough.

Had Millicent persuaded herself that he wasn't serious? Had she assumed she could win him anyway, despite his reluctance?

Perhaps he should begin nudging Millicent to consider a new direction for herself. With Warwick in the army, and Penny about to be a wife and leave too, he didn't need Millicent hovering. Had that situation already dawned on her? Was it fueling her surly mood?

He reached his bedchamber and was met by his valet, but he sent the man off to join the servants' party down in the kitchen. He changed his own clothes, donning a comfortable shirt and trousers. Then he poured himself a whiskey and went over to stare out the window, but it was cloudy, so there wasn't much to see.

It was very quiet, and for once, he was lonely and chafing over how small his world had grown. The realization surprised him. He wasn't keen on self-assessment. His antics as a young man had proved that he had an unrestrained side to his personality. He'd learned to ignore it until, gradually, it had vanished.

But the fascinating Miss Carstairs, with her poignant performance, had ignited a fire of emotion in his breast. He was reminiscing over squandered possibilities. Her cousin, Mr. Falcon, was spurring him to recollect what it had been like to be rich and wickedly handsome and brazenly prancing about in London.

After that interval had collapsed in scandal, he'd forced himself to become stodgy and boring, but he wasn't dead. He wasn't feeble or decrepit. He was only forty-six, and it had been so bloody long since he'd truly enjoyed himself. The house was filled to the rafters with people who were making merry. Why shouldn't he be one of them?

He downed his whiskey, then poured himself another and downed it too. He spent a few more minutes staring outside, and he knew what was bothering him: Edwina Fishburn was bothering him. And she was right down the hall. She was like a thorn he couldn't pluck out.

The first evening after she'd arrived, he'd tried to convince her to walk in the garden with him. It had been a huge blow to his ego to have her decline. He'd avoided her ever since, but why had he?

The manor was his castle, and he was king of it. Why not approach her again?

He'd been suffocating at Roland for two decades, but he hadn't forgotten how to tempt a lady to misbehave. A gentleman never really lost that sort of skill, and his had merely been hidden out of sight. It was time to pull it out and let it fly free.

Poor Fish didn't stand a chance.

WHEN THE DOOR FROM the hall opened, Fish was loafing in a chair, drinking a brandy, and gazing out at the cloudy sky. A fresh breeze was wafting in, and she could smell rain in the air. She was ready for bed, attired in just her nightgown, her hair down and brushed out.

She hadn't been given a fancy suite like Libby, so she didn't have a sitting or dressing room. Her bedroom was tiny and modest, the type offered to an unwelcome guest in the hopes that it would encourage a short stay.

"Hello, Fish," Charles said from behind her.

She sighed and glanced over her shoulder. "Hello, Charles. Hurry and close the door, would you? I don't suppose you ought to be observed sneaking into my bedchamber."

"No, I shouldn't."

When Simon had initially mentioned the invitation to Roland, she'd figured Charles wouldn't even remember her, so it would be safe to visit. But apparently, they had unfinished business to resolve. Where would it lead? How would it end?

She couldn't imagine, but they had to deal with their old issues, or she'd always regret it.

"What are you doing here?" she asked.

"What do you think I'm doing?"

"I have no idea, but you were always a fool. I'm sure you've concocted a totally ridiculous excuse to explain yourself."

He grinned. "Maybe."

That grin still had the power to knock her sideways. Where he was concerned, she'd never been able to keep a level head. One would presume, after twenty odd years as an adult, she'd start making more sensible choices, but perhaps—in light of how she viewed the world—that wasn't possible.

She was at Roland, and he was at Roland, and she'd be in residence for a quick sojourn. Why not enjoy a bit more entertainment than she'd originally planned?

She stood and walked over to him. She held out her glass of brandy. He grabbed it and downed the contents.

"After you first arrived," he said, "I invited you to walk in the garden with me, but you refused."

"I've been wondering how long it would take you to decide I had no right to disobey your grand self."

"You will be in my home for a fortnight."

"Probably."

He scowled. "Why *probably?*"

"I mean Libby has other irons in the fire, and I go where she goes."

The sole hot iron for Libby was her brewing affair with Lord Barrett. The man was absolutely obsessed, to the point where he was willing to ruin his future just to have her.

The reckless pair would eventually be caught, then a huge brouhaha would erupt. Fish, Simon, and Libby would most likely have to slither away in the dark of night. Lord Barrett would have completely disgraced himself, while also managing to destroy his cordial relationship with Charles.

Fish would watch it all unravel, praying the bricks in Lord Barrett's wall of chaos didn't pummel her as they fell.

"You're not leaving Roland before the party ends," Charles said.

Fish tsked with annoyance. "You are just as bossy as you were twenty years ago."

"And you, dear Fish, are just as stubborn. It's silly to argue with me on any topic. Haven't you learned that by now?"

"You haven't seen me in two decades. Why would you automatically assume I'll succumb to your dubious charms?"

"I assume it because you could never resist me."

"I repeat," she said, "you are bossy as ever."

"I'm older and much less patient. These days, I reach out and seize what I want."

She rolled her eyes. "You always acted that way. Don't pretend your haughty character is a new development."

"It's not new, but it's been tamped down forever, and it appears you've lit a fire under it."

He stepped in and wrapped an arm around her waist. Suddenly, her entire front was pressed to his, and he'd definitely aged well. He was tall and fit as ever, his shoulders wide, his legs long and lean, so he towered over her. She gazed up at him, and the Devil must have been sitting on her shoulder and urging her to perdition.

Why not? a strident voice was whispering in her ear. Why not trifle with him? He was offering. Why decline such a delicious invitation?

She wasn't a green girl who had to mind her manners and keep her legs tightly crossed. She was an independent, modern spinster who could behave however she pleased, and he was correct that she couldn't resist him.

She'd warned herself to avoid him while she was at Roland. The broken heart she'd suffered in the past had been too grueling, so she'd spent the intervening years allied with scoundrels who hadn't deserved her regard. She'd ceased being imprudent and gullible.

Men weren't a mystery to her, and she was never surprised by any conduct they perpetrated. Yes, she could dabble with Charles Pendleton, then waltz away unscathed when they parted. She was certain of it.

"It's your lucky day, Charles," she said.

He smirked. "Oh, really? And why is that?"

"I've decided to give you a chance to make me like you again."

"You always *liked* me, Fish. In fact, if I recall, you were once madly in love with me."

"I might have been," she blithely said.

"I predict I can stir that sort of hot emotion all over again. Shall we bet on it?"

He was smiling down at her, still gorgeous, still thin and dapper, and still smart enough to desire her—even after so much time had passed.

"We don't need to bet, Charles," she told him. "I'm positive we can stir quite a bit of emotion—and some passion too—with no effort at all."

"That is the answer I was waiting desperately to hear."

He lifted her off her feet, tossed her onto the bed, and followed her down. In two seconds flat, it seemed as if they'd never been separated a single minute.

～～

SIMON PEEKED DOWN THE deserted hall, then slipped into Penny's bedchamber. He spun the key in the lock so no one could bluster in after him.

She'd continued to refuse to tell him where her room was located, but she'd claimed—if he could figure out where it was on his own—she wouldn't complain if he snuck in. How could a fellow ignore a dare like that?

He hadn't even had to bribe a footman to spill the beans. As she'd headed to bed, he'd simply tiptoed after her, with her being too naïve to glance over her shoulder to see him standing there. He hadn't entered immediately, but had had to dawdle until her maid left.

Her suite was just as grandiose as he'd imagined it would be. The outer room was a sitting room, and there was a bedroom behind it. The whole place was packed with fussy furniture in varying shades of pink. He wondered if the color was a holdover from when she was a child and had liked a frilly décor.

He hoped it wasn't a recent choice. If he managed to attach himself to her—which he had every intention of doing—the feminine ambiance would drive him batty.

A few dolls were perched on a shelf, but then, she was only eighteen. Maybe she hadn't matured quite as much as he'd assumed. The notion was disheartening. Then again, if she remained so juvenile in her tastes and habits, it would be much easier to coerce her into debauched conduct.

He went over and leaned against the door jam, and he studied the bedroom with a jaundiced eye. He was only twenty himself, but due to his shocking upbringing, he felt a hundred years older than her.

Even though he was a young man, he'd loafed in many beautiful women's bedchambers. The rooms always fascinated him, and he learned many tidbits he could use to persuade them to give him things they shouldn't.

His opinion of the fairer sex had been skewed by his growing up around Libby and Fish. They weren't ordinary females, so there'd never been a bedroom like this in any of their homes. Normally, they were busy performing in the evenings, earning an income to keep a roof over their heads. They didn't huddle by the fire at night, knitting shawls or embroidering pillowcases.

With his father, Harry, having directed their every step, they'd moved constantly too, traveling with circuses and acting troupes, so they'd never had the space to accumulate many possessions. If they filled up a wardrobe, it was usually with costumes necessary to play their parts.

There was a dressing room in the back, and Penny was in there and humming to herself. He waited right where he was, his amusement spiraling as he debated over how she'd respond when she saw him.

Finally, she strolled into view, and he was delighted to report that she didn't scream with alarm.

"Simon Falcon!" she quietly scolded. "Why are you in my bedchamber?"

"You told me—if I could determine where it was—that I'd be welcome to visit you."

"I wasn't serious!"

"Weren't you? Are you sure about that?"

"I'm reasonably sure."

She frowned, her consternation clear. As with most girls, she'd never met a man like him. He was tantalizing her with thoughts of how her life could be, rather than how it was. She was destined to marry Lord Barrett, that disgusting roué who'd just been lifting Libby's skirt.

If Penny didn't wind up betrothed to Lord Barrett, her father would shackle her to another tedious aristocrat just like him. Didn't she deserve better? Wouldn't Simon be better?

He was spurring her to start asking herself that question. Every person in the kingdom would vehemently insist he wasn't *better* by any standard, but he was keen to have her suppose he was.

He sauntered over to her, and she stood her ground. She was no shrinking violet, and he preferred females who were bold instead of timid.

"If you're caught in here," she said, "how will I explain it?"

"I locked the door."

"Yes, but my maid might come back to check on me."

"Will you let her in? Should I leave? Is that what you want?"

He grinned a cocky grin, being certain she wouldn't send him away, and if she did? He'd try again on a different night. He had all sorts of tricks up his sleeve, and he'd continue tormenting her until she couldn't resist.

She assessed him forever, her moral inclinations at war with her reckless ones. According to rumor, her father had had a wild side when he was young. Had she inherited any of his wicked habits? So far, she hadn't exhibited many dissolute tendencies, but it was early.

"No, I don't want you to leave," she ultimately said.

"Of course you don't."

"But I'm not convinced you should stay either."

"You're conflicted about what's best, so I will have to help you decide."

"Let me guess," she scoffed. "You'll persuade me that it's *best* if you tarry."

"I'm betting I won't have to work very hard."

He dipped in and kissed her, just a quick brush of his lips to her own. He'd kissed her before, and she'd reveled in it. He'd reveled in it too, and he would be thrilled to walk down the decadent road they appeared bound to travel.

"You're going to get me in so much trouble," she said as he drew away.

"I'm not planning on it."

"It's a large house, but it's a small house too. The servants always know everything that's occurring. There's no way to keep an affair a secret."

His grin widened. "Is that where I am with you? Are we having a secret affair?"

She sighed with disgust. "I'm about to become betrothed to Lord Barrett, and my father has promised me that he will be the perfect husband.

Yet if I carry on with you, and we're discovered, my reputation will be ruined, and I'll likely never marry."

Simon waved away the comment. "Why would you be so eager to wed Lord Barrett? He's so much older than you."

"My father claims that's beneficial, that an older husband can guide a young bride in a good direction."

"That's nonsense. Barrett is stuffy and stodgy, and you're so vibrant and vivacious. He could never love or understand you. You'd suffocate as his wife."

"You can't be sure of that, and I shouldn't listen to you about it. You make me doubt my father, and I'm very fond of him. He wouldn't steer me wrong."

"Wouldn't he?"

The query hung in the air between them, and it had the desired effect. She glowered at him, quite ferociously too.

"I've upset you," he murmured, and he kissed her sweetly, tenderly, keeping on until she relaxed against him.

"You bewilder me," she said.

"Aren't you yearning to live happily ever after?" he asked.

"Isn't everyone?"

"Would you really be happy with Lord Barrett? Be honest with me."

"I barely know him, so I can't imagine if I'd be happy or not."

"You're only eighteen."

She bristled. "Don't cite my age as if I'm a child. How old are you?"

"Twenty."

"You're not exactly a wise old elder."

"I simply mention it because I've seen more of the world than you. I'm certain you have a very romantic view of marriage."

She shrugged. "Maybe."

"You expect to have the wedding of the Season, then you'll retire to Barrett Manor, and eventually, Lord Barrett will fall madly in love with you. It's how girls picture these things."

"First off, I'm not a *girl*, and I'm not deceived about my future."

"I apologize. You're a young lady who's anxious to be a bride, but might I suggest that you have some skewed ideas as to how matrimony will unfold with Lord Barrett?"

"Why couldn't he fall in love with me? It could happen."

Pity slid into his expression, and he scrutinized her in a gentle way, as if she was precious and might break into a dozen pieces if he wasn't careful with her.

"Should I confide a secret about him?" he asked. "Could you bear to learn a hard truth?"

"I'm not sure," she tentatively replied, "and how would you have learned any of his secrets? As far as I know, you're not acquainted with him."

"That's as may be, but I've unearthed one tidbit that's shocking. Would you like to hear it or not?"

She debated, then said, "I'd like to hear it."

"He loves someone else."

She gasped. "Who is she?"

"I probably shouldn't name names."

"No, no, now that you've blurted out the news, you have to tell me who it is."

His pitying expression grew remorseful. "I'm sorry, but it's my cousin, Libby."

"Miss Carstairs?"

"Yes."

"Oh ..."

"Even if he weds you, I don't believe he intends to give her up. Could you live like that? I realize it's common for men of his class to have mistresses and second families, but I deem it to be horrendous behavior. It seems so ... *duplicitous* to me."

She staggered over to a chair and sank down, and she studied the floor. He hoped he hadn't wrecked Libby's sojourn at Roland, hoped

Penny didn't demand their immediate departure, but he didn't think she would. If Libby left, Simon would go with her, and Penny wouldn't want that.

"It's not a mystery why he would love your cousin," she said. "She's so exotic and beautiful. What about Miss Carstairs? Does she return his affection?"

"Unfortunately, yes. She's always had scoundrels circling her like vultures, but she's never been interested in any of them—until Lord Barrett came along."

"I see." She pulled her gaze from the floor and settled it on him. "Might my father have discovered their affair? Might he be aware of it, but he pursued the match anyway?"

"They've been very discreet, so he couldn't have found out."

"If Lord Barrett proposes after all, and I asked Miss Carstairs to part with him, would she?"

"*She* might oblige you. She's a kind person, and she never likes to hurt anyone, but Lord Barrett is quite determined about her. He might not be willing to end it, and he's such a wily character. He'd make it difficult for her to break it off."

"He's that besotted?"

"I'm afraid so."

"What should I do? What would you recommend?"

"At the moment, you can't really *do* anything, can you? You have a house full of guests."

"I can't exactly call off the party and send them home."

"No, you can't, and there's no guarantee that Lord Barrett will forge ahead. I mean, he might figure out that you're completely incompatible. But if he doesn't change his mind, you could have a word with your father. You could explain that *you* have changed your mind."

"That announcement wouldn't go over very well, and what would happen to me then? My father would have to find another candidate. It might take forever, and I was so eager to marry this year. All my friends are having weddings. I want to join in the fun."

Her comment underscored how deluded she was about matrimony, and he was compelled to counsel, "You can't pick a husband merely because you're in a hurry to be a bride."

"No, I suppose not."

"You have to select the *right* husband. He has to be the type who will put you on a pedestal above all other women. Lord Barrett never would. You could never matter to him in any significant way."

"I understand that now."

"I'll be here for the next week or so," he said, lightening the tone of the conversation. "We can discuss the sort of spouse you need and deserve."

"I wish I could wed someone young and handsome like you."

She flashed a hot look that he felt clear down to his toes, and he was greatly encouraged by it.

"I'd marry you if I could." He oozed regret. "I can guarantee we'd have a lifetime of pleasure and excitement."

"You're too far beneath me, Simon." She sounded like the spoiled brat she was. "My father would never approve."

"If a girl is clever, she can obtain what she wants. And haven't we already agreed that your father doesn't know who would suit you? Just remember that he picked Lord Barrett! He has no idea of the kind of man you require."

"You might be correct about that."

He'd planted enough seeds for one evening. He'd water them and watch them grow. He had ten more days to flirt with her. When she was so naïve, it was an eternity. Who could predict where they'd be when the party ended?

Simon was certain of one pertinent fact. He would walk away from the relationship much wealthier. She'd wind up as his wife or—if she got cold feet—he'd persuade her father to pay him to go away. Lord Roland would likely cough up a small fortune to rid himself of a cad like Simon.

In the interim, he was positive he'd scuttled Lord Barrett's chances with Penny, so Libby's road with Barrett was suddenly wide open. Simon nodded with satisfaction, delighted to have done her such a good turn.

He stuck out his hand and said, "Come with me."

"To where?"

"To loaf on your bed of course."

She blanched. "We can't!"

"Yes, we can. The door is locked, and we're alone. No one will stumble on us."

"It would be wrong. It would be a sin."

He chuckled. "It's only a sin if we're caught. And we're *not* about to be caught."

She didn't move, and he clasped hold of her arm and raised her to her feet. He began kissing her again, and he kept on and on until her limbs were rubbery and her curvaceous front was pressed to his all the way down.

He thought she'd be a splendid bride. She was beautiful, elegant, and refined, and she was very rich too, and a rich girl was always prettier than a poor one. As he pictured her dowry money flowing into his purse, he scooped her up and carried her over to the bed.

She scowled. "I told you we can't do this."

"I know," he arrogantly retorted, "but give me a few minutes to show you how much fun we can have, and I'm betting you'll be glad I insisted."

He dropped her onto the mattress and followed her down.

Chapter

11

"WHAT DO YOU THINK of Lord Barrett?"

At the question posed by Lady Penny, Libby was stumped over what her reply should be. They were alone in the park, strolling arm in arm, their heads pressed together.

Penny constantly begged to chat and seemed intent on becoming friends, but Libby was torn over the notion of their socializing too intimately. She wanted to be closer to the younger girl, but she didn't want to be closer too.

A picnic was about to be served on the lawn. Tents had been erected, chairs and tables arranged. The servants were bustling to and fro, anxious to ensure that every little detail was perfect. As the preparations had grown frenzied, Penny had suggested they slip away for a few minutes, and Libby couldn't have refused.

"Lord Barrett?" Libby said, feigning nonchalance. "I don't really know him. Is it appropriate for me to offer a comment?"

"You've spoken to him on several occasions. What is your opinion of him?"

"He's very . . . polite."

"That's not much of a compliment. How else would you describe him?"

"I doubt I could or should." Libby frowned. "Why are you asking me about him?"

"I like you so much."

"I'm flattered, and I like you too."

"You're so much older than me."

Libby chuckled. "I'm not *that* old. Aren't you eighteen? I'm only twenty-five."

"You're so sophisticated compared to me."

"I suppose that's a valid assessment." Libby was responding carefully, not eager to engage in the conversation Penny was determined to have. "My upbringing was unconventional and nothing surprises me."

"Just so, Miss Carstairs. And may I call you Libby?"

"I would like that very much."

The snobby girl didn't extend the same courtesy, didn't request that Libby call her simply Penny, rather than *Lady* Penny, and she bit down a sigh. What had she expected? Every aristocrat she'd ever met had been extremely vain. Lady Penny was no different.

"You have a unique perspective that I don't possess," Penny said, "so I thought you might be able to give me advice I can't get otherwise."

"About what? About Lord Barrett?"

"Yes. My father and my aunt are pursuing a match between us, and the Watsons have been our neighbors forever. When Father told me Lord Barrett was interested in me, I never wondered whether we should marry or not. I simply assumed Father was correct."

Libby felt as if she was tiptoeing across a bog, and if she took a wrong step, she'd fall into the muck and be swallowed whole. She had no business discussing Lucas Watson with Penny Pendleton.

"I'm sure your father knows what's best for you," Libby tepidly said.

"He doesn't understand the kind of person I am. What if Lord Barrett turns out to be a horrendous choice? What then?"

"I see what you mean."

"I'm vexed, Libby, and I don't have anyone to confer with about it. I can hardly mention it to Lord Barrett."

"No, that wouldn't do at all."

"My aunt would just say Father is always right and I should listen to him."

"What is it you're actually asking me?" Libby inquired.

"What sort of husband would you imagine he'd be?"

"I couldn't make a prediction. No bride can ever be certain. Women roll the dice when they shackle themselves. It's the reason I've never considered it."

Penny stopped and pulled Libby around to face her. She looked serious and concerned. "If *you* could marry him, would you?"

Libby laughed breezily. "Me? Marry Lord Barrett? Well, yes, if he proposed, I'd probably jump at the chance. Who wouldn't want to wed a rich earl?"

"Forget about his wealth and title. Why would he be a good husband? Men like him have affairs and mistresses. They sire bastard children and have second families. What if I proceeded only to discover that he loved another woman?"

Libby was frightfully glad she'd spent so many years on the stage. She was adept at hiding her emotions. "I really can't answer you, and I hate that you're worrying. Are there any other acquaintances here who know him better than I do? Perhaps there are others who could supply the information you seek."

"Yes, there are others, but I couldn't ask them. Just tell me your opinion about him in general. You're constantly surrounded by handsome men, so you're an excellent judge of character. Would you wed him if you could?"

Penny was studying Libby intensely, and her severe expression was unnerving. What, precisely, was Penny trying to learn?

"How about this?" Libby said. "I would never wed him. I'm not a romantic, so I can't envision an ending with someone like him. I'd have to believe in fairytales and persuade myself that I could become Cinderella."

"Have you heard any rumors about him? Might he have a . . . a . . . mistress to whom he's inordinately attached?"

Libby blanched with dismay. "I'm sorry, but you and I shouldn't gossip about such a scandalous topic."

Penny took a deep breath, then she eased away from Libby. They started strolling back toward the party. Whatever the purpose of Penny's odd interrogation, it appeared to have concluded, and Libby couldn't figure out if she'd responded correctly or not.

As they approached the tents, Penny said, "May we walk again in the future?"

"Of course."

"And if I think of other issues, about being an adult and about matrimony, may I raise them?" Libby must have looked as if she'd refuse, for Penny hurriedly added, "I don't mean to make you uncomfortable, but I'm anxious to receive guidance only you can furnish."

"I'm delighted you assume I can guide you, but I don't feel I've offered a single remark that was helpful."

"You're been incredibly helpful," Penny said.

Several of her friends rushed up to greet her, and Libby shifted away, eager to let her be swept off. She had no idea why Penny would quiz her about Luke. Had they been seen together? Were stories swirling? If so, how could she tamp them down?

She went to a nearby table and had a footman pour her a glass of punch. She stepped to the side and was drinking it when she sensed she was being watched. The person's focus was so penetrating it was like a dagger in the back.

She glanced around and there, skulking behind the bushes, was Luke. He was trying to be inconspicuous, but there was no way to conceal his heightened regard.

After her peculiar discussion with Lady Penny, she couldn't have him hovering and staring. What if he came over to her? What if he insisted they chat?

At the moment, she simply couldn't oblige him. She sidled away and headed for the house, keen to reach her bedchamber where she could claim she needed to change her clothes. She might be able to waste hours and not be found.

She kept on at a brisk pace, and she didn't peek over her shoulder to check if Luke had followed her. In broad daylight, he wouldn't dare.

Would he?

~

CHARLES WAS LOAFING BY the window in his bedroom suite, peering down at the garden where the afternoon festivities were just beginning. Lawn games had commenced, but he hadn't yet mustered the energy to put in an appearance.

He'd spent the night with Fish, a development that was shocking and thrilling. It had been an eternity since he'd enjoyed such a wicked assignation. Not since he'd shackled himself to Florence. He'd sworn to her—and to himself—that he'd give up his vices and doxies. Otherwise, she wouldn't have married him.

He'd lived modestly and discreetly in the country, being determined to never cross paths with a female he might find tantalizing. But now, Fish was in residence, and her presence had stirred every depraved impulse he'd ever possessed.

He'd sneaked away from her at dawn, but he'd only departed after wringing a promise from her that they'd have a private breakfast later.

It had been a reckless request, but he'd tendered it anyway. He hadn't expected her to show up, but she'd tiptoed in right on time. She was over at the table in the corner, finishing her tea.

With his not wishing to fuel speculation in the kitchen as to who was joining him for the meal, he hadn't ordered breakfast for two. He'd had a tray delivered with one plate, napkin, and fork, so they'd had to share everything. The entire interval had been amazingly romantic in a way he'd relished much more than he should have.

Though it was ridiculous to admit, he felt as if he'd been reborn, as if he'd been unconscious and had been violently shaken to life. Colors were brighter, sounds louder, the sky so blue, the sun so vibrant. For once, he was disgustingly happy.

Two women were strolling in the park, away from the other guests, and as he assessed them, he realized it was Penny and Miss Carstairs.

He glanced over at Fish and said, "Have you noticed how Penny and Miss Carstairs look alike?"

"No."

"Come here. They're out in the garden."

Fish walked over, and he draped an arm over her shoulders and snuggled her to his side. He was intrigued by how easily they'd fallen into their prior pattern of fond acquaintance. It seemed as if they hadn't been parted a single day.

She studied them, then said, "They do look alike, don't they?"

"In a few years—when Penny is a bit older—she'll be Miss Carstairs's exact double."

"Yes, but Libby is much more flamboyant than your daughter. There are similarities in their features, but they're not really that similar."

The girls were having an intimate discussion, the resemblance becoming more pronounced. They were standing with the same posture, their heads cocked at the same angle, and a shiver slid down his spine. Suddenly, there was the eeriest perception in the air that powerful forces were at work and that he ought to pay attention to them.

"What can you tell me about Miss Carstairs's past?" he asked. "I don't remember how those three *lost* girls resolved their fates. Was there ever any news about her family?"

"She was claimed by an uncle. Her parents were missionaries, sailing for the Caribbean, but their ship sunk in a storm. He raised her."

"Is that the fellow to whom you were attached? Harry, wasn't it?"

"Yes, Harry. He's mostly responsible for how she turned out. He honed her talents so he could make money off them." Fish snorted with disgust. "He was never one to let a financial opportunity go to waste."

"She probably would have burst out into some sort of fame no matter what. Somehow, I can't imagine her being ordinary. I can't see her tucked away in a cottage and rearing a dozen brats."

Fish chuckled. "No, neither can I."

"You're sure her parents were missionaries?"

"It's the story Harry always told, but with him, you could never be certain if he was being truthful."

"She's simply so stunning. I can't picture her springing from humble beginnings."

"I agree. It's utterly possible that she has lofty kin. If I ultimately discover that she's actually a king's natural child, I wouldn't be surprised."

"You don't suppose . . ."

A demented notion riveted him, and his voice trailed off.

His crazed first wife, Amanda, had fled England with her lover, and she'd taken his daughter, Little Henrietta, with her. He'd been a detached, disinterested father, and when Amanda had vanished, he'd been separated from them for months. He'd cut ties so he'd had no idea where they were living or how Amanda was supporting herself. Weeks had passed before he'd learned they were gone.

He'd been too angry at Amanda to keep track of her, but he should have. Henrietta hadn't been safe with her, yet he'd left her with her mother anyway.

He'd barely known Henrietta and hadn't exhibited any paternal tendencies toward her, but he'd fretted over her plight. Where was she? How was she faring? Was she still alive?

No, she wasn't, and in fact, she'd been declared deceased by the courts.

Now, on observing Miss Carstairs with Penny, he wondered about her. Was there a bizarre chance in the universe that Miss Carstairs might be Henrietta?

He shoved away the fantastical prospect. As if Henrietta would waltz into his life after twenty-three years! As if Libby Carstairs was his long-lost daughter! The whole scenario was preposterous.

"Suppose . . . what?" Fish inquired when he didn't finish his sentence.

"Nothing. I was woolgathering. Don't mind me."

He continued to watch Miss Carstairs though, his disquiet increasing as they returned to the party, and Penny was whisked off by her friends. Miss Carstairs tarried and drank some punch. After a bit, she frowned and peeked over her shoulder.

Luke was lurking a few feet away and avidly staring at her. They shared a heated visual exchange that was so torrid and filled with lust and yearning that he noticed it even though he was quite a distance away.

Miss Carstairs scowled at Luke, flashed a warning, then rushed off.

"Did you see that?" he asked Fish, but she'd briskly slithered away and was seated at the table and pretending not to have witnessed the odd encounter.

"No, what?" Her tone was much too casual.

"Lord Barrett and Miss Carstairs appear to be very cordial."

"Do they?"

Her nonchalance was alarming, and he said, "Spill your secrets, Fish. Are they . . . involved?"

"Don't ask questions you don't really want the answer to."

"I'll take that as a *yes*. How close are they?"

Fish shrugged. "Close enough, I guess."

"What does that mean? I'm hoping he'll propose to Penny. If it comes to fruition, will there be a third person in the middle of their matrimonial relationship?"

Fish was silent forever, pondering the situation. She'd always been very loyal, and she would never disparage Miss Carstairs.

"I don't have a comment on that topic," she said.

"Your reply terrifies me."

"If you're curious about Lord Barrett and his habits, you should speak to him directly."

"I intend to."

"But again, Charles, are you sure you should pry? It might be better to leave well-enough alone."

Fleetingly, he tried to envision having a conversation with Luke on the issue of monogamy and adultery. He simply couldn't fathom it, and he realized she was correct. He couldn't bear to hear the answers Luke might supply. He'd offered Penny to Luke because Luke had claimed to possess Charles's same aversion to scandal and vice. Had the younger man been lying?

Luke was rich, titled, thirty, and he'd been a navy sailor. It was entirely expected that he would have affairs, but if he would, was it wise to push Penny into his arms?

Apparently, the subject had been too much for Fish. She tossed down her napkin, sauntered over, and kissed him on the mouth.

"Libby will change her clothes for the picnic," she said. "I have to help her."

"I refuse to let you go."

"It's not up to you, and we're lucky no servants have knocked. I can't imagine being discovered in here with you. It might rock the house to its foundations."

"I don't care if we're discovered."

"Of course you don't. You're a man, and it's your home. You can act how you please. I, however, am a woman who's little more than a servant. I can't be caught with you."

"Let's spend the day in my bed."

"You are deranged, my dear Lord Roland, and I have chores."

"Ignore them. Miss Carstairs can dress herself for once."

"I don't want her to have to tend herself. She might figure out that she doesn't need me."

"You're aware of how vain I am. I view myself as being much more important than her."

Fish scoffed at that. "You know where my room is located. I'm certain you can find it again—whenever you're in the mood."

She went over and peeked into the hall. Seeing no one, she winked at him, waved goodbye, then hurried out. He dawdled in the empty room, irked that the fun and excitement had ended with her departure. It had been so long since he'd succumbed to carnal temptation, and he'd forgotten how overwhelming it could be.

With her having left, he was too depressed to tarry. He grabbed his coat and headed downstairs, and he wandered through the mansion. It was quiet, the servants busy with the outside activities. Finally, he slinked to a side door, thinking he might sneak to the stables, saddle a horse, and take a ride, but as he was about to exit the manor, Miss Carstairs was approaching.

He was delighted to bump into her. Since she'd arrived, they hadn't had an opportunity to chat in a meaningful way, and he was dreadfully curious about her. He didn't believe the story her uncle had spread about her parents being lowly missionaries, and he agreed with Fish that he wouldn't be surprised if she had drops of noble blood running in her veins.

He wondered too whether a Pendleton relative might have sired her.

Before he could hail her, a man stepped from behind a carriage that was parked in the grass. He was a fussy-looking fellow, short and rotund, wearing a brown suit, bowler hat, and spectacles.

"Miss Carstairs!" he gushed. "Fancy meeting you here!"

She halted. "I apologize, sir, but I don't recognize you. Are we acquainted?"

"I've watched you on the stage in London. I'm your biggest admirer."

"How nice."

She flashed a tight smile and attempted to walk on, but the oaf wouldn't allow her to pass by.

"Actually, Miss Carstairs, my name is Howard Periwinkle. I write for the London Times."

"Oh." She frowned. "How did you track me to the country?"

"It wasn't hard. I stopped by the theater in town, but your booking there was over. I asked one of the actors where you were."

"You've been trying to talk to me, haven't you? My cousin has chased you off on several occasions."

"Yes, but it's about the anniversary! Surely you'd like to reminisce! You can provide a few remarks for me to quote."

"My cousin has been very firm with you, Mr. Periwinkle. I don't wish to discuss my past with you."

"It's been twenty years, Miss Carstairs! The whole kingdom would love to hear how you're faring."

She chuckled. "I doubt that very much, and you'll have to excuse me. I'm needed at an event, and I must get ready."

Periwinkle was undeterred. "Have any new memories come to light? Have you uncovered information about your parents? About your *real* parents?"

"My parents were missionaries, Mr. Periwinkle. You're aware of that."

"What if your Uncle Harry lied about them? He was a cad and a bounder. That's what I've been told. What if he tricked everyone—especially you?"

"My uncle was kind and generous"—Charles had learned from Fish that that wasn't true—"and I won't listen to you denigrating him."

She pushed by him and, when she saw Charles in the doorway, she sagged with relief.

As he stared into her eyes, he suffered the strangest wave of vertigo. He grew incredibly dizzy, as if the ground had shifted under his feet, but as swiftly as the unsteadiness bubbled up, it vanished when Periwinkle called to her again.

"Should I tell you about your two companions from the shipwreck? Caroline and Joanna, right?"

Miss Carstairs blanched and whipped around. "No, I'm not interested."

Periwinkle was a nuisance who wouldn't shut up. "My newspaper would like to arrange a reunion for the three of you."

"I wouldn't consider it," she responded. "Not it you paid me a thousand pounds. Now please leave me be—or I'll have my cousin speak to you. He'll be quite a bit less polite next time."

Periwinkle would have continued his harangue, but Charles blustered outside, saying, "Miss Carstairs! There you are! I've been searching for you everywhere."

"I'm so glad you found me," she said.

"Is this dolt bothering you?"

He cast a scathing glower at Periwinkle, but the cretin had no shame and didn't slither away.

Miss Carstairs cast a glower that was very similar to Charles's own. "Yes, as a matter of fact, he is bothering me."

"I am Lord Roland, Mr. Periwinkle," Charles said to him. "You're trespassing, and you've been harassing my guest. Depart at once or I'll have my footmen escort you off the property."

"Hello, Lord Roland," the cheeky dunce replied. "How about you and your anniversary? Hasn't it been twenty-five years since your . . . *troubles* occurred? Would *you* like to reminisce for me?"

Charles marched over, grabbed him by his shirt, and lifted him off his feet. He pulled him up until they were nose to nose. "Go now! Don't make me tell you twice."

Charles flung him away. Periwinkle staggered, then straightened. He grinned at Charles and said, "People are eager to read about their betters. I could pen a very sympathetic story—about both of you."

Charles didn't waste his breath answering. He simply spun away, took Miss Carstairs's arm, and they went into the house. He didn't glance back.

"You're distraught," Lord Roland said. "Would you like a glass of sherry? Would it soothe your nerves?"

Libby smiled at him. "I can't abide sherry. Would you view me as being terribly debauched if I had a whiskey instead?"

He snorted. "Ah, a girl after my own heart."

They were sequestered in a small parlor, the door closed to shield them from any intruders. She didn't suppose Periwinkle would enter the manor, but if he dared, he wouldn't find them.

Besides, Lord Roland had whispered to the first footman they'd encountered and had told the boy to round up some other male servants and chase Periwinkle away. Libby was thrilled by the order. She had no desire to have the intrusive fiend accost her ever again.

There was a liquor tray on a table in the corner, and Lord Roland poured two glasses. Libby stood by the window and gazed out at the garden where the afternoon festivities were progressing. She couldn't see Luke anywhere, and she wondered if he was mingling in the crowd.

Her yearning to talk to him about what had just happened was so tangible that it seemed like a physical need she couldn't slake. Clearly, her fixation was ridiculous, and she had to shuck it off, the problem being that she had no idea how.

Lord Roland came over and handed her a glass, and they sipped their beverages and stared out at the revelers.

"Has Mr. Periwinkle been stalking you for long?" he asked.

"He's been *trying* to stalk me, but my cousin, Simon, has kept him away."

"I hadn't realized it was the twentieth anniversary of your rescue."

"Neither had I—until Periwinkle started hounding me."

The comment was a bald-faced lie. There was never a minute of the day that she didn't ponder her rescue by those navy sailors. Because Uncle Harry had turned her tragedy into a performance monologue, she was never able to *not* think about it. The event had defined her life, but she didn't remember much about what had actually transpired.

Any authentic recollection had been dragged out of her by Harry when she was tiny, then he'd enhanced her memories so it sounded even more catastrophic than it had been. She couldn't guess which portions were genuine and which were faked for dramatic effect.

Occasionally, at night when she couldn't sleep, she'd struggle to recall reliable details. There were things like her gripping a piece of wood and floating in the ocean in the dark. Adults had been shouting at her to hold on tight so she didn't slip away.

She assumed it was a valid image. She hated bodies of water and the dark, and she never placed herself in a spot where there was shouting. That sort of experience lit a huge fire under her anxiety.

She remembered being on the island with Caroline and Joanna, remembered snuggling together like puppies. When she shut her eyes, she could feel their warm skin against her own.

But she didn't remember her parents, didn't remember the ship they'd been on, leaving England, or being out on the ocean. It was as if the frightening incident had been wiped clean. A doctor had once told her that it was a typical reaction after a calamity. A person could only handle so much scary information, then she buried the rest.

She would love to see Caroline and Joanna again. They'd been closer than sisters and inordinately attached. Then, when Harry had arrived to claim her, they'd been ripped apart. She hadn't been allowed to tell them goodbye, and it was a wound that still hadn't healed.

Did they suffer the same nightmares as Libby? Would they like to meet her? What would a reunion be like? What might they remember that she didn't?

The prospect was too daunting to consider, so she never considered it. Periwinkle's offer to put Libby in contact with them was tempting, but she remained too fearful to follow through. So she wouldn't follow through.

Men liked to talk about themselves, and she *didn't* like to talk about herself. She had a thousand questions she'd like to ask Lord Roland, and for once, there was no one to interrupt or distract them. If she was shrewd in her queries, what might he confide?

She peered up at him and said, "You survived a disaster, didn't you, when you were younger? Apparently, you're facing a big anniversary too. We have that in common."

"I hadn't really thought about it. I never dwell on that appalling period."

"May I inquire about it? Or would you rather I mind my own business?"

"You can inquire. It played out very publicly, so there aren't many facts that haven't been chewed over. If you dig into something you shouldn't, I'll absolutely order you to butt out."

She chuckled, and they clinked the rims of their glasses.

"I'll just be very bold," she said, "and mention your first wife. She left you, and you ended up divorced and disgraced."

"I will defend myself by insisting I was stupid and wild, and no offense, but I eloped with a singer. It was such a stunning misstep that I'm amazed I didn't send the Earth spinning off its axis."

"Weren't you ever apprised that disparate people shouldn't wed? Down through the centuries, there's been plenty of evidence that it never works out. What's the old adage? Like should stick to like."

He smirked. "I didn't want that adage to be true, but I learned my lesson in a very hard way."

"You had a daughter with her, didn't you?"

"Yes, Little Henrietta. My wife absconded with her."

Casually, Libby asked, "What happened to them?"

"My wife abandoned me for a handsome gambler."

"Did you know him and see it coming? Or was it a complete surprise?"

"I knew him, but he wasn't a friend. I certainly never suspected their affair or I'd have tried to stop it. I'm not sure I could have. My wife was quite insane."

"Insane! My goodness."

"She had many problems, mostly with how her emotions would swing out of control."

"You're being very frank with me," Libby said, "and I can't decide if I should be flattered or disturbed."

"I was in the middle of it when it occurred, but now, it's so far in the past it seems as if some other clueless idiot wreaked that havoc."

"Where did the shameful couple go after they fled England?"

"They sailed to Italy."

"You must have hunted for them."

"Not for them so much. I didn't care about them, but I searched for Henrietta. She would have been imperiled by her mother, and I hoped to rescue her."

"You never found her?"

"Her mother's paramour died in an accident in Rome, and after that, their trail went cold. My lawyers finally convinced me that they had to be dead too. My wife was very flamboyant, and she could never have hidden herself away, but there was never a trace of her."

"Did you love Little Henrietta?"

"Will you think I'm horrid if I confess to being an awful parent? When she was born, I was an irresponsible dandy who wasn't ready to be a father. I wasn't concerned about her in the slightest."

"Yet you searched for her . . ." Libby wistfully said. "You weren't successful, but you *tried*."

The interval grew awkward, and he downed his liquor and moved away from her. His cheeks were flushed, indicating he was embarrassed to have been so candid.

"Has the liquor fortified you, Miss Carstairs?" He gestured to the garden. "Will you go outside?"

"Yes, I'm feeling much better, but I have to head upstairs to change my clothes. I'm always on stage, even during a picnic."

"You constantly look fabulous."

"I appreciate you noticing, but it's none of my doing. My companion, Miss Fishburn, is in charge of my wardrobe."

"I'm acquainted with Fish from when I was frolicking in town decades ago. She and I are old friends, and it's nice to have her at Roland. We've been able to reminisce."

"I'm so glad," Libby said, not meaning it.

His use of Fish's nickname was distressing, and it was obvious Libby needed to have a chat with Fish. Fish was the one who urged caution in romantic affairs. Libby didn't suppose Fish would be reckless, but Libby had to counsel restraint.

She downed her drink too and handed him her glass. As he placed them on the tray, she said, "Thank you for taking a few minutes to calm me."

"It was my pleasure."

"Would you call me Libby?"

"I'd like that."

As with Penny, he didn't suggest she call him Charles. Not that Libby would have. She couldn't imagine them being on such familiar terms, so she shook off her disappointment.

She wanted to stay in the small room with him forever, but she'd been too blunt in her interrogation, and he was anxious to end their private discussion. Once he'd declared it to be over, she could hardly argue that they should continue.

"Will *you* go out to the party?" she asked as he opened the door and they walked down the hall to the front foyer.

"I guess I have to."

She laughed. "Don't be so glum. In another week or so, we'll all have left."

"Yes, you will have, and then, I'll probably mope and complain that the house is too quiet."

"If you see Fish, tell her I require her assistance up in my bedchamber."

"I will, and you've given me the perfect excuse to track her down."

He appeared so delighted by the prospect that Libby was a tad alarmed.

She wasn't sure if there was an appropriate comment to utter. After all, she was in no position to scold him for being too friendly with Fish, but she lingered a moment, then a moment more, until the delay became uncomfortable. She spun away and started up the stairs. She'd reached the landing when he called to her.

"Libby?"

She halted and stared down. "Yes?"

"What do you know about your parents?"

"Mostly just what my Uncle Harry shared with me. He was the relative who claimed me after I was returned to England. I lived with him and he raised me."

"Fish told me they were missionaries."

Libby shrugged. "It's what Harry always said."

"Do you think he was being truthful? Do you think they were missionaries?"

For the briefest instant, there was an eerie stillness in the air, as if every being in the universe was waiting to discover what they'd say next.

Libby broke the silence. "That's a very strange question. Why would you ask it?"

"You're much too remarkable to come from ordinary stock. If you announced that your father was a king, I would absolutely believe it."

She forced a smile, the one that brought audiences to their feet so they cheered and applauded. "I've heard statements like that all my life, Lord Roland. Perhaps I should pretend my father really was a king."

She kept on, and she didn't glance down, but she sensed him watching her. His curiosity was intense, and she couldn't bear to observe it. If she did, who could predict what might happen?

Chapter

12

LIBBY GALLOPED DOWN THE rural lane, bent over her horse's neck, the animal cantering at its fastest speed. Her hat had flown off and her hair had fallen from its pins so the blond locks were wildly flowing behind her. Anyone who observed her would likely wonder if a madwoman hadn't just passed by.

She'd parted with Lord Roland in his foyer and had intended to socialize with Penny and her guests, but she'd been too disconcerted. After her confrontation with Mr. Periwinkle, then her conversation with Lord Roland, she'd felt as if the hounds of Hell were chasing her. A reckless act had been required to outrun them.

She'd written a note for Fish, then had snuck away from the manor as rapidly and as furtively as she could.

It was always disturbing to bump into a man like Periwinkle. He was determined to hash out the truth about her past. And as to Lord Roland, well . . .

She'd been yearning for a private chat with him, and now, she'd had it. His daughter, Little Henrietta, was dead, so what was the point of anything?

She was adept at fleeing uncomfortable situations. Harry had taught her that neat trick. Whenever circumstances had become too dicey, he'd always had them pack their bags, and they'd tiptoed away from the problem that was plaguing him. His ability to disappear had kept him from getting arrested, from getting pummeled by creditors, from getting shot at by angry husbands.

He might not have been her uncle by birth, but she certainly exhibited many of his worst tendencies.

The sky had been growing darker, and suddenly, lightning flashed and thunder rumbled. Her horse shied, causing her to frantically grapple for purchase. She tugged on the reins and slowed him to a walk. Sprinkles dampened her shoulders.

Momentarily lost, she peered about, and she was dismayed to find that she was sitting at the gate to Barrett. At the realization, a shiver slid down her spine. Was it a warning or maybe an evil portent?

She glanced down the road, and a rider was trotting toward her. Of course it would be Luke heading to his home just as she was at that very spot. He'd seen her, so she couldn't whip around and race off in the other direction. If she tried, she was positive he'd chase her down.

As he neared, it seemed as if great fortune was approaching, as if doom was approaching. Which would it turn out to be in the end?

He kept coming until they were side by side, and he leaned over and pulled her close so he could deliver a passionate kiss.

When they straightened, he was scowling like a grumpy nanny. "Why are you gallivanting across the country without a maid or a groom?"

"I had to escape the party for a while. I had to clear my mind."

"That doesn't explain why you're alone."

"I'm not a fussy debutante," she said. "Don't scold me as if I have rules to obey."

"What if you suffered a mishap when you were off by yourself? What then? How would we guess that you were imperiled?"

"I never have trouble, and if I did, I have my pistol in my pocket."

"Your comment alarms me."

"Why? I know how to use it."

"I'm sure you do, but I am incensed to hear that you believe you're invincible."

"Perhaps I am invincible. My history proves I can survive any ordeal."

"Well, people supposedly have nine lives, and I fear you've squandered several of them already. Stop tempting Fate."

"I've always tempted Fate," she breezily said. "Why quit now?"

He studied her and frowned. "You're upset. What happened?"

"Nothing."

It was her typical answer to that question. For much of her life, she'd been anxious or aggrieved, but she'd had to pretend she was fine. Harry had insisted that no one liked a complainer, so she'd proficiently learned how to bury tons of petty grievances and bad attitude.

Luke scoffed. "Liar. Your distress is plain as the nose on your face, so I repeat: What happened?"

"I was accosted by a reporter." She waved away the remark, as if the encounter had been silly.

"From a newspaper?"

"Yes. What other kind is there?"

"What did he want?"

"He wanted to talk about the shipwreck."

"My goodness, why?"

"It's the twentieth anniversary this year—of my being found? I'm trying to ignore it, but he's been pestering me."

"What is he expecting you'll say?"

"He's tracked down the other two lost girls. Caroline and Joanna? He'd like to print a retrospective, and he asked if he could arrange a reunion for the three of us."

"Would you like to speak with them?"

"I might—if it was private." For some reason, tears flooded her eyes, which was embarrassing.

"Don't be sad." He leaned over and kissed her again.

"I'm not. I'm just...annoyed. I can't bear to be harassed. I don't need the sort of publicity he'd generate."

He grinned, eager to lighten her mood. "Are you certain about that? You've thrived on sharing your story with audiences. You might create a whole new crop of admirers."

She snorted at that. "I have too many as it is. I can't escape some of them."

She meant him, and he understood that she did.

"After you were drinking punch in the garden," he said, "I waited for you to return to the picnic, but you didn't. I finally bribed Fish to reveal your whereabouts, and she admitted you'd gone for a ride."

"You didn't bribe Fish. She wouldn't have succumbed to blackmail."

"Maybe not. Maybe she's simply a romantic at heart, and she hoped I'd find you so we could spend some time together."

"I doubt that very much. She thinks we're both mad."

"She's probably right."

"Is that how you found me? You nagged at Fish until she told you where I was? I assumed our meeting was an accident, but apparently, you deliberately sought me out."

His grin widened. "I might have."

"Your fixation has spiraled to an outrageous height, and I must inform you that you are dancing on a very perilous ledge."

"You've forced me to realize that I like to live dangerously. I didn't recognize that trait in my personality, so I must categorically state that you are having an interesting effect on my character."

"I don't want to have an effect."

"What do you want to have?"

"I want sanity to be restored."

"So long as you are present in my world, there's no chance of that."

Thunder rumbled again, so loudly that they instinctively ducked. Then the clouds opened, and a torrent of rain began to pelt them. In an instant, the deluge was so intense that she could barely see.

"Roland is too far away." He had to shout to be heard over the noise. "Let's head for Barrett."

"I can't join you there," she replied, but the storm swallowed her words.

He likely would have ignored her comment anyway. He spun and rode through the gate, and he didn't peer back to guarantee she'd tagged after him. He was so gallingly confident in his ability to command her.

She was a modern, independent woman who made her own choices in all matters. She could have braved the tempest and continued on to Roland, but she went with him like a trained puppy, being happy to go wherever he led. What could it hurt to tarry, warm and cozily, as they waited for the gale to wane?

They raced by the orchards and were quickly spit out at the door. He helped her down as a footman rushed out to tend the horses. She was whisked into the manor, the butler and others hurrying up to fuss over them. All the while, she was scolding herself for being such an idiot, for letting him coerce her.

She had no business being in his home. Not when he was about to betroth himself to Lady Penny. Servants couldn't keep a secret, and gossip of their arrival would spread swiftly in the neighborhood. How long would it take for it to float over to Roland?

His servants were incredibly competent, and she was escorted up to a guest bedchamber. Maids scurried about, eager to assist her, as if they hadn't seen a female in ages. Barrett Manor was a bachelor's residence, so perhaps they hadn't.

They lit a huge fire, and she was positioned on a chair in front of it. Hot chocolate was produced, as were a wool shawl and slippers. She was stripped of her wet gown and a dry one magically furnished. It was a bit too long and a bit too big, but it was much more comfortable than the drenched dress they had removed.

Her own garments were carried away, with promises that they would be cleaned down in the kitchen. Then, once she was in a better condition, a footman delivered the message that Lord Barrett had been dried and cleaned too, and—if she was amenable—he hoped she'd have a whiskey with him in a downstairs parlor.

The maids were furtively studying her, and she couldn't decide if it was because they were astonished that Luke had a woman in the house or if it was because her identity had been revealed. There weren't many places where her name *wasn't* recognized.

They'd also have heard from the servants' grapevine that she was staying at Roland. The prospect had her anxious to protect Luke from himself. He was determined to jump off the cliff where they were standing, but she truly believed she should stop him from toppling over the edge.

She thanked the maids who'd aided her, and her compliments showered over them like golden flower petals, as if they'd never been praised before. The footman guided her down to the parlor, but the maids quietly followed, watching her every step so they could describe the moment at supper later on.

Luke was pacing and impatient, irked that she'd been so slow to appear. Another huge fire was roaring, and a tray of liquor and other refreshments had been arranged on a table. He shooed everyone out, and they were definitely sluggish in their departure, their furtive glances becoming less furtive until they were openly gawking.

As the door closed behind them, he said, "Your reputation precedes you, Miss Carstairs."

"Sometimes, I wish it wouldn't. I wish I could have snuck in as an anonymous person."

"No, you don't. You would hate being anonymous."

"I can't have rumors drift to Roland that I was here alone with you."

"We can't prevent it. I'm certain the whole county will soon know you visited, but we have the storm to use as an excuse. We can insist we met on the road, and when the rain started, we fled to the nearest shelter, which was Barrett."

She scoffed. "No one will think it was an innocent trip."

"I don't care."

With that, he pulled her into his arms and conveyed a stunning kiss that went on and on. She didn't hesitate to participate. Why would she? She reminded herself that *she* had no losses to incur if their mischief was uncovered.

She was a theatrical performer, so she was constantly painted with an illicit brush. If she traipsed off with him, it wouldn't be surprising, but *he* could lose quite a bit, specifically his pending engagement to Penny.

Yet he wasn't concerned about it. If he wasn't worried, why should she be?

Eventually, they tumbled onto a sofa. He drew her onto his lap, and she snuggled there, content to loaf with him in a way that was completely improper, but she had to cease focusing on her misgivings. She had to simply be glad for the interval they'd been able to steal for themselves. It wouldn't last.

"You've kidnapped me," she said.

"I didn't kidnap you. As I vividly remember it, I merely suggested we ride to Barrett, and you obliged me."

"I didn't complain because I was positive—if I'd refused and had headed in the opposite direction—you'd have chased after me."

"You could be right about that."

"What if this tempest continues for an entire week? Will I be your prisoner until it abates?"

"Yes. Now that I've finally ensnared you, I might never let you go."

"I was afraid that would be your opinion."

She scooted away and hurried over to the window to peer outside. It was raining even harder, so how long would she dare to tarry? He was relaxed on the sofa like a lazy king and assessing her as a lion would a rabbit—as if he was about to gobble her up. That look always thrilled her.

"Your servants dressed me in dry clothes," she said. "Whose gown am I wearing?"

"I have no idea."

"It didn't belong to one of your mistresses, did it? I'd be really annoyed if that was the case."

"I've never brought a woman here, so I can't imagine where they found it."

She smirked with disgust. "I can't decide if you're telling the truth or not."

"I won't claim to have ever been a saint, but I've never had a mistress."

"Should I believe you?"

"Why would I lie about it?"

"Why would a man lie about any fact?"

"*Touché.*" He patted his thigh. "You're too far away from me. Come over and sit down."

"I shouldn't."

"Why not?"

"When I'm close to you, it stirs wicked notions I hadn't ought to contemplate."

"I like the sound of that."

The quiet room was too much for her. It fostered an intimacy she didn't like. It felt as if they were the only two people on Earth and any misconduct would be allowed.

She walked to the refreshment tray and poured them both a whiskey. As she handed him one, he grabbed her wrist, but she skittered away and hovered over by the window, braced like a panicked virgin who would bolt at the least sign of trouble.

"Will you ever release me from this dungeon?" she asked him.

"Maybe not."

"What if it rains all night?"

"I could have a carriage harnessed, and we could travel to Roland in it, but I'd hate to impose on my servants when the weather is so inclement."

"Yes, that would be cruel."

"Give it an hour or so. If it doesn't improve, we can discuss the situation again."

"You hustled me into the house so fast that I've barely had a chance to snoop. May I have a tour? It would pass the time."

"You can have a tour, but you're incredibly nervous. Why?"

"This is too odd," she said. "I can't figure out how to act."

He smiled a delicious smile. "If you sit on my lap, I'll show you how."

"I'll just bet you would."

"What do you suppose will happen between us?"

"Nothing good. I'm sure of it."

He sipped his drink, his warm regard washing over her and easing some of the tension. After a bit, he said, "That reporter really upset you."

"Yes, very much."

"Why is that? You've spent so many years telling your story. I'd think it would seem very blasé to you by now."

"A lot of it is invented."

For a moment, he looked shocked. "Don't say so."

"My Uncle Harry pried some memories out of me when I was small and had first been brought back to England, but he significantly embellished them."

"I'm stunned to hear it."

"I have some real memories though, but they're hidden deep down inside. If I focused on them, I might recollect something terrible. It scares me."

"What might you recollect?" he asked.

"If I wanted to recall, I would," she said more testily than she'd intended.

"After suffering a trauma, it's common to bury the details. I saw it regularly in the navy, but a doctor once apprised me that it's therapeutic to reminisce about an incident. Apparently, distress will wane with the remembering."

She bristled. "He was probably a charlatan."

"Your parents weren't missionaries, were they? Isn't that what you told me?"

"I swear, that question has been put to me a dozen times today."

"By who besides me?"

"The newspaper reporter and Lord Roland. They assume I'm too flamboyant to have sprung from ordinary folks."

"They're correct. You are." Appearing sly and crafty, he asked, "How did you answer them?"

"I didn't. There's no point in piquing their curiosity. It's not as if I can change my history."

"Your Uncle Harry wasn't even your uncle. Aren't you concerned about what else he might have concealed?"

From perusing the box of Harry's old letters, she knew what he'd concealed, and the whole sad saga surged to the tip of her tongue.

She yearned to open her mouth and let it spill out, but she couldn't force herself to confide in him. What if he ridiculed her? What if he laughed with derision? What if her tale ignited a chain of events that destroyed the entire world? Wasn't it better to remain silent?

Oh, she was so conflicted!

"Your devious mind is whirring," he said.

"My mind is not devious, and it's not whirring."

"Yes, it is. You're debating whether to unburden yourself over some issue. What is it?"

She scowled. "Why would you think that?"

"I can read your thoughts clear as day. You're not a mystery to me."

"That news alarms me. I'll have to try harder to be enigmatic."

"It won't work. I've figured you out."

"What have you—in your infinite wisdom—deduced about me?"

"You're not as tough as you pretend to be," he said.

"Maybe not."

"And you're lonely. You're constantly surrounded by people, but you're always alone. You're tormented by your past, and you'd like to shuck off the weight your uncle demanded you carry, but if you did, you can't imagine who you'd be afterward."

Her jaw dropped in astonishment. "You couldn't possibly have guessed all that. Are you about to tell me you're a clairvoyant?"

He chuckled. "No. I was merely blowing smoke, but from your reaction, I take it I hit the mark."

"Don't gloat. It's annoying."

"Will you come and sit down? Or will I have to walk over and drag you back?"

"I should stay where I am, and *you* should stay where you are."

"If you get much more prim on me, I'll accuse you of having moral tendencies."

"I have some," she said. "Not a lot, but some."

"We have so few chances to be together like this. Once the rain stops, we'll have to return to Roland and act like strangers. Why waste these precious minutes?"

"We're not wasting anything. We're chatting."

"I'm bored with chatting, and I want to dally."

"Of course you do." Her tone was scolding. "You're a man. It's all you dolts think about."

"Not me. Before you strolled by, I was never overly consumed by passionate rumination. But since I met you, I've become a raging ball of lust. I feel like a randy adolescent who just discovered that girls are pretty."

"You're blaming me for your obsession?"

"Absolutely, and because you're responsible for my discomfort, I insist you slake it."

Her defenses were wilting. The room was cozy and dark, the fire casting intriguing shadows and creating an ambiance that encouraged mischief. If she relented and offered what he sought, who would ever know? What if she sauntered over, took his hand, and told him to escort her up to his bedchamber?

She had a fairly precise idea of what would happen there. Fish had been extremely blunt in describing the carnal deeds women were required to perform. Nearly every female had to engage in them sooner or later. Why not Libby?

As Simon had mentioned, it wasn't as if she was saving her virginity for a husband. Why not bestow it on rich, dashing Lucas Watson? She could view it as a type of scientific experiment, and she had no doubt that he would be incredibly adept at showing her how enticing sexual play could be with the right partner.

But if she yielded, she understood one salient fact: Much of his infatuation was fueled by the pesky detail that she kept refusing him. If she gave in, he'd quickly weary of her, and before she could regroup, he'd decide it was over.

It was humiliating to admit, but she wasn't ready for that moment to arrive. She enjoyed how he gazed at her so fondly, as if she was fabulously remarkable, and she was relishing every second of his delectable fascination. She wouldn't deliberately hasten the end of it.

Better to share torrid kisses, but naught more. Better to stand across the room and fill her eyes with the sight of him. Better to be safe than sorry.

"Unfortunately for you," she said, "I won't be doing any slaking."

He snorted with feigned affront. "You wound me with your disregard, Miss Carstairs."

"It's the method I've devised for dealing with a man who's besotted."

"I'm quite a bit beyond besotted."

It was a stunning declaration, and they were disconcerted by it. She, because she was suffering from the same heightened affection. He, because it had been a proclamation of sorts, and he was much too manly to have confessed it.

"We're a pathetic pair," she teasingly said.

"We are. I can't deny it."

"If we make it through the next week without setting the whole world on fire, it will be a miracle."

"You are a master of understatement."

They smiled, a poignant sense of connection flaring between them. It was the worst point yet for her. She had to physically work to keep herself right where she was. If she rushed over to the sofa, he'd instantly have her flat on her back, and he'd never release her. She wouldn't try to escape either.

She downed her whiskey, put the glass on a nearby table, then headed for the door.

"Where are you going?" he asked. "I'm not finished with you."

"I thought I'd have your butler give me a tour of the manor. What's his name? Mr. Hobbs? Will you come with me?"

"Don't be such a pest," he complained. "I'm eager to misbehave, and it's the perfect afternoon for it. We're alone, and we've snuck off from all those prying eyes over at Roland."

"Well, I'd like to snoop around in your house. You don't seem to realize this about me, but I always get my way."

"So do I, and my wishes should take precedence over yours."

"Why?"

"Because I'm a man and you're a woman. Because I'm an earl and you're not."

"You are such a spoiled baby." She laughed and hurried out, calling, "Mr. Hobbs? Where are you."

Behind her, she heard him sigh, then grumble under his breath, but he didn't chase after her, which was probably for the best. If she spent an hour with his butler, perhaps she would gain control of her inappropriate yearning.

She could only hope.

Chapter

13

LUKE MARCHED DOWN THE hall to Libby's guest bedchamber.

His servants were absolutely agog to have her visiting, and she had an interesting way with them. He supposed the knack had developed from her experience on the stage. She knew how to captivate an audience, how to make people like her. And his servants definitely *liked* her. It meant that, so far, he hadn't been able to get her alone.

She'd slyly surrounded herself with them, and everyone had been charmed and hanging on her every word. With each step she'd taken, a hoard of admirers had followed her through the house, with all of them eager to have a chance to assist her.

She'd ended the afternoon by giving them a show that would have them chattering for years.

Luke had hovered on the edge of the crowd, a sort of unwanted voyeur who was anxious to drag her off to a deserted parlor so they could engage in mischief.

Because the servants were such gossips, he'd had to pretend she was just an ordinary guest and he was merely a gracious host who'd bumped into her out on the road as the storm was commencing. But he'd exceeded his limit as to how much longer he'd allow himself to be ignored.

It was evening already, with the deluge having grown worse as the hours had passed. Ultimately, he'd had a footman bundle up and ride to Roland with the news that he and Libby were stranded at Barrett and would return in the morning if the rain abated.

The message had been conveyed to Fish, with Luke practically begging her to reveal the information carefully and, if they weren't missed, to not reveal it at all. He had ulterior motives toward Libby—why claim otherwise?—and his patience for her nonsense was exhausted.

He knocked on her door, and finally—finally!—she emerged from the room, and there wasn't a servant in sight to provide a barrier. She sauntered over, approaching until they were toe to toe. He wrapped an arm around her waist and pulled her close for a quick kiss.

"We're having supper," he told her. "Don't argue about it."

"I won't argue. I'm starving, but why are you glowering at me? Let me guess. I haven't showered you with nearly enough attention today, and your feelings are hurt."

"Precisely. Now come."

He escorted her to his bedroom suite, arriving so rapidly that it hadn't occurred to her that she should decline to join him in it.

The servants had set a table in front of the fire, and they'd arranged a small buffet on another table so he and Libby could serve themselves. The butler, Mr. Hobbs, was hovering, and he straightened as they entered.

Hobbs could gossip as fervidly as anyone, but Luke had requested he supervise the preparations in the hopes that it would subdue some of the speculation down in the kitchen. But it was probably ludicrous to imagine it could be quelled.

"This looks cozy," Libby said, as she waltzed in.

If Hobbs was shocked or scandalized by the private meal, he didn't reveal it. He held the chair for her, then for Luke, as he asked, "Shall I serve you, my lord?"

"What's your opinion?" Luke asked Libby. "Shall we keep him? Or can he slink off to his bed?"

Libby flashed a smile Hobbs would remember forever. "You don't need to wait on us, Mr. Hobbs. It's late, and we can fend for ourselves."

"Are you sure, Miss Carstairs?"

"I'm sure, and the food smells delicious. Tell the chef that I was incredibly pleased."

"I will. And if I may be so bold as to say ...?"

"Yes?"

"Thank you for entertaining the staff. We were all enthralled, especially the younger housemaids."

Libby reached out and squeezed his hand, leaving him so giddy that Luke was surprised he didn't faint.

"I'm delighted Lord Barrett furnished the opportunity," she said. "The servants here are the most gracious audience I've ever had."

Luke had tolerated all the gushing he could stand. He waved Hobbs out, and once he'd left and it was quiet, she collapsed in her seat, as if the air had rushed out of her. She grabbed the wine decanter and poured her goblet full to the rim before Luke could offer to do it for her.

"What a day," she muttered as she took several gulps. "Did you send a note to Fish so she won't worry?"

"Yes, I sent it."

"You have some gall to automatically assume I'd dine with you in your bedchamber."

"Yes, I'm renowned for my gall. It's an aristocrat's prerogative to be audacious."

"Your servants will know I'm locked in with you."

"I don't care. You won't quail like a trembling virgin, will you?"

"No. Just feed me. When I told you I was starving, I wasn't joking."

"Your wish is my command," he facetiously retorted.

He rose and went to the buffet, lifting the lids to check on what had been delivered.

"We have a bit of everything," he said, "and if I recall correctly, you like everything."

"This is our second meal. Is it your intent to make a habit out of feeding me?"

"Yes."

"Isn't food the way to a *man's* heart? Can the same ploy work on a woman?"

He grinned. "We'll see, I guess."

He dished up plates for both of them, then brought them over. He served hers with a flourish, then sat across from her. She picked up a fork, but didn't eat. As was typical of her, she simply pushed the food around. He studied her, deciding she looked exhausted.

"You're tired," he said.

"Of course I am. I've been on stage all day. It's not easy being me. People have expectations, and I like to live up to them."

"Are you ever just yourself? Or are you always putting on an act?"

"I'm myself with you—if that's what you're asking."

He snorted with amusement. "You are never *yourself* with me. You are the most enigmatic person I've ever encountered. I can never tell from one minute to the next if I'm viewing the real Libby Carstairs or if I'm staring at a false façade."

"If I showed you the *real* me, you probably wouldn't like me quite so much."

"I doubt it. I'm certain I'd be besotted no matter what."

"I like your servants," she said, deftly changing the subject.

"They like you too. In fact, I can safely state that they're all in love with you."

"You mention their heightened regard as if it's a bad thing."

"You expended all your energy on them, and now, none remains for me."

"You are so spoiled."

She smiled one of her glorious smiles, and he reached across the table and linked their fingers. She stirred the oddest impulses, and he wanted to protect and cherish her forever. He couldn't deduce why he'd be plagued by such a feeling, and he definitely didn't like it, but he had no idea how to suppress it. He'd given up trying.

"Will you quit fussing with your food and eat some of it?" he asked.

"I'm too fatigued to enjoy it."

"Ha! My grievance is valid. You spent hours strutting for my servants, and I must survive on the dregs of your attention."

"I have a bit left for you."

"If you don't eat, my chef will be crushed. He'll likely never recover."

She smirked and nibbled at the edges, but mostly, she sipped her wine and gazed at him over the rim of the glass. Her focus was so penetrating he had to ask, "Why are you looking at me like that?"

"I'm struggling to figure out why I let you coerce me. No one is ever able to boss me. Why you?"

"I'm more determined than anyone else. When there's something I crave, I don't relent until I receive it."

"I suppose that explains it. You dragged me to Barrett when I was opposed to coming. You forced me to dawdle until it was too late to head for Roland."

"I didn't *force* you. Don't exaggerate."

"You arranged a private supper for us—in your bedroom, no less!—and I'm still here. For the life of me, I can't ascertain why."

"Perhaps I've merely lured your sweeter, more feminine side to the surface, and you're being amenable for once."

"Or perhaps—where you're concerned—I'm completely spineless."

"If you are, I will admit to being delighted. It will be simpler than ever to seduce you."

It was too aggravating to watch her *not* eat, so he took her plate away and refilled their wine. She could barely stifle a yawn, and he scoffed at his stupidity.

He'd presumed he could feed her, ply her with wine, then march her into his bed, but she'd exhausted herself, enticing everyone in the manor, while he'd loafed in the background like a grouchy chaperone.

She stifled a second yawn, and he asked, "Are you about to fall asleep on me?"

"I'll try not to be that rude."

"May I complain about how much your cleverness annoys me?"

"What do you mean?"

"The entire afternoon, you engaged in tactics that would guarantee we were never alone."

She batted her lashes in a teasing way. "I can't believe you noticed."

"Now, when I finally have you all to myself, you're so weary you can't keep your eyes open."

"I'm sorry." She didn't look sorry.

She leaned forward, her elbows on the table, her chin in her hand. They stared for a long while, a hundred unvoiced remarks swirling. He couldn't imagine what she was thinking, but when she spoke up, he had to laugh.

"When you marry Lady Penny," she said, "I'll hate you for all eternity."

"We've previously agreed that we're not talking about Penny Pendleton."

"We're *not* talking about her. I simply thought I should clarify my position—so you'll always remember what it is."

He could have launched into a diatribe about how he hadn't settled on Penny, but it would probably be a lie. He'd been a guest at Roland for several days, and nothing about the visit had dissuaded him from his goal of marrying her.

If he didn't pick her, he'd have to stagger to town and find another aristocratic girl, and the prospect of beginning a new search was too grueling to consider. It was the sort of chore his mother or some elderly aunties should have dealt with for him, but he was on his own and having to forge ahead with very little guidance as to how he could achieve the best ending.

Wasn't Penny the best ending?

If he had to select a facet of the process that appealed the most, it was that the whole mess could be accomplished with scant effort on his part. He was willing. She and her father were willing. She had the attributes required of a countess, and she'd been raised to embrace that exact kind of life. Why not marry her?

But he wasn't about to discuss the situation with Libby.

"Would you be terribly disappointed if I went to bed?" she asked.

"You could never disappoint me." He offered the comment with much more affection than he should have displayed.

"I'm glad."

"A maid has been assigned to tend you. Actually, three have been assigned. They were arguing so vehemently over who would have the privilege that the housekeeper told them they could all pitch in—just so they'd stop bickering."

"I'm shaking up your staid existence."

"I didn't need it shaken."

"Yes, you did."

He stood and lifted her to her feet.

"I'll let the maids put you to bed," he said, "then I'll sneak in and kiss you goodnight more properly."

"You can't come in. I refuse to allow it."

"Don't pretend to be virtuous. It's so irritating."

"I should at least act as if I have some moral inclinations. If you continue to run roughshod over me, I'll be crushed by the weight of your inflated ego."

"Am I gaining that much ground on you?"

"I'm serious," she said. "You can't come to my room."

"I won't. I promise, but will you join me for breakfast?"

"Yes, if we can meet down in the dining room like civilized people."

"I suppose we can manage it. How about nine o'clock."

"That sounds fine."

He walked her out to the hall and around the corner to her room. It was just two doors down from his own. The trio of housemaids was waiting for her to arrive. They avidly observed every detail of his parting from her, so he couldn't even squeeze her hand. He simply bid her good evening—as if they were casual acquaintances—then he returned to his own bedchamber.

He left his door open though so he could hear when they departed. Then he headed over again. He'd promised her he wouldn't slither in, but she was mad to imagine he'd been telling the truth. She was a female and a very stubborn one at that. She harbored completely skewed ideas about what should happen, so why would he listen to her on any topic?

He knocked, spun the knob, and went inside.

Libby was about to crawl under the blankets when Luke snuck into the sitting room. She sighed with exasperation. Why would she have assumed he'd heed her request to stay away? Deep down, had she been hoping he'd ignore it?

Her day had been spent avoiding him, with her being unclear how to impose distance between them except to use others as a barrier. It hadn't been so much that she needed to keep him at bay. No, she'd erected obstacles that would force *her* to behave.

She wanted to be closer to him—in ways that were wrong, in ways that were dangerous, in ways that were sins. Her yearning had escalated to such a fevered pitch that she suspected she'd try whatever he suggested for the sole reason that it would make him happy.

She feared she might have lost the ability to say *no*, and she might have reached a spot where she would stop fighting the inevitable. But if she succumbed to his advance, where would she be in the end?

The answer to that question was very frightening indeed.

He appeared in the doorway, and for a charged moment, they stared at each other. There were words on the tip of her tongue—words to scold him, words to order him out—but she couldn't speak them aloud.

The maids hadn't been able to find a nightgown for her, but they'd provided a thick, warm robe instead. She'd blithely donned it, having them strip her so she was wearing it and nothing else. Her hair was down and brushed out, and she felt like a young bride about to greet her husband for the first time.

Or maybe she was like a wanton paramour whose favorite rake had just strolled in after an evening of revelry. She wasn't nervous in the slightest, and the notion was terrifying and thrilling.

"I told you not to visit me," she said.

"How could you think I'd listen to a comment that silly?"

With that, he came over to her. He pulled her into his arms and tumbled them onto the mattress so, in a fleet move, they were stretched out, and she was neatly tucked beneath him.

Evidently, her antics throughout the day had quashed his restraint. Further conversation wasn't necessary. They'd said what needed to be said, and they had to cease dithering and race to the location where Fate was determined they go.

She might have been out of her body and watching some other deranged woman carry on precisely as she shouldn't. Most other females had trod the path she was about to walk. Shouldn't she learn what all of them had discovered?

Forever after, she would comprehend adult secrets. When other women talked about men and amorous conduct, she would smile and nod. She'd no longer be a curious virgin. From this point on, she would *know* the details of a passionate dalliance.

He was kissing her, touching her all over, and she was touching him. For once, he was giving her all the physical stimulation she could stand.

He was dressed casually in shirt and trousers, his boots still on, while she was attired only in her borrowed robe. Gradually, he was loosening the belt, tugging on the lapels to open the front so the middle of her torso was exposed. He broke off their torrid kiss and nibbled a trail down her neck, across her bosom, to her breasts.

He began to toy with her nipples, laving them, biting them, until she was squirming with excitement. His naughty hand sneaked down her tummy to her womanly hair, then he slid a finger into her sheath. From Fish's descriptions, she recognized that this was common, but despite Fish's technical explanations, Libby was unprepared for how deliciously wicked it would feel.

Before she could fully focus on what was occurring, she was soaring to the heavens, goaded into a paroxysm of pleasure that was beyond imagining. It was as if she'd been struck by lightning, as if every inch of her anatomy, down to the smallest pore, had been electrified with a powerful current of energy.

She cried out with delight, and she flew up and up, finally reaching a peak of bliss that was perfect and stunning. Then she careened down and down, landing safely in his arms. He was the vainest male who'd ever lived, so he was preening over the havoc he'd wrought.

He smirked. "I suspected you were a lusty creature. You've proved me right."

"I can't believe I let you do that to me."

"There was no other way for it to conclude. We're destined to be together like this. Can't you sense it?"

"Yes, I guess I can."

"You have to be mine. If you don't agree, we might explode with unquenched desire."

"I doubt we'd explode."

He grinned. "I'm not willing to risk it. Are you?"

"No, we probably shouldn't."

He sat on his haunches and yanked off his shirt, throwing it over his shoulder so it fluttered to the floor. Then he lay back down and stretched out on top of her. Her robe was still open, so she was bared for his prurient perusal, and as he snuggled down and their chests connected, she was glad she was prone. If she'd been standing, she might have fainted from the titillation pelting her.

He gazed down at her, and she didn't quail or try to hide herself. She used her body to tell stories, and she'd never been shy. Besides, he'd just touched her intimately. Weren't they past the point of modesty?

"You're so beautiful," he said, "more beautiful than I envisioned in my wildest dreams."

"Flatterer."

"You've ruined me for every other woman. You realize that, don't you? After I've been with you like this, what woman could compare?"

She was accustomed to receiving compliments from handsome scoundrels. In light of her profession, it came with the territory, but she hadn't heard them from a man she cherished, from a man to whom she was miserably attached. His words stoked a fire of yearning that was startling in its intensity.

She wished she could tarry forever on the plush mattress, while he showered her with praise. She was certain he'd never claim he loved her, but she was merrily eager to settle for admiration and regard. It was easy for him to say she was beautiful, and she was ecstatic to let him.

He rolled on top of her again, and he kissed her thoroughly, enticing her until she was baffled over what she'd like to have occur. She was feeling pummeled, her limbs rubbery, as if her bones had melted. She couldn't slow down what was transpiring, and she wasn't interested in slowing it down.

Wherever he led her, she was content to follow. In the morning, she'd fret about consequences and wonder if she hadn't gone mad. But just then, she was thrilled to continue. She was an independent adult who could pick her own path. She'd picked him—to show her how amour could truly be.

Their kisses became more heated. He was driving her up the spiral of pleasure again, caressing her, playing with her breasts. The sensation was so compelling that it distracted her so she didn't pause to consider where they were headed.

Vaguely, she noted he was unbuttoning the flap on his trousers, then tugging them down to his haunches. He pulled out his cock, the hard male rod that men never grew weary of contemplating. He centered the tip in her sheath, and she took a deep breath and blew it out, determined not to blanch or cower.

For a moment, she frowned, trying to figure out if she was ready. Was she?

Apparently yes. She couldn't conceive of a single reason to retreat.

"I want to make you mine," he said.

"I want that too."

"Do you know what's about to happen?"

"Yes."

Her assertion was offered in a hazy manner, from a virgin who'd had it explained verbally, but who wasn't clear on the details.

"Everything will be perfect now," he said.

They smiled, then his wily thumb found the spot at the vee of her thighs. He flicked at it, once, twice, and as she soared to the heavens again, he gripped her hips and shoved his phallus into her.

She barely had an instant to brace for what was coming, and she'd assumed it would hurt, but she was wet and relaxed from his ministrations. As he breached her maidenhead, she scarcely felt it.

He immediately realized the import of what he'd done: She'd been a virgin and he'd deflowered her. He halted, frozen in mid-thrust, and he glared down at her as if she'd tricked him.

"This was your first time," he murmured, and his tone was scolding.

"Yes."

"Why didn't you tell me?"

"I did tell you, over and over, but you're a man so you never listen. I'm not loose, and I never have been."

"Then why...? Why me? Why?"

He looked perplexed, and she cradled his cheek in her palm.

"I wanted you to be the one," she gently replied, as if clarifying a difficult concept for a child.

"But...why?" he repeated.

"I like you much more than I should. I predicted it would be marvelous with you, and I was right."

"I can't marry you," he blurted out. "Is that what you're hoping?"

Trust a man to say exactly the wrong thing! She should have hit him. "Don't be an idiot. I was never hoping for that."

"This is too precious of a gift. What am I to do with it?"

"You said you needed me to be yours. Now I am."

He studied her for an eternity, then he nodded. "You *are* mine, and I'm not sharing you with anyone."

"No, not with anyone. Not ever."

"Swear it to me. Swear you'll always be mine alone."

"Always yours," she vowed, and she meant it.

The joining of their bodies was much more intimate than she could ever have fathomed. She would never attempt it with a subsequent partner.

He kissed her tenderly, saying, "I can't hold back."

"I don't want you to."

"It should be more special for you."

"It's special enough," she responded. "Don't ever think it's not."

With a groan that sounded near to despair, he started flexing into her. He would push in all the way, then pull out to the tip, then push in again. She participated eagerly, following his lead, but then, he made it incredibly easy. She simply held on tight—as if she was on a raft on a rampaging river—and she struggled to keep track of every detail.

Much before she was ready, much before she'd gotten the hang of it, he shoved in, and with another intense groan, he spilled himself against her womb. She was aware that a man could withdraw at the end to prevent a babe from catching. Had he known that? If he had, he certainly hadn't been concerned about it.

The copulation had spiraled so rapidly and concluded so rapidly that she hadn't had a second to ponder the problem. Nor had she thought to discuss it with him. How did a passionate couple converse over that sort of topic?

She had no idea, but...?

She wasn't sorry. In the morning, she'd panic, but just then, she wasn't worried about any possible ramifications.

He collapsed onto her, his weight pressing her down, but he didn't feel heavy. He felt welcome, and she felt safe and cherished. They rested like that for a bit, then he rolled away and dropped onto his side. She rolled too so they were nose to nose.

"I'm completely flummoxed," he said.

"Why?"

"I wasn't worth it."

She smiled. "Probably not, but I convinced myself to do it with you anyway."

"You're deranged, Libby Carstairs."

"Perhaps."

He sighed, and she sighed too, then tears flooded her eyes. On seeing them, he appeared stricken.

"Are you sad about this?" he asked.

"No. I'm simply overwhelmed. It was more...more...personal than I'd expected it would be."

"You silly girl! You should have told me to slow down. I would have, but I didn't know I needed to control myself."

"I didn't want you to slow down or control yourself."

He snuggled her closer, hugging her as if she was very dear to him, which was precisely the reaction she was anxious to receive.

"What did you think of it?" he asked. "Tell me the truth."

"It was different from how I assumed it would be. I had heard it was very physical, but I didn't understand just *how* physical."

"It gets better with practice."

"I thought it was wonderful this time."

He snorted at that and said, "I'm glad we did this. I'm glad we got it out of the way."

"So am I."

"Maybe now our lust won't rage quite so hotly."

"Maybe," she agreed, but she wasn't sincere. She'd never stop desiring him.

"No regrets. Promise?" he said.

"I promise."

"It would kill me if you decided later on that we shouldn't have proceeded."

"I won't ever decide that."

"Good."

"What do we do now?" she asked.

"We loaf for a while, then we try it again. If you're not too sore...?"

"I'm not sore. I'm...I'm..." She broke off and chuckled miserably. "I don't know what I am, but I'm not sore."

She hadn't realized how draining the sexual event would be, and she was growing extremely lethargic. He was too. Would they fall asleep? Was it allowed? Would it be rude or inappropriate?

"You can't drift off in here," she said. "If we doze off, I'm afraid we won't awaken until a housemaid wanders in to open the curtains in the morning."

"I won't let that happen."

He shifted onto his back, and he drew her nearer so she was draped over him, their feet and legs tangled together, her ear directly over his heart so she could hear it beating.

"I'm happy," he said. "*You* make me happy."

"That's the sweetest thing you could have told me."

Those pesky tears bubbled up again, and if she didn't watch out, she suspected she might cry like a baby.

There were always stories about a deflowering being very distressing, but she'd presumed she was made of sterner stuff than ordinary females. She'd figured she could march through the episode with nary a ripple in her composure. Where was her carefree deportment when she needed it?

"What will become of us?" she asked, working to keep her voice casual.

"I can't imagine, so let's just enjoy this moment. Tomorrow, we can talk about where we stand."

He was so nonchalant, as if he ruined virgins every day. And who could guess? He'd probably had dozens of lovers in his life. He might have had hundreds of them! Of course he'd be nonchalant.

As to herself, she felt raw and disturbed, as if the Earth had shifted off its axis and she couldn't find her balance.

"I want you to always be mine," she brashly declared, a huge surge of possessiveness sweeping over her. "I won't permit any other woman to have you. I couldn't abide it."

"I like the sound of that."

After that comment, she didn't know if he said anything else. Sleep claimed her, and she plummeted into a deep slumber. Her next cogent thought came in a nightmare, and it was one she'd frequently suffered over the years.

She was little and back in the middle of the shipwreck. It was dark, and she couldn't see. People were screaming, and she was desperate to stay afloat. It was very cold, and someone was shouting at her: *Hold on! Hold on!* Then, *Grab her! She's sinking under!*

But she couldn't hold on. Her hands were too small to grip the log, and it was too slippery. Waves were crashing over her head, and she swallowed a gigantic gulp of water. She couldn't breathe! She was drowning, and she'd never learned to swim!

Help! she pleaded, but the storm was so loud the wind whisked the word away.

Another wave crashed over her, and she reached for a . . .

She bolted upright, her pulse pounding, a moan escaping from her lips. Frantically, she glanced around, several seconds passing before she remembered where she was: in the guest bedchamber at Barrett. She was naked, her robe lost in the blankets, and she clutched them to her chest.

She struggled to calm herself and gain her bearings. In her nightmare, she'd been yelling. Had she called out? Oh, if she'd been overheard, she'd die of embarrassment.

Without peering over, she sensed that Luke was gone. Instead, there was a single rose on his pillow, along with a note that said, *Don't forget we're having breakfast at nine. Can't wait until then.* He'd signed it with the letter L for Luke.

She wondered when he'd tiptoed out. She certainly hadn't noticed, and she tried to picture him, roaming through the quiet house, searching for a flower in a vase, locating a quill and ink, then writing her the note.

Out the window, dawn was breaking. It was cloudy, but the rain
had stopped. She considered dawdling until nine o'clock, having breakfast with him, chatting over eggs and tea as if all was fine between them,
but it wasn't fine.

She'd given herself to a man who wasn't her husband, a man who
would never marry her, a man who was hoping to betroth himself very
soon. What if she was with child? What then?

She'd assumed she understood all she should know about carnal
matters, but she'd been so wrong. She hadn't grasped how intimate it
would be, how dear and tender. She hadn't grasped how profoundly she
would be affected.

It was possible she was madly in love with him now. She felt filled
up with gladness, which was bizarre. Where was she to put all the feelings that were churning inside her? How could she stagger into a relationship with him when she could never have him for her very own?

She couldn't meet him at nine. What would they discuss? Would
they parlay over the bastard babe he might have planted?

No, she couldn't tarry. What she urgently needed was to confer
with Fish. Immediately. That's what the situation required.

She threw off the covers and hurried to the dressing room where her
borrowed gown hung on a hook. It was a simple garment that she could
don without a maid's assistance. In a few minutes, she'd be on her horse
and on her way to the safety of her bedchamber at Roland—with Fish
present to tell her what to do.

Chapter
14

"Father, may I ask you a question?"

Penny had caught him in the breakfast parlor alone, as she'd been hoping she might. She'd gotten up early for that specific purpose. He was seated at the table, and she pulled up a chair across from him.

She'd tossed and turned until dawn, her mind awhirl with problems she'd never contemplated in the past.

Ever since she'd met Simon, she'd been confused about her path. She'd always been a dutiful daughter, and because of her father's tragedy as a young man—when her little half-sister, Henrietta, had vanished—Penny had grown up with the implicit understanding that she should never upset him.

Yet she'd learned how to coerce him into giving her whatever she desired, and he'd never been able to refuse any of her requests. She'd wanted to become engaged, and she'd begged him to pick a husband for her. Luke had seemed like a perfect choice until Simon had pointed out that he might not be.

Luke was so much older than she was, and he was stern, polite, and unbending. He rarely smiled. He never joined in the afternoon lawn games, never danced at night. No, he lurked in the corner, watching the crowd as if trying to figure out how he'd stumbled into it.

It was clear they had nothing in common except the fact that their families were neighbors. Was that really a viable basis for a marriage? She no longer thought so.

Then there was the *other* issue about what would happen in the bedchamber. She had several friends from school who were already wed, and they whispered alarming tales about what a spouse expected from his wife. Nudity was required, as were various physical acts that were too shocking to describe.

She pictured herself in a bedroom with Luke, pictured herself removing her clothes and being naked in front of him. The idea was disturbing on every level.

I could do it with Simon though . . .

The wicked notion flitted through her head before she could tamp it down. For Simon Falcon, she might consent to any risqué conduct. She was that fascinated.

Her father had been reading the morning newspaper, and he put it down and grinned at her. "Dear Penny, you're aware that you can ask me any question you like, and I will attempt to answer it to your satisfaction."

"I'm glad to hear it."

She'd planned to blurt it out, but it was incredibly hard to proceed. She'd been demanding he select a husband for her, and he had. How could she now claim she didn't want that husband?

Her consternation must have been evident because his grin altered to a frown. "What's wrong? Is someone vexing you?"

"I guess my topic is more difficult than I realized."

"Just spit it out. I generally find that it's the easiest way to begin. Once a subject is voiced, it's never as tough as we were imagining."

"You're probably correct." She took a deep breath and let it out, then she asked, "Are you sure I should marry Luke?"

"Yes, I'm absolutely sure, so why inquire? What's this actually about?"

"I recognize that I'll sound like a spoiled brat."

"You don't so far, but keep going. We'll reassess my opinion after you're finished."

"Well, it's just that Luke is so much older than me, and we're practically strangers. What if we're not compatible?"

"Oh, I see." He leaned over and patted her hand. "You're having pre-betrothal jitters. Every bride has them, and I can guarantee they'll get worse as we march toward the wedding."

"They're not jitters, Father. I am having second thoughts."

His eyes narrowed. "You're having *second* thoughts? Why?"

"I told you why. You settled on Luke immediately, so you couldn't have considered whether he'd be a good match for me. What if he's not?"

He flashed an angry look she'd never previously witnessed from him. "Where is this bizarre sentiment coming from? We're hosting a party for Luke so he can ascertain what an excellent wife you'd be. You can't sit here and announce that you're not interested."

"He's in love with someone else!"

"Who is? Luke?"

"Yes. I can't agree to have him when he's ardently attached to another. What kind of life would I have? The whole time, there would be a third person in the middle of it."

"Who is she?" he snapped. "Tell me her name—if you can."

"It's Miss Carstairs."

He blanched. "Where did you hear that?"

She couldn't decide if she should admit it, but he didn't appear to believe her. "From her cousin. Mr. Falcon? Apparently, they've been involved for ages and Luke has no intention of giving her up after he's wed."

A muscle ticked in her father's cheek. "Mr. Falcon told you that?"

"Yes."

"If that's the case, then I fear you are being entirely too cordial with him."

"Why would he lie about it?"

Her father muttered, "Why indeed?"

"Obviously, you doubt it's true, but what if it is? I wouldn't blame Luke. Miss Carstairs is so beautiful and gracious. Who could resist her? But if they're in love, and I marry him, where would it leave me?"

Her father sighed. "I'll talk to Luke. I'll ask him about her and judge his reply."

She was aghast. "You'll ask him? You can't! I'd die of shame!"

"I'm positive this rumor is ridiculous, and I must caution you to stay away from Mr. Falcon. If you won't promise me you will, you'll wind up stirring a dilemma I'd rather not have stirred."

"What dilemma?"

"First off, I'd have to quietly demand he vacate the premises. Then I'd have to alert the footmen to watch for him so he couldn't slink back to fraternize with you again. It would also mean I'd have to evict Miss Carstairs, and I won't encourage that sort of gossip. It would be so awkward."

"You're being absurdly dramatic. Mr. Falcon and I are just friends!"

"You are about to become engaged, so any relationship with Mr. Falcon—even the most innocent one—is completely inappropriate."

"I can't marry Luke! I've changed my mind about it."

"I'm sorry, but it's not up to you. It's up to *me*, and at the end of the party, I'm confident he'll propose. Your future as Mrs. Lucas Watson is briskly winging in your direction. You can't stop it, and *I* don't want to stop it. I'm happy to have Luke as my son-in-law."

"You picked him without thinking about me for a single minute!"

"I always think about you," he said, "and Luke is the very best man I could have found. Would you calm down so I can finish my tea? Your complaints are giving me a terrible headache."

He grabbed his newspaper and began reading it again. He studiously ignored her, while she seethed with fury.

She and her father never quarreled because he *wouldn't* quarrel. It was impossible to fight with him. This was their most bitter conversation. She'd explained her reservations about Luke, had explained about Miss Carstairs, and her father had discounted her every comment.

How dare he scoff at her grievances! How dare he treat her like a child!

She had to locate Simon and apprise him of how shabbily her father had behaved. He'd have plenty of advice as to what she should do about it.

She jumped up and stomped to the door. As she was about to exit the room, Miss Fishburn entered. She was naught more than a glorified servant, and when she greeted Penny, Penny was rude for what was probably the only time ever. She continued on without acknowledging the other woman.

She stepped into the hall, and she glanced back, curious if her father had noticed her uncouth conduct. It would have provided him with evidence of how thoroughly he'd enraged her, but he'd already forgotten she'd been present.

He peered up at Miss Fishburn as if she hung the moon, gracing her with a look so warm and intimate that Penny was astonished.

"Good morning, Fish." He used the casual nickname Simon and Miss Carstairs used.

"Good morning, Lord Roland."

Miss Fishburn had utilized the proper mode of address, but they both chuckled, as if it was a private joke between them.

"You're *up* so early," she said to him, her voice oozing an innuendo Penny didn't understand.

"I had a busy night," he replied, "so I should be exhausted, but I'm filled with energy."

"So am I."

Her father winked at Miss Fishburn, and as she walked by him to dish up a plate of food, she passed his chair. Discreetly, she brushed a hand across his neck, as if she had every right to touch him in such a personal way.

There was an aura being generated that Penny couldn't identify, but it was very disturbing. They seemed much closer than they should be. What did it indicate? What was Penny observing?

His gaze moved from Miss Fishburn and landed on Penny. He grinned a sly grin that was full of secrets, and her heart literally skipped a beat. She whipped away and rushed off, determined to find Simon as quickly as she could.

⌒

"Luke! You're finally back. I'd been wondering if we'd see you today."

Luke flashed a wan smile. "Hello, Charles. You weren't worried about me, were you? I was caught in the rain yesterday, so I spent the night at Barrett."

"I heard, so I wasn't concerned."

It was early afternoon, and Luke had just arrived at Roland. After loafing for hours in bed with Libby, he'd tiptoed off to his own room just before dawn broke. He'd managed to fall asleep, but only after extensive reflection about what the event might mean for them.

Now that they'd proceeded to the worst—or perhaps the best—possible ending, she'd have to change her mind about an affair. Wouldn't she?

He'd arranged to have breakfast with her at nine, but he hadn't staggered down until almost ten. He'd assumed she would have dined without him, but when he'd been informed that she hadn't been down either, he'd figured she'd overslept too.

He'd sent a housemaid to rouse her, only to be notified that her room was empty and she'd left without a goodbye. He was still trying to deduce what her actions signified, but who could guess what the accursed female was thinking?

"Could I talk to you for a minute?" Charles asked. "Alone?"

Luke couldn't conceal a wince. He was in no condition to engage in a confidential chat with Charles, but he forced out, "Of course. What did you need?"

"Let's confer in my library, shall we?"

"Certainly, but if we have to lock ourselves away, I hope it's nothing awful."

"It's not awful." Charles frowned. "At least it's not awful yet. I simply have to probe your opinion on an important topic."

"Lead the way."

They were in the front foyer at Roland, and as Charles turned and marched down the hall with Luke stumbling after him, he received the distinct impression it was no accident that he'd bumped into Charles the moment he entered the house. Had Charles been watching for him? Gad, what could have happened?

The butler went by, and Charles said to him, "Lord Barrett and I will be speaking privately. We're not to be disturbed."

The request heightened Luke's apprehension. What could Charles intend to discuss? Whatever it was, Luke was sure he wouldn't like the subject matter.

Once they were sequestered in the ostentatious room, Charles sat at the desk, and Luke pulled up the chair across. Out the windows behind Charles, he could see the picnic tents. Everything was drenched from the rain the prior day, so there would be no outside reveling.

He supposed he was facing another afternoon of cards, duet singing, and book reading. It definitely made him wish he hadn't resigned his commission in the navy. He had no aptitude for idleness and sloth, and the hours stretched out like the road to Hades. He simply wanted to find Libby and figure out why she'd run away.

"Would you like a brandy?" Charles asked.

"No, thank you. It's a bit early for me."

"Would it bother you if I have one?"

"No. Go ahead."

Luke waved him to the sideboard, observing as he poured himself a tall drink. As he sat again, he studied Luke, then he scoffed with amusement. "You're staring at me so morosely that I might be your headmaster and about to paddle you for an infraction."

"It feels that way."

Charles wasn't that much older than Luke, only sixteen years, but he seemed much older. Wiser too. Luke had spent most of his life in the navy, following orders and doing what he was told. Charles had been wed twice, sired three children, been divorced, survived scandal and the death of a daughter, debated in Parliament, served on government councils, and advised kings.

Their experiences were so different that it was difficult to view them as being part of the same species.

"I'm sorry," Charles said. "I'm not handling this very well."

"Handling what? Am I about to be scolded for a transgression? I must admit I don't remember committing one."

"It's not that. It's ... it's ..." Charles cut off his comment, then he tsked with annoyance. "This is harder than I thought it would be."

"Just say it."

"All right." Charles took a deep breath, slowly let it out, then asked, "Are you having an affair with Miss Carstairs?"

It was the last question Luke had expected, but after Libby had passed the whole night at Barrett, he probably should have been prepared to answer it. He frantically considered what his response should be and ultimately settled on, "What makes you inquire about her?"

"I notice you didn't deny it."

"And *I* notice you haven't explained yourself."

"Are you in love with her? It's the rumor that's circulating."

"Well..."

"I don't think it's a rumor," Charles said. "I saw you gazing at her in the garden yesterday. Your affection was so blatant that it was almost embarrassing to witness it."

"I like her." It was such an understatement he was surprised the Good Lord didn't swoop down from Heaven to call him a liar.

"But are you in love with her?" Charles pressed. "Again, you haven't denied it. If you love her, and you propose to Penny, where will it leave my daughter?"

"Who told you about this?"

"Does it matter?"

"It matters to me," Luke said.

"Actually, it was Penny herself."

Luke's jaw dropped. "What?"

"Have you met Miss Carstairs's cousin, Mr. Falcon?"

"Oh, yes, I've met him."

"Apparently, he spilled the beans."

Luke scowled. "Why would they have been discussing such an inappropriate topic?"

"Precisely," Charles mused.

He sipped his liquor, evaluating Luke over the rim of the glass. It was so quiet, Luke could hear a clock ticking down in the foyer, could hear his heart pounding in his ears.

"I hate to tell you this," Charles finally said, "but Penny is no longer keen to wed you. She believes you're in love with Miss Carstairs, and— if you won't agree to part with her—there would be another woman standing in the middle of her marriage. She's not eager to live like that, and I can't blame her."

"No, I wouldn't blame her."

Charles continued. "*I,* on the other hand, am still delighted by the prospect of having you as my son-in-law. It's my decision as to who her husband will be, and I deem you to be an excellent choice."

"I'm so relieved. I couldn't bear to discover I'd squandered your esteem."

"It would take quite a bit more than a romance with a beautiful female to dampen my regard, and girls like Penny can be so silly. I don't suppose I have to listen to her when she's being a brat."

"I'm mortified that I've caused this discord," Luke said. "I realize how much you detest conflict."

"I appreciate the sentiment, but I haven't received an acceptable answer from you about Miss Carstairs. Where are you in terms of your relationship? Is it just beginning? Or have you been together for ages? If you're contemplating matrimony, are you ready to split with her? Is that what's happening? What are your plans?"

Luke chuckled miserably. "I have no idea."

"You and I have had conversations in the past about the kinds of men we are, and you're aware of my opinion about moral rectitude and avoiding scandal."

"I haven't forgotten."

"I'm much older than you are, but I'm not dead. I vividly remember what it's like to leap into an amour with a vixen as alluring as Libby Carstairs."

"I only recently crossed paths with her, and I'm bowled over."

"She was with you at Barrett," Charles said.

"Yes."

"I won't pry for details, but I assume you tarried there—with her—for illicit purposes."

Luke didn't respond, but his cheeks heated to such a degree he was amazed he didn't ignite. Charles's assessment was forceful, and he couldn't abide the scrutiny. It felt as if he'd failed a great ethical test, as if his fatal flaws had been exposed.

He was thirty years old, an earl and a decorated navy captain. He didn't bow down to anyone, but—by consorting with Libby—he'd disappointed Charles in a significant manner that could never be repaired. He was embarrassed and ashamed.

He went over and poured himself a whiskey, then he strolled to the window and peered outside. It was cool and cloudy, and a wet pall hung over the park, painting the landscape in gloomy shades of gray that perfectly matched his dour mood.

Charles's probing gaze cut into his back, and Luke yearned to spin around and demand the man stop judging him, but Luke was in the wrong and he recognized that he was. He was Charles's guest, his presence requested so he could socialize with Penny in order to determine whether they should wed. But so far, he'd hardly focused on her. Instead, he'd been completely fixated on Libby.

"When I was young," Charles said, "I lived a full and degenerate life in a very short interval."

"I know."

"My debacle entitles me to offer advice in this arena."

"What arena?"

"The arena of lust and the bad consequences it can bring."

Luke glanced over his shoulder. "Are you about to tell me I have to give Libby up? For if that's your ploy, I must confess that she and I are barely acquainted. We're at the beginning of something, but I can't describe what it is."

"I wouldn't presume to scold you."

"It feels as if you are."

"Please don't take it that way. I simply ask this: If you're so eager to philander with her, are you sure you're ready to marry?"

Luke shrugged. "I thought I was."

"Then you met Miss Carstairs."

"Yes."

"With you being so besotted, you're not in any condition to be a husband. You shouldn't be pondering matrimony for a single second."

"Should I go home and leave Penny alone? Is that your wish?"

"No! As I previously mentioned, I want you to join my family, but I don't see how we could proceed if you intend to pursue your flirtation."

"I understand."

"And the type of passion that's flaring with her? It's not real, Luke. It doesn't last, and when it burns out, you have just the ashes for company. I'm living proof of that."

"Should I ignore what's bubbled up? Should I walk away from her? Is that what you're suggesting? If so, it definitely makes me wonder what it would be like to have you as my father-in-law. Would you constantly butt into my private business?"

"Penny is my daughter. I could never be silent as you shamed her by chasing after loose women."

Luke felt duty-bound to defend Libby, even though he should have kept his mouth shut. "Libby isn't *loose*. Yes, she's an actress, but she doesn't possess the low morals attributed to those doxies."

Charles didn't argue the point. Instead, he said, "You have to decide the best path for yourself, but it can't be Penny and Miss Carstairs riding in the same boat with you. You don't have a parent to guide you in your marital search, and I can provide counsel that might benefit you in your choices."

Luke tucked away his fit of pique. "I'm being an ass, Charles. I apologize."

"Apology accepted, but you aren't being awful. I'm cognizant of what it's like to be mad for Miss Carstairs. Your fascination doesn't surprise me, but such ardent attachment ruins men like you and me. We're not cut out for such all-consuming obsession."

"Probably not, so what should I do? Shall I return to Barrett? If I depart, it will stir rumors as to why I vanished. I'd hate to put you in such an awkward position."

"We have a whole week left of this accursed party."

"Now, now," Luke facetiously said, "don't be grouchy about it. We're meant to be having fun."

Charles scoffed at that. "You have to spend a bit more time with Penny. Let's get you back in her good graces."

"Are you certain she'll be amenable to socializing?"

"She'll be amenable. If she's not, I'll set her straight at once."

Luke sighed. "This is a disaster."

"It's not a disaster until *I* declare I don't want you as my son-in-law. For the moment, we're marching down the same road."

"Fine."

"But I'll have to ask Miss Carstairs to leave. I'll regret it, but I will. It wasn't appropriate to have her as a guest. A Pendleton cousin invited her without apprising me, so I didn't realize she was coming. We have too many impressionable young people here. If I'd been notified, I'd have quashed the idea."

At hearing that Charles would ask Libby to go, Luke suffered a wave of panic. He couldn't bear it! Yet what had he expected? With their affair being exposed, what other option was there?

"Must you kick her out?" Luke asked. "Isn't that rather harsh?"

"I'm afraid so, and I doubt you'll believe me, but I'm doing it for you. You need to separate yourself from her for a bit. When she's close by, she's the center of your attention. You can't focus on what's important."

"Yes, I suppose that's true."

"You're assessing Penny with an eye toward marriage. I'd like you to ponder that notion and no other. You owe me that much, don't you think? Miss Carstairs will only distract you."

"I suppose that's true too," Luke glumly concurred.

"Mr. Falcon should go with her. He's entirely too friendly with Penny, and he's a bad influence."

Luke wouldn't be sorry to see the cheeky oaf disappear. "I wasn't aware that he'd ingratiated himself to her. I've chatted with him quite extensively, and he's not a boy who should be flirting with her."

"I agree."

"Would you like me to meet with Miss Carstairs for you?" Luke asked. "You're so polite, and I can't picture you ordering her to pack her bags. This is my fault, and I should take care of it for you."

"I'll handle it," Charles said. "She and I have grown cordial enough to have a frank discussion."

Luke blew out a heavy breath. "When will you confer with her?"

"Later today. It's already after two o'clock. I can't force her out when supper is approaching. I'll request she depart in the morning."

At learning she'd be in residence one more night, Luke was like a condemned felon who'd just discovered his life had been spared by the king.

"I feel terrible about this," Luke said, and Charles shrugged.

"These things happen."

Charles stood and gestured to the door. "Shall we head out and bluster into the middle of the party? The festivities were moved into the house because the grass is so wet."

Luke motioned to his whiskey. "If you don't mind, I'll finish this, then I'll catch up with you."

"Thank you for talking about this with me. It's was extremely difficult, but we staggered through it without embarrassing ourselves."

Luke snorted with disgust. "Speak for yourself. I'm incredibly embarrassed."

Charles started out, and at the last second, he halted and glanced back. "Miss Carstairs's presence in the manor this evening will be a huge temptation for you. Don't disgrace yourself under my roof. I can put up with a lot, but I have to draw the line at you sneaking into Miss Carstairs's bedchamber. This is Penny's home after all."

"I won't misbehave. I respect you too much to act that way."

"Good." Charles nodded. "I'm glad we cleared that up."

Then he was gone, and Luke was left to fuss and stew all alone.

Libby would depart, and apparently, *he* would stay right where he was. He'd have to pay more attention to Penny, would have to play the part of doting swain so she stopped despising him. He wanted that, didn't he? He wanted to please Charles. Didn't he? He still wanted to wed Penny for her dowry. Didn't he?

Charles was correct that Luke should remember what mattered—and that was Penny. For pity's sake, he'd only known Libby a few weeks. Would he sever his fond acquaintance with Charles just for her? Would he relinquish Penny's fortune just so he could continue to roll around on a mattress with her?

He asked questions to the quiet room. "Would Libby be worth that much turmoil? Would I be mad to cut ties with the Pendleton family—just for her?"

When voiced aloud, there was no denying that he sounded deranged.

What kind of man made those choices? *He* certainly didn't, and he had to get a grip on his unruly fixation before he carried on like a lunatic. As Charles had advised, he had to separate himself from her so he could determine if he might not be as besotted as he assumed.

Except what if—when the party ended and he followed her to London—she'd vanished and he never found her again? What if? What if?

The prospect sent such a wave of terror racing through him that he stumbled over to a chair and plopped down. He sipped his whiskey, thinking that he must have been bewitched by her. There was no other explanation, and if she'd cast a magical spell, how could he free himself?

He had no idea, and truth to tell, he had no desire to free himself. If he couldn't have Libby Carstairs by his side for as long as he could keep her there, what was the point of anything?

<hr />

PENNY STROLLED DOWN THE hall to a rear door that led onto the verandah. It was cool and wet, and she was bundled in a cloak and intending to walk to the stables where she would pretend nonchalance as she arranged carriage rides—weather permitting—for her guests the next day.

In reality, she would slyly eavesdrop on the grooms to discover if they might know where Simon was hiding. She'd been searching for him everywhere. It had been hours since she'd quarreled with her father, and she was anxious to discuss the situation with him. He was the only one who would commiserate.

She stepped outside, but she immediately pulled up short. Luke was leaned on the balustrade and staring out at the park. She hadn't seen him all day and didn't mind that she hadn't. In her current mood, she couldn't bear to speak with him.

He hadn't noticed her, and she thought about sneaking away, but the wind banged the door shut behind her, and he glanced around. On viewing her, his expression was completely blank, and his obvious lack of regard had her temper soaring.

He was at Roland to decide if he would like to wed her. Was he so sure of his position that he imagined he didn't have to expend any effort to win her?

As Simon had bluntly clarified, he was after her money. He didn't care about her as a person and would never love her. In fact, he was in love with someone else—a problem that would have crushed Penny if she didn't like Miss Carstairs quite so much. Penny comprehended why a man would be smitten by Miss Carstairs, but honestly!

Luke was an idiot if he presumed Penny would marry him when he was obsessed with another woman.

"Penny! Hello," he said, and he started toward her.

It was too late to dash down the stairs and run off, so she said, "Hello to you too."

"Are you taking a walk? The grass is soaked, so you'll ruin your shoes."

"I'm off to the stables, so I can stick to the gravel paths. I'll be fine."

"May I join you?"

She gnashed her teeth, not convinced she could be civil, but she forced a smile. "I'd enjoy it if you would."

He extended his arm, and she grabbed hold. They went down into the garden, even as she irritably recollected that it was the first time she'd touched him since the party had begun. He treated her like a pesky little sister, while Simon was so besotted he brashly crept into her bedchamber so he could shower her with torrid kisses.

Penny cherished him for it, and on pondering his heightened affection, she grew even more aggravated by Luke's tepid display.

"Since I arrived," he said, "we've hardly had an opportunity to chat."

"I invited too many guests. We'd have been better off with a small family gathering."

"I'm not much of a one for large crowds. I spent too many years on a ship at sea. I'm afraid it's made me unsocial."

You're right about that! she silently fumed.

She peered up at the sky and inquired, "What is your prediction as to what the weather will be like tomorrow? I'd like to offer carriage rides for people who would like to tour the neighborhood."

"My groom swears it will be sunny and dry."

"Wonderful."

Their conversation dwindled after that, and she couldn't conceive of a topic to keep it going, but why was it up to her to stir the dialogue between them?

It was another sin to lay at his feet. Why must she do all the work?

Again, she couldn't help but compare him to Simon. When she and Simon were together, they didn't stop talking for a single second. He understood her as no one ever had, and she felt as if they'd been acquainted forever.

There were so many comments churning inside her. She was like a pot on a stove and the lid about to blow off. What if she simply blurted out her reservations? What if she simply told him exactly what she was thinking?

He'd likely drop dead of shock, and she'd have murdered him with her flippant attitude. Then again, if he dropped dead, she'd be shed of him once and for all.

She snorted with a grim amusement, and he asked, "What has you laughing?"

"Nothing important. I was merely reflecting on a horrid thought."

"I hope it wasn't about me."

"No, no, it wasn't about you. Why would you suppose that?"

"Your father waylaid me"—she could barely tamp down a wince—"and he mentioned that I'd vexed you. I hadn't realized it, so I probably ought to apologize."

She wasn't aware that her father had accosted him, and she could picture them, snickering about her over a brandy. They'd have clucked their tongues about how young she was, how immature she was, how she needed the firm hand of an older husband. They'd have congratulated themselves on how Luke was the perfect spouse for her and how they'd been smart enough to recognize it.

The entire scenario was galling and infuriating.

If she hadn't been so irked, she'd have minded her manners, but she suspected—if she acted in the proper way, in the expected way—she'd always regret it.

"Can you answer a question for me?" she asked.

"I will if I can."

"Are you in love with Libby Carstairs? If you are, why would you consider marrying me? Why would you put me through that sort of misery?"

The query was so inappropriate and so impertinent that she was surprised she didn't swoon with astonishment. What had come over her?

He stepped away from her so quickly he might have suddenly learned she had the plague. A muscle ticked in his cheek as he debated his possible replies. The one he picked was precisely what she should have anticipated.

"We shouldn't discuss a topic like that."

"Of course that would be your opinion!"

She whipped away and started for the house. He called to her retreating back, "Penny, wait!"

She halted and glared over her shoulder. "I asked a valid question that shouldn't have been that difficult for you to address, but I notice you conveniently failed to offer a response—or a defense."

"I'm sorry you're angry, but could we not bicker? It will upset your father."

"Ooh, my poor, poor father," she caustically said. "Heaven forbid that we displease him."

Luke shrugged. "He's always been my friend."

"Well, then, I'm sure matters between us will work out swimmingly."

"He informs me that you and Mr. Falcon have been gossiping about me, and I'm worried Falcon may have filled your head with nonsense. I wish you'd calm down."

"Believe me, Lord Barrett, I am very, very calm, and I suggest you carefully ponder this dilemma so you can figure out how we are to deal with it. Until then, this party is over for you. Why don't you return to Barrett? I'm positive you'd be much more comfortable there."

She whirled away and continued on to the manor. She marched up the stairs and slammed inside without glancing back.

Chapter

15

"Where have you been? I sent for you hours ago!"

Libby glared at Fish, then went over and closed the door to her bedchamber. She spun the key in the lock. For this conversation, she didn't dare encourage any eavesdroppers.

"I was busy," Fish blithely said, "and I'm not your maid. What did you need?"

"I have to talk to you."

"Well, I'm here now. What's wrong?"

Fish plopped down onto a chair, and she looked totally at ease while Libby felt raw and exposed, as if her skin had been scraped away and all her flaws revealed.

Dawn had just been breaking when she'd returned to Roland from her night of frolicking at Barrett. She'd snuck into the manor and had tried to start her day, but she'd been too disturbed to engage in any ordinary rituals.

Once a housemaid had arrived to light the fire, she'd ordered breakfast, but had been too distracted to eat it. Then she'd ordered a bath, but she'd been too anxious to enjoy it. She'd dressed in her most comfortable clothes, but they hadn't helped to calm her down.

Finally, when the morning had advanced sufficiently that she wouldn't seem like a shrew, she'd summoned Fish, but none of the maids had been able to find her.

After relentless pacing and fretting, she'd staggered to her bed and had taken an unsatisfying nap. On waking, she was more unsettled than ever.

Every time footsteps echoed in the hall, she braced, being sure that it would be Luke, that he'd have realized she'd left Barrett—and him—and he'd be determined to scold her. He was brazen enough to stroll up to her bedchamber, but it hadn't ever been him, and she was struggling to figure out what it indicated.

She understood that much of his attraction to her had been fueled by the fact that she had constantly refused his advances. Now that she'd succumbed, was he already over her? She would hate to imagine a man could be that fickle, but the pathetic reality was that they were.

She was ruing and regretting and completely in love with him. If he was bored by what had transpired and keen to move on, she'd be crushed to death by disappointment. She'd yielded to temptation. What if he decided he'd gotten what he craved and could proceed with his betrothal to Penny? If that occurred, Libby truly couldn't guess how she'd survive it.

"Where were you?" Libby said. "Dare I ask? From the gleam in your eye, I'm not certain I want to know."

"I don't care if you know. I've stumbled into a torrid affair."

Libby frowned. "With who?"

"Who do you think?"

Libby was focused on her own dilemma, but it wasn't difficult to deduce who it was. She collapsed onto a chair, her gaze caustic and condemning. "You're having an affair with Lord Roland?"

"Yes."

"I forbid you!" she ludicrously said. "Stop it immediately!"

"You're not my mother, Libby, so it's not up to you. And I have no desire to stop it. I'm having a grand time."

"How did this happen? Why did it happen?"

"He and I were cordial years ago. I told you that."

"How cordial? Clearly, I was mistaken about the level of your attachment."

"For a bit, I had flirted with the idea of marrying him, but by then, he was on a different path."

"What do you mean?"

"It was during that terrible period after his wife had fled and he'd filed for divorce. He was marching down the road to marrying his second wife as his father and friends were demanding. I probably could have saved him from that fate, but after what he'd been through, I didn't suppose I ought to be that greedy."

"You let him go? You set him free?"

Libby's tone was snide, but she couldn't help it. She was too overwhelmed to think rationally, and she couldn't have Fish entangled with Lord Roland. It would simply add to the weight of the burdens she was carrying.

"Yes," Fish replied, "I very nobly set him free, but with my traveling to Roland, we've rekindled our affection. We're both unattached adults. What's it to you if we're dallying? It's not any of your business, and I fail to comprehend why you're in such a snit about it."

"You can't be involved with him."

"Your opinion is noted, but as I previously mentioned, it's not up to you." Fish had never been a person who would fight over an issue. "What's wrong? You still haven't told me."

"I spent the night at Barrett with Luke."

"Yes, I received a message from him that you were stranded by the rain."

"I finally did it," Libby muttered, eager to spill the dreadful confession out into the open. "I'm no longer a maiden."

"You didn't ruin yourself!"

"I did." Tears sprang into Libby's eyes. "I wish I hadn't."

"Why? Didn't he know his way around a mattress? He's such a handsome rogue. I would have bet ten pounds he'd make it interesting."

"It was splendid. It was perfect and . . . and . . ."

Libby broke off. She was wretched and desolate, feeling as if she was all alone, without a single friend. She was anxious to talk to Luke and have him tell her everything would be fine, but she wasn't brave enough to have a conversation with him about what they'd done.

In the cold light of day, she was positive she shouldn't have participated, but then, she was frightfully glad she had. She kept studying herself in the mirror, expecting to look altered and not able to believe she could have experienced such a colossal event and still be exactly the same.

Fish pointed out the obvious. "You're distressed."

"Very distressed."

"It's a common sentiment. A virgin's deflowering is a big moment in a girl's life." Fish smirked. "Was he any good at it?"

"He was."

"I suspected as much, so why are you fuming and fretting?"

"I'm not sure what I should do now."

"What would you like to do?"

"I'd like to vanish. That was my plan when we were in London and I still want that."

"No, you don't. If I had to describe your condition, I'd say you're madly in love with him. Why would you disappear just when your affair is heating up?"

"He'll engage himself to Lady Penny and wed her very soon."

"I'm certain he will," Fish slayed her by concurring. "His kind never behaves any other way."

"I can't stay on the fringe of his world and watch him proceed. I didn't realize how intimate fornication would be."

"I tried my best to explain it."

"Evidently, you weren't adept at clarifying because I am thoroughly bewildered."

"Why? Did he hurt you? Did he scare you?"

"No. It was very romantic."

"Then why this anguish? In my view, you're being very silly."

"It was very...*special* to me, and I'm terribly afraid it won't have been special to him at all. It would kill me to discover that it wasn't."

Fish shrugged. "I've told you about men and their drives. It's just physical conduct for them, and you have to separate your feelings from the bodily antics he showed you. Otherwise, your yearning will consume you."

"I can't muster your callous attitude about it, Fish."

"Yes, I see that."

Fish had never been a maternal female. She was pragmatic and practical, and she never offered sympathy when Libby could desperately use some. In that, she'd always been very much like Uncle Harry.

With Harry, if Libby had voiced the most paltry complaint, he'd ordered her to buck up and cease her whining. He'd remind her she had a great life and she ought to be more thankful for it. His heartless disposition had pushed her to develop a very hard shell, but deep down, she was a gentle soul, and emotional issues wounded her.

Fish didn't possess the traits necessary for this type of discussion, but if Libby didn't talk to her, who would she talk to? It wasn't as if she had a dozen confidantes waiting in the wings. Her immoral act was sinful—and illegal too. She could be arrested and prosecuted for her night of debauchery.

"Could you simply commiserate?" she asked. "Could you be sorry for me?"

"Why would I be sorry? You philandered with a rich, handsome scoundrel. It's not the end of the world."

"It feels like it might be."

"Well, it's not. Don't read so much into it. Just . . . relax."

"I don't think I can."

"Has Lord Barrett returned to Roland with you?"

"No. I snuck out at dawn and came back by myself. I've been agonizing all day."

"About what? About Lord Barrett?"

"Yes, I can't bear to ever see him again, but I can't bear to *not* see him again either. I'm a complete mess."

Fish tsked with disgust. "I'm so surprised to find you in this agitated state. Aren't you tougher than this?"

"Usually, but I never had anything like this happen to me before."

"You can't let him have such a potent effect on you."

There was a liquor tray on the table, and Fish stood and filled a glass with brandy. She handed it to Libby.

"Drink that," Fish said. When Libby wrinkled her nose, Fish added, "Drink it all. You can't force yourself to calm down, so the liquor will do it for you."

Libby downed the contents, shuddering at the strong taste, but it worked quickly. She felt warmer and more in control.

"Better?" Fish asked.

"A little."

"Then are we finished? If so, I'm busy and need to leave."

Libby sighed. She'd never had anyone to empathize over any situation, and Fish had definitely never been her mother. Why would she have anticipated a different result?

"What has you so preoccupied?" Libby asked. "Are you hoping to jump back into Lord Roland's bed?"

Fish grinned. "Yes—if I can catch him in it—but I don't believe he's still there. I think he's down in the front parlor, pretending he's enjoying the party."

"What if his sister-in-law stumbles on your mischief? Hasn't Miss Pendleton sunk her claws into him? I doubt she'd be keen to discover you'd horned in on her territory."

"What she doesn't know won't hurt her."

"It might wind up hurting *you* though, and I'm betting she'd be a vicious adversary."

"I'm not worried about it."

"Perhaps you should be."

Fish rolled her eyes in exasperation. "Are we *finished*, Libby? I won't be scolded by you. I'm happy about what's occurred with Charlie."

"Charlie! Is that what you call him? Oh, my lord."

"He's very fond of me, so if you simply intend to complain and chastise, then I can't listen."

Libby gazed at her old friend, and she was sad for her. Nothing good could come from her infatuation. It would lead to grief in the end, but under Lord Roland's shower of attention, she'd forgotten what she'd learned about men. She was eager to forge ahead and damn the consequences.

"I can't bear to quarrel," Libby said.

"Neither can I."

"But I have to tell you a story."

"Fine, but would you get on with it? From the minute I walked in, you've been wringing your hands like a trembling virgin, but you're *not* a virgin any longer, and your new condition won't kill you. You have to regroup so you can figure out how to deal with Lord Barrett. I wish I could help you with your dilemma, but you're not ready to hear the advice I'd supply."

"Which is what?"

"You should grab hold of him and have as much fun as you can— for as long as you can. It's what I'd choose."

"I want him to fall in love with me. It's the only way I could keep on with him."

Fish finally displayed some sympathy. "He won't ever love you, Libby. You have to lower your standards about it. He seems besotted though, and you have to persuade yourself that you can be satisfied with that level of attachment."

Libby could just picture that sort of arrangement. He'd rent a house for her in London, and she'd see him a few times a month when he traveled to town on business or for social events.

She'd strut about on his arm at decadent soirees, where the rogues of High Society brought their own mistresses. All the while, back at Barrett, he'd be married to Penny and working hard to plant a babe in her womb and get his nursery started.

She absolutely could not live like that.

"I couldn't abide a tepid relationship," she said. "It's not enough for me, so we need to leave Roland. We'll go in the morning. Yes?"

"No. The party is scheduled to continue for another week, and I intend to revel until it's over."

"We can't stay here."

"Maybe *you* can't, but I certainly can. Head to London if you're so anxious. I'll join you there later. If you decide to vanish, write me a note so I have some idea of where you are. I'll chase after you once I'm done."

Libby blew out a heavy breath. "There's a secret I must tell you about Lord Roland. It's important."

"There's no secret you could share that would change my mind about tarrying, and I wish you could be glad for me. My romance will be over soon."

"We shouldn't have come to Roland."

"Speak for yourself. I'm tickled silly to have arrived."

Suddenly, a knock sounded on the door. She and Fish jumped as if they'd been caught engaging in illicit behavior.

"Who is it?" Libby called.

"Libby?" Simon jangled the knob. "For pity's sake, why is your door locked? Let me in."

Libby went over and spun the key, and he strutted in as if he owned the place. He was naturally flamboyant, plus he had a flair for fashionable clothes—inherited from Harry—and with wardrobe guidance from Fish, he always looked amazing. But Libby thought, on this occasion, he appeared particularly dazzling, as if he was walking on air.

"Why are you two hiding up here?" he asked.

"Libby is upset," Fish said, "and she had to discuss it with me. We're finished though."

He frowned at Libby. "Who upset you? It better not have been that roué, Lord Barrett. If he was awful to you, I'll pound him into the ground. Should I?"

"I don't need you to pound on Lord Barrett."

Fish chuckled with amusement. "Definitely not—since she's in love with him. If you rearranged his pretty face, she'd be devastated."

"What are you talking about?" Simon asked. "Libby is not in love with that wastrel. She's too smart for that."

"She spent the night in bed with him at Barrett," Fish announced.

"Fish!" Libby scolded as Simon said, "Really? How wildly marvelous!"

"How is it marvelous?" Libby inquired, not liking his cunning expression.

"If he's sweet on you, he'll delay his betrothal to Lady Penny, and I'd like it to be postponed."

"Why?"

"Because I have a few plans of my own for dear Lady Penny."

"What plans?" Libby demanded, her alarm rising.

"She doesn't want to wed him. He's old and stuffy and too much like her father. In fact, at the moment, she and Lord Barrett are fighting."

"Why?" Libby said again.

"Because he doesn't dote on her. Because he doesn't treat her as if she's special. Because he will never love her." He grinned a dangerous grin. "It didn't take much convincing. They're a horrible mismatch."

"Meaning what?"

"Meaning she's decided she might not be cut out for a cold, impersonal aristocratic marriage. It's dawned on her that she deserves a husband who is young, dashing, and fun." He snorted with delight. "I'm available."

Libby's heart literally skipped a beat. "You're running a scheme on her?"

He shrugged. "I wouldn't refer to it as a scheme. We've been flirting, and she's becoming besotted. With a tad more effort, I'll be able to persuade her to do whatever I suggest."

"To what end?" Libby said. "Are you thinking you could get her to marry you?"

"Maybe."

Fish chimed in with, "Her father might have quite a vehement opinion about that."

Simon scoffed. "It's not as if we'd ask him."

Libby gaped at him, wondering if he'd actually elope with the wealthy heiress. Could he really be that brazen? That reckless?

It was exactly the sort of thing Harry would have attempted, but how could Simon assume he'd succeed? How could he suppose there would be no consequences?

The nobility was a tight-knit bunch. They didn't take kindly to interlopers absconding with their daughters. There were laws to prevent such mischief. It was called kidnapping, and a titled lord like Charles Pendleton had enormous power. He could have vicious punishments inflicted on Simon, and Libby couldn't bear to envision what some of them might be.

"No, no, no," she murmured, vigorously shaking her head. "You are not eloping with Penny Pendleton. I forbid it."

Simon retorted as Fish had earlier, "It's not any of your business, is it?"

"I'm making it my business."

He laughed. "If Lady Penny throws her life and her dowry in my direction, why would you care? It doesn't have an effect on you one way or the other—except that I'll be rich and have the money to support you. You'll never have to worry or struggle again. I'll support Fish too. From this point on, you'll both be safe. I'll see to it."

"You're mad," Fish said to him.

"I agree with Fish," Libby said, "and we never should have come to Roland. We're leaving in the morning, and I won't argue about it."

Fish sighed with exasperation. "I already told you I'm not going."

Simon swiftly sided with Fish. "Don't be ridiculous. Of course we're not leaving. Not when everything is just falling into place."

"You two listen to me," Libby said. "I can't have you imposing yourselves on Lord Roland or Lady Penny. I can't, and here's why!"

She'd thought she could blurt it out. Months had passed since she'd stumbled on the box of Harry's old letters, and from the minute she'd read through them, she'd been biting her tongue.

Her tale was fantastical, like a plot in a novel, and she'd been so afraid that she wouldn't be believed or, even worse, that she'd divulge the information and it wouldn't change anything.

"Why are you in such a dither?" Fish nagged. "I'm not interested in departing Roland, so if you have some reason that will convince me, please get on with it."

"This is hard," Libby said. "I have no idea where to begin."

Fish's patience was exhausted. "Just tell us, Libby!"

"Yes, Libby," Simon concurred. "Spit it out so we can figure out where we are."

He poured himself a glass of liquor, then sat next to Fish. They glared at Libby, almost daring her to voice a remark they were determined not to like.

"After Uncle Harry died," she tentatively started, "I found some letters."

"And . . . ?" Fish pressed.

"They were from Harry's brother, Kit Carstairs. I know who I am now. Harry lied to me about my identity. All these years, he lied."

"That's not a surprise," Simon said. "He was always a liar."

"So who are you?" Fish asked. "Weren't your parents missionaries who were off to preach to the natives in the New World?"

"They weren't missionaries," Libby told them.

She felt as if she was running toward a high cliff and about to jump over. Where would she be when she landed at the bottom? She couldn't imagine, but once she spoke the words aloud, there could be no retracting them.

"I am Little Henrietta, Lord Roland's lost daughter."

Fish and Simon froze and gaped at her, then Simon's jaw dropped. "No bloody way! You're joking!"

Fish simply studied Libby intently, as if checking for Pendleton features. Then cautiously, as if testing how the comment would sound, she said, "Harry had letters that claim you're Little Henrietta?"

"They don't *claim* it, Fish," Libby said. "They prove it."

"This is so brilliant!" Simon practically crowed. "I can't believe you thought of it!"

"It's the truth," Libby insisted.

"We can make a fortune off this story!" he said.

"We will not make money off it," Libby sternly replied. "I merely need the two of you to tell me how to proceed."

"I know how we'll proceed," Simon said. "Is this a ploy to snag Lord Barrett?"

Libby scowled. "What?"

"He would never wed you because of your low status, but if you're an earl's daughter, you're perfect for him." Simon clucked his tongue like an annoying hen. "It's so cunning! If you're Roland's long-lost daughter, think of how we can use it to ingratiate ourselves to him!"

"Simon!" Fish chided. "Calm down. We're not scheming on Lord Roland."

Simon, the craftier of the three of them, hurried over to the door and spun the key, locking them in again. Then he sat back down.

"I'm stunned that Libby concocted this before I did!" He turned to Libby. "Why didn't you confer with me about the details? I could have rounded the edges so there aren't any flaws."

"Simon, hush!" Fish sharply snapped, and she shifted her attention to Libby. "Explain this to me," Fish said. "I'm trying to understand."

"My mother was Amanda Pendleton, Lord Roland's runaway wife. The man with her when she perished at sea was Harry's brother, Kit Carstairs."

"When your ship sank in that storm," Fish asked, "weren't you bound for Jamaica? That's what I always heard, but Amanda went to Europe. It's an established fact, and Lord Pendleton had investigators search there."

"She fled to Europe with her lover—when she first left the marriage—but he died in an accident in Rome. She was destitute, desperate, and alone, and she bumped into Kit Carstairs who was a university student on holiday. She begged him to save her, and it seems as if he was a young, gullible idiot. Harry warned him to stay away from her, but Kit was besotted, and he ignored his brother's advice. They sailed for Jamaica, and they concealed their plans so Lord Roland could never find her."

"Why would Harry hide that news?" Fish asked.

"Why did Harry do any insane thing?" Simon rhetorically responded.

Fish kept on. "If this is true, when you were returned to England, why didn't Harry admit who you were? Why didn't he give you back to your father?"

"My mother had regaled Kit Carstairs with dreadful stories about Lord Roland and how terrified she was of him. Mr. Carstairs presumed he was rescuing a damsel in distress from a violent ogre."

Fish huffed with offense. "Charles Pendleton wouldn't hurt a fly."

"It's how my mother persuaded Mr. Carstairs to help her, and he made Harry promise to never tell a soul their destination. He assumed—if Lord Pendleton found me or my mother—we'd be endangered."

Fish scoffed with disgust. "So Harry—the confirmed bachelor and confidence artist—decided to secretly raise you, rather than hand you over to your rich, important family?" Fish's incredulity was depressing. "I'm sorry, Libby, but you're aware of what Harry was like. He didn't have a benevolent bone in his body, and he wouldn't have cared if your father was a fiend. He wouldn't have aided you out of the goodness of his heart. If anything, he'd have sold you to your father."

"When he took custody of me," Libby said, "it wasn't exactly altruistic, was it? I spent my life earning the income that supported us. I did all the work, and he collected all the benefits."

Fish frowned. "Are you claiming that he figured out—from the very start—that he could fabricate your identity, then use you for his own financial purposes? Even for Harry, that's too calculating. He couldn't have invented a plot that devious. He wasn't smart enough."

On hearing the derogatory comment, Libby felt as if all her energy had drained out. She sank onto her chair and gripped the arms so she didn't simply slide to the floor.

"You don't believe me."

"It's just so far-fetched," Fish said.

"You think I'd lie about it?" Libby asked.

Fish shook her head. "No, I don't think you'd lie. Do you have the letters with you? Could I look at them?"

"They're in London."

"I want to read them. I want to see them for myself."

"I'm happy to show them to you—the instant we're in town again."

After Simon's initial outburst, he'd been silent. He'd been listening to Libby and Fish argue, turning to and fro as if watching a ball being swatted back and forth.

He jumped into the conversation. "Wait a minute. If Kit Carstairs wasn't your father and if Lord Pendleton is, then *you* aren't my cousin. Don't tell me that. You've always been my cousin, and I refuse to let you state that you're not."

To Libby's surprise, Simon appeared crestfallen, and she leaned over and patted his hand. "You've always been my cousin, and you always will be. A few old letters can't change that."

"You'd better mean it," he said. "If I didn't have you and Fish, who would I have?"

"That might be the sweetest remark you've ever uttered in my presence."

He grinned a cocky grin. "Don't get used to it."

Fish was still studying her, and she said, "What now, Libby? What is your plan?"

"I don't have a plan. I'm merely determined to head to London."

"Why? It seems to me you have several matters to address with Charles. You have to speak to him about this."

"How can I? You've known me for ages, and you think I'm lying. He and I are practically strangers. If I couldn't convince you, how could I convince him? It would be pointless to try."

"I'd just like to read the letters you found," Fish said. "We'll go from there."

"It was wrong for us to come here," Libby said. "I'd been anxious to meet Lord Roland, and when Simon originally mentioned this party, I thought it was a good idea for us to attend." She chuckled miserably. "I assumed I could assess the situation, then announce who I was, but I was mad to suppose I could."

"What's happened during your visit that would make you decide that?"

"He's certain Henrietta is dead!" Libby was nearly wailing. "I explicitly inquired about her, and he's positive she's been dead for years. After that declaration, how can I claim that *I* am Henrietta? Wouldn't that be cruel? Wouldn't it be viewed as a trick or a swindle? I'd likely be hauled off to prison as a criminal or to Bedlam as a lunatic."

They were all glaring, contemplating, then Libby asked Simon, "What should I do?"

"You should do whatever will bring us the most money in the end."

Libby's irritation spiraled. "Would you be serious?"

"I am being serious. If you're Roland's daughter, the news is worth a fortune to us. I say we shout it to the whole world and fill our purses with the blessings that will rain down."

"And you, Fish?" she asked.

"I think Simon is the very last person whose advice you should seek on any topic—but especially this one. And *I* need to ponder the dilemma. You've just sprung it on us, and I have to consider the angles before I offer an opinion."

"While we figure it out," Libby said, "I have to swear both of you to secrecy."

"I'll definitely keep my mouth shut," Fish told her. "I have no desire to wade into the middle of this bog unless I know the safest route to the other side."

"What about you, Simon?" Libby asked. "You can't tell anyone until I give you permission."

"You can't expect me to be quiet. Not with a story this big."

"For a bit. Please?"

Libby stared him down so he began to squirm, then he said, "All right, all right. I won't breath a word until you tell me I can."

"Thank you, and we'll go home in the morning, yes? We'll leave, so I can reflect on what my path should be."

They scowled at her as if she were insane, and Simon said, "No way am I leaving Roland tomorrow. Get over yourself, Libby."

"I'm not leaving either," Fish said. "I've been very clear about it."

"We can't stay here!" Libby insisted. "I won't stay."

"So go," Fish said. "We're not stopping you."

Fish's blithe response irked Libby to her limit. After what she'd just revealed, she'd yearned for them to be supportive, and their dismissive attitudes were infuriating. One of their rare fights might have erupted, but there was a knock on the door, and they froze.

"It's Miss Carstairs," Libby called. "May I help you?"

"It's your maid, Miss Carstairs. Lord Roland asked me to fetch you down to the library. Will you come?"

Libby stood and went to the door. She unlocked it and peeked out. "I'm indisposed at the moment and not participating in social engagements."

"He'd like it to be now, Miss Carstairs. He said to mention it's important."

Libby stared at the maid, then at Fish and Simon who were glowering at her like angry sentinels. Ultimately, she sighed.

"I'll be right down."

"He's in the library. Would you like me to escort you?"

"There's no need."

The girl left, and a heavy silence descended. There was the worst sense of dread in the air, as if something bad was about to happen, that it would be awful and they'd never be the same afterward. But that was silly. Lord Roland would probably request she perform after supper. It would be a subject that mundane. Wouldn't it?

"What could he want?" Simon said.

"I have no idea."

Libby looked at Fish, seeking an answer, but Fish shrugged.

"Will you change your clothes?" Fish asked. "Shall I pick out a gown for you?"

"The one I'm wearing is fine."

"Track me down when you're finished," Fish said. "Let me know what you discussed."

Libby snorted at that. "Yes, I'll inform you immediately. You two are at the top of my list of what's worrying me."

"You don't have to be so snippy," Simon said. "We only want what's best for you."

"Somehow," Libby retorted, "that doesn't reassure me in the slightest."

She pulled the door wider, motioning for them to slither out. They bristled and fumed, but finally obeyed her. She watched as they vanished around a corner, then she spun and went into the dressing room to check herself in the mirror.

She dawdled forever, being in no hurry to rush downstairs. Lord Roland would simply have to cool his heels until she was composed enough to face him.

What was about to transpire? How hideous would it be?

In her interactions with him so far, he'd been polite and considerate, but then, she'd felt horrid since she'd awakened at Barrett. In the intervening hours, her condition hadn't improved.

Would the blasted day ever end?

PEGGY HAD BEEN A housemaid at Roland from the year she'd turned seven. Her mother had served Florence Pendleton, the second Lady Roland, and she'd been able to bring Peggy to work in the manor at a very young age. Yet after Lady Roland had passed away, then Peggy's mother, Peggy had never achieved the status her mother had managed.

Miss Pendleton had never liked Peggy, and Peggy constantly tried to ingratiate herself, but to no avail.

She should have been down in the kitchen, waiting for the house-keeper to send her to clean another guest chamber, but instead, she was lurking outside Miss Carstairs's suite.

When they'd been apprised that the famous celebrity would visit, Peggy had fervidly hoped that she'd be assigned to tend the woman, but as usual, Peggy had been overlooked. Other, more senior girls had received the posh task, and Peggy was incredibly jealous.

The hall was empty, so she could casually stroll past Miss Carstair's door without being observed. Her costumer, Miss Fishburn, was with her, and they were talking in an animated manner that—when Peggy tarried at just the right angle—was audible.

Apparently, Miss Carstairs was no better than she had to be. She'd mis-behaved with Lord Barrett and was feeling guilty, but Peggy wasn't about to chastise her for the lapse. Actresses had no morals, and Peggy wouldn't begrudge any female for dallying with Lord Barrett. She might have tried any ruse if it would have guaranteed the handsome lord noticed her.

She was curious as to how Lady Penny would view the relationship though. Would she like to know that her likely fiancé was immersed in a fling with Miss Carstairs? Would she be glad or incensed? Would she kill the messenger?

Peggy debated the issue, wondering if there could be a benefit in telling. *Probably not . . .*

This was a delicious secret she would keep to herself. It was like a plot in a scandalous theatrical play.

Footsteps pounded up the stairs behind her, and she continued on as if she had a destination in mind. When she glanced back, she saw that the cheeky scoundrel, Mr. Falcon, had arrived. Miss Carstairs let him in to join the conversation.

Mr. Falcon was another handsome devil who'd tantalized Peggy. The other housemaids were all in love with him, but he was busy flirt-ing inappropriately with Lady Penny.

Had her Aunt Millicent realized what was occurring? Should she be informed? Could there be an advantage to speaking up?

Probably not . . .

She wandered toward the door, desperately anxious to discover what sorts of topics the three fascinating people would discuss. To her great delight, the door hadn't closed tightly when Mr. Falcon had entered the room. She could hear some of their comments and didn't even have to press her ear to the wood.

Suddenly, Miss Carstairs said, "I am Little Henrietta, Lord Roland's lost daughter."

Peggy bit down a gasp, as Mr. Falcon gushed, "This is so brilliant! I can't believe you thought of it! We can make a fortune off this story!"

Peggy's heart was hammering so loudly that she could hardly discern any words, but Miss Carstairs definitely said, "I merely need the two of you to tell me how to proceed."

Mr. Falcon responded with, "I know how we'll proceed. Is this a ploy to snag Lord Barrett? He would never wed you because of your low status, but if you're an earl's daughter, you're perfect for him. It's so cunning! If you're Roland's long-lost daughter, think of how we can use it to ingratiate ourselves to him!"

Peggy lurched away, feeling afraid, and very, very excited. She could never get Miss Pendleton's attention, and she always dickered over how to curry favor. Well, she'd certainly found a stellar route.

Miss Pendleton had to be notified immediately, and—Peggy was sure—when the devious scheme was exposed, Peggy would wind up the heroine for revealing the whole sordid charade.

She reached the stairs and raced down them, eager to locate Miss Pendleton and confess what she'd learned.

Chapter

16

MILLICENT RUSHED DOWN THE hall toward Charles's bedroom suite, hoping he was in it. There were too many blasted guests observing her every move, so she couldn't run around hunting for him.

The housemaid, Peggy, had just revealed the most appalling story about Miss Carstairs and her two dubious companions. They were a trio of scheming confidence artists who were about to play a terrible trick on all of them, but especially on Charles.

Millicent had warned Charles about them, but he'd refused to heed her, and look where it had left them!

While he could be stern and unbending when the situation called for it, he could also be extremely gullible, particularly where women were concerned. If Miss Carstairs had already managed to speak to him, there was no predicting what catastrophe she could set in motion. He might make promises or hand over money or ... or ... who could guess what else before Millicent intervened to stop him.

The door to his sitting room was open, and she hurried in, seeing that it was empty, the bedroom too. He probably wasn't in the dressing room behind it, but to be sure, she went over and peeked in.

To her great astonishment, she came face to face with Miss Fishburn. Millicent blanched so violently she was surprised she didn't fall down. As to Miss Fishburn, if she was discomfited by being found—quite alone—in Lord Roland's private quarters, she gave no sign at all.

She was holding a glass of liquor, and she brazenly toasted Millicent with it. Then she stared blandly, as if it was perfectly normal for her to be where she was.

Millicent's immediate and urgent thought was to wonder if Miss Fishburn was a thief. Had she been pilfering Charles's dressers? Charles's most valuable jewels were locked in the family vault, but he had diamond cufflinks and other items in a top drawer.

What might she have taken?

"Miss Fishburn!" Millicent's tone was shocked and firm. "Why are you in Lord Roland's dressing room?"

"He asked me to wait for him, so I'm waiting."

"You can't have the nerve to tarry in here. Tell me your business— and be quick about it."

"He had an important meeting downstairs, but I expect him shortly. What is it you need? Can I help you?"

Miss Fishburn strolled by Millicent and out to the bedchamber where she flopped down in a chair by the window. She sipped her drink, appearing very relaxed, as if she'd loafed there a thousand times prior.

Millicent felt as if she'd been turned to stone. Never in her life had she witnessed such brash conduct, and she'd like to search the woman's pockets. Dare she? Or should she summon a footman to assist her? Or should she send a servant to bring Charles upstairs so they could search her together?

Finally, Millicent shook herself out of her stupor, and she stomped over to stand directly in front of the shameless harpy. "You still haven't told me why you're in here. I suggest you offer an explanation at once!"

Miss Fishburn pondered the request, and ultimately, she said, "You should probably talk to Charles about it."

At her using his Christian name, Millicent sucked in a sharp breath. "Why would I waste any energy discussing you with Lord Roland?"

"I won't clarify any issue with regard to him and me. I doubt he'd want me to."

Millicent had never been so flummoxed, and her mind raced. There was only one reason Miss Fishburn would be so confident in her current location. Were they . . . they . . . philandering?

The notion didn't bear contemplating.

Charles belonged to Millicent! She'd decided on that ending when she'd been little more than a girl and jealously watching her older sister marry him. Florence had been all wrong for him, and after she'd died, Millicent had jumped at the chance to correct his mistake.

She'd frittered away the decades, pretending to be his wife. She'd served as his hostess, had raised his children, and supervised his home. She'd engaged in every act she could devise that would push him to recognize the obvious.

They were supposed to wed. She, Millicent, was supposed to be his next wife. Miss Fishburn—this interloper, this glorified seamstress, this . . . this . . . trollop who tended an actress—couldn't have him! Millicent would commit murder to keep it from occurring.

Without another word, she whipped away and dashed out, sweeping down the hall, then the stairs. She bellowed like a lunatic at every servant she passed, demanding to be informed as to Charles's whereabouts until, blessedly, she was pointed to the library.

By the time she reached it, she was in a frenzied state, her combs falling out, her chignon sagging down her back.

He was seated behind the desk, and she bustled over, sliding to a very ungracious stop against the wood. Frantically, she glanced around, seeing that they were alone. Luckily, there was no sign of Miss Carstairs, and Millicent hoped she'd arrived before it was too late.

He frowned up at her. "Millicent, my goodness. You look distraught. What's happened?"

"In the past few minutes, have you spoken to Miss Carstairs?"

"No, but I'm about to. Why?"

The butler huffed in, so most likely, the servants who'd observed her running like a madwoman had tattled to him and he was checking to learn what problem had flared.

"Shut the door!" she snapped at him. "Don't let anyone in. Especially not Miss Carstairs. She can cool her heels until we're finished."

At her sharp tone, he inhaled stiffly, but obeyed and sealed them in.

Charles's frown deepened. "Honestly, Millicent, there's no need to be rude to the servants. You're aware that I don't like that kind of behavior."

"He'll get over it," she caustically said. "Now be silent and listen to me."

"I can see you're upset. What is it?"

"A housemaid was walking by Miss Carstairs's room when she was inside with her cousin and her costumer." Millicent wouldn't debase herself by uttering Miss Fishburn's name aloud. "She overheard an outrageous conversation, and you have to hear it too."

"Fine. I ask you again: What is it?"

Millicent leaned nearer and lowered her volume. "Miss Carstairs and her cousin are preparing to implement a hideous hoax that will devastate you."

"You're being incredibly melodramatic. Would you calm down?"

"This is not a moment for *calm*. They are about to claim that Miss Carstairs is Little Henrietta."

He froze, blatantly confused, as if she'd babbled in a language he didn't understand. "She's about to what?"

"She will declare herself to be Henrietta. She and her cousin, that awful Mr. Falcon, intend to shout the story to the whole world."

"In the hopes of accomplishing what goal?"

"Why, to pressure you into accepting her as your daughter, of course. And get this! She's obsessed with Luke, and apparently, he's fascinated with her too. She thinks—if she can coerce you into believing her—he'll marry her instead of Penny. He'll realize she's an earl's daughter rather than a common slattern, and he'll make her his bride."

Charles shook his head with derision. "That's madness. Henrietta is dead. The courts and all of my investigators have said so."

"None of that matters to her. She'll dangle her bait anyway."

"She wouldn't pursue such a despicable scheme. I've chatted with her, and we've discussed personal topics. She wouldn't hurt me in such a painful way."

Millicent threw up her hands in frustration. "She was playing a part, you demented fool! She's an actress! She was ingratiating herself so you'd grow fond. She's roped you in, and now, she'll spring the news on you, figuring you'll announce that she's your long-lost girl."

"I wouldn't consider that," he murmured, but she knew he wasn't serious.

"Yes, you would. You'd pay any price to have Henrietta back in your life. Don't deny it."

"I won't, but I don't want it to transpire like this. I don't want charlatans to burst into my home and improperly gain my sympathy."

"Precisely, Charles! So this is how you should proceed."

"Yes, you have to apprise me. For I must admit, I am bewildered by this revelation."

"We shall immediately remove her from the manor."

"I had already planned on that. You were correct that there's an issue with her and Luke, and I decided it would be best if she left. It's not wise to have her around and tempting him when he should be focused on Penny."

"I'm glad you're taking action, but you must be very firm with her. You can't let her run to London and start telling tales. You can't let her cousin open his mouth either. Think of the gossip that would spread. The entire kingdom would be agog, and people would demand you claim her—even if she isn't Henrietta. The masses would love that ending."

"Yes, I suppose they would."

"You have to nip this in the bud. You have to scare her so she is too afraid to disseminate her lies. I mean, what if she went to the newspapers? Can you imagine?"

The butler knocked and peeked in. "Miss Carstairs is here, my lord."

"I'll be with her in a minute," Charles replied, and the butler slithered out.

Millicent stared at him, a thousand unaddressed comments flitting between them. She felt as if she was competing in a race and falling farther and farther behind.

"You'll never stand up to her, will you?" she fumed.

"Yes, I will. I promise."

"I'll stay with you. She's adept at batting her lashes, and I'll prevent any manipulation."

"I can handle one young girl."

Millicent scoffed. "You've never been able to handle any female."

"I won't argue the point with you. Why don't you leave so I can talk to her? I'd like to finish this."

"Why don't *you* delay for a bit? This is a dangerous circumstance, and we should review the ramifications more thoroughly. We should develop a response. We must counter her lies, and you should have your threats ready to unload."

"I'm not about to threaten her, and I'm sure you're wrong about this. I predict there's a perfectly valid explanation for what your maid overheard. Now please depart and allow me to conclude this as quickly and quietly as possible."

"You'll never convince her to be silent."

"I'll try my best. It's all I can do."

"She must understand the power you can wield. She must fear that you could ruin her. It's the only way you'll shut her up."

"I will deal with it as I see fit."

Millicent glared at him across the polished oak desk, and her temper soared. She thought of all the years she'd wasted on him, all the effort and energy. And for what?

That very moment, a harlot was loafing in his bedchamber. If he would blithely consort with such a disreputable doxy—right in the house where Millicent and Penny resided!—then it was clear he was reverting to his old habits. How could Millicent, who was a moralistic, decent Christian woman, ignore the sordid scenario?

There was a loud voice in her head, goading her to speak up for once. But there was a softer voice too, and it was urging caution.

How many times had she bitten her tongue and pretended to be happy? How many times had she acted like the contented partner, the contented *wife*—who wasn't a wife? Her pathetic situation was too wretched to abide.

The louder voice won. "Before I came downstairs, I stopped by your bedchamber to check if you were there. I was searching for you so I could share this terrible news."

"I'm sorry you were searching, but you found me, and you've imparted your information. I'll take it from here."

His impatience was evident, but she forged on. "To my enormous surprise, Miss Fishburn was loafing in your bedroom, and she appeared to be quite comfortable."

"Oh."

"Is that the sole remark you can muster? Oh? Initially, I worried that she might be a thief, but she insisted she'd tarried with your permission."

She studied him caustically, and finally, he said, "Yes, I seem to remember asking her to wait."

"Would you like to clarify why she was there?"

He sighed. "No, Millicent, I wouldn't, and you shouldn't be concerned over it."

"Not be concerned!" Her fury wafted out. "Am I to have no opinion about it? There is a scandal brewing under my very own roof, and you expect me to tolerate it without complaint."

He crushed her by saying, "It's not *your* roof. It's mine, and whatever deed I decide to perpetrate under it, it's my business. Not yours."

"All these years, I've stayed for you."

"And I've been grateful."

"I raised your children. I ran your home."

"Yes, and you were a great help to me."

"I thought we would ... would ..."

She couldn't spit out what she'd thought: that he'd notice her devotion and reward her with marriage.

"What did you think?" His tone was gentle, but galling. "I'm inquiring because it's recently dawned on me that you might have misconstrued your position here."

It was the scariest statement he could have uttered, and she didn't dare respond, for it might force them to dicker over topics she was too cowardly to confront.

Instead, she said the only thing she could say, the only thing she truly wanted to know. "Are you in love with Miss Fishburn? Is that it?"

He chuckled. "No, I'm not in love with her."

"What's happening then? You're simply having a ... a ... fling?" She hurled the word *fling* as if it were an epithet.

"As I mentioned, Millicent, it's not any of your business."

He stared her down, his expression stern and implacable, and she had so many emotions bubbling just under the surface. It occurred to her that she'd never really been angry in the past. For once, she grasped how a person could be driven to commit murder. She was close to launching herself across the desk and physically attacking him.

Then what ...?

The question echoed in her mind, and she had no answer to it.

Women were mostly impotent. They had no money or power, no authority or control. She was no exception.

She lived at his mercy, and he'd been generous—because he'd needed her assistance. She'd gladly offered it, but she had to accept that he'd never planned to give her the benefit she'd desired in return, that being a ring on her finger.

She swallowed down the bile that was choking her, and she pushed back her chair and stood.

"Enjoy your *chat* with Miss Carstairs," she nastily said. "I hope you get just what you deserve from her."

She whipped away and marched out, viewing it as quite a dramatic exit.

"Millicent, wait!" he snapped, but she didn't halt.

She yanked the door open and stormed out. The hussy, Miss Carstairs, was standing there, and she smiled and said, "Hello, Miss Pendleton. It's nice to see you today."

Millicent's rage boiled over. She was much taller than Miss Carstairs, and she loomed in. "You can play games with your precious cousin, Mr. Falcon, but hear me and hear me well! If you harm me or mine, I'll make you pay forever."

As a parting comment, it wasn't bad, and it completely captured her foul mood. Miss Carstairs blanched, and Millicent continued on, leaving the other woman slack-jawed with astonishment.

⸻

"COME IN, MISS CARSTAIRS." Charles rose and waved her into the room. "You'd previously given me permission to call you Libby. Is that still all right with you?"

"Yes, that's fine."

After bumping into Millicent out in the hall, she was wary, as if unsure whether she should enter or not. If she'd spun and dashed back to her bedchamber, he wouldn't have blamed her.

He could have told her that Millicent's vitriol wasn't actually aimed at her. Millicent had been annoyed with *him*, but too gutless to vent her fury in the proper direction.

Obviously, she'd been harboring feelings Charles didn't share. How long had she suffered in silence? Fish had warned him that he'd misconstrued his relationship with Millicent, but he'd scoffed at the notion. Fish had proved yet again that she understood people better than he ever had.

Libby hesitated in the doorway, and he said, "Don't mind Millicent. She's upset with me, and she took it out on you. I apologize for her outburst."

"Don't worry about it. I've often been shouted at. I've survived in the past, and I expect I'll survive this time too."

She walked over and sat down, and he studied her, pondering Millicent's story. It was fantastical and improbable, but he had to admit it was very gripping. He and Libby were barely acquainted, but he liked her very much. If she was about to drag him into a swindle, she'd figured out the precise method to torment him.

How had she managed to identify his weakest spot so perfectly?

He perceived an interesting connection to her, one that could have developed into a genuine friendship. He thought she could use a loyal friend. She was constantly surrounded by crowds, but he suspected that she was very much alone.

He wished he could advise her as she maneuvered through her very public life. And gad, if he'd been twenty years younger, he'd have been half in love with her already. No wonder Luke couldn't resist.

She exuded a forlorn air that made him want to take care of her. She oozed vulnerability, a damsel in distress who should have a strong shoulder to lean on. There wasn't a man in the kingdom who could ignore that kind of pull.

"You look tired," he said. "Have our many events fatigued you?"

"No. I've been quarreling with Fish and my cousin. It exhausts me."

"I hope the subject wasn't too intense."

"It's never too intense with us. They're my only family, and we squabble occasionally—like affectionate siblings."

He was curious as to what they'd been fighting about. Had it been the ploy Millicent claimed they were fomenting? He truly yearned for Millicent to be wrong and that Libby would never have agreed to conspire in such an awful scheme. If she was immersed in it, he'd be crushed.

"You sent for me," she said. "What is it you need?"

"I had to talk to you about one issue, but another has suddenly arisen, and they're both difficult. I can't decide where to start."

"I'm so grateful to have been your guest, and I sincerely pray I haven't offended you somehow."

"No, no, it's not that. It's ... it's ..."

He stumbled, unable to begin. Her eyes were wide, her expression innocent, and he sensed that harsh words would deeply wound her, and he couldn't bear to.

His cheeks heated. "I guess this will be harder than I imagined."

"I realize I look like a wilting violet, but I'm really quite sturdy. Whatever the topic, I'm certain we'll muddle through."

"All right. Here goes."

But still, he hesitated. Once he spoke up, they'd be marching down the road to their separating. After she left, there would be no reason to socialize with her ever again. The prospect depressed him, as if there was a weight on his back, as if he was about to assume a burden that would be very heavy.

When he liked her so much, when they had such a potent bond, why kick her out? He was never cruel, and he didn't want to be cruel to her, so why proceed? So far, she hadn't done anything but befriend his daughter and grace his home with her lovely presence. As a reward, Charles would order her to pack her bags.

"Just tell me, Lord Roland," she said, and she smiled.

Her smile was his downfall. She resembled Penny so much that he had to tamp down a shiver. Could Millicent's tale be true? Could Libby be Little Henrietta? Was it possible?

The wild questions wedged into his head, and he shoved them away. He wouldn't and couldn't give them any credence. Millicent had been correct about one blatant, indisputable fact: If he learned that Henrietta might be alive, if there was even the slightest chance of it, he'd work to make it a reality—even if it wasn't.

"I was chatting with Lord Barrett a bit earlier," he said.

"And . . . ?" She was very composed, not providing the least hint that she'd misbehaved with him.

"I'm aware that you spent the night with him at Barrett."

"Oh."

He was glad she didn't deny it. It saved them an awkward flurry of prevarication, and he could get straight to the point. "I'm aware too that he's very fond of you."

She winced with dismay. "He told you that?"

"Yes, and he's admitted that you're very fond of him too."

"I'm trying not to be, but I'm not having much luck."

"Luke is on a different path than you are. You understand that, don't you?"

"Yes, I understand."

"He's thirty, and he has to wed this year."

"Yes, he's been very blunt about it."

"I hate to be blunt as well, but he desperately needs the money in Penny's dowry. When you're in residence and distracting him, he forgets what matters."

"I see." She fiddled with her skirt, her fingers tracing over and over the fabric. "Did he ask you to talk to me about this?"

"No. *I* noticed what was bubbling up, and after I heard about your sojourn at Barrett, I had to intervene. By inviting you to our party, I've placed you in a horrendous situation. You're both suffering from an incredible attraction, and it's creating problems we simply can't stir at the moment."

"I understand," she said again.

"I'm afraid too that it will wind up causing issues with the betrothal. What if Penny found out about your affair? What if she refused the engagement? It's difficult for a bachelor to find an heiress. What would Luke do then? I think you care for him. Could you bear to put him in such an untenable position?"

She studied him for an eternity, and he received the distinct impression that she wanted to share a secret about Penny and Luke, but she swallowed it down, choosing instead, "What are you telling me? Are you asking me to leave?"

His shoulders slumped with regret. "I'm sorry, but yes, I am."

"I'll go immediately. I just need a few minutes to pack."

She stood as if she'd race off that very instant, and he felt awful. "Please, Libby, sit down."

"I'd rather not. I've never been more embarrassed in my life, and I heartily apologize. I appreciate your hospitality, and I'm mortified to the marrow of my bones that you had to mention any of this to me."

"Sit, please!" he said more sternly, and he waved to her chair. She dithered, then sank down, and he warned himself to ignore the guilt that was swamping him. "Don't be embarrassed. I was young once, and I discovered how hotly passion can burn, so I'm not judging you."

"I must clarify that I've struggled valiantly to avoid a relationship with Lord Barrett. It's why I was arguing with Fish and my cousin. I'm anxious to return to the city, then vanish before Luke can follow me. I've been trying to save him from himself."

"I'm delighted to hear it, and it makes me like you even more." He forced a smile. "It's my goal to help him too. I comprehend how amour can overwhelm a person's common sense. I'm certain, if the two of you part for a while, his ardor will wane."

"I'm certain of it too."

"So you don't have to run upstairs and pack. It will be fine with me if you depart in the morning."

"You're being very kind," she told him, "much kinder than I deserve."

"You're the type of girl who has men eager to assist you, but it doesn't appear you have many people to give you sound advice."

"No, I don't. There was just my Uncle Harry, but he wasn't good at anything, particularly dispensing advice."

"I hope you can view me as a friend, Libby. If you ever need guidance, you can always write to me. I'd be happy to correspond. Promise you'll contact me."

"Again, you're being very kind, and I can assure you that I won't ever pester you in the future. You shouldn't worry about that."

"I wouldn't consider it pestering. I would consider myself aiding a young lady who very much requires shrewd counsel."

Tears flooded her eyes, and he cringed, hating that he'd pushed her to such an emotional ledge. It occurred to him that she was even prettier when she was distraught.

"Could I categorically state that I'm not loose?" she said. "I'm ashamed to have you believe I am. I've never been in love before. I've never even had a beau. I'm surrounded by men, but Lord Barrett is the only one who's ever enticed me into misconduct."

"I've known Luke since he was a baby, so you don't have to explain to me how he's beguiled you. Don't forget that I picked him to be Penny's husband. That's an indication of the level of my regard for him."

"I shouldn't have misbehaved with him though, and I'm begging you not to think badly of me for it. I try to be honorable and decent. Up until I met him, I'd never disgraced myself."

"When I was your age, I engaged in many scandalous activities, so I can't condemn you for it."

He was suffering from a strident urge to walk around the desk and hug her. She looked bewildered, lost, and alone, like a tiny child who'd fallen and skinned her knee.

"Thank you for being so sympathetic," she said, "and I'll go in the morning. I swear. I'll get up early—so no one realizes what I intend—and I'll stay in my room this evening too. I won't join in the festivities."

"You don't have to hide yourself away from the other guests."

"I probably should."

He gazed at her, and unbidden, he was rocked by an old memory. Suddenly, it seemed as if he was staring at Amanda, his insane wife who'd caused him so much grief.

At the time of their doomed marriage, she'd been younger than Libby was by a few years, but she'd had dark brown hair, while Libby had blond, so he hadn't noticed any similarities, hadn't compared them. But he was definitely comparing them now. He felt as if he was gaping at a blond replica of his first wife.

He recalled seeing Libby in the garden with Penny and noting how much alike they'd been. He'd doubted ordinary missionaries could have produced such a magnificent creature. He'd wondered if she hadn't been sired by a Pendleton relative. Then the crazed notion had surfaced that Libby might be Henrietta, but he'd shoved it away.

Yet what if his initial assessment had been correct? What if Libby was Henrietta?

If he could stumble on Henrietta—alive and fine—it would wash away decades of guilt. He blamed himself for what had happened to her. Whatever her fate had ultimately been, he was positive it had been horrid, and her mother wouldn't have eased her through it.

He hadn't wanted to be a father, so he'd abandoned Henrietta to her disturbed mother's whims. If he could find her, maybe he'd finally be able to forgive himself.

He understood all those issues, and he possessed an inexplicable affection for Libby, so he had to tread cautiously. She had a peculiar, powerful effect on him, as well as on most men, but it wasn't passionate emotion plaguing him. No, it was paternal and fatherly. He'd like to shield her from the slings and arrows the world would shoot at her.

"Before you go," he said, "I have to address one other topic."

"You mentioned there were two things, didn't you? What is it? Might I hope it won't be as awkward as what we just discussed?"

He chuckled miserably. "It's worse."

He was about to accuse her of nefarious scheming, of being in league with her cousin in order to tantalize him about Henrietta, but if there was a plot hatching, he was convinced her cousin would have initiated it. He couldn't blame her for Mr. Falcon's mischief.

"Please don't keep me in suspense," she said.

He exhaled a heavy breath. "A rumor is circulating, and Millicent demanded I question you about it. It's why she was so angry a bit ago."

"I can't imagine how I might have irritated her. Since I arrived, she and I have hardly spoken. She's not exactly the warmest person."

"It's not what you did to her specifically. She's very protective of me, and she never likes to see me hurt or upset."

"*I* haven't hurt or upset you, have I? If I have, I might simply curl up in a ball and die of shame."

"A housemaid eavesdropped on you and your cousin when you were talking in your bedchamber. Evidently, your cousin has persuaded you to approach me and claim you're my lost daughter, Henrietta." He forced a laugh. "I defended you to Millicent. I told her you would never play such a terrible trick on me. I told her that we'd become friends, and you would recognize how deeply such a flagrant lie would wound me. I told her you'd never behave so reprehensibly."

"A housemaid overheard us?" was her only reply.

He noticed she didn't deny the charge. "Tell me you weren't considering such a regrettable ruse. I'm sure your cousin is responsible, and it would devastate me to learn that you'd agreed to be involved. You haven't, have you?"

She peered into his eyes, and it was the strangest thing, but Time seemed to stand still. His heart seemed to quit beating. The wind in the trees stopped blowing, the birds stopped chirping.

Her mind was whirring, as she debated whether to share an important remark. It would change his life forever, would rock his world to its very foundation. But ultimately, she drew in on herself, as if tucking away whatever it had been.

"I have no idea why a housemaid would spread such a tale," she said. "My cousin never suggested it, and I hold you in the very highest regard. I realize how badly such a lie would distress you. Believe me when I insist that I would never disseminate it."

Millicent had urged him to threaten Libby, that he scare her into silence, but he wasn't such a bully that he'd frighten her. He struggled to formulate a final comment, but he couldn't determine what would be appropriate, and apparently, they'd chatted to the bitter end.

She rose from her chair, curtsied low and perfectly, then said, "Thank you for being kind—and goodbye."

She swept out, regal as any queen, and he was left all alone, feeling like a fool and an ass.

Chapter

17

Libby swept into her bedroom suite, praying it was empty. She'd never been more embarrassed in her life, and she couldn't bear to speak with anyone.

Lord Roland, Charles Pendleton, the man who was actually her father, had kicked her out of his home. She'd disgraced herself with Lord Barrett, so he thought she was too disreputable to remain and socialize with his *real* daughter.

Then he'd killed her a bit more by mentioning Libby's quarrel with Simon. A duplicitous housemaid had reported their conversation, and Lord Roland had felt compelled to state that he'd heard about the lie and was certain she'd never spread it.

She'd gazed at him, practically in a stupor, and she'd wanted to shout, *Look at me! Can't you tell I'm your daughter too? Will you send me away?*

But she hadn't uttered a word.

Ever since she'd stumbled on that stupid box of letters, she'd been on pins and needles, yearning to share the shocking news she'd uncovered, but she'd been afraid she wouldn't be believed. It was galling to realize how right she'd been.

Lord Roland was willing to allow her to depart in the morning, but she wouldn't inflict herself on him another minute. Not when he was convinced she was a harlot who was too notorious to tarry under his roof. She would pack a satchel, have her carriage harnessed, and be off within the hour. Fish could bring the rest of her belongings whenever she deigned to haul herself away.

Fish and Simon could pursue their ridiculous affairs. Libby had tried to persuade them *not* to debase themselves, *not* to stir trouble, but why worry about them?

When Libby had needed their support the most, they'd scoffed and had refused to supply it, so they could dawdle at Roland until they choked. Fish could trifle with her precious earl, and Simon could flirt to exhaustion with Lady Penny. But Libby was heading for London. Immediately. Then she would vanish for several months.

By the time she resurfaced, the disloyal, tattling Lord Barrett would either be a happily married man, with Lady Penny as his bride, or he'd have gotten over Libby to the point that he barely remembered who she was.

She wouldn't accept any other ending. She was Libby Carstairs, one of the most infamous women in the land, and she was finished with letting the people she loved treat her badly.

She slammed the door, determined that Fish and Simon not wander in to bother her. Nor could she have any housemaids hovering and offering their dubious assistance. It would be too difficult to discern which one had eavesdropped, then rushed to inform Millicent Pendleton of Libby's secrets.

She stormed into her bedchamber, feeling as if she'd been pummeled with clubs.

She'd fornicated with Lord Barrett and was reeling from the experience, but the treacherous cad had blithely discussed the event with

Lord Roland. He'd been so effusive with his descriptions that Lord Roland had decided it was necessary to chastise her for it.

She had to leave so Lord Barrett would be saved from the wicked impulses he suffered when she was nearby. She'd struggled—as valiantly as she was able—to deflect Lord Barrett's advances, but it had been impossible to dissuade him.

Had Lord Barrett any responsibility for what had happened? Why shouldn't *he* be asked to leave? Why must Libby slink out like a mongrel dog? If Lord Roland was so offended by what had occurred, why would he still want Lord Barrett as a son-in-law? Why would he still hope the marriage went forward?

Well, she knew why. Lucas Watson and Charles Pendleton were peers, were part of the same elevated social sphere. They were so far above her she was surprised they could see her from their lofty perches.

She'd always loathed their kind of snobbish, entitled prigs, and nothing about the past few days had changed that opinion.

"Hello, Libby," Luke suddenly said from over in the corner.

She'd been so distracted by her furious musings that she hadn't been paying attention to her surroundings. She jumped a foot and pounded a fist on her chest, urging her thundering pulse to slow down.

He was seated in a chair as if it was perfectly appropriate for him to have snuck in. He was grinning, as if he'd played an amusing trick, and clearly, it hadn't dawned on him that he might not be welcome.

"Lord Barrett! Why are you in my bedchamber?"

"Where have you been? I've been searching for you forever."

"I have been in the library, being scolded by Lord Roland for my having had the audacity to fornicate with you."

"What?"

"Evidently, I am a harlot who has seduced you against your will, and you are such a gullible boy that you couldn't ward off the temptation I present. I must stop enticing you at once, lest you be completely corrupted by me."

"What are you talking about? I never denigrated you to Charles."

Her rage soared to a fevered pitch. "How dare you gossip with him about me! How dare you share details of our night together! I swear—if I was holding my pistol—I would shoot you right between the eyes."

He scowled, looking bewildered by her ire. "Would you calm down?"

"No. I am very, very angry, and I suggest you slither out—this instant!—or I can't predict how I'll behave."

"I didn't gossip with him."

"Then how did he know about it?"

He shrugged. "He was aware that you'd been at Barrett with me, and he figured we hadn't been drinking tea and chatting about the weather."

"So he accosted you and . . . what? You merrily admitted our tryst? Have you no spine? No discretion? What about my reputation? Were you concerned about it for a single minute?"

"He's a friend of mine, and we've been acquainted for ages. I wasn't about to lie to him."

"Heaven forbid that you lie to Lord Roland. Heaven forbid that you protect me."

"I didn't need to *protect* you. He was very sympathetic in how he raised the subject."

"If I'd been a fussy, aristocratic debutante, I bet you'd have denied it quite vehemently."

"Charles and I are friends," he repeated. "We always have been, and we merely had a very private discussion about how I've been acting. You're making too much of this."

"Since *I* was the center of that conversation, I beg to differ. I'm not making nearly enough. Get out of here."

"No."

"Get out!"

She was trying to keep from shouting. After how Lord Roland had castigated her, she couldn't have another snooping servant hear that she had a man in her bedroom. The news would immediately be conveyed to Millicent Pendleton, and Libby would be even more disgraced.

"We have to confer about numerous issues," he said.

"I have no idea why you'd think that."

"You're not serious. After last night, we have a thousand topics to address."

"You are mad! Now go away!"

He didn't budge, but gaped at her as if she were a toddler throwing a tantrum. She was a tiny woman, and he was a very large man. She couldn't physically toss him out, and he wasn't about to heed her verbal entreaties. So to Hades with him!

She whipped away and marched into her dressing room. She opened a traveling trunk and retrieved her pistol. It was still loaded from when she'd been riding the prior afternoon, which seemed to have been a lifetime ago. It was wet from the rain, so she doubted—if she pulled the trigger—it would even fire, but she was more than ready to find out.

She stomped back to the bedroom, the barrel pointed at the middle of his cold black heart. If he felt threatened in the slightest, he didn't exhibit any sign. He simply frowned as if she was deranged.

"What are you planning?" he said. "Will you shoot me merely because I've refused to leave?"

"Yes. I'm not joking. I have had it—with you, with your precious Lord Roland. If I have to murder you to be rid of you, then I am happy to take that drastic step."

"You just might be the most astonishing female in the world. How should I view such bizarre conduct?"

He laughed, and her rage burned even hotter. "Yes, that's what I've always heard about myself. I'm astonishing, but my bad temper is never mentioned. At the moment, I've had all the turmoil and insults I can abide, so get going! Don't make me tell you again!"

She bellowed her sentences, beyond caring if there was a housemaid spying in the hall. Before she could react though, he leapt up, and in a sly, smooth move, he yanked the gun away and pitched it onto the floor behind her. It slid across the polished boards and crashed into the wall, causing it to fire toward the dressing room.

A huge puff of smoke filled the air, and her ears rang from the loud bang. They were frozen in their spots, wondering if the commotion had been noticed, if people might rush up to knock on the door and ask what had happened. But no one came and no one knocked.

He broke their stunned silence. "Do you feel better? You could have killed me with that thing."

"I wish I had!"

"I can't believe it was loaded." He looked irked, but impressed too. "You would have shot me. You really would have!"

"You'd have deserved it," she spat.

He swooped in and drew her into his arms, and he tried to kiss her, but she wiggled away. She couldn't let him. Despite how furious she was, despite how he'd upset her, she was putty in his hands. No matter what he did, her obsession would never completely wane.

If he kissed her, if he was kind and sweet, she would never muster the fortitude to separate herself, and she'd sworn to Lord Roland that she would.

Her assignation at Barrett had sealed her fascination. She was madly in love and yearned to be by his side forever, but as Lord Roland had gallingly clarified, she could never grab the spot she was hoping to occupy.

She was too lowly to have Lucas Watson for her very own. She'd started out at the right level, but circumstances—and her insane mother—had plucked her out of it, so she was too common and too shameful to attach herself.

"Would you tell me what's wrong?" he said.

"You still don't know? I thought I was quite clear."

"Yes, you were, but could we deal with it in a rational manner? I don't understand why we have to shout and quarrel."

"You wouldn't," she seethed, and the anger finally drained out of her.

She felt as if she'd deflated, as if her bones had turned to rubber. She'd never been a fighter, but he simply drove her to extremes she'd never previously experienced.

She staggered over to a chair and eased down, worried—if she didn't sit down—she might fall down. Of course he was too pompous to leave her alone so she could lick her wounds in private. He picked up a second chair and dragged it over, and he sat too, but much too near so their feet and legs were tangled together.

He clasped her hand and linked their fingers, and she let him do it. Even now, even when she was too livid for words, she couldn't erect any walls and keep them in place.

From the minute she'd fled Barrett, she'd wanted to tarry in a quiet room and talk to him. Here they were, by themselves, and she supposed it would be the last occasion she talked to him about anything.

"I'm sorry I discussed you with Charles," he said. "When he raised the issue of our night at Barrett, I was taken off guard and too flummoxed to deny it."

"Fine. I will accept your explanation of what occurred."

"I never meant to embarrass you."

"Fine," she said again.

"Charles thought you should depart Roland. He figured—when you and I were in such close proximity—we're just courting trouble."

"I specifically noticed that he didn't ask *you* to depart. It's obvious he deems me to be at fault for this mess." Sarcastically, she added, "I'm such a temptress!"

"He doesn't view either of us as being at fault, and he was hardly judgmental. He was young once, and he had his own torrid affair."

"He certainly did," she caustically stated.

She pondered her crazed mother and wished she had an acquaintance who'd been cordial with her parents back when they'd met. How had stoic, polite Lord Roland ever been lured to such folly? In any scandal involving amour, the woman was always blamed, so her mother must have been fantastically beautiful and exotic to have coaxed him to such blatant ruin.

"Charles is not exactly in a position to condemn us," he said.

"He seemed plenty condemning to me."

"I hate to hear it, but would you stop fuming over it?" He sighed with exasperation. "You're making this much more difficult than it has to be."

"How am *I* making it difficult? I've been accused of being loose and immoral, and I've been ordered to vacate the premises. I've agreed that I would, and since I'm prepared to behave precisely as has been requested, please clarify how I'm being difficult."

"Charles has been through a situation like this, and he thinks we could both benefit from an interval apart."

"He thinks *you* could benefit. I've constantly tried to avoid you, but you pestered me until I relented and gave you what you sought."

"It was grand though, wasn't it?" He snorted with amusement. "Don't you dare claim it wasn't. If it were up to me, I'd carry you back to Barrett, toss you in my bed again, and keep you in it forever."

She almost said, *You could take me there if you wanted,* but she swallowed down the comment.

He was a rich, powerful nobleman who could act however he liked. He didn't have to listen to Charles Pendleton, and his decision to obey Lord Roland was an overt indication of his true opinion.

Oh, he could whine and insist he was just being courteous, but the reason Libby had to slink away was so he could focus on whether he'd still like to propose to Penny.

Libby had fornicated with him, but he hadn't been careful at the end. He'd spilled his seed into her womb, so he'd placed her in incredible jeopardy. What if she wound up with child? By the time she discovered that the worst had transpired, he'd likely be wed to Penny. What then?

"You'll leave as Lord Roland suggested?" he asked.

"Yes, of course. How could I refuse?"

"Will you return to London?"

"Yes."

He nodded as if she'd supplied the correct answer. "I told Charles I'd stay here for the remainder of the party. I'm the guest of honor after all, so I shouldn't vanish."

He chuckled, then paused, as if he expected her to chuckle too, but she simply gaped at him as if he were a stranger who'd wandered into her room by accident.

"No, you shouldn't vanish," she snottily retorted. "Not with your presence being so important."

"Will you go back to the theater where you were performing last week? What are your plans?"

"Yes, I'll go there," she lied. "I can't afford to be unemployed."

"I'll come to town as soon as I'm finished. Promise me you'll be there. Promise me you won't do something crazy—like disappear on me. I'll be aggravated if I have to search for you."

She wondered, once she hid herself away, how long it would take for his obsession to wane. Hopefully, if she ever bumped into him again—in the far distant future—he would be married, with Penny having already delivered many babies to his nursery.

She asked, "What are you imagining will happen between us when you arrive?"

She wasn't about to connect with him in the city, but she was curious about how his mind was working. He seemed to truly believe he could keep on with her *and* Penny, that Libby would ultimately agree to that sordid scenario. She couldn't make him realize how revolting it sounded.

Then again, she was an *actress,* and everyone knew that actresses were harlots. Why wouldn't he assume she'd debase herself in any manner he requested? In her dealings with him, she hadn't exhibited much of a moral spine, but that was about to change.

He frowned, as if it was a trick question. "What will happen? What would you suppose? We'll continue on as we have been."

"What about Penny?"

"What about her?"

He threw the query out casually, as if Penny were a dog by the side of the road, rather than the girl he was about to wed.

"You're staying for the rest of the party," she said. "It tells me you're still on track to propose to her."

He debated his reply, then settled on, "I have no idea what I intend. I told Charles I would tarry until the bitter end. He asked me to, and I swore I would. After that, I can't guess what will occur."

"You need an heiress. You need Penny's dowry."

"I won't claim I'm eager to pass up the money she can provide."

"You're such a smart man, Luke. Why can't you admit how awful this predicament is for me?"

"It's only *awful* if I forge ahead into an engagement. I haven't decided that I will."

"If you don't wed Penny, you'll wed someone else just like her." He looked as if he'd argue the point, and she cut him off. "You will. Don't treat me as if I'm stupid."

He sighed. "This is becoming an impossible problem."

"Yes, it is, and I'm tired of bickering over it."

"I'm not too keen about it either." He forced a smile, one that begged her to smile too, and when she didn't, he said, "Tell me what to do, Libby. I can't bear that I've made you so unhappy."

"What if I wind up with child?"

He blanched, as if he'd never pondered the notion. "You won't. A babe rarely catches after just one attempt."

"What if it's one of those *rare* occasions? If I was increasing, would you still betroth yourself to Penny?"

She sat on the edge of her seat, waiting for him to announce that he'd never behave that despicably. She waited for him to declare that he'd marry her in an instant, that he'd forsake Penny and Charles and pick her instead.

But that vow didn't arrive.

"Let's not worry about it now," he said. "We can cross that bridge if we ever have to."

"It's because I'm a lowborn actress, isn't it?" Her tone was scathing. "If I was a rich earl's daughter like Penny, you wouldn't hesitate."

He grimaced. "Could you not talk like that? I think you're remarkable, but you understand the world where I reside. You realize the kind of bride I'm meant to have. I've constantly told you how extraordinary I deem you to be, so I won't enter into this sort of discussion. I can't win it."

She pulled her hand from his, and she slid out of the chair and away from him. He reached for her, but she was too quick. She studied him, certain it was the last time she'd ever see him, and she was anxious to catalogue every detail so she'd never forget.

"I have to tell you a secret," she said. "I should shut my mouth about it, but in case there's gossip later, I want you to hear it directly from me."

He exhaled heavily, as if she was a great burden, then he stood too and faced her. The bed was between them, like a barrier he wouldn't dare climb over.

"Fine, Libby. What is it?"

"After Uncle Harry died, I found a box of old letters. I learned the truth about my past and my parents."

"You mentioned it when we first met, and I'm glad for you."

"My mother was a flamboyant singer who enticed a nobleman, and eventually, they eloped."

"My, my, that must have created quite a scandal."

"It was definitely a scandal. She was a lunatic who likely should have been locked in an asylum to prevent her from causing my poor father so much anguish."

"I'm sorry you have to feel that way about her."

"After how she fell apart, I can't convince myself to picture her as being particularly stable."

"I'm conflicted as to what I should say about your mother, but I'm not surprised to discover that your father was a nobleman. You're so incredible. I always suspected you had blue blood running in your veins. Who is he? Is he British? Would I be acquainted with his family?"

"Yes, as a matter of fact, you're intimately acquainted. You've known him all your life."

He scowled, not able to unravel the puzzle. "Who is it?"

"It's Charles Pendleton. I'm his lost daughter, Little Henrietta."

His jaw dropped, and he scornfully scrutinized her. Then he provided the exact response she'd expected.

"Libby Carstairs, you are not Henrietta Pendleton."

"I am," she firmly stated, "so you see, *Lord* Barrett, my father is an earl, and Lady Penny is my sister. With that information on the table, are you still desperate to wed her rather than me?"

"You're not Henrietta," he repeated. "Why would you tell such a whopping falsehood?"

"People have been calling me a liar all day, so I shouldn't be irked by your attitude, but I must admit that I am sincerely crushed by it."

He clucked his tongue with disgust. "Libby, you have to recognize how bizarre this sounds. Who persuaded you to make such a claim? Was it Mr. Falcon? I consider him to be a shady character. I hope you haven't permitted him to drag you into an untenable morass."

"He didn't persuade me of anything. *I* learned about it from my uncle's letters. I couldn't decide how to proceed, so I kept the news to myself until this afternoon."

"Gad, you can't have apprised Charles. It would be such a cruel trick to play on him. He'd be devastated."

"Lord Roland just happens to be my father."

"Would you stop saying that?"

"Yes, I will stop. For now. I simply want you to hear—from my own lips—that my father is an earl, that I was born with very high blood. And Penny is my sister, and you're about to marry her. If my world had spun in a different direction, I would have been the perfect bride for you, but Fate and my mother snatched it all away. So you'll pick Penny instead of me, and it will kill me forever."

"I can't imagine how I should reply to such a peculiar outburst."

"I'm feeling a tad hysterical, so you probably shouldn't stand too close. Who can predict what I'll do next?"

He stared at her across the mattress, an impasse as vast as the ocean opening up between them.

He could have shaken off his stupor and told her he didn't mean to denigrate her, that he believed her and was certain she would never lie about such a monumental topic. He could have rounded the bed, pulled her into his arms, and told her he was excited for her, that he would help her maneuver through the harrowing future that would arrive after the truth was disseminated.

But he didn't round the bed. He didn't pull her into his arms.

"You mentioned this to Charles?" he asked.

"No, *he* mentioned it to me. I guess a housemaid was spying on me while I was talking about it with Simon. She tattled before I could reveal the secret in my own way, but just so you know, Lord Roland thought I was lying too. His only concern was to be sure I didn't blab to anyone."

"I can understand why. Have you any idea of the upheaval this will stir if it spreads?"

"Oh, yes, I'm prepared for it. I've been the *Mystery* Girl of the Caribbean for twenty years. I have a fairly clear notion of what that entails."

"Don't tell people about this, Libby. Please don't. It can't end well for you."

"I'll keep that in mind."

She waited a second, then another and another, dying a little when he didn't take a step toward her.

Ultimately, he said, "I should check on Charles. He's likely quite distraught over this situation."

"We can't have Charles distraught, can we?"

"You stay right here," he ludicrously commanded, as if she was prone to following orders. "I'll be back in a bit. We'll discuss this further."

"I won't move a muscle until then."

"Good."

He dawdled, appearing as if he'd offer a profound remark, as if he'd apologize for calling her a fraud, but it wasn't voiced.

He whipped away and left, and she listened as he exited the suite. She wondered if he'd bothered to look in the hall first before he strutted out. What if he'd been observed by her nosey housemaid?

Well, it was *his* problem. Not Libby's. She wasn't the one who was about to become engaged to an earl's daughter. She was single and free, and he was the least of her worries.

"Pompous idiot," she muttered as his strides faded away.

She went into the dressing room to dig out a satchel so she could pack a few clothes for her trip to London.

Chapter

18

Penny arrived at Libby's bedchamber, and she peeked into an empty sitting room, but in the bedroom beyond, Libby was next to the bed. There was a satchel on the mattress, and she appeared to be stuffing clothes into it.

She hurried in, saying, "Libby! What are you doing? You can't be leaving. Please tell me you aren't."

Libby froze, then crudely muttered, "I should have locked the bloody door." Then she turned around. "I'm sorry, but I can't have a visitor right now."

Penny bustled over, and she studied Libby. It was very strange, but from the moment they'd met, she'd felt such a potent connection to the beautiful female.

It wasn't just that Libby was famous and glamorous. She was the woman Penny would like to be when she was older. Penny had always been the quiet daughter, the perfect child, but a stubborn streak bubbled below the surface.

She envied Libby her autonomy and freedom. Libby didn't answer to anyone, didn't heed silly orders or edicts. She made up her own mind and chose her own path. No female in Penny's world was ever allowed such liberty.

Penny intended to watch and imitate Libby, so she would gradually learn how to display the exact sort of brazen attributes.

"The party isn't over for a week," she said. "You can't abandon me. You're the only guest I truly want in residence."

"I can't stay here another minute."

"Why not? Was someone rude to you? Who was it? I shall deal with him or her at once."

Libby stared, and Penny received the distinct impression that she was biting down many comments that Penny ought to hear. Clearly, there were events occurring that involved her, but they were likely being kept from her for her own good.

She rolled the dice and asked, "Is it my father? Or is it Lord Barrett? Which one of them has vexed you?" Libby's eyes widened imperceptibly, and Penny said, "Was it both of them? If so, I will wring their stupid necks."

Libby chuckled, but glumly. "Your father suggested I depart, and I agreed that I would. He decided it would be for the best if I left."

"The *best* for whom? My opinion wasn't sought, and I don't want you to go."

"I shouldn't have attended in the first place. In light of my profession, I'm not suitable company for you and your friends."

Penny's jaw dropped in astonishment. "Did Father say that to you?"

"Not in so many words, but I understand his reservations."

"I'm stunned that he'd insult you that way. How dare he!"

Libby sighed. "You're a nice girl, Penny, but you don't have to defend me, and I would hate for my presence to cause a rift between you and your father."

"The rift has already been created, but it wasn't your fault."

"I like your father, and I *don't* like to have the two of you quarreling."

"Can I tell you something, Libby? Will you listen?"

"I'm not sure I should be your confidante. There are many issues with us that shouldn't ever be addressed."

"I know what some of them are."

Libby smirked. "I doubt that very much."

"How about this? I know Lord Barrett is in love with you."

Libby blanched. "No, he's not."

"How about if I describe his sentiment as inordinately devoted. Is that better?"

"No."

"I wish you wouldn't deny your relationship with him. Your cousin, Mr. Falcon, told me all about it."

Libby sniffed with offense. "If that's even remotely true, then Simon needs to shut up."

"I'm glad he revealed it. People in this accursed manor treat me like a baby. If I continue to obey my father, I'll be marching to the altar with Lord Barrett before I can blink."

"It's probably a good plan for you," Libby tepidly said.

"No, it's not! Not if he's in love with you instead. Would you put me out of my misery and honestly admit that he's besotted?"

"You constantly mention Lord Barrett to me, but you and I shouldn't discuss him."

"We have to, don't you think?" The question hung in the air, then Penny stepped in and clasped Libby's hand. "Father is determined that I wed him, but I won't. It wouldn't be fair to you—or me. Why would I pick a husband who's in love with someone else? If that's where I'd stand right at the beginning of my marriage, what kind of life would I have?"

"There are expectations for you," Libby said, "and the rules are different. You don't get to marry for love, and Lord Barrett would be an excellent husband."

"I suppose—if you don't count his being obsessed with you! You can't mean I should be content with a philandering spouse. You can't believe that."

"No, I don't believe it."

"I told Father—and Lord Barrett too—that I won't marry him so long as he's infatuated with you."

"You didn't!"

"I did, so I'm fighting with them. They're so annoyingly arrogant."

"I won't argue the point," Libby furiously said.

"They assume they can command me, but I won't let them. I can't figure out why, but I'm so desperately fond of you. I could never hurt you, and if I wed Lord Barrett, I'm certain you'd be crushed."

"Maybe," Libby murmured, unwilling to dive in any farther than that.

"Since that's the case, I *won't* marry him. My father can rant until he's blue in the face, but he won't change my mind."

"I'm very impressed by your bold attitude."

"I have to watch out for my best interests. Father has proved that he won't. If I'm not careful, there's no predicting who I'll wind up shackled to."

Libby sank down on the bed, her hips balanced on the edge of the mattress, her feet on the floor. She gazed at Penny with her magnificent blue eyes, and she looked weary and very sad. Penny was still holding her hand, and she linked their fingers and squeezed tight, eager to shift some of her own vigor into the troubled woman.

"I'm going to tell you two things I shouldn't," Libby said. "It will stir even more discord with your father, but in the future, there may be wild rumors circulating about me, and I want you to hear the truth."

"I'm delighted you feel that way. I can see that you're distressed. Please unburden yourself."

"First, you're correct about Lord Barrett and me. I can't speak to his level of attachment, but as for myself, I'm madly in love with him."

"I knew it!" Penny staunchly declared.

"When I came to Roland, I had no idea about your connection to him. I swear it! Nor was I aware he'd be a guest too *or* that he was about to betroth himself. I especially wasn't aware of that. He didn't bother to apprise me."

"Of course he didn't!" Penny suffered a wave of indignation on her behalf. "Isn't that just like a man to trick you over it?"

"I had actually traveled to the country to escape him. Our amour bubbled up so swiftly that it scared me. I couldn't deduce how to tamp it down so I thought—if I disappeared from London— he'd grow tired of the chase. But then, I arrived here, and he was here too. It's an impossible situation."

"You can put your mind at ease about it. I won't wed him! I promise you. If you part with him later on and can assure me it's over, I might consider him as a husband, but not until then."

Libby smiled. "If I didn't already like you so much, I would cherish you for that comment alone."

At learning of Libby's heightened regard, Penny beamed with pride. If she could have picked an older sister for herself, she'd have picked Libby Carstairs. Who wouldn't want such a flamboyant, stunning female for a sibling?

"What is the other thing?" she asked. "You said there were two topics. And be extremely blunt, for whatever it is, if you don't inform me, no one else will."

Libby snorted at that. "I fear this one will generate intense gossip—for it's very shocking. If you don't choose to accept my account, I'll understand, but I hope you'll at least contemplate the ramifications. No matter what you think, I'd appreciate it if you wouldn't call me a liar. I've been through enough of that today."

"Who has been calling you a liar?"

"Mostly your father and Lord Barrett."

Penny scoffed. "I've stated my opinion about them. If they've deemed you a liar, then I'm positive *I* shall view you as the most honest person in the kingdom."

"After I reveal my secret, you might not be so convinced of my veracity."

"Try me. Let's see what reaction you get."

Without hesitating, without debate, Libby announced, "I am your lost half-sister, Little Henrietta. I'm not dead, and I'm not missing. I'm right here."

Penny studied Libby's features, then said, "It only makes sense, doesn't it? I mean, look at us! We could practically be twins. It definitely explains the bond we've shared from the very start. Have you told Father?"

"Yes, but he didn't believe me. Neither did Lord Barrett."

"Ooh, they are such idiots!"

"Your Aunt Millicent was quite incensed too."

"Then I add her to my list of despicable people."

"They presume I devised the story in order to extort money from your father."

"Have I mentioned that they're idiots?" Penny said.

"I'm not surprised by their rancor or skepticism, but it's why I have to depart. I can't tarry when my presence is so divisive."

"This is my home too!" Penny huffed. "I refuse to let them chase you away."

"Penny..." Libby sighed. "You're not thinking clearly about this. Imagine how your father feels. Imagine the drama this will stir. I need to absent myself so everyone can come to terms with the news."

"They might not ever come to terms with it. Your supposed *death* has shaped our lives. If we didn't have you to mourn, what would we talk about?"

"My goodness, don't ever repeat that. I've caused enough trouble, and I simply have to leave. I'm incredibly enraged over how I've been treated."

"I don't blame you, but won't you delay so I can speak to Father? I'm certain I can smooth things over with him. With Lord Barrett too. I'll persuade them to apologize."

"I don't want them to apologize," Libby said.

"The afternoon is waning. You can't traipse off when evening is approaching. That would be very reckless."

"I can't bear to dawdle, but this doesn't have to be farewell for you and me. You can visit me in London. You'd always be welcome."

"I'd like that! I will visit, and I don't care how much Father complains about it."

Libby stood and motioned to her satchel. "Why don't you let me finish packing? It's painful for me to linger."

"All right. I'll cease my nagging, but I won't cease being offended about this."

"It's nice to know I have one friend in the world, and she's on my side."

"I'll always be your staunchest ally! Don't allow Father or Lord Barrett to drag you down. They're not worth it."

"I'm sure they're not."

Astonishing them both, Penny stepped in and gave Libby a tight hug. She doubted Libby had had many hugs in her life. Nor had Penny.

"I'm glad we're sisters," Penny whispered in Libby's ear.

"So am I."

"I will travel to town to visit you the minute this party is over. Would next week be too soon?"

"No, it wouldn't be too soon."

"I won't say goodbye then, not when we'll be together again shortly."

"I'm looking forward to it."

Penny smiled with satisfaction, then she hurried out, determined to find her father and inform him just what an obtuse ass he'd become. How could he be so blind about Libby? Penny would set him straight, and she wouldn't listen to any nonsense to the contrary.

FISH SAT IN CHARLES'S bedroom. She was sipping a whiskey, waiting for him, and curious about what would happen when he arrived. He'd invited her to tarry, and she liked loafing. It furnished her with a chance to snoop through his belongings.

Though it was foolish to daydream, she was anxious for Charles to fall in love with her again. It was dangerous fantasizing that would only lead to heartache in the end, but she couldn't stop herself. Why not wish for the best for a change? What if the *best* actually occurred for once?

Unfortunately, her brash decision to dawdle had landed her in a precarious spot. His shrewish sister-in-law, Millicent, had stumbled on Fish precisely where she shouldn't have been. She'd glared at Fish as if she were a thief, then she'd run off, probably to locate Charles and demand to know why Fish was in his private suite.

Fish would like to have been a mouse in the corner during that conversation. She'd warned Charles that Millicent viewed herself as his wife, but he wouldn't admit she had any designs on him. How had he explained Fish's presence? He likely *wouldn't* have explained it, which would put Millicent in a permanent snit.

If she was enraged, then the house would be pitched into an uproar, so Fish's sojourn might be about to conclude. The realization was incredibly depressing, but she wasn't stupid. If her relationship with Charles started to cause problems, he'd ask Fish to leave. She yearned to hope he wouldn't behave that way, but she wasn't exactly a female he would fight to keep by his side, despite how they were carrying on.

Finally, she heard him coming. He closed the door and called, "Fish, are you here?"

"Yes, Charles, I'm in the bedroom." He marched across the floor, his strides slow and measured, as if he was exhausted, and she seized the initiative. "Millicent caught me, and she was livid. Did she find you?"

"Yes, she found me."

"I'm betting it wasn't pleasant."

"As always, Fish, you are a master of understatement."

He walked over and sat in a chair next to her. There was a small table between them, a liquor tray with a decanter and a glass on it.

"Will you have a drink with me?" she asked.

He nodded, and she poured it for him and handed it over. They sipped in silence, and they were so compatible they might have been an old married couple. She could have lazed there with him forever and died a happy woman.

After a bit, he sighed and murmured, "What an awful day."

"You look absolutely devastated. Dare I inquire about your chat with Millicent? I'm sorry she bumped into me. If I'd had any idea she would barge in, I'd have crawled into the wardrobe and hid until she departed."

He smirked. "She's worried we might be having an affair."

"Did you confirm the worst? Or did you deny it?"

She tried to appear as if she was teasing, but if he'd claimed they weren't involved, she'd be very hurt. She wasn't an innocent maiden who had a reputation to preserve, and she didn't care about Millicent Pendleton. But she cared about Charles and his opinion. If he couldn't confess his mischief with Fish, what would that indicate about how he viewed their amour?

"I neither confirmed nor denied it," he said, "so she was left wondering."

"Considering I was in your bedroom, I doubt she's wondering very hard."

"I don't like to upset her."

"You don't like to upset anyone."

"I won't stir discord for any reason."

"That's because you stirred plenty of it when you were young."

"Yes, and I didn't like how it thrust my life into the public eye."

"You could have admitted we were dallying," she said. "I wouldn't have minded. I'm barely acquainted with your sister-in-law, and after the party ends, I'll never see her again. If she believes I'm a slattern, it wouldn't bother me."

She shifted in the chair so she could watch him and judge how he assessed the remark. She'd given him several openings where he could have insisted she was staying on after the party, but he didn't latch onto any of her overtures.

Instead, he frowned and said, "Millicent told me the most disturbing story, and I have to ask you about it."

"I should be able to drum up an answer for you."

"How long have you known Libby?"

"Eight years maybe? Or nine? Her Uncle Harry hired me to dress her after she turned sixteen. Why?"

"A housemaid was eavesdropping on her and Mr. Falcon. She tattled to Millicent."

"About what? From your expression, it must have been terrible, but I can't imagine Libby speaking offensively about you. She likes you very much."

"They were talking about Little Henrietta. Evidently, Libby is preparing to announce that she's my lost daughter."

"Oh."

Fish was very self-centered, and in all of her musings about Millicent and Charles, she'd conveniently neglected to ponder Libby and her wild tale about her paternity. It had been too fantastical, and Fish had resolved to focus on it later, once they were in London and she could read the letters.

Charles studied her strangely, then asked, "Had Libby mentioned it to you?"

"Yes, she mentioned it."

"How long ago?"

"Just this afternoon. I was with her when you sent a maid to fetch her downstairs. She informed me right before she went to meet with you."

"Prior to that, you had no idea?" He looked extremely skeptical.

"No."

"According to the maid who overheard them, it's a scheme she and Mr. Falcon cooked up to extort money from me. They're hoping I'll accept that she's Henrietta or perhaps that I'll tender a bribe so they'll go away." He sipped his drink, scrutinizing her over the rim of his glass. "You're intimately acquainted with both of them. Which scenario would you deem to be more likely?"

Fish huffed with aggravation. "Libby wouldn't trick you like that. She doesn't have a dishonest bone in her body."

"What about Mr. Falcon? Would he trick me?"

Fish wasn't keen to wade into those murky waters. Simon possessed all of Harry's dubious traits and then some. He might engage in any wicked plot.

"After Harry died," she said, "Libby found a box of letters he'd stashed away. That's all I can tell you about it. I haven't seen them."

"If the housemaid hadn't accidently stumbled on their discussion, I wouldn't have been apprised in advance. When Libby came forward, I'd have been blindsided."

"You weren't though."

She didn't like how he was evaluating her, as if he was checking for details that might catch her in a lie. He'd already judged Libby and Simon to be guilty, and suddenly, she felt as if she was skating on very thin ice.

"Would you ever have told me about this?" he asked. "Or are you so loyal to Libby that you'd have kept it a secret? Would you have remained silent and let her shout her falsehoods to the world?"

"I wasn't keeping anything from you! I've known about this a few minutes longer than you have. I thought it was very far-fetched, and I asked if I could read the letters once we return to London. She agreed that I could, and I had decided I would proceed from there—depending on what they say."

"If she spreads her nonsense, have you the slightest clue of the inferno that will ignite?"

"I can imagine how explosive it would be."

"I would hate it, and I don't mean to insult you, Fish—"

"Then don't."

"—but I need you to look me in the eye and swear you weren't part of this. When you showed up at Roland, I was so excited, but now, I'm wondering if it wasn't terribly convenient for you to have arrived with Libby."

She bristled. "What are you implying? I suggest you be very, very clear."

"Was this a scheme they fomented prior to traveling here? Were they aware that you and I are old friends? Did they invite you along to help them ingratiate themselves?"

Her jaw dropped. "Of all the despicable, rude, vile—"

He held up his hands, warding off her fury. "I'm simply curious about what's happening. Somehow, Libby has figured out the exact way to entice me into believing her. I would cut off my right arm to find Henrietta, but I won't be manipulated like this."

"I only just learned about it myself! You have more information about it than I do. How dare you accuse me of bad conduct!"

"I've asked her to vacate the premises."

"Oh, Charles. You didn't."

"She's involved in a torrid affair with Lord Barrett, and it's distracting him from proposing to Penny. I thought it would be best if she departed."

"You've seen how he gazes at her," Fish said, "so if you think you can tamp down his fascination by sending her back to town, you're mad. He's wild for her, and I doubt you can persuade him to leave her alone."

"You'd watched their amour unfold, yet you brought her here anyway."

"I didn't know the enamored scoundrel would be at Roland! Libby didn't either. We were attempting to hide from him, but when we rolled in, he was standing in your driveway. Don't blame me because he's a rutting dog who can't control himself."

"You have to speak to Libby for me."

"About what?"

"You must dissuade her so she doesn't circulate these bizarre tales about being Henrietta. It would stir a scandal that would never die down, and she has to promise she'll never mention it to anyone. She has to realize that there would be dire consequences for disseminating baseless rumors."

"Are you threatening her?"

"No." He scoffed as if the notion was absurd.

"It definitely sounds to me as if you're threatening her. What if I read the letters and they seem genuine? Have you considered that for a single second?"

"Letters can be forged."

"And some letters might not be. What if she's your daughter? Aren't you concerned about that possibility? What if you spurn her now, only to discover in the future that she was telling the truth? How will you ever convince her to forgive you?"

"Henrietta is dead," he callously stated. "She's been dead for two decades, and I won't have Libby Carstairs and Simon Falcon dredging up this painful issue." He paused, then added with a grim finality, "I *won't* tolerate it."

"Fine. I'll talk to her for you."

Fish wasn't serious precisely, and in any dispute, she'd side with Libby. Harry had certainly been wily enough to perpetrate such a fraud, but he could never have coerced Libby into being the bait. And if he was planning to run a swindle, why hadn't he begun much earlier? Why wait until Libby was grown?

Charles had offered a huge reward for Henrietta's safe return, so Harry would have profited financially if he'd handed her over, and it wasn't like him to ignore his worst impulses. Could the reality be that a very deranged Amanda Pendleton had glommed onto his brother Kit, then Kit had perished at sea, while trying to *rescue* her from Charles?

Afterward, had Harry wound up with Libby dumped in his lap, but not sure of what to do about it?

Might he have debated and pondered, but as the months—then years—went by, perhaps he'd lost the chance to come forward? Or had he actually suffered a fatherly affection for Libby? They'd been very close. Had she gradually become the daughter he'd never had?

With Harry deceased and unable to explain, who could guess how his devious mind had worked? Should Fish theorize over any of that? Probably not. In light of Charles's angry mood, she wasn't about to expound on cunning, deceitful Harry Carstairs.

She was anxious to smooth over their bitter words, so she was stunned when he said, "I think you should depart with her."

She bristled. "You're kicking me out too?"

"Let's not say I'm *kicking* you out. Let's just say I need an interval away from you while I digest what's transpired."

"Why is any of this my fault?"

"I'm not claiming it's your fault. I'm simply bewildered by events, and I refuse to be dragged into a quagmire by your two acquaintances."

"I haven't caused any trouble. I just crawled into your bed because you're a randy goat who can't keep his trousers buttoned."

"We shouldn't have rekindled our affair. It was a mistake."

She was surprised she didn't slap him. "It's a little late for you to decide it was a mistake, but it's what I should have expected from you. Twenty years have passed, but you're still a pompous ass."

"I'm sorry." His cheeks heated, so apparently, he was capable of some shame.

"You don't look sorry," she fumed.

She downed her whiskey, slammed the glass on the table, then stood and marched out.

As she reached the door, he said, "Fish!"

She halted and glared over her shoulder. "What?"

"I'll write you in a few days or . . . or . . . next time I'm in town, we'll get together." He forced a smile. "I apologize for upsetting you. Once I calm down, I'll contact you."

Could he assume she'd want to hear from him again? After he'd insulted and offended her? After he'd accused her of duplicitous conduct? After he'd threatened Libby and accused her of awful conduct too?

"Don't put yourself out on my behalf, *Lord* Roland." She hurled the comment with an incredible amount of venom. "Should you ever deign to lower your grand self to write me, I will always be too busy to respond."

She whipped away and continued on, and to her great annoyance, he didn't call to her again. Nor did he chase her down to stop her from going.

Chapter
19

HOWARD PERIWINKLE, WHO PICTURED himself as the most dedicated of newspaper reporters, lurked in the woods near the gate that led onto Lord Roland's estate. Previously, after he'd tried to speak with Miss Carstairs, the earl had had a pair of burly footmen run him off. Lord Roland probably assumed he'd fled back to town like a scared rabbit, but he didn't have to be in London until the next day, so he hadn't left the area.

Instead, he'd been loafing on the lane to the village and buying people drinks at the local tavern. He'd heard many stories about the party at Roland, and he remained dreadfully curious about Miss Carstairs. Everyone in the kingdom was curious about her, and with it being the twentieth anniversary of her rescue, interest was even higher than usual.

Apparently, at Lady Penny's request, she'd given the guests a private performance, and he'd have paid a thousand pounds to have seen it. He'd been in the audience in London several times when she'd been on the stage there. She was just so beautiful, and it was thrilling to watch her. He was fascinated and not about to abandon his quest to obtain an interview.

A housemaid was approaching, and it was a girl he'd strolled with twice as she'd completed errands for the housekeeper. She was a lazy, sullen creature who wasn't very bright. His attention made her feel important, so no effort had been required to befriend her.

She was quite greedy too, and he always slipped a few pennies into her palm when she finished gossiping. He wondered if Millicent Pendleton knew how much she liked to talk about her betters. If her tendencies were ever revealed, he doubted she'd be employed very long.

"Ho, ho, Miss Peggy!" he said, and he waved. "Are you off to the village again? May I accompany you?"

"I'm not walking there this afternoon. I just had to tell you something."

He removed his hat and placed it over his heart. "You were thinking of me? I'm flattered."

"If I don't share this with someone, I might bust from holding it inside. I can't mention it to any servants at the manor, so I thought of you."

"My goodness! I'm all ears."

"You can't ever admit how you learned of it."

"I never would. I promise."

"And you have to swear you'll protect Lord Roland. He's a kind man, and I won't have him hurt by swindlers and frauds."

"Who would want to hurt him?"

"I can hardly believe it, but it's that Miss Carstairs. The whole time she stayed with us, she seemed so nice."

"Libby Carstairs, behaving badly? No! I don't believe it either."

"Mostly, it's that cousin of hers. Mr. Falcon?"

"I know him well," Periwinkle said. He'd been attempting to confer with Miss Carstairs for weeks and Falcon had been a staunch barrier, preventing it.

"They have cooked up a scheme whereby Miss Carstairs will claim she is Lord Roland's long-lost daughter, Little Henrietta."

Periwinkle blanched with astonishment. "She'll claim she's Little Henrietta? Oh, oh, oh, this is shocking!"

"Mr. Falcon told her it was a *brilliant* plan. That was his exact word: brilliant."

"How did you stumble on this information?"

She hesitated and her cheeks flushed. "I can't say, but they were very clear."

Which meant she'd eavesdropped when she shouldn't have.

"Why tell me about it?" he asked. "I work for a newspaper. There's no way I'll keep this a secret."

"What if *they* go to the newspapers? I'm convinced they will, and if you have advance warning, you'll be able to send them packing. You can print that it's a lie."

"Yes, I see what you mean."

The more likely scenario was that she loathed Lord Roland and was anxious to stir trouble for him, while acting as if she was being noble. Periwinkle wouldn't try to decipher her motives, but he was delightfully glad that he'd curried her favor.

"Now then," she said, "I have to get back."

She didn't head off though, and he realized she was waiting to be paid. He sighed, reached into his pocket, and withdrew his purse. As he slapped the coins into her palm, her avaricious eyes gleamed with glee.

"Thank you for confiding in me," he said.

"The minute I heard them conspiring, I was sure you'd be eager to know."

"If you discover any other outrageous tidbits, find me at once. My purse is full, and you're welcome to empty it."

She grinned and strutted away. He watched her until she vanished down the lane, then he blew out a heavy breath.

"Little Henrietta," he mused to the quiet forest. "Home at last. What an exciting tale this will be."

He didn't waste any energy debating whether it was true or not. Libby Carstairs had intrigued the nation from the instant she'd been found on that deserted island. And Lord Roland was a tragic figure with whom the whole kingdom had grieved when his mad ex-wife had disappeared with his tiny daughter.

It was the perfect ending for both of them, and he, Howard Periwinkle, would be the man to share it with the world.

"MILLICENT, WILL YOU COME in here please?"

She halted, gnashing her teeth, and desperately wondering if she dared to continue on, but it was Charles who had summoned her. She had no idea how to ignore him.

He was in his library, sitting behind the desk where he'd been when they'd quarreled earlier. If she'd suspected he might still be there, she'd have walked down another hall.

"What do you want?" she demanded.

"I won't shout at you from across the room. Come in here!"

She stomped in and pulled up a chair, but she was perched on the edge of her seat, ready to march out at the least provocation. She glared silently, not inclined to make the conversation easy for him. *He* was the one consorting with a trollop while they had a house full of impressionable young people. He could spit it out or not. At the moment, she was beyond caring.

After a bit of dithering, he said, "I have asked Miss Carstairs to leave for London, and she's agreed she would. She'll depart first thing in the morning."

"Good. I won't be sorry to see her go. Will that be all?"

"Miss Fishburn will go with her."

Millicent wouldn't touch that comment with a ten-foot pole. "Fine."

"I've instructed Miss Fishburn to speak with her about the rumors she's keen to spread. Miss Fishburn will advise her that there will be dire consequences if she defames me."

"I'm certain that will scare the daylights out of her."

"I think it will too," he concurred, not noting her sarcasm.

"What about her cousin?" Millicent inquired. "That odious Mr. Falcon? He's in the thick of their plotting."

"I'd completely forgotten about him. I suppose he'll accompany them, won't he? Why would he tarry at Roland without them?"

"Why indeed?" she caustically seethed. "Perhaps he hasn't yet stolen any of the silver, and he needs a few more hours to learn where we keep it."

"Don't be shrewish. It was difficult for me to be rude to them, and I never like to be discourteous."

Except to me! she nastily thought. "You're positive you've handled Miss Carstairs appropriately? You've successfully crushed their scheme?"

"I'm as sure as I can be without physically gagging her."

"Well, then, it should work out swimmingly."

Her mockery was biting, but she couldn't tamp it down. She was just so angry! After all the years she'd sacrificed for him! After all the years she'd tried to make him happy! Her reward was that he'd allowed himself to be seduced by a seamstress!

At her snide retort, a glimmer of fury flashed in his eyes. They never fought, mostly because he refused to exhibit strident emotion, but they were both grouchy and feeling unfairly harassed.

An uncommon argument might have erupted, but suddenly, Penny rushed in. She dashed over to the desk and fumed, "Father! How could you!"

He sighed with what sounded like exhaustion. "Whatever it is, Penny, I can't listen to it now. Your aunt and I are having a private discussion. Would you excuse us?"

Of course the spoiled brat ignored him. "You kicked Libby out of the house! I'm so ashamed of you!"

"Penny," he said, "this entire day has been horrific. Would you cease your nagging? We can chat about it later, when I'm in a better mood."

"I've notified Luke that I won't marry him," she blithely announced. "He's in love with Libby, so there's no reason to proceed with a betrothal."

Millicent bristled. "The choice is not up to you, Penny."

"Stay out of this, Aunt Millicent! This is between me and my father." Penny turned her livid gaze on Charles. "You kicked Libby out, so *I* kicked Luke out. We don't need him here."

Charles sighed even more heavily. "I wish you'd talked to me first."

"I talked to you, and you were dismissive of my every complaint."

Charles's shoulders sank. "I'm sorry. I should have been more understanding."

"Don't you dare beg her pardon!" Millicent sharply said. "She doesn't get to voice an opinion as to whom she marries. Nor does she get to insult Luke this way. She will not defy you! Not in my presence." Millicent glared at her niece. "Apologize to your father at once!"

Penny rolled her eyes at Millicent's command and addressed Charles instead. "Libby told me the news."

"What news?" Charles asked.

"She's Little Henrietta."

Charles and Millicent gasped in unison. Charles was too stunned to respond, but Millicent managed to inquire, "When did she tell you that?"

"Just now. I stopped by her room as she was packing. She's been lost for over two decades, but she's finally home where she belongs, and you—Charles Pendleton—kicked her out without wondering if her story might be true."

"We wondered," Millicent firmly stated, "and it's not."

"Says who?" Penny sneered. "Says you?"

"Your father and I already decided that she's a liar. It's why he forced her to leave. We can't have her strutting about and ruining our lives with gossip and innuendo."

"It's not a lie," Penny insisted.

"Have a care for your father, Penny," Millicent warned. "Have you any idea what this would do to him? Have you any idea of the circus that would ensue? We won't be part of it, and you've distressed him plenty for one afternoon. Go away and let us finish our discussion."

Charles seemed to have been struck dumb, and Millicent snapped, "Charles! For pity's sake, speak up for yourself. Explain to Penny why she's wrong. We can't have her disseminating these unfounded rumors."

Penny was undeterred. "They're not unfounded."

Charles shook himself out of his stupor. "Miss Carstairs swore to me she wouldn't mention this to anyone."

"She didn't mention it to just *anyone*," Penny said. "She told me! She told her sister, and I'm glad she did."

Millicent had had enough. "You need to shut your mouth about this. Head to your room and remain there until you've calmed down and thought this through."

"You can't send me to my bedchamber as if I'm a misbehaved child," Penny said. "You're not in charge of me anymore."

"Charles!" Millicent protested. "Will you allow her to sass me? Do you see what I put up with from her?"

He didn't answer her, but said to Penny, "I'm very troubled. Could we please not fight?"

"I believe Libby," was Penny's reply.

"You shouldn't," Millicent scolded. "She's a fraud, and it's precisely the reaction she's hoping to elicit from you."

"Be silent, Aunt Millicent!" Penny raged, then she said to Charles, "Aren't you curious, Father, about how you'll repair this if she's really Henrietta? She came home, and you evicted her. How will you ever sufficiently apologize?"

She whipped away and stormed out, and they were too astounded to call her back. She was such an obstinate nuisance that she wouldn't have halted anyway.

Once the tension settled, Millicent smiled a tight smile at Charles. "You certainly have it under control, don't you? I'm so delighted with how you threatened Miss Carstairs so she obeyed you. You have her trembling in her boots."

Millicent scoffed with disgust, stood, and stomped out too. He dawdled behind his desk, frozen in place like a bump on a log.

<hr>

CHARLES WAS WALKING ACROSS the foyer, intending to slink to his bedchamber to lick his wounds in private, when he happened to glance out a window. Luke was in the driveway. His horse was saddled, and it was obvious he was leaving.

Charles marched out to him and said, "Penny informed me that she'd ordered you to return to Barrett, but I didn't imagine you'd listen."

"It's not so much that I've obliged her," Luke said, "but I agree with her. My presence is stirring problems."

"Let's go inside and talk about it." Charles was practically begging. "Penny doesn't get to choose her husband. You and I will come to terms—or not. Don't slither away simply because she's being a brat."

"It's not that, Charles. She knows about my affair with Libby."

Charles winced. "She mentioned it to you?"

"Yes. She was very blunt about it, so you and I can't proceed toward an engagement. We can confer in the future—when she's not quite so livid and I'm not quite so distracted."

"I suppose that's better," Charles grudgingly concurred.

"It's not as if I'm about to run off and wed someone else. At the moment, I just can't continue on with *her*. When she's so irate, it would be too awkward."

"You're correct of course."

"I didn't mean to sneak away," Luke said. "I looked for you, to apprise you, but I couldn't find you."

"I've been hiding. I have a few *issues* that are plaguing me, and I'm not dealing with them very well."

"Yes, Libby told me she's claiming to be Little Henrietta."

Charles blanched. "Oh, no. Is there anyone she hasn't told?"

"It's why I was trying to locate you. I thought you might like to chat about it." Luke studied his morose expression, then said, "Or maybe not. What are you thinking?"

"I'm *not* thinking. I'm completely flummoxed. I only learned about it because a housemaid eavesdropped when Libby was conspiring with her cousin. It definitely sounds as if they're hatching a plot to cheat me out of a ton of money."

"Mr. Falcon is a dodgy character, but Libby has always seemed very straightforward to me. Despite what nonsense her cousin might pursue, I doubt she'd join in if it was duplicitous."

"Did you ask her if she was Henrietta?"

"I accused her of lying," Luke said, "so she's furious with me. Penny is furious with me too, and I can't abide this quarreling. I just want to head home so matters can cool."

"You're lucky you can escape. I'm stuck here."

"How about if we meet in a few days and figure out where we are?"

"I'll stop by next week," Charles said. "How about that?"

"That's fine, but in the interim, what about Libby?"

"So far, I've misplayed my hand with her. I had Miss Fishburn advise Libby that there would be consequences for spreading a false story about me."

"You had Miss Fishburn threaten Libby for you?"

Charles huffed with offense. "I didn't have her threatened! I simply had Miss Fishburn clarify the dangers of slandering a man in my position."

Luke snorted with amusement. "Libby's not the kind of girl you could scare easily."

"I wasn't trying to scare her!" Charles insisted. "I was trying to reason with her."

"You can't *reason* with a female like her. She's too independent."

"You've got that right, and Miss Fishburn is even worse."

"What will you do now?" Luke asked.

"Now I'll . . . I'll . . ." Charles cut off his sentence, feeling befuddled and at a loss. "I have no idea what I'll do, but I can't have her waltzing around London and spewing these wild tales. Have you any notion of the ruckus it would create? But I haven't been able to persuade her to be silent."

"Have you offered her money?" Charles was aghast, and Luke hurriedly explained, "If it's a blackmail scheme, the sooner you pay her, the sooner it will go away."

"What if it's not blackmail, Luke? What if she's telling the truth?"

They froze, pondering the prospect, then Luke said, "I have no answer to that question, and I'm glad *you* have to wrestle with it rather than me. Have you noticed though that she and Penny look exactly alike?"

"Yes, I've noticed."

Charles might have stepped away then, to let Luke be on his way, but a rider was trotting up the lane. In his brown suit and bowler hat, he was familiar, but Charles couldn't recall who he was. As he neared, Charles realized it was the reporter who'd been harassing Libby. He bristled with aggravation.

The cheeky devil pranced directly up to Charles, and he climbed down and tipped his hat.

"Lord Roland," he said, "I apologize for bothering you again."

"If you don't leave at once, I will have my footmen drag you off."

Luke frowned. "Who is this?"

"He's a newspaper reporter who is pestering Miss Carstairs."

"Howard Periwinkle." The oaf brazenly introduced himself, grinning at Luke as he said, "And you are . . . ?"

Luke ignored him and told Charles, "You don't have to summon any footmen. I'm happy to drag him off myself. I'll pummel him first though."

Periwinkle was undeterred. "There's no need for violence, sir. I'm off to town this very moment, but before I depart, I just had to seek a comment from Lord Roland. You see, I have it on good authority that a miracle has occurred."

"What are you talking about?" Charles asked.

"Apparently, Little Henrietta has returned, and lo and behold, she's England's darling, Miss Libby Carstairs! Henrietta has been hiding in plain sight as the Mystery Girl of the Caribbean! It's the most fantastical ending in the world. Who could have fathomed it? You must be overwhelmed with joy. Would you like to provide a few remarks for our readers?"

The insolent idiot had disgorged so many shocking statements that Charles couldn't decide where to begin in addressing them. Who had tattled? And so quickly too! It had to have been Libby. With the rumors circulating so widely, how would Charles ever tamp them down?

Luke grabbed Periwinkle by his coat and lifted him so they were nose to nose.

"I can't guess where you received such ludicrous information," Luke fiercely said, "but Henrietta has not been found, and Miss Carstairs is not Lord Roland's lost daughter. If you publish one word of such outlandish gossip, Lord Roland will have your newspaper shut down, and you'll be jailed for the rest of your days."

"I can't be jailed for printing the truth!" Periwinkle said.

"It's not the truth," Luke countered, "and your bravado only proves that you have no clue as to how much power Lord Roland can wield when he's really, really angry."

Luke tossed Periwinkle away, and Periwinkle staggered, almost fell, then straightened. He scooped up his hat and smashed it onto his head.

"All righty then." He said to Charles, "I take it you have no reply, but if you change your mind and would like to furnish our readers with your side of the story, please contact me."

He whipped a card out of his coat and offered it to Charles, but Charles glared at it as if it were a venomous snake. Periwinkle dropped it, and it fluttered to the dirt. Then he jumped on his horse and galloped away.

They didn't stop him, although it had been very tempting to have Luke administer the thrashing he'd been eager to supply.

"What an impudent cretin," Luke said. "How will you silence him? You can't permit him to print his lies. Can you imagine the uproar that would ensue? You'd have to hire armed guards to keep the crowds at bay."

"This is a nightmare!" Charles moaned.

"Shall I chase after him? Shall I beat him bloody? If I knock out some of his teeth, he won't be quite so keen to torment you."

Charles tried to picture the repercussions of such a brutal act. Yes, he was an earl and, yes, he was very powerful, but he wasn't the type to have underlings flogged or beaten. In England, there were laws to prohibit an influential man from inflicting his own brand of punishment.

"I don't need you to batter him," Charles said. "I think the better route would be to speak with his boss, so I'll travel to London immediately. His superiors will be sensible, and I'll convince them to see reason."

"And if you can't?"

"I'll have my lawyers meet with them. A hefty lawsuit always gets a person's attention."

"Would you like me to come with you?"

"No. I can handle one measly reporter on my own."

"Let me know when you're back. I'll be anxious to hear the details, and I'm sorry about all of this. I'm sorry Libby caused this trouble. I'm sorry I've upset Penny."

"Don't be sorry. None of it is your fault." Charles forced a smile. "If I was your age, I'd be in love with Libby too. I believe she's gone to town. Will you follow her?"

"I'm conflicted about my feelings for her. If she's tricked you about being Henrietta, I have no idea where that will leave me."

"I can't figure out where it leaves me either," Charles sullenly stated.

They chuckled wearily, then Luke mounted and rode off. Charles watched until he was swallowed up by the trees, then he went inside to find the butler and declare that he was off to London as fast as his carriage could convey him there.

***

"Where have you been?"

Simon pulled up short and grinned at Penny. They were behind the manor, on a gravel path that led from the barns to the house. The afternoon was waning, the sun drooping in the western sky.

From the frantic tone of her query, it was obvious she was growing overly attached, which he was delighted to observe. At least he assumed he was delighted.

He'd commenced his flirtation as a lark, as a jest. She was rich and pretty, and he'd been sure he could persuade her to give him all sorts of things she shouldn't. But should he proceed?

He genuinely liked her, and for once, he was suffering qualms. He'd had to absent himself for several hours so he could deduce what he'd like to have happen. If he kept walking down the road he was currently walking, he might wind up married to her. He'd dangled the prospect of an elopement, and she'd been amenable. Could he whisk her away from her family?

He couldn't predict if Lord Roland would cut ties and disinherit her over such a rash deed, but Simon couldn't envision her living in reduced circumstances. Was he reckless enough to put her in such jeopardy?

Unfortunately, he thought he might be, but she deserved a different conclusion than the one he would provide.

"Did you miss me?" he asked, his grin widening.

"Don't be pompous," she said. "My patience for your vain posturing has vanished."

He laughed. "Well, excuse me then. What's wrong?"

"A thousand tragedies have cropped up, and I've been searching for you so you could help me sift through them."

"I took a ride. Your father has the most beautiful animals in his stable. I couldn't resist."

"I wish you'd told me you were going," she said. "I'd have gone with you."

"I figured you'd be too busy with your guests. Perhaps we can try for tomorrow, but can you really suppose your aunt would let you traipse off with me?"

"I can bring my groom or I can have some friends tag along."

"If we have to bring chaperones, they'll suck the fun out of it."

Dare he be alone with her again? They'd already misbehaved in numerous ways that would get him shot by her father if their antics were discovered, and he was wondering if he shouldn't yank her off the ledge where she was perched with him. Should he save her from herself?

He couldn't decide, and the fact that he was questioning his motives was so out of character that he was worried he might be ill.

"Libby headed back to London," she said without preamble. "Miss Fishburn went with her."

"What? Why?"

"My father kicked her out. He didn't like how Lord Barrett was mooning over her. He claimed it was distracting Luke from proposing to me."

"It probably was. I've explained how besotted he is."

"But also, we've learned a shocking secret about Libby, and it will create a huge scandal, which my father hates. He was livid about it, so he sent her away."

Simon was certain as to what the topic would be, and he debated his reply. Libby had ordered him to remain silent about her sudden insistence that she was Henrietta. Initially, he'd accused her of plotting a swindle, but Libby wouldn't engage in duplicitous conduct. Simon would, but not Libby.

If she had documents to prove she was Lord Roland's daughter, then she likely was, but what should his comments about it be to Penny?

"What was the secret?" he tentatively asked.

"Don't pretend to be confused. She's my lost sister." When he didn't confirm the news, she said, "You can admit it. I was convinced the minute she told me."

"I didn't realize she planned to announce it."

"She didn't. A housemaid eavesdropped when you were talking to her. People deem you to be a confidence artist who might involve yourself in any nefarious mischief."

He smirked. "They might be right."

"So they're painting her with the same bad brush. They contend she's hoping to blackmail my father."

"She wouldn't do that."

"I know that, and you know that, but my father and aunt are in an absolute snit."

"I can imagine."

"Why didn't you tell me about her? You concealed it from me, so I'm concerned about the level of your attachment."

"She only apprised me earlier this afternoon," Simon said. "After my father died, she found some old letters he'd hidden, and she's been struggling over how to come forward."

"You haven't been deceiving me?"

She studied his eyes, hunting for dishonesty, and he gazed back intently and said, "Of course I haven't been deceiving you. How could you think I would?"

Apparently, she located the candor for which she'd been searching, for she nodded. "I believe you."

"You'd better."

"And I believe Libby, about her being my sister."

"She wouldn't lie about it."

"I can't fathom why my father doesn't understand that fact."

"It has to be a lot for him to absorb. Once he calms down, he might change his mind about it. She's always wanted to be part of a big family, and it would make me happy to have her settled with you."

It was the appropriate sentiment to offer, but he wasn't serious because—if Lord Roland broke down and accepted Libby as his daughter—what would it mean for Simon? If her story was true, then Simon wasn't really her cousin, but she was very loyal and would never leave him behind.

If Lord Roland relented and embraced her, Simon would constantly rub elbows with the Pendletons. Penny would be wedged into the middle of his life, and with her being willing to have him there, was there any reason to avoid her? Her father would never permit them to wed, so perhaps an elopement was a viable plan.

Her smile turned sly. "Guess what else?"

He was almost afraid to ask. "What?"

"I sent Lord Barrett home. I pressed him about his affair with Libby, but the coward wouldn't even discuss her, so I told him I'm not interested in a betrothal."

"He left?"

"Yes. I demanded it, so I'm free and available to do whatever I'd like instead."

He snorted at that. "Not exactly *whatever*, I don't suppose."

"If I choose to encourage the attentions of a younger man who is much more to my liking, I can, and I won't be branded a flirt."

"Is there a *young* man who's tantalized you?" he cockily inquired.

"You know there is."

"If we keep on, it has to be a secret. You can't let your father find out. If he suspected we were growing too close, he'd have me kidnapped and dumped onto the first ship bound for the Orient. I'd never see you again."

"My dear Simon Falcon, that will never happen."

"I will pray that you're correct."

He stared up at the manor, wondering what was winging in his direction. He felt a terrible perception of peril lurking, as if he'd tiptoed out as far as he dared onto the wobbly cliff where they were hovering, but then, he liked to live dangerously.

"Am I kicked out of Roland too?" he asked. "Was I expected to slither away with Libby and Fish?"

"No one has remembered you. In everyone's haste to be shed of Libby, no one thought about you at all."

"I usually hate to be ignored, but for once, maybe I'm glad of it."

"After supper," she said, " I shall have a headache, so I'll retire to my bedchamber much earlier than normal."

"You, Penny Pendleton, are such a tease."

"Will you join me there after it's safe to sneak in?"

He realized he shouldn't, that it was mad to agree, that it was stupid to agree, but he was Harry Carstairs's son. When had he ever behaved in a sane manner?

"Yes, I'll join you."

He dipped down and stole a quick kiss. He shouldn't have, but the garden was empty, so there were no observers. She grinned, winked, then whipped away and sauntered into the house. He stood in his spot until she disappeared, then he followed after a bit so it wouldn't seem as if they'd entered together.

If he'd had any sense—and he'd always possessed very little of it—he'd proceed to town, even though night was falling. He'd catch up to Libby and Fish and escort them the rest of the way.

But evidently, he wasn't departing Roland just yet. He still had business to conduct with Penny, and until he'd had his fill, he wasn't about to flee.

⌒⌒

MILLICENT PACED IN HER bedchamber, and her temper was on a slow boil.

Charles had derided her warnings about the scandal that was brewing. He'd trusted Libby Carstairs not to spread her falsehoods about being Henrietta, but the instant his meeting with her had ended, she'd started shouting the lie in every direction.

Penny had heard it. Luke had heard it. A London newspaper reporter had heard it and had already accosted Charles.

The housemaid, Peggy, knew it too, and Millicent was no fool. The tidbit about Henrietta would be too delicious for Peggy to resist. Before supper was over, she'd be whispering it to the staff.

Charles had trotted off to London on a mission to thwart Miss Carstairs. His strategy was to bully and sue anyone who refused to be silent about her story, so Millicent had no idea when he'd be back.

Miss Fishburn was in town now too, thanks to Charles insisting she slink off with Miss Carstairs. He loathed London and never went there if he didn't have to, so Millicent couldn't help but fear that Miss Fishburn was a hefty portion of the reason he'd been so eager to rush to the city.

Charles, Penny, and Penny's brother, Warwick, were Millicent's family. She'd abandoned her own for them. She'd given her life to them, and for her efforts, she was ignored by Warwick, scorned by Penny, and disregarded by Charles. He'd rather carry on with a trollop than make a moral commitment to Millicent.

She had to reestablish her position in the family. She had to remind them that she was a valued member, and they were lucky she was so loyal and faithful, but how could she rekindle their esteem?

Clearly, Charles had no ability to deal effectively with Miss Carstairs. He'd blatantly threatened her, but she wasn't afraid of him, apparently recognizing that he would never be genuinely cruel.

Well, Millicent never worried about being too cruel. Nor did she worry much about how others viewed her. She was perfectly willing to force Miss Carstairs to respect Charles as she ought. In the process, she was positive she could get Miss Fishburn's attention too.

The wicked slattern had waltzed into Millicent's home and assumed she could latch onto Charles, but Charles belonged to Millicent, and she wouldn't blithely surrender what was hers.

What would be best? What course of action would inflict the most damage on both women?

Her mind racing with possibilities, she wandered to the window and stared down into the garden. It was a beautiful summer day, and the vista always soothed her.

Penny was there, dawdling on the path, and to Millicent's great aggravation, Simon Falcon was there too. Charles had rid them of Miss Carstairs, but he'd forgotten to ensure Mr. Falcon left too.

Even from the far distance of Millicent's bedroom, it was obvious the pair was much friendlier than they should be and that Penny was encouraging him. Was she insane?

Mr. Falcon was little more than a criminal. He'd spent his life around circus performers, actors, and other dubious people. He was worldly and flamboyant and much too sophisticated for Penny. What scheme was he hatching? Had he asked her for money? Had she promised to give him some? Or might he have sought other favors? What might they be?

The answers to those questions were terrifying.

Suddenly, Mr. Falcon leaned down and kissed Penny. Right on the lips! Right in the garden where there could be witnesses! Then Penny grinned and sauntered toward the house.

Millicent gasped with dismay and lurched away from the window so Penny wouldn't glance up and see her spying. She braced herself against the wall, her pulse pounding, her temper flaring to an even hotter temperature.

Libby Carstairs had burst into their lives with her horrid seamstress and her devious cousin. Could Millicent stand idly by and let the trio wreck Millicent's bucolic existence? Could she rely on Charles to take charge and handle them?

No, she could not.

Drastic measures were required, and she had to figure out what they should be, then implement them in the quickest manner she could devise.

In the end, Charles would be glad she'd assisted him. She would free him from the machinations of the brazen pests, and he would be grateful for her intervention on his behalf. Perhaps once she'd imposed all the punishments they deserved, he would finally realize how much he cared.

Chapter

20

"I THINK MY HEART is broken."

"It's the normal conclusion to a love affair with an aristocrat."

Libby glared at Fish. "I don't need philosophy from you. I just need you to commiserate for once."

Fish shrugged. "Lord Barrett is a rich, handsome scoundrel who would never have fallen in love or married you, but you involved yourself anyway. In a situation like that, heartbreak is the only option."

They were in London, in the front parlor of their rented home. They were licking their wounds and not yet ready to figure out their next steps. They'd been too battered by their experiences at Roland.

"What about you?" Libby asked. "Is your heart broken?"

"By Charles Pendleton? Are you joking? I let him torment me when I was twenty. I'm smarter now."

"Really? You're not devastated by his tossing you over?"

"I'm feeling a tad low," Fish confessed, "but it will pass."

Libby scoffed. "You're such a liar. You're as forlorn as I am."

"I won't admit that you're correct."

"I hate him!" Libby fumed.

"Who? Charles? He's your father. You can't hate him."

They'd been back for four days, and they were like lost puppies who couldn't find their mother. The house seemed particularly empty, the rooms echoing in a way that underscored their misery. They'd always worked for a living, and it was odd to be loafing, to have no evening show to occupy their hours with preparation.

They jumped at every sound, expecting it to be Simon returning from Roland or perhaps Luke or Charles rushing to apologize. They were wallowing in the same fantasy: that the two men would realize how horridly they'd behaved, and they'd be anxious to proclaim how profoundly sorry they were.

But that type of ending only happened in fairytales, and this was real life. If Libby had to guess, she'd predict that both men had come to their senses and were delighted to have had the liaisons terminate with so little fuss.

"Maybe I don't hate Charles," Libby said. "Maybe I merely loathe him to the marrow of my bones."

"He's complicated. He's persnickety about status and class, but deep down, he's kind, and he worries about how he's viewed by others. He constantly tries to do the right thing."

"You couldn't prove it by me."

Libby was aggrieved over how she'd been evicted. Luke wasn't a gullible boy. He'd leapt into their amour, but *she* had been blamed for it.

She was aggrieved too over how Charles and Luke hadn't believed her about her parentage. She comprehended Charles's reluctance to instantly accept her story, but she'd assumed Luke knew what sort of character she possessed. How could he doubt her?

Where was he at that very moment? Was he still at Roland and ingratiating himself to Penny? Was he about to propose? Would Libby pick up the newspaper some morning and read their engagement announcement? The whole scenario left her sick at her stomach.

The box of Harry's letters was on the table between them, and Fish gestured to it. "I'm stunned by how Harry kept your past a secret. He was such a conniver—and a talker too. How could he have swallowed down this information for so many years? If I had to bet, I'd wager that he'd have blabbed simply so he could be the center of attention when the gossip spread."

"His brother, Kit, insisted Charles was violent, so Harry must have been protecting me."

"Harry—being altruistic? Don't be daft."

"It's not entirely beyond the realm of possibilities."

"Yes, it is," Fish said. "The more likely scenario is that—if he'd come forward—Charles would have yanked you away from him, and he'd have had to surrender the income you generated. If he'd lost yours, he'd have had to generate some of his own, and he was too lazy to support himself. You were his breadwinner."

Libby smirked. "That explanation is probably the closest we'll ever get to a valid answer."

A carriage rattled to a stop out on the street, and they perked up, hoping it would be Simon. They figured he'd tarried at Roland, but if he hadn't, they had no idea where he might be. They were beginning to fret.

Libby went to the window to peer outside, watching as several officious-looking men emerged from the vehicle. They milled and muttered, assessing her house as if they were about to throw her out of it.

"Is it Simon?" Fish asked.

"No. It's a group of men in uniform, but I don't know any of them."

She never liked to have strange men stroll in. It was an old fear, fueled by Harry and his wicked habits when she'd been a child. He'd always had creditors circling, so they'd had to brace for any catastrophe.

Finally, one of the men marched up and banged the knocker. Libby frowned at Fish, wondering what new calamity was about to arise, then she walked over and pulled the door open.

"Yes?" she said. "May I help you?"

He gaped at her, temporarily tongue-tied, then he asked, "Miss Carstairs? Miss Libby Carstairs?"

"Yes, I'm Miss Carstairs."

"I most humbly apologize, but I'm here to arrest you."

"Arrest me?" Libby cocked her head as if he'd misspoken.

"Yes, Miss. For spreading lies about Lord Roland?"

Libby gasped with affront. "Are you joking?"

"It's called slander. A common person such as yourself can't defame such a top-lofty fellow. It's not permitted."

Fish leapt to her feet, and she appeared mad as a hornet. "Charles is accusing her of slander?"

"Are you Miss Fishburn?" was his reply. He flushed, as if he was embarrassed by his task.

"Yes, I'm Fish."

"My apologies to you too, ma'am, but I have to arrest you along with Miss Carstairs."

"On what charge?" Fish demanded.

"On stealing cufflinks from Lord Roland? Apparently, you were caught red-handed in his bedchamber."

Fish's jaw dropped in astonishment as the other men barged in, and they looked much less civil. One of them blustered up and said, "Let's go, ladies. We won't brook any argument or delay."

"May I pack a bag?" Libby asked. "I should grab my reticule too, so I have plenty of money once we're at the facility."

"Yes, you can fetch your things," the first man said, as the second man said, "No, you can't pack anything."

The first man waved her to the stairs. "Fetch what you require, but don't dawdle."

"I'm sure this is in error," Libby insisted. "May I write a note to my cousin and have you mail it to him? He'll post our bail, so there's no need to take us into custody."

"You won't be allowed any bail, Miss Carstairs. I've clarified the gravity of your crimes. You can't commit a felony like this against a nobleman. You'll be lucky if you don't wind up hanged for it."

Libby blanched, but Fish glared and said, "If you stumble on Lord Roland before I do, tell him I will kill him for this. I will absolutely kill him!"

"In light of your situation, Miss Fishburn," the second man huffed, "you shouldn't issue threats. It will only make matters worse for you."

"Who's threatening?" Fish retorted. "I'm deadly serious. I will kill him when I next have the chance."

Fish stomped up the stairs, and as Libby followed, she sighed with disgust. She'd previously spent a night or two in jail. Harry hadn't been all that honest, and whenever he'd been incarcerated, she'd been swept up with him as his ward.

It wouldn't kill her to be detained, but after she was released, she agreed with Fish. She definitely might kill Charles Pendleton.

❧

"Mr. Falcon? I would have a word with you."

Simon glanced over his shoulder, seeing that Millicent Pendleton had spoken to him, which was a bad sign. From the minute he'd arrived at Roland, she'd treated him as if he were invisible, but he hadn't minded.

She didn't like him anymore than he liked her. She thought she was better than he was due to her having posh relatives like Lord Roland, but he deemed himself to be any man's equal and never bowed down.

He pasted on a smile and spun to face her. "Yes, Miss Pendleton, I would be delighted to chat."

"Please join me."

She was standing in the doorway to Lord Roland's library, and she gestured into the ostentatious room. He couldn't wait to hear her comments, and he'd already guessed what the topic would be.

She sat behind the desk, and he sauntered in after her and plopped into the chair across. He kept his gaze locked on hers, and she struggled to appear very firm, but she wasn't succeeding.

Ultimately, when she began to fidget, he inquired, "Are we about to discuss my scorned cousin, Libby? Or will we talk about Penny?"

She was taken aback that he'd blatantly toss out Penny's name, but she quickly regrouped and straightened in her seat.

"We shall discuss both young ladies," she said.

"Fine. What did you wish to tell me?"

"Miss Carstairs has departed the premises, and it's time for you to leave too. Immediately. I expect—when we're finished—that you will pack your bags."

"I certainly will, Miss Pendleton."

His tone was incredibly sarcastic, and she bristled. "You think I can't make you go?"

"It's always been difficult for women to *make* me do anything. I blame it on my horrid upbringing, but if you're nice about it, I might oblige you."

"Your presence here is no longer necessary."

"Yes, I'm getting the general impression that I've overstayed my welcome." He winked at her. "I'll ask Penny for her opinion."

"You cheeky devil! You will not ask Penny, and it's *Lady* Penny to you."

"She's happy for us to be on more familiar terms than that."

He wasn't normally so rude, but he just really didn't like her, and he couldn't abide such snobbery.

"It's come to my attention," she said, "that you have become entirely too cordial with my niece."

"Yes, she and I are great chums."

"You're a bit more than *chums*."

He grinned. "Maybe."

"Your scheme has been exposed, Mr. Falcon."

"What scheme is that?"

"When you were plotting with Miss Carstairs as to how you would deceive Lord Roland, you were overheard by a housemaid. Your duplicitous conduct has been revealed, and your swindle has unraveled."

"What are you claiming? Speak in plain English, would you? I've never been clever enough to solve riddles."

"From your own devious mouth, we have learned that Miss Carstairs will step forward and pretend to be Lord Roland's lost daughter, Little Henrietta. This very moment, she is being arrested in London, and I—"

"Whoa! What did you say?"

"Lord Roland is having her prosecuted for blackmail and slander. She's already been jailed. You will be swept up too—unless you behave exactly as I bid you."

"What is it you think you can pressure me into doing?"

She pulled a bag of coins out of a desk drawer, and she tossed it to him. "You are a confidence artist, Mr. Falcon, and you have glommed onto our family for nefarious purposes. I will not let you hurt Lord Roland, so I am willing to pay you so you'll cease your torment. I'm sure that's the ending you've been angling for all along."

"Oh, yes, I've definitely been hoping to blackmail you."

"You will take this money and depart Roland at once and forever. You will not confer with Lady Penny about it. Go now—before I summon the law and have you imprisoned too."

"I will go—as you've requested." He grabbed the bag and stuck it into his coat.

"You also have to sign a binding contract that states—in exchange for the compensation I've forked over—you will never mention Lord Roland or Little Henrietta ever again."

"I won't ever mention them. I swear."

"Should you break your vow—which I'm positive you'll consider—I will have the contract that proves you're a fraud and a liar."

He'd suspected she was an idiot, and she'd just convinced him of it. For some bizarre reason, she assumed she could negotiate with a criminal, and the criminal would keep his word.

She retrieved the document from the same drawer, and she placed it between them. She dipped a quill in the ink jar and asked, "Can you read and write?"

"Yes, ma'am. It's the great thing about England. Even a rogue like me can be educated."

"Is your full name Simon Falcon?"

"No, it's Simon Carstairs. Falcon is my stage name."

"I am not surprised by your subterfuge."

He stood, leaned over, and yanked the pen away from her. He grabbed the document and signed it with a grand flourish. Then he straightened and started out.

Behind him, he could sense her stewing. He hadn't groveled, so she'd be eager to hurl a few more insults, but he wasn't about to listen. All he cared about was the fact that she'd handed over a small fortune, and if Libby had really been incarcerated, he'd post her bail with it.

"You're leaving, aren't you?" she called.

He halted and glared at her. "Miss Pendleton, you shouldn't attempt to coerce someone like me. You're awfully bad at it, but thank you for the money. I'll put it to good use."

He reached the door, and she sputtered with offense. "What do you mean? We have a deal! You've agreed to shut your mouth."

"I was lying," he cockily said.

He exited into the hall, and she shrieked, "Mr. Falcon! Get back here!"

He marched to the foyer, and she ran after him, bellowing for him to stop. Servants and guests peeked out of parlors, curious to discover why there was such a ruckus.

As luck would have it, Penny was coming down the stairs, and she frowned at him and asked, "What's that noise? Who's shouting?"

Her aunt rushed up to Simon, and on observing Penny, she clasped his arm and tried to drag him back to the library. He shook her away and told Penny, "Your aunt has bribed me to vanish."

Penny huffed with derision. "Aunt Millicent! You didn't!"

"You will *not* consort with him," her aunt seethed. "I will not permit it, and when your father arrives home from town, you will learn your lesson about where you stand in this house!"

Penny rolled her eyes and continued down to the foyer until she was next to Simon.

"Ignore her," Penny said.

"I intend to, but get this. She informed me that your father has had Libby arrested for slandering him."

Penny scowled. "Father wouldn't have done that."

"It's what your aunt is claiming."

Penny whirled on Millicent. "*You* had Libby arrested, didn't you? How dare you!"

Millicent wasn't cowed. "If Miss Carstairs is in trouble with the law, it is only what she deserves. After what she planned to do to your father, I hope she rots in Hell."

Millicent whipped away and retreated to the library, then Simon said, "I have to head to London immediately. I have to check the situation there."

"I understand."

"I'll be back as soon as I can."

"You'd better be."

"Beware of your aunt."

"I'm not afraid of her."

"You should be. She might lock you away so we can't be together."

"I'd like to see her try."

"I'll sneak in, but if you've disappeared, how will I find you?"

"Don't worry about that," she said. "*I* will find you. Now go to Libby. If you need my assistance, send a messenger. I'll come to town and aid you if I can."

"I'll post her bail, and I'll have her out like that." He snapped his fingers, the sound echoing off the high ceiling. "I'll use the bribe money your aunt gave me."

"Good, and I'll pray you won't encounter any difficulties."

"In the meantime, you should talk to your father. If he's behind this, he might have to withdraw his complaint before any of it will calm down."

"I'll deal with my father. You just help Libby. Tell her I'll visit her shortly."

"I will tell her."

They had quite an audience by then, with guests staring as if it were an exciting theatrical play.

"What's happened?" one of Penny's friends asked. "Why is Miss Carstairs under arrest?"

"Libby Carstairs is my father's lost daughter," Penny announced to the assembled company. "She is Little Henrietta, and there are some people—my aunt for instance—who want to deny it and hide her away."

The declaration brought gasps, titters, and even a few shouts of astonishment.

"Is this some kind of party joke?" another friend asked. "Is it a trick?"

"No, it's no joke," Penny said. "Libby Carstairs is my sister, and my father and aunt are working hard to keep the news from spreading."

Millicent stepped into the hall, and she was aghast as she demanded of Penny, "What have you done?"

"I've admitted the truth, Aunt Millicent. This isn't a secret you can conceal. It's too big."

"The story is *not* true!" Millicent insisted to the gaping crowd. "Penny hasn't been well, and she's babbling nonsense."

Spectators mumbled their disdain, and several openly laughed at her, but others were slipping outside, eager to ride to London as fast as they could so they could brag about how they'd been present when the information was first disseminated.

When Libby had originally told Simon about her being Henrietta, he hadn't known what to think, but that cat was out of the bag. From this moment on, the whole world would believe she was Henrietta, so he'd believe it too.

"I have to go," he said to Penny.

"Go! But hurry back!"

"I will."

He dipped down and kissed her right in front of everyone. Some of the onlookers gawked with amazement, but most of them were rushing upstairs to pack so they could return to town and join in the frenzy over Libby. The party was definitely over.

As he and Penny drew apart and she smiled up at him, it dawned on him that he might like having her for his very own. In fact, he might like it just fine. His seduction had started as a lark, but maybe it would be much more than that. He might wind up obscenely rich too and that would simply be icing on the cake.

He spun away and skipped out the door. Libby needed him, and he'd always been the one man who could keep her out of trouble.

"Were you successful?"

"Yes, much more than I thought I'd be when I initially departed for town."

Luke sighed with relief and nodded at Charles. It was a chilly day, and they were sitting by the fire in the small family parlor at Barrett.

Charles had stopped by on his way home from London so he could report on how he'd fared in tamping down Libby's rumors. They were having a brandy, and Charles was warming himself, then he would continue on to Roland.

"I managed to reach the newspaper office," Charles said, "and chat with the owner before that weasel, Mr. Periwinkle, arrived. He was a very rational fellow, and he realized how a whiff of innuendo would set off pandemonium we couldn't control. He agreed to ignore it."

"You didn't have to bribe or threaten him?" Luke asked.

"No. He was extremely reasonable. Years ago, he'd published articles about Henrietta's disappearance, as well as about Libby and those other girls being rescued. He recognized how fascinating both tales were to the masses, and he swore he would never distress me by reigniting the controversies."

"I don't imagine Periwinkle will be too thrilled to have this quashed. He didn't seem the type to give up easily."

"Apparently, he's a loyal employee, and if he's ordered to forget about it, he will."

Luke snorted at that, not trusting the cretin for a single second. "What will you do about Libby? You've suppressed a public airing of her claims, but you still have to deal with her inclination to share it more quietly."

Charles blew out a heavy breath. "I haven't decided the best route. I've been fussing about it the entire trip to the city and back."

"What if she's telling the truth, Charles? Have you considered that possibility?"

"I've reflected on nothing else since I left for London."

"She could be your daughter."

"You don't have to remind me."

Luke liked having an excuse to discuss Libby. The prior time he'd been at Barrett, she'd been there with him. It had been the rainy day when they'd been caught in a deluge out on the lane. He'd slyly convinced her to tarry, then he'd taken advantage of their isolation and her affection. After that marvelous night, everything had fallen to pieces.

The last occasion he'd seen her, they'd fought quite viciously. She'd surprised him with her shocking assertion about being Henrietta, and he'd been so astounded—and so dubious—that he'd basically called her a liar and a fraud. They'd been stupid words uttered in the heat of the moment, and he hadn't meant them.

Or maybe he'd meant them, but with him having calmed down, he was fervidly wishing they could be retracted.

What if he saddled a horse and rode to London to talk to her?

He was positive—if he could even locate her—she'd refuse to speak to him. If he forced his way into her presence anyway, she'd likely slap him silly for being an idiot, and he was too proud to suffer such a humiliating rejection.

Yet he was so pathetically morose without her. He'd been incessantly pondering his miserable condition, and gradually, it had dawned on him that he might be in love with her. He couldn't deduce any other explanation for why he'd be so glum.

He ought to be glad they'd separated. He ought to be celebrating, but the pitiful fact was that he was hideously despondent. He'd never been close to a woman before. He'd never been . . . been . . . *in love*. That was the problem.

He'd been struck by Cupid's arrow, but then, he'd behaved like the biggest ass in the world, so how did he beg her forgiveness? Why would he expect to receive it? Then again, perhaps she was as forlorn as he was. Might she be missing him as dreadfully as he was missing her?

He kept wondering—if he showed up at the theater and waltzed into her dressing room—how she'd react. What if she tried to shoot him again? Or . . . what if she'd been pining away, hoping he'd muster the courage to chase after her? How was a fellow to guess what a crazed female like Libby Carstairs might be thinking?

Charles interrupted his wretched reverie. "I'll let things settle for a few weeks, then I'll go to town and meet with Libby."

"That's a good plan."

"I became a bit...friendly with Miss Fishburn while she was at Roland."

Charles's cheeks flushed, and Luke smirked. "How friendly?"

"Never you mind, but I'll ask Fish about Libby. Fish is an excellent judge of character, and she'll have some pertinent comments about all of this. I didn't treat either woman very kindly, so I'm not sure they'd allow me in the door."

"I was just contemplating the same response from them," Luke said. "We're a ridiculous pair, aren't we?"

"Yes. I always hate to distress anyone, and I like both of them so much. I feel terrible."

Luke's butler, Mr. Hobbs, knocked once, then entered without waiting to be summoned.

"Lord Barrett!" He rushed over to Luke. "I apologize for barging in, but you have to read this immediately." He was holding the London newspaper, and he laid it in Luke's lap. "Miss Carstairs has been arrested!"

"What?" Luke and Charles said in unison.

Hobbs glared at Charles, his expression unusually caustic. "Evidently, Lord Roland arranged for it to occur."

Charles frowned. "I most certainly did not. Let me see that!"

He yanked the paper away from Luke, and they perused it, their ire and astonishment spiraling.

The main headline was huge and exasperating: *LITTLE HENRIETTA FOUND AT LAST!*

The others were smaller, but no less infuriating: *Libby Carstairs, Mystery Girl of the Caribbean, Revealed as Little Henrietta!* and *Lord Roland Denies His Long-Lost Daughter!* and *Libby Carstairs Under Arrest! Lord Roland Determined to Hide the Truth!*

"I thought you discussed this with the owner," Luke said. "I thought he agreed he wouldn't print any articles."

"He swore he wouldn't! How dare he trick me like this! I'll have that bloody rag shut down as a public nuisance!"

Hobbs bristled, being entirely too blatant with his opinions. "Miss Carstairs stayed with us, Lord Barrett. Remember? She was lovely and gracious, and the whole staff is heartsick. To think that she's Henrietta, and she's been scorned and disbelieved by those who should know better!"

"Hobbs!" Luke warned. "That will be all. This information is a shock to us. Please leave us so we can digest it in peace."

Hobbs bristled again, looked as if he'd jeopardize his job with another inappropriate remark, then he marched out. Luke and Charles froze, listening as his footsteps faded away, then Luke said, "What now?"

"This is a disaster! Have you any notion of the frenzy it will generate?"

"I can imagine."

"No, you can't."

"Why have her imprisoned, Charles? That's rather harsh, isn't it? It definitely didn't tamp down the gossip."

"I *didn't* have her imprisoned! I have no idea what's happening."

Suddenly, from out at the front of the house, doors were slamming and people were shouting. Then booted strides were audible and briskly stomping toward them. He and Charles leapt to their feet, braced for any eventuality.

Hobbs hurried in. "I'm sorry, Lord Barrett, but you have a visitor, and he wouldn't—"

Before Hobbs could finish his sentence, Simon Falcon stormed in. His appearance was so odd and startling that Luke had to blink and blink to be sure he wasn't hallucinating.

Falcon was dashing as ever, dressed in traveling clothes: leather trousers, knee-high boots, a warm coat and jaunty red kerchief tied around his throat. His color was high, his temper visible.

He honed in on Luke and said, "Have you heard about Libby?"

"We were just reading about it in the paper."

Falcon whipped his hot gaze to Charles and said, "You! I'll kill you for this!"

The demented boy actually lunged for Charles as if he might physically attack the older man, and Luke jumped between them, a palm on Falcon's chest.

"Whoa, Falcon!" Luke ordered. "Back down! Right now!"

"He had her arrested!" Falcon said. "I tried to post her bail, and he's such an important prick that no bail is being allowed!"

Charles threw up his hands. "It wasn't me!" When they both glowered skeptically, he insisted, "I swear! I can't guess what's caused it."

"Fish has been detained with her!" Falcon said.

Charles was so flabbergasted that Luke was surprised he didn't faint.

"On what charge?" Charles asked.

"Apparently, she stole some of your precious cufflinks. I bribed a jailer who told me she was caught in your bedchamber with the items on her person!"

"If she was in my room," Charles admitted, "she was there at my invitation."

Luke was stunned to have Charles confess it aloud, and if Falcon was too, he didn't show it. He was too angry.

He whipped his irate gaze to Luke and said, "Lord Roland—being the arrogant bastard that he is—is demanding that Libby be transported to the penal colonies. Fish too! He's requested speedy trials, so he can be shed of the matter as quickly as the courts can manage it!"

Falcon was too incensed to restrain himself, and Charles was too bewildered to defend himself. Luke pushed Falcon away and said, "Stand behind that chair and don't move unless I give you permission."

Falcon dithered, nearly refused, then obeyed, and Luke said to Charles, "Sit down, Charles, before you fall down. We have to figure out the best course, and I need you lucid and participating in our discussion. You can't collapse on me."

Charles eased onto a chair, his expression distraught. "I know what might have occurred."

"I *know* what occurred," Falcon seethed. "Libby finally announced who she really is, and you can't bear to discover that you have an actress as a daughter, but the tale is all over London. You'll never make it go away. You can't."

"If Fish is implicated for being in my bedchamber," Charles calmly stated, "then it has to be my sister-in-law, Millicent, who perpetrated this debacle."

"You blame her?" Falcon said. "I was with her at Roland when this began, and she conveniently claimed *you* had arranged it. According to her, it's all your fault."

Charles sighed. "It wasn't me. I went to the newspaper office in London and simply asked them not to print the story. I was aware of the chaos it would stir, but I wouldn't have harmed Libby over it. I wasn't livid. I was . . . flummoxed more than anything."

"Your name and seal are on the legal documents," Falcon said.

"Oh, no." Charles sighed again. "Millicent had to have forged my signature and used my seal when she shouldn't have."

Luke shook his head with disgust. "It sounds as if you have some trouble to deal with at Roland."

"Millicent is very protective of our family," Charles said. "By ridding us of Libby, she would view herself as helping me."

Luke scoffed. "If she would have Libby jailed, then she's a bit beyond supplying you with *help*. She's mad as a hatter."

"I can understand her wrath against Libby," Falcon said, "but why pick on Fish? What did she ever do to Miss Pendleton?"

Charles and Luke shared a grimace, with Charles silently begging Luke to change the subject. It appeared that plain old female jealousy might have played a part in Millicent's decisions.

"Millicent doesn't like Fish very much," Luke said. "Let's just leave it at that."

Falcon was very cunning, and he scowled at Charles and said, "You seduced Fish? Gad, I ought to kill you for that alone! I'd have expected her to have better sense."

Charles bristled and started to rise—as if he'd had enough of Falcon's uncouth remarks— and Luke cut off a confrontation by saying, "Here is how we will proceed."

Falcon's retort was very snide. "I am absolutely on pins and needles waiting to hear."

"You and I," Luke told Falcon, "will ride to London and get Libby and Fish released."

"How will we?" Falcon caustically inquired. "There's been a denial of bail!"

"We'll take a letter from Charles, asking that the prohibition be lifted, and don't forget: *I* am a lord too. They wouldn't dare tell me I can't walk out with her."

At the comment, Falcon's temper visibly waned. He looked younger, less cocky, and quite relieved. "Can we depart immediately? I don't want them to spend an extra minute in that foul place."

"Yes, we can go at once." Luke was warming to the notion of saving the two damsels in distress.

"I'll accompany you," Charles said. "I'm anxious to inform them that I wasn't responsible for their incarceration. I'm bereft that they would believe I was."

"You're not coming," Luke said to him. "First of all, if scandal is swirling in town, you can't show your face there. Your presence would only stir more gossip, and if you were observed with Libby, imagine the frenzy that would erupt."

"Gad, I hadn't thought of that."

"Second of all, you and Mr. Falcon can't travel to London together. I'd have to constantly keep him from pummeling you."

Charles huffed with indignation. "I'm not the decrepit codger you assume I am. I'm betting I could match him blow for blow, and if he doesn't shut his mouth and mind his manners, he's about to find out how hard of a punch I can throw."

"No one is throwing any punches." Luke sounded like a fussy tutor struggling to discipline some recalcitrant boys. "You have to head to Roland and rein in Millicent. I'm in no mood to discover she's plotted further mischief. You have to ensure that Falcon and I won't receive any other surprises."

Charles glared, pondered, glared some more, then said, "Yes, I suppose that's a big worry. Who can predict what else she might have instigated? I'm stunned by what she's managed so far. I wouldn't have guessed she had it in her to be this devious."

Charles stood then, and he peered over at Falcon. "When you see Fish and Libby, please tell them I'm not culpable. It's important to me that they understand."

Falcon fumed, clearly not keen to accept Charles's olive branch, but in the end, he said, "I will tell them."

Charles added, "Send a fast messenger to Roland as soon as you've won their release and they're safe."

"I will," Luke said. "Now why don't you hurry on to Roland? Falcon and I have to get going to London. We'll rescue them; I swear it to you."

"Thank you." Charles stared at Falcon and said, "And I swear to you that Millicent will answer for what she's done."

"Good," Falcon replied.

Charles nodded, then left.

Luke turned to Falcon and said, "Are you ready?"

"I was born ready."

"Vain ass," Luke muttered.

He and Falcon marched out too, with Luke calling for Mr. Hobbs, calling for his horse to be saddled, calling for a bag to be packed.

For days, he'd dawdled at Barrett, frozen with inaction and out of ideas as to how he should proceed with Libby. It felt so bloody grand to finally have a plan. He would pry her out of the jail, and she'd be so grateful for his assistance that he'd be able to apologize and they'd start over. It would have to conclude that way. Wouldn't it?

He refused to envision any other conclusion.

Chapter

21

"It ain't right, Miss Carstairs! It just ain't right!"

The complaint was voiced over and over as Libby and Fish crossed the courtyard at the prison. A guard had come to fetch them to the warden's office, so something positive was about to happen. As she walked by the other inmates, they parted like the Red Sea to let her through.

Prisoners of all ages were crammed together, and they were reaching out to her—as if she could perform miracles. She nodded and waved, sauntering slowly, like a benevolent queen bestowing favors.

"Henrietta! Little Henrietta! Bless me, would ya?"

"Henrietta! Touch my boy! Touch my son!"

Men doffed their caps and bowed. Women curtsied and sighed. They were gazing as if she were a saint, as if she'd been raised from the dead, and in a way, she supposed she had been.

She and Fish had only been in the facility for a few days, and it hadn't exactly been a horrid experience. Nor had she been mistreated. An important person wasn't meant to suffer. She and Fish had each brought a trunk of clothes, plus plenty of money to pay bribes and purchase amenities.

In fact, as her identity had spread, they'd been moved to an even nicer apartment than the one that had originally been supplied. Jailers had constantly stopped by to ask if she was comfortable and if they could be of service.

She had no idea how the news about her being Henrietta had spread in the general population. She hadn't spoken a word about it, but with the story disseminated, it was as if a dam had broken. People were absolutely agog.

"Do you hear that?" Fish leaned in and murmured.

"No, what?" Libby asked.

Then the noise hit her. A crowd had gathered outside the walls, and a chant of, *Let her out! Let her out!*, filled the air.

"You like being the center of attention," Fish said, "so this is the perfect conclusion."

"Would you rather no one knew who I was? We'd have been common prisoners with common privileges."

"Gad, no." Fish scoffed. "I'm content to grab onto your coattails and stay tightly attached."

"Our bail must have been posted," Libby said. "Who do you figure managed it?"

"I'm betting on Simon. I can't imagine who else would have bothered. It wouldn't have been that philandering dog, Lord Barrett, or that treacherous fiend, Lord Roland."

"Neither of them would dare show their sorry faces in our presence."

"I like to think they wouldn't," Fish said, "but they're both so arrogant. They probably assume we'd be glad to see them."

"I wish our jailers would have allowed me to keep my pistol," Libby told her. "If it's one of them, I'd be delighted to use it to indicate how *glad* I am."

They were being guided to the main office located near the front entrance. The inmates they'd passed surged forward, anxious for a final glimpse of her.

"We're on your side, Miss Carstairs!" they cried repeatedly.

"Lord Roland is a monster!" others added. "Don't forgive him for this! We certainly won't!"

She hadn't mentioned Lord Roland having her arrested, but there must have been gossip about it. She was terribly hurt by his tactic, and she received enormous consolation from learning that others were outraged on her behalf. His ploy to lock her away hadn't worked. Evidently, the rumor about her being Henrietta had circulated far and wide, so his attempt to silence her had been pointless.

She wondered if he regretted his decision. Or—now that his first scheme had imploded—would he implement a different penalty? How desperate was he to prove that she *wasn't* Henrietta? What other methods might he employ to thwart her? Would she always have to look over her shoulder?

She hoped he'd simply leave her alone. His message had been loud and clear. He didn't believe she was Henrietta, and he had no desire to welcome her into the family. Since he was obviously opposed to any reconciliation, she wouldn't push herself at him. She was a very proud woman, and she wouldn't put herself in a position where he could spurn her ever again.

From the moment she'd opened the box of Harry's letters, she'd comprehended how hard it would be to have Lord Roland accept her. It was why she'd shut her mouth for so many months, but she wasn't a glutton for punishment, so she intended to continue shutting it.

They were led into the warden's office. It was a small, unadorned room, with a desk, three chairs, and some filing cabinets along the wall. He was seated at the desk, and he stood and smiled a fake smile. He came over to her, his hands extended in greeting as if they were old friends.

"Ah, Miss Carstairs!" he said. "There you are! May I call you Libby? Or should I call you Henrietta? Which would you prefer?"

"You may call me Miss Carstairs," she imperiously replied.

Apparently, he'd presumed she'd be grateful to have been summoned, so he was taken aback by her haughty tone. His smile slipped, but he pasted it on again. "I've seen you on the stage several times, and we've been so honored to have you lodged in our establishment."

Libby was afraid she might slap him, but Fish saved her by asking, "Why were we brought to you? Has our bail been posted? Is that it?"

"Yes." His cheeks flushed as if he was embarrassed. "We apologize for the delay, but there was an issue over the amount and who would pay it. The problem has been rectified though."

"How?" Fish caustically inquired. "Did someone browbeat Lord Roland until he stopped acting like an ass?"

The warden scowled. "Let's not disparage our betters, shall we?"

"Are we free to leave?" Libby asked, too impatient to endure their bickering.

"Yes, you're free," he said. "We're just waiting for your escort. There's such a crowd on the street that it was difficult to maneuver your carriage up to the gate."

Suddenly, they heard many men approaching, as if it would require a phalanx of guards to whisk her out to her vehicle. Then Simon burst into the room, which she was thrilled to observe, but when she realized who had accompanied him, she grimaced with distaste.

"Lord Barrett?" she said to Luke. "Why are you here?"

"Are you all right?" He looked frantic and concerned. "I've been worried sick."

His expression was warm and fond, as if they hadn't quarreled, as if he hadn't mocked and grievously wounded her. Had he forgotten their prior conversation? Could he assume *she* had forgotten it?

He reached out as if he'd hug her, and she scooted behind Fish so Fish could be a barrier. He frowned, appearing confused and upset, but Libby couldn't care less about his precious feelings.

"Are we going?" she asked Simon.

"Yes, but there's a mob out there. It's insane!"

"I don't understand this ruckus," she said. "Why is everyone outside? Why are they clamoring for my release?"

"It was in the newspapers about your being Little Henrietta!" Simon said. "That reporter, Howard Periwinkle, who was pestering you learned of it somehow. The whole country is buzzing!"

Fish muttered, "The entire kingdom has gone mad."

"We'll get you out," Simon said, "*if* we can guide you through the protesters."

"I'm not scared of my admirers," Libby said. "They'll permit us to pass unmolested."

"I certainly hope so."

Simon gestured toward the door, and the guards leapt to attention and started down the hall. She swept out after them.

For an instant, Lord Barrett moved forward as if he expected her to take his arm and allow him to walk her out, but she had no intention of letting him.

During her incarceration, she'd had many hours to engage in some soul searching. Gradually, it had dawned on her that she had to separate herself from him. She'd recognized that situation before she'd traveled to Roland, and she grasped it even better now.

With her father disavowing her, she'd been painfully reminded that she didn't belong in the sphere occupied by the likes of Charles Pendleton and Lucas Watson. She might have initially been born into it, but as a child, she'd plunged from her lofty spot, and there was no way to reclaim it.

She was too tarnished, too notorious, to demand a position in their snobbish, aristocratic world. And why would she yearn to have a position there?

Her life was grand. The streets were packed with people shouting her name and wanting only what was best for her. That was enough.

For a few brief months, she'd wondered if she required more than that to be happy, but she didn't. As Fish had wisely counseled, it was pointless to love a man who couldn't love her back. When she was around him, she acted like a ninny who couldn't control her emotions. But she was Libby Carstairs, was Little Henrietta Pendleton, and she'd always controlled them.

Lord Barrett had made her forget how strong she was, but her short stint in the prison had her vividly recollecting an important truth about herself: She was fine just as she was, and she didn't need a waffling, disinterested beau in order to feel complete.

She scowled at Lord Barrett as if he was a stranger who'd wandered in by accident, then she took Simon's arm instead. Fish took his other arm, and the three of them—her *real* family—strolled out together. She supposed Lord Barrett trailed after them, but she didn't glance back to find out.

They were marched to the gate. More guards were there, and they yanked it open so her retinue could clear a route to her carriage. It was parked very close, but they would have to push through the horde to reach it.

The nearest spectators saw her, and a cheer went up. *Libby! Libby! Libby!* There were also assorted cries of, *Henrietta!* Still more of, *Let her out! Let her out!* and *Shame on Lord Roland!*

She was curious how Charles Pendleton—a man who detested scandal and strife—would fare with his reputation in tatters. He wouldn't like to be so thoroughly disparaged, and she smiled with a grim satisfaction, thinking it served him right for being so horrid, not just to her, but to Fish who had fallen in love with him again and who was suffering from the betrayals he'd inflicted.

Then they were at the carriage. The door was jerked open, and she, Simon, and Fish were lifted in, then it was slammed shut again. Their driver cracked the whip, the horses snorted and complained, then the vehicle lurched away, sending her audience dashing away to avoid being run over. In a quick minute, they were rolling down quieter streets to her rented house.

Lord Barrett hadn't been lifted in with them. He hadn't been permitted to sequester himself with her, so she was snuggled between the only two people who mattered to her at all.

If she'd been a sillier female, she might have mourned that fact, but she was glad they'd left without him. She was glad! And she wouldn't pretend otherwise.

CAROLINE GREY STOOD IN the milling throng outside the prison. She was a petite woman, so it was difficult to discern what was happening around her.

Once she'd read in the newspaper that Libby had been wrongfully arrested, she'd visited the facility on several occasions. It had been a fool's errand, but she'd asked to be admitted so she could talk to Libby, but the jailers had jeered and told her that dozens of purported acquaintances had been claiming a connection to Libby and demanding to speak with her, so Caroline's attempts had been soundly rebuffed.

Rumors were rampant that Libby was finally going to be released, and Caroline was making her way toward the front. Up ahead, a carriage was parked, and the gate came into view. Suddenly, it swung open, and the spectators surged forward. She was whisked off her feet and carried with them.

There was no opportunity to worry that she might be crushed in the melee; it occurred too fast to fret. A line of guards rushed into the bystanders, and they began shoving and hitting with fists and clubs, clearing a path for someone approaching behind them.

Then . . . ? There she was! Dear Libby! Her oldest friend. Libby, the fearless companion who had haunted her dreams for two decades. Libby, the lone female in all the world who would comprehend the challenging life Caroline had led after their terrible ordeal in the Caribbean.

Caroline recalled Libby being very pretty, but she was even more beautiful now. Her adult years had added drama and elegance to her gorgeous face so she could have been a princess or maybe an angel who would have been painted on a church ceiling.

She was being hustled along, intent on reaching the safety of the carriage, so she wasn't focused on any of the unruly bystanders. She didn't so much as peek at Caroline, and why would she have? Caroline was filthy, her palms scraped raw, her skirt torn and in need of washing. With her hand extended in Libby's direction, she was aware that she appeared to be a beggar, pleading for alms.

"Libby!" she shouted, but it was impossible to be heard over the noise. "Libby! It's me! It's Caroline Grey! Do you remember me? You can't have forgotten!"

But Libby was hustled into the vehicle, and she vanished so swiftly she might never have been there.

Upon her departure, the clamor and bellowing ceased. The protesters circled about, still filled with the energy that had been generated on Libby's behalf. Their shared outrage had proved effective. Hadn't it? She'd been set free, but they weren't sure of how to act now that she'd left. They chatted in groups, their expressions beatific, as if they'd witnessed a miracle.

"I didn't see her!" a woman complained. "I'm not tall enough! Did you see her?"

Another said, "Yes! She stared right at me! Imagine that!"

Yet another said, "The Mystery Girl of the Caribbean—she was right in front of me!"

Caroline snorted with disgust and yearned to reply, *I'm a Lost Girl too. I was with her when we were found on that stupid island,* but when Libby was such a glorious celebrity, who would listen? Who would believe her? Who would care?

She wondered where Libby lived and whether she could find out. If she knocked on Libby's door, would Libby even recognize her? When Libby's life had proceeded down such a grand and important road, why would she recollect a few frightening months she'd passed with Caroline when they were five?

No doubt Caroline and Joanna—and their sojourn on the island—were but a distant memory. How could Caroline have hoped for any other ending?

Her shoulders slumped with defeat, and she staggered away.

LUKE DAWDLED LIKE A dunce in the middle of the boisterous horde, watching as Libby's carriage vanished around a corner. Her exit had been hectic and brutal, with guards shoving and whacking spectators with clubs. He'd gotten separated from her and hadn't been able to catch up.

It was obvious she didn't notice and wasn't concerned. She hadn't bothered to glance back to be certain he'd followed her, and at the realization, he couldn't decide if he was hurt, surprised, or insulted. He figured it was a mixture of all three.

He and Simon had galloped to town together, and with very little effort, they'd arranged for Libby's release. There had been no arguing or attempts to block him. As news of her arrest had spread, as the mob outside had swelled to an uncontrollable size, prison authorities couldn't manage it. They'd been glad to be shed of her.

He was so vain. He'd convinced himself that she'd be thrilled to see him. He'd assumed they'd snuggle in her carriage as they hurried to her rented house. He would have profusely apologized, received her forgiveness, then he'd have had her pack a bag so they could travel on to Barrett and spend several splendid days locked in his bedchamber.

Evidently, the prospect had never occurred to her.

How had he so thoroughly misjudged her mood and feelings? He'd thought it would be easy to begin again. He'd thought she'd understand how sorry he was, but she'd been rude and dismissive.

How was he to respond? Was he supposed to chase after her? He was an arrogant prig, so she had to grasp that he *wouldn't* chase after her. He wouldn't plead with any woman.

So . . . to hell with her!

For once, he'd attached himself to a female, and look where he'd wound up! He'd let himself grow besotted, but why had he? Was he mad? Very likely yes.

She was an actress! She played on people's sympathies so they'd give her money for a ridiculous incident that had happened when she was a tiny child. It was bizarre to carry on in that manner. She also seemed to believe she was Charles's lost daughter, but if she was, her blue blood had been so diluted by circumstances that it had to have been totally washed away.

Yet if her claim to be Henrietta was a deception, then she was a terrible liar, so why was he mooning over her? Didn't he have better sense? His horse was down the street, a boy holding the reins until he returned. He could dash to it, mount, and trot after her, but why would he?

If he showed up at her door, he was positive she'd be just as dismissive as she'd been in the jail. Why would he put himself through such a humiliating ordeal?

His temper flared. He never permitted anyone to treat him as she'd treated him. He didn't have to. It was clear she was over him, that their affair hadn't meant to her what it had meant to him, so why prostrate himself?

She could wallow in her pathetic life, with her dubious acquaintances. He had chores to attend at Barrett. He had an heiress to marry and a dowry to stick in his bank account so he could make the necessary repairs at the estate.

What he *didn't* need was a snooty, beautiful shrew driving him crazy.

He spun to stomp off when a woman stepped in his way. She was pretty, but apparently, had fallen on hard times. Her dress was torn and her palms scraped as if she'd tripped or had been pushed to the cobbles by the rowdy crowd. Her face was smudged, and she could have used a bath.

"Pardon me, sir," she said to him, "but you were gazing at Miss Carstairs so fondly. Do you know her?"

"Yes, I know her."

"I know her too."

He bit down a scathing retort of, *I seriously doubt that.*

"Good for you," he muttered instead.

"I called to her, but she couldn't hear me."

"Yes, it's been very loud."

He tried to walk by her, but she clasped his arm. "Can you tell me where she went? Are you going there now?"

"No, I'm not going there," he firmly stated.

"Where does she live? How would I find her lodging?"

He scowled. "I can't tell you any of that."

"When you talk to her, will you inform her you spoke to Caroline Grey? I've been searching for her."

The name sounded familiar, but he couldn't place it. "Yes, I'll be sure to apprise her for you."

It was a lie. In light of his current foul mood, he didn't think he'd ever converse with Libby Carstairs again.

He wasn't normally cruel though, so he could have mentioned that Libby was always working at various theaters, that Miss Grey could probably track her down at one of them. But in her bedraggled condition, she didn't seem like a person Libby would want showing up to pester her.

He circled by her and kept on, and she said, "It's Caroline Grey! Little Caro! Don't forget! I've missed her desperately!"

She offered another comment, but there was too much noise, and he couldn't hear what it was.

He marched past the teeming crowd, and no one was leaving. Their darling Libby had been freed, but they looked bewildered. How would they rid themselves of their pent-up energy? He hoped they didn't start a riot merely because they didn't have anything better to do.

His horse was right where he'd left it. The boy tending it was anxiously watching for him. Luke tossed him more coins than he should have, then he jumped into the saddle and turned the animal so he could travel in the opposite direction from the one Libby had taken.

Heaven forbid that he catch up with her. Heaven forbid that they cross paths again.

He rode away from her, from the prison, from London, and headed home to Barrett.

Chapter

22

Millicent stormed into Charles's library. She was boiling with fury, and she blamed him for every mistake they'd committed so far.

It was bad enough that she'd been forced to wrestle with that wretched Libby Carstairs by herself, but while Charles had been away, Simon Falcon had been toying with Penny's affections and convincing her that Luke wasn't a viable option to be her husband. Luke—who was a titled earl! Luke—who was head of one of the oldest, most prestigious families in the land!

The immature girl likely deemed herself in love with the despicable creature. Had it occurred to her that he was simply after her dowry? Was she expecting Charles to blithely offer it to the petty criminal?

Charles had just returned from town, and he was sitting behind his desk and drinking a whiskey. She hadn't realized he was back, and she'd been rudely summoned to speak with him immediately. Apparently, he planned an urgent conversation, so she'd had to instantly march down the stairs to oblige him.

She had so many complaints to voice that she felt as if she was choking on them, and if he didn't side with her for once, she didn't know how she'd react.

"We've had the most shocking situation develop," she said, seizing the offensive as she marched over to sit in the chair across from him. It didn't matter what he was eager to discuss. She had too many issues of her own, and she had to get them out on the table before they reviewed any of his paltry problems.

"What is it?" he asked.

"Penny has been misbehaving with that scoundrel, Simon Falcon."

"Oh, no."

"I bribed him to go away and leave her alone."

He sighed with aggravation. "Millicent! I wish you wouldn't have. You should have let me handle it."

"I would have been glad to, but you weren't here. He took my money, and he insisted he'd heed me, but he hasn't. What should we do?"

"I'll deal with it."

"Really? As you dealt with Miss Carstairs? I'm sorry, but I don't trust you to manage it appropriately. If we're not careful, I'm afraid the irresponsible pair might elope."

He scoffed with derision. "Penny is not about to elope with Simon Falcon. She would never be that reckless."

"Are you sure about that? She's your daughter, so she has your same blood running in her veins. You were just a few years older than she is now when you dashed off with Amanda."

"Penny isn't *me,* and she wouldn't hurt me that way. She understands how distressed I'd be."

"If that's what you assume—that Penny would never engage in mischief—then you're a fool."

He shrugged. "Probably."

"Mr. Falcon is a confidence artist! I believe he intends to abscond with her so he can glom onto her dowry."

"I would never sign it over to him, and Penny would recognize that. She would never traipse off to live in poverty with him. She's been too spoiled by life."

Millicent clucked her tongue in disgust. "Is that your answer? She's spoiled so she won't be negligent? Mr. Falcon is a handsome, flamboyant cad, and she's clearly besotted."

He shrugged again. "I'll talk to her."

"Then I'm certain it will all work out brilliantly," she snidely said.

"I'm certain it will too," he agreed.

It was pointless to criticize Penny. She'd been growing more recalcitrant and stubborn by the day, but he refused to accept what she was truly like. Well, Millicent had warned him. If he wasn't concerned, why should she be? She shifted to the other topic that had left her consumed with rage.

"Have you seen the London newspapers?" she asked.

"Yes, I've seen them."

"Miss Carstairs has successfully spread her lies. There will be no tamping them down."

"No, I don't suppose there will be."

"People will demand you claim her—even though she's a fraud!"

"It's already started." He was studying her over the rim of his glass, his expression curious and probing, as if he couldn't quite remember who she was, then suddenly, he said, "You had her arrested. Would you like to explain that to me?"

She hadn't expected the accusation, so she hadn't been prepared for it, and she blurted out, "Of course I had her arrested."

"You had Miss Fishburn arrested too."

Millicent's cheeks flushed. "She's a thief. I caught her in your bedchamber, riffling through your jewelry."

"What was stolen?"

She couldn't reply because—as far as she was aware—nothing was missing. But Miss Fishburn was a slattern, so she *would* have stolen something if given the chance.

"I haven't checked your dressers," she said. "Besides, I wouldn't know what was there in the first place. I'm not the person to make a list of the items."

"The legal papers mentioned cufflinks."

"Hmm . . ." she mused. "I recollect an allegation to that effect."

"You had them jailed, and you forged my signature on the complaint. Then you used my seal—very much without my permission—so you could pretend that *I* was seeking the harsh treatment."

"Don't blame me for acting in your stead. I alerted you to Miss Carstairs's scheme. I dumped the entire mess in your lap, but you ignored my advice. You didn't threaten her. You didn't buy her silence. You let her waltz off to town and inform the whole world. Gad, it was reported in the newspapers! I've never been so mortified."

"What an odd statement." His assessment became even more intense. "Why would you have been mortified? If anyone should be affronted, shouldn't it be me? It's my reputation and my lost daughter. How does the story impact you in the slightest?"

"Not impact me! Am I a member of this family or aren't I? Am I your staunchest friend or not? If my efforts on your behalf can be so easily discounted, what have I been doing here all these years?"

The bitter words were out before she could swallow them down. They seemed to reverberate off the walls, and with her tiptoeing out onto such a dangerous ledge, his response was exactly what she could have predicted.

"I've been asking myself that very question," he said. "Why have you been here?"

"I've been assisting you! I raised your children and ran your home. I shouldered the burdens a wife would have carried, and I won't be denigrated for it. I've always had your best interests at heart."

"Have you?" he blandly inquired.

"Yes, and don't you dare deny it. In every instance, I've toiled away as hard as I could to make you happy."

He frowned and shook his head. "That excuse won't work this time. I'm a lazy lord. I admit it, and I've let you assume more and more authority rather than fight about it. Evidently, you now believe you have power that's equal to mine."

"I would never presume that."

"You were eager to harm Miss Fishburn—simply because you were jealous."

His affair was at the root of her pique, but she had no idea how to debate the issue. Who wouldn't be jealous? She'd persuaded herself he would eventually marry her, but obviously, he never would have, so where did it leave her? Why couldn't he comprehend how deeply she'd been wounded?

"You've shamed me with her," she said. "You engaged in illicit conduct with a harlot—right under our roof—and you never paused to wonder how I might feel about it."

"I thought I was very clear with you about my relationship with Miss Fishburn, but I guess I have to repeat myself. If I choose to grow friendly with her—or any other woman for that matter—it's none of your business."

"I'm to have no opinion?"

"No."

She might have been a puppy he'd kicked to the curb, and she yearned to curl up in a ball and die.

"I'm not sure what to do with you," he said, "and I'm curious to hear your suggestions. You've stepped over so many lines this week that I can't count them all."

"I've stepped over no lines! I've been helping you. Why can't you understand that fact?"

"I figured that would be your defense—you were *helping* me—but you've provided aid I don't want and would never have allowed."

"What is that supposed to mean? Are you about to claim that charlatan, Libby Carstairs, is Henrietta?"

"I can't imagine how I'll proceed, but *I* will decide. Not you."

"What about Miss Fishburn? Will you convey her to Roland so you can renew your affair? Will you force me to watch while you disgrace yourself?"

"I don't plan to make you watch me ever again."

There was a grim finality to his words that halted her in her tracks. "What are you talking about? Don't speak in riddles."

"It's time for you to move home and reside with your brother again. It's time he took charge of you."

"Move . . . home? You're being absurd. *This* is my home. It has been since Florence passed away."

"I shouldn't have permitted you to live with us."

She huffed with offense. "Isn't it typical that you'd reach your conclusion after I've sacrificed my best years for you?"

"I told you—on many occasions—that you shouldn't waste your life on me, and I have to correct my mistake. I'm sending you back to your brother."

"No! I refuse to obey you. He's married to a harpy who rules the roost like a vicious quartermaster. What would I do there?"

"I don't believe that's my problem."

"I doubt they'd *let* me come. They assume I belong with you."

"You convinced yourself that you belong here, but I never thought you did."

It was the cruelest comment ever uttered in her presence, but he wasn't cruel. Normally, he was kind and polite, so he was more upset than she'd realized. She pushed off her chair and rounded the desk. She fell to her knees and clasped his hand.

"You're distraught," she said, "and I recognize why you are. You can't bear to be embroiled in a scandal, so you're lashing out at me—when there's no reason to blame me. Try to see this from my point of view. I was merely keeping you safe from Miss Carstairs's machinations."

"It's what is vexing me, Millicent. I didn't need you to keep me safe. Whatever happens with Miss Carstairs, it's between her and me. The situation with Miss Fishburn is the same. Now get up. You're embarrassing yourself—and me."

He stood and yanked her to her feet, as behind them, the door opened. She glanced over and frowned when she noticed who'd entered. It was the slothful, impertinent housemaid, Peggy, who'd eavesdropped on Miss Carstairs and Mr. Falcon. She was dressed for traveling in a cloak and hat, and she was carrying a heavy portmanteau.

"I'm ready, Lord Roland," she said to Charles.

"Ready for what?" Millicent asked him.

Charles answered with the most bizarre reply. "Millicent, you are departing Roland immediately, and Peggy will accompany you."

"I'm not leaving." She laughed as if it was a horrid joke.

"I've rented a room for you at the coaching inn outside the village. You'll stay there while I write to your brother and schedule your journey to his estate."

"Don't be silly. I won't tarry at a coaching inn. I'm not going to my brother's."

She was very firm, but he ignored her and continued. "If he won't consent to your return, I will rent you lodging in town. However, your circumstances will be quite reduced, so let's hope he's amenable."

Millicent's wary gaze shifted from Charles to Peggy, and she asked, "Why is Peggy here?"

"The butler informs me that you and Peggy have become great chums recently, so she's the perfect servant to tend you as you transition into the next phase of your life."

Millicent bristled. "Are you mad? She's lazy and incompetent."

"Yes, she is, and she's also a tattle. She was observed chatting with a newspaper reporter out on the lane. I can't imagine why she'd have been talking to him. Can you?"

Millicent swung to Peggy and fumed, "You shared our private business with a reporter? What is wrong with you?"

Peggy stared back, looking bored, and Charles said, "She'll accompany you because—if she remains at Roland—she'll be fired."

"So fire her," Millicent said. "It's fine with me."

"Instead of being terminated, she's agreed to this arrangement. I won't supply you with any other staff from the manor, so it's her or no one."

"I pick no one!" Millicent seethed.

Charles said to Peggy, "Miss Pendleton doesn't need your help, so you may take your things and go."

The girl didn't have the good sense to be silent. "It was all Miss Pendleton's fault. She stirred the trouble for Miss Carstairs. Not me, and I've never gossiped about you." Then she had the audacity to inquire, "Will you pen a reference for me?"

Charles scoffed. "No, now get out of my sight or I may lose my temper."

Peggy hesitated for a second, then spun and stomped out. The butler was there to lead her away.

Their strides faded, and a dangerous calm settled in. She and Charles were standing very close, and she peered up at him, searching for some hint of affection or sympathy, but he glared coldly—as if he didn't know who she was.

"Don't treat me like this, Charles," she begged. "Please don't. I've always loved you!"

"Well, I have *never* loved you, and you have to go too. A carriage is waiting out in the drive. You'll be conveyed to the coaching inn, and I'll contact you in a few days, after I've heard from your brother."

"Charles! Stop it."

She would have fallen to her knees to beg him again, but he'd had enough. He seized her arm and marched her out, and she was so stunned she didn't have the mental wherewithal to protest or even drag her feet.

They passed numerous servants, and they gaped at her, their expressions condemning. Were they all aware of what she'd done to Miss Carstairs? They were servants! Why would they have the gall to revile Millicent over any issue?

Charles kept on until they were outside and down in the driveway. As they approached the carriage, a footman whisked the door open. She didn't move toward the vehicle, so Charles simply lifted her in and shut the door behind her. She would have grabbed the latch and jumped out, but before she could gather her wits, the driver cracked the whip and the coach lurched away so rapidly she was flung off the seat.

She grappled for purchase and righted herself, so she barely managed a final glimpse of the manor as it was swallowed up by the trees. Charles was watching her depart, looking cool and placid, as if nothing egregious had occurred.

The traitorous shrew, Peggy, was walking down the lane, her portmanteau banging on her hip. She didn't glance up, didn't step out of the way, and they skirted around her without slowing.

Millicent sagged against the cushion, wishing she was dead.

       ❧

"Don't make a sound."

At the whispered warning, Penny awoke from a deep sleep. A hand was clamped over her mouth, and a large man was pressing her down. Her fear cleared quickly as she realized it was Simon.

"What time is it?" she asked.

"Late."

"How did you sneak into the house?"

"I found a window that wasn't latched. Your servants should be more careful."

"Your reply has me worrying that you possess criminal tendencies."

"I absolutely have them. My father, Harry, taught me all his best— or worst—habits, depending on your viewpoint. I can pick a lock or pick a pocket or swindle an unsuspecting dunce out of his money. If shady conduct is required, I'm the fellow for the job."

He was perched on the edge of the mattress, and she pulled him down so he was stretched out beside her. He kissed her fiercely, and as he drew away, they both sighed.

"You've been gone for ages," she said. "What have you been doing?"

"First, I went to London to bail Libby and Fish out of jail, only to learn that no bail was being allowed."

"Who ordered that?"

"Originally, we assumed it was your father, but it turned out to be your aunt."

"You won't believe what happened to her."

"Ooh, I hope it was horrid. Is there a torturer's rack in the basement?"

"By her standards, it was just that bad. Father kicked her out of Roland and sent her to live with her brother."

He grinned and facetiously asked, "Are you missing her?"

"Don't be daft. I never liked her, and I'm so glad to be shed of her." She snuggled nearer and asked, "What else have you been doing?"

While he'd been gamboling in the city, she'd been awash with jealousy. She'd spent every minute contemplating the beautiful girls who might have crossed his path when he was away from her. He'd thrown himself at her until she'd caught him, and now, he was hers. What, precisely, was she supposed to do with him?

"After I discovered no bail could be posted," he said, "I raced to the country and enlisted Lord Barrett to help me free them."

"Tell me he pitched in or I'll be so aggravated."

"Yes, he helped me, and he was quite majestic about it too. Libby and Fish are at our London house and recuperating from their ordeal. Libby wasn't grateful for his assistance though. I guess, when she told him about her being Henrietta, he called her a liar."

"The dolt!" she fumed.

"She's vexed with him, so I'm not sure if they're still having an affair or not. If they've split apart, it would mean your father could start pushing you about becoming engaged to him."

"He never could. Even if she spurns Luke for all eternity, I don't want him."

"Are you certain?"

"I have other ideas about my future."

"What are they?"

The question hung in the air between them, and as she studied his handsome face, she wondered if she hadn't gone mad. She'd had years to ponder the sort of man she yearned to wed, yet the crop of available aristocratic boys was a shallow pool. She craved an amazing husband, and she'd never met anyone more amazing than Simon Falcon.

Then again, she'd had scant experience with amour. Luke had been the sole candidate her father had presented, so she hadn't been able to make many comparisons. It was such an important decision, which was why a girl's father selected her husband, but she'd let him handle it, and he'd chosen distracted, aloof, much older Lucas Watson.

Luke had been all wrong for her, so her father couldn't be counted on to settle on a candidate she'd agree to have. Dare she forge ahead on her own?

Her father's wild proclivities were flowing in her veins. Was this how he'd felt about his wife, Amanda, when he'd eloped with her? Had he felt—if he couldn't have Amanda—his life might not have been worth living?

His marriage to her had been a disaster, but he'd survived, and he'd relentlessly repented his error. If Penny staggered forward into reckless conduct, she'd only be doing what her father had done, so he could hardly condemn her for it. And if it collapsed later on, he'd welcome her back; she was convinced of it.

But she refused to think it would end in catastrophe. She would bluster into it, assuming it would be perfect.

"I have to tell you something," he said, and suddenly, he looked much too serious. "Let's sit up, shall we? When I explain this to you, I should be standing on my feet."

He slid off the bed, and he drew her up to rest against the pillow, then he went to the window and stared outside. It was a cloudy night, but the moon was up, so it wasn't completely dark.

He appeared as if he was about to confide a terrible secret. Or perhaps he was leaving her. If she'd been a trembling ninny, her heart might have been pounding, but she wasn't concerned about any issue he might raise. She was in control of the entire situation.

"Well?" she said when he couldn't begin. "You're obviously distressed. What's bothering you?"

He whipped around and admitted, "I seduced you with wicked motives."

"I know that. I'm an heiress, and I've ceaselessly been cautioned about scoundrels like you. I hadn't imagined for a single minute that you had *pure* motives."

"I was planning to persuade you to elope to Scotland with me. I would have slyly suggested you bring some money to pay for our trip, then—when you weren't watching—I would have stolen it and vanished."

She smirked, not surprised that he'd planned it, but surprised he'd confessed it. "Would you have left me enough to get home to Roland?"

He bristled with offense. "Of course I would have. I'm not an animal."

She chuckled, finding him to be absurd and marvelous. "So now what? You said you *were* thinking of behaving badly. What are you thinking instead?"

"I'm thinking we have to part. I intend to climb out the window, jump on my horse, and ride to London."

"I'll never see you again?"

"I have to save you from yourself. I've toyed with your emotions, but I'm *good* at toying with a woman's emotions. It's another trick my father taught me, but with you, I'm sorry I enticed you. I like you so much, and I shouldn't have been hideous to you."

"Have you developed a moral conscience?"

"I guess I have."

"Am I supposed to simply bid you farewell, then it will be over between us?"

"Yes."

She pretended to mull the notion, then she frowned. "There's a problem with your decision, and it's this: You can't treat me like a child. It's what drives me insane in my dealings with my father. I'm an adult. Not a baby. I am fully capable of making up my own mind. I don't need you to make it up for me."

"I realize that, but you haven't considered the ramifications of shackling yourself to me. I'm a petty criminal! I have no funds of my own, and my only skills are those best performed under a circus tent. I rely on Libby to support me." He threw up his hands. "That's how useless I am! I have to be supported by a woman! How could I provide for you?"

"You're forgetting one important detail."

"What is it?"

"You may be poor, but *I* am very, very rich."

"If you run off with me, your father will never offer us your dowry. You're deranged if you presume he will."

"He'll give us some of it. He would never allow me to be imperiled because of my relationship with you."

"What if you're wrong? What then?"

"Then . . . ah . . . I figure we'll move in with Libby, and she'll have to support you *and* me. Fish will have to teach me how to sew, so I can earn my keep by stitching Libby's fantastic apparel."

"You're not thinking clearly, Penny. If you allied yourself with me, you'd regret it forever. Not at first. At first, it would seem like a lark, but when times were tough, after we were struggling financially, and we fought about it constantly, you'd grow to hate me. We shouldn't walk down that road."

"How long have you been reflecting on your change of heart?"

"All the way from town. I didn't expect to be noble. I was ready to beg you to elope with me. I brought a horse for you and everything, but the farther I traveled from London, the more I recognized you can't ruin yourself over me."

"That is the prettiest speech I've ever heard, but you're being ridiculous." She tossed off the covers and stepped to the floor. She was attired in just her nightgown, her hair down and brushed out, and at abandoning her warm bed, she shivered. "Am I correct that you have two horses tied out in the woods? Am I correct that you were planning to convince me to ride to Scotland this very night?"

"Well . . . yes."

"Then give me a minute to get dressed. We'll depart at once."

"Penny, would you stop it? Please?"

"I'm about to roll the dice and take a chance on you." She waltzed over and kissed him on the mouth. "Don't you dare disappointment me in the end."

"I've disappointed people my whole life, so you oughtn't to risk it."

"You're turning over a new leaf with me."

"What if this winds up being as horrid as I've painted it?"

"I'll declare myself sick of you and come home to my wealthy, wonderful father who will welcome me back without saying, *I told you so.* But why are you so certain it will be dreadful? Here at the beginning, can't you at least attempt to picture it as being grand? It's what I intend to do."

She whirled away and headed for her dressing room. He followed her, watching with elevated interest as she lit a candle and riffled through her clothes. What, exactly, should a girl wear when she was eloping? She supposed dark-colored and comfortable were best. She grabbed a black gown, sewn from a soft wool, and held it out to him.

"You'll have to help me with the buttons," she said.

He gaped at the garment, but didn't reach for it. "Are we really proceeding? After what I confessed, you still want to?"

"For pity's sake, Simon, don't try to talk me out of it. I'm determined to have you for my very own."

Finally, he grinned his devil's grin. "I might actually enjoy this."

"You'd better, and before we leave, I have to set one rule for you. You have to agree to it. The terms are nonnegotiable."

"I'm awful at playing by the rules, so don't pick one that would make it hard for me to comply."

"It's just this: While we're together, you can't have any other women. None! I'm afraid I have to put my foot down about it. If you decide in the future that you wish to stray, tell me in advance, and we'll part without a fuss. But so long as you're with me, you're mine. I'm possessive that way, and I won't share you."

He bowed with a flourish. "Lady Penny, I am all yours. Let me help you with those buttons."

Chapter

23

FISH SAT IN THE parlor of their London house. It was late in the afternoon, the street finally quiet, the crowd out front having called it a day and headed off to their suppers.

People had always been fascinated by Libby, but now, with her being Little Henrietta too, interest had spiked to an even higher level. Libby had been besieged by admirers and newspaper reporters, but also by various charlatans who were anxious to glom onto her with spurious intentions. They were claiming prior friendships or prior business dealings where she owed them money.

She couldn't step outside without being hounded to death, but she'd been feeling claustrophobic, so she'd risked jumping into her carriage to run some errands.

As she'd departed, the most devoted of her retinue had chased after her, particularly the reporters who were cataloguing her every move for their readers. Once she'd left, the other stragglers had gradually left too. With Libby gone, what was the fun of dawdling?

Fish wondered how long the chaos would continue, and she hoped some other, more delicious scandal would erupt. She'd like focus to shift to some other unlucky woman.

A knock sounded on the front door, but she ignored it. She was relishing the chance to be alone with her thoughts. She'd been sucked into Charles's life and bed, but their affair had ended abruptly, and with it over, she couldn't figure out how to proceed.

For most of a decade, she'd trailed after Libby, designing her clothes, dressing her, and advising her when she needed shrewd counsel. It had been a stable, enjoyable existence, but she was chafing, bored, and dissatisfied with her choices.

Why hadn't she made better ones? She could have wed several handsome rogues over the years. Why hadn't she?

She could have had a home of her own and a few children to keep her company in her old age. Instead, she'd rejected all suitors, and she'd picked Libby and Simon to fill the role of the children she'd never birthed. What if they weren't enough?

Her world—of sewing, theatres, and actors—suddenly seemed small and pointless. The perception wasn't true, and she had to quit thinking so negatively, but her low mood was causing her to question everything.

She wished she could climb onto a ship and sail to a tropical island. She'd wallow in the sun and rearrange her attitude. She'd start over as a different, more intriguing female.

The knock sounded again, but no one rushed to answer it. They had three servants, but they were having tea in the kitchen at the rear of the house, so they wouldn't have heard the summons. When their visitor—likely a reporter—knocked a third time, indicating he was very determined, her temper sparked.

She went over and yanked the door open, ready to vent her pique at the stupid idiot who'd dared to bother her, but when she saw who'd arrived, she froze.

"Hello, Fish," Charles said.

"Charles."

There was an awkward pause where they studied each other, struggling to deduce what their next comment should be, and Charles broke the silence.

"I thought we should talk. May I come in?"

She'd planned to deny him entrance, but her tongue seized control of her mouth, and she said, "I suppose."

He strolled in, but didn't bluster or strut, and she realized he'd been reduced somehow, as if much of his haughty aplomb had leaked away when he wasn't paying attention.

He looked a tad lost, as if he didn't remember how to sit down, and she waved him to a sofa. He was nearly relieved that she'd provided instructions, and he staggered over to it and flopped down.

"I was about to have a whiskey," she said. "Will you join me?"

"Yes, an alcoholic beverage would be perfect."

She poured two glasses, handed him one, then moved to the chair across. There was a table between them that would serve as a barrier. She couldn't imagine why he'd blundered in, and she wasn't about to make it easy on him. She simply stared, waiting for him to speak up or leave.

"How have you been?" he ultimately asked.

"Fine."

"And how is Libby?"

"Fine too."

"Is she here?"

"She's out running errands."

Her tone was overly surly, but she couldn't help it. He'd kicked her out of his home, as if she were a scullery maid who'd been lifting her skirt for a penny. It had been a malicious act that she suspected would always sting.

"I hope your ordeal with her wasn't too awful," he said. "Lord Barrett told me it wasn't. He insisted you'd muddled through with no difficulty."

"Yes, Charles, jail is just fun and games."

His cheeks flushed with shame. "I know you assumed I signed the papers to have you arrested, but it wasn't me."

"We were informed that it was your sister-in-law."

"I'm stunned that she implemented such a wicked scheme. I would never have expected it from her."

"You're gullible about women, so I believe you."

At least she thought she believed him. He wasn't generally a cruel person, but so what if he hadn't signed the papers himself? He'd still evicted her—as if she'd been too disreputable to tarry. She was so embarrassed she might never fully recover.

"I didn't end things very well with you," he said.

"I beg to disagree. From my perspective, you were quite thorough."

He snorted with disgust. "I deserve that, I guess."

They stared again, and she couldn't bear it. She asked, "Why are you here, Charles? What is it you want? Forgiveness? All right. You're forgiven, so your mission is accomplished. You can go."

He scowled. "Would you stop being such a shrew?"

"I'm sorry, but I'm not sure how to act in this sort of situation."

"Neither am I, but I'm trying. Could you try a bit too?"

"I'll rein in my temper, but clarify your purpose so we can get it over with."

He sighed heavily, as if she wasn't behaving correctly. Was she about to be scolded for an infraction? If he dared, she'd escort him to the door.

"Tell me about Simon Falcon," he said.

She was taken aback by the query and instantly on guard. Simon had vanished days earlier, and they weren't certain where he was or what he might be doing. He might have perpetrated any insane deed, and she braced for the worst.

"Why are you curious about Simon?" she asked.

"Would you describe him as a fortune hunter?"

"Yes, absolutely."

"Has he had any schooling? Has he any antecedents worth mentioning? Has he any prospects? Or is Libby his sole support? I'm anxious to receive details about his character."

"Why?"

"He's eloped to Scotland with Penny."

Fish's jaw dropped. "You're joking!"

"I'm not joking."

"Of all the stupid, preposterous, outlandish . . ." She couldn't finish the sentence. There weren't enough words to define how shocking it was.

"Will he marry her? Or will he simply ruin her, then abandon her at a coaching inn along the road?"

"I can't predict what he'll do. He was flirting outrageously with her, but matrimony? It seems outside the realm of possibilities."

"I can't decide if that's good news or not. Would it be better if they're wed or wouldn't it?"

"Libby warned him to stay away from her, but once he gets an idea in his head, it's hard to dissuade him from pursuing it. In that, he's just like his father who was as reckless as they come."

"If he actually marries her, what kind of man is he? Is he a drunkard? Is he a philanderer? Would he be violent or abusive?"

"He doesn't have many bad habits—except for his being a rogue and a charlatan. He's generous to a fault and incredibly flamboyant. He works tirelessly so people will like him, so he's funny and interesting. He doesn't drink to excess, and he's never angry. For the most part, he's a very happy fellow who loves life and enjoys reveling. In many ways, he'd be a grand husband for a young girl like her. She'll never be bored with him. I can guarantee it."

"Will he presume I'll hand over her dowry?"

"I positive that's a motivating factor."

"I won't give it to him."

Fish shrugged. "But then, Penny would be left in the lurch financially. I can't imagine you being so spiteful."

"No, I couldn't be," he glumly agreed.

She smirked with amusement. "They'll likely return to Roland very soon, so you'll have a son-in-law in the house—and it won't be Lord Barrett."

"Gad, don't remind me! I'll have to tell Luke she tossed him over for a circus performer. His ego might not survive it."

"In my opinion, he has too much ego. He'll bear up."

She was still fuming over Lord Barrett and what an arrogant prig he was. When they'd been freed from the jail, they'd trotted away without him, and he hadn't bothered to ride after them. He hadn't visited, hadn't tried to rekindle Libby's affections. So...

A pox on his sorry hide!

"Could you chase after them?" she asked. "You might be able to find them so it doesn't conclude in calamity."

"She had a huge head start before we realized she was missing. I doubt I could have caught her, and even if I had, she's very stubborn. She'd have told me to sod off and allow her to continue on her merry way."

"She's just doing what you did all those years ago. You recognize that, don't you?"

"Of course, but it doesn't make the debacle anymore palatable."

"The damage is done, so you have to figure out how to deal with it. I can't see you fighting with them. Nor can I picture you cutting ties."

"No, I never would."

"Look on the bright side. Maybe she'll be happy forever with Simon. She wouldn't have been with Lord Barrett, so maybe this is a blessing in disguise. Simon is a good boy—when he's not swindling someone—and Penny will have the most dashing husband of all her acquaintances. I'm betting she'll be delighted."

"Until it dawns on her that this was a terrible mistake."

Fish couldn't muster any concern for rich, spoiled Penny Pendleton. "If it crashes down later on, you'll be there to pick up the pieces."

"I suppose."

"It's not the end of the world, Charles. Daughters wed the wrong men all the time. Even when the father selects a stellar candidate, it can wind up in disaster. Let's hope for the best."

He nodded firmly. "That has to be my attitude, doesn't it?"

His misery was painful to observe, and she'd always been a sap when confronted by a distraught male. She always leapt to their rescue, which had caused her countless problems in her life. She had to stop behaving like such an idiot.

She changed the subject. "I have to show you something."

She went to the desk where the box of Harry's letters lay like a bomb ready to explode. She brought it over and placed it on the table.

"Open it," she said.

"Why? What's in it?"

"It's the letters Libby stumbled on after Harry died—the ones that clear up her past."

Charles didn't reach for it, but glared as if wishing he had magical eyes that could peer into the wood. "I can't fuss with this right now."

"If not now, when?" she asked.

The question hung in the air between them, and still, he didn't move. He was frozen, almost fearful over what he was about to learn, and she bristled with aggravation, then shifted to sit next to him on the sofa. She lifted the lid and began reading them to him.

Initially, he wouldn't glance at them, but as she commenced the third one—written by Amanda to Harry—he peeked down and gasped.

"That's Amanda's handwriting," he said. "I'd recognize it anywhere."

He took the stack from her and perused the others on his own. She nestled by his side, watching the emotions that swept over his face. The facts he'd sought for so long about what had happened to Henrietta were finally revealed.

Amanda had vanished from London with her lover, but the oaf had perished in Italy. Amanda had been penniless, friendless, and alone. She'd met Harry's brother, gullible Kit Carstairs, who'd been a university student on a tour of the country.

Poor Kit had believed Amanda's story about being an abused wife who was fleeing her brutish husband, and he'd been determined to save her. While Charles had fruitlessly searched for Amanda in Europe, she and Kit had sailed for the Caribbean. Their ship had sunk in a storm and the rest, as they say, was history.

As Charles finished the last letter, posted from the Canary Islands before the sinful pair continued across the Atlantic, he put them back in the box and secured the lid so they were shielded from his sight.

He sat like a marble statue, and they dawdled in the silence. Eventually, he said, "Libby is my daughter, isn't she? She's Little Henrietta."

"I'm afraid so."

"Did Harry leave any explanation as to why he hid her from me?"

"Not that we've found. It will probably always be a mystery, but he was incredibly fond of her, Charles. He truly was. Perhaps it's no more complicated than that."

"Oh, my Lord, she's Henrietta, and I kicked her out of my house!"

Fish didn't have a reply to that remark, so she kept her mouth shut. He leaned forward, his elbows on his knees, his head in his hands. An eternity ticked by, and after a lengthy interval, he straightened and turned to her.

"Will she ever forgive me?" he asked.

"I think she will. She's a kind girl. She's stubborn—sort of like Penny, so maybe obstinacy is a family trait—but she's kind. I can't guess if you'll ever have the relationship with her you're hoping, but I expect some type of connection will form."

"What should I do?"

"Invite her to Roland for an extended stay. Spend some time getting acquainted. Simon and Penny will be back from Scotland soon, and they'll want to live with you. Libby and Simon are affectionately close, so it might help to have her there to smooth things over."

On mentioning the idea, Fish felt sick at heart. Libby and Simon were her family, the children she'd never had. If she allowed Charles to have them, if they joined his life rather than hers, she'd be all alone. If they left her to become Pendletons, where would she be?

After another excruciating interval, he said, "If I invite Libby to come, would you come with her?"

Her pulse fluttered as if she were a gushing debutante. Apparently, she was still so smitten that she'd jump at the chance to be humiliated all over again. Where was her pride? Where was her sense of self-preservation?

"I don't know, Charles. I'd have to think about it long and hard."

"I've sent Millicent away—if that's what is worrying you."

"You *sent* her away? I thought the two of you were attached at the hip."

"When I discovered her mischief toward you and Libby, I was so incensed. I finally had to accept that she isn't the person I deemed her to be."

"I told you so," Fish mumbled under her breath.

"Yes, and I decided she should move on. I delivered her to her brother—and good riddance."

"I don't suppose she was very happy about it."

"She wasn't, but she's gone, so you needn't be concerned about her."

Her mind raced with a hundred pretty visions. She could picture lazy afternoons and nights of passion where their frolicking never ended.

There would be quiet chats and emotional bonding and poignant intimacy that would keep them occupied until . . . when?

She scowled at him. "What would I do there, Charles?"

"I don't have any answers, but my bedchamber is so bloody empty without you. Won't you come home?"

It was a dangerous question, and she tamped down the eager response that yearned to burst out.

"I have to ponder your request," she said, "and I have to discuss it with Libby. If I agreed to tarry for a bit, I'd grow too besotted, and I don't trust how you'd treat me or where I'd be when you were through with me."

"What if I was never through with you? What if every minute was grand and you stayed forever?"

"I'm not a green girl, Charles, and you're not the only aristocrat who ever seduced me. The word *forever* doesn't exist for a disparate couple like you and me. Don't pretend about it."

He leaned over and kissed her. She hadn't expected it, so she hadn't realized she should ward him off. She'd always been an easy target for him, so she kissed him back with much more enthusiasm than she should have displayed.

He drew away, and they both sighed as if she'd consented, but she hadn't. If she went to Roland, how long might she remain? No doubt, once gossip spread that he was scandalously consorting with a mistress in the manor, he'd kick her out again.

Would the joy of the sojourn cancel out the subsequent despair? She'd never been one to rue and regret. Should she relent? Might it be worth it?

"I can't decide," she said. "There are too many ramifications to consider."

He grinned, wearing her down. "Without Millicent, I'm in desperate need of a female to run my house and serve as my hostess. It could be you."

"In your dreams maybe."

"We could lie to the neighbors and insist you're simply my special *friend.*"

"Yes, I'm sure they'd believe it was entirely innocent—right up until they tarred and feathered you for being an immoral libertine."

"I might risk any punishment to have you back."

"Don't tell me that," she said. "If you spew nonsense, I'll start liking you again."

"I've behaved like a saint for too many years, and it's probably time for me to behave badly. Say *yes.* Say you'll come."

She gazed at him, studying his handsome face, and the Devil was whispering in her ear.

Why not go to Roland? Why not love him for as long as he'll allow it?

But he was urging her to walk down a hazardous road, and she had to be careful.

"Let me think about it," she said. "That's all I can promise for now."

"I won't quit pestering you until you give me the correct answer, so I don't understand why you don't put me out of my misery and agree immediately."

"I'll *think* about it," she repeated more sternly. "And there would have to be some rules in place first."

"Rules about what?"

"About how we'd end it after you're weary of me. You'd have to swear you'd never evict me on the spur of the moment merely because you were angry."

His cheeks flushed. "Gad, I'm such a pompous ass, aren't I?"

"You definitely can be, but I'm fond of you anyway."

"I have to try harder to ingratiate myself."

"I admit you're not making much progress. How will you rectify the situation?"

She shouldn't have inquired. Once he'd kissed her, it was all over but the shouting. A hot gleam flooded his eyes, the one that flared when he was contemplating sexual activity.

On observing it, she shook her head in exasperation. "We're fighting, and I'm still irked by what a callous bastard you can be, but you're focused on carnal mischief."

"I'm a man. It's all we think about. For years, I had *stopped* thinking about it, but you've enticed me, and it would be cruel of you to refuse to keep my flame lit—and you've never been cruel."

"No, just gullible."

"Is your bedroom upstairs? Let's sneak up there and roll around like a pair of naughty adolescents."

"Can you really suppose I'll fall into your lap simply because you're begging?"

"Yes, I really suppose that, and I'm not *begging*. I'm asking. I haven't had you flat on your back in ages, so I view it as a perfectly valid question."

She glared at him, then at the foyer where she could see the stairs leading up to her room. "I'll show you where it is, you irritating roué, and it doesn't matter what you say. You're begging, but then, I love it when a man begs. It's gotten me in all sorts of trouble in my life though."

She stood, clasped his hand, and dragged him away.

CHARLES TIPTOED INTO LIBBY'S foyer, and he was grinning, but preening too. He'd left Fish sleeping in her bed, and he'd crept out, feeling happier than he could ever remember being.

Before he'd arrived, a dalliance had been the last thing on his mind. On learning of Penny's brash deed, he'd been anxious to talk with someone who would commiserate, and Fish had been the only one who'd seemed appropriate to the task. But after they'd kissed, he'd realized that a torrid romp with her would cure much of what was currently ailing him.

She'd spent a week at Roland, but he'd grown used to having her around. He relished her sassy attitude and pithy conversation, and she'd never been in awe of him. She never gushed or fawned, and she was always just who she appeared to be: a shrewd, practical, and independent female who tantalized him beyond his limit.

He'd pressured her to return to Roland, but he hadn't yet convinced her. He'd give her a few days to relent, but if she didn't, he truly thought he might travel to town and kidnap her. He was that determined to have her by his side.

After she was there though, he couldn't imagine what he intended. He wasn't about to wed again. Nor would he shock the nation by wedding *her*, but he simply couldn't bear to carry on without her. Especially with Penny and Simon figuring they could bluster to Roland without consequence. With Fish present, the reconciliation would go much more smoothly.

He was tugging on his coat, when suddenly, the door opened, and Libby strolled in. She hadn't expected anyone to be standing in her foyer, and he hadn't expected to bump into her, so they both blanched with surprise.

He regrouped first. "Hello, Libby. May I still call you Libby?"

"Hello, Lord Roland. To what do we owe the pleasure?"

Her tone was chilly and unfriendly, and he glanced down to check that his buttons were buttoned correctly.

"I was chatting with Fish," he said.

Libby peered over his shoulder, but Fish was nowhere in sight. "You were *chatting*? Really?"

He wondered how much Fish had revealed about their antics. "She was tired, so she's . . . ah . . . upstairs in her bedroom. Resting."

"She doesn't usually take naps."

"For some reason, she . . . ah . . . was fatigued."

He sounded like a dunce, and he decided to shut up about Fish. Besides, he and Libby had more important topics to address than his sexual misconduct with her companion.

She whipped away from him and yanked off her cloak and bonnet, and she made a great display of hanging them on the hook by the door. He sensed her aggravation, and he couldn't fault her for her fit of pique.

What must it have been like to know for months that she'd found her father? Then to have him instantly reject her so she couldn't even mention the possibility? He wished he had a machine that would whisk him back in time so he could retract the terrible comments he'd uttered that last afternoon.

"I had news to share with you," he said. "It's why I'm here."

She turned to face him again, coolly asking, "What is it?"

"Your cousin, Simon, has eloped to Scotland with Penny."

Her shoulders slumped. "I'm very sorry, and I hope you don't blame me. When I was at Roland, I learned that he was flirting with her, and I ordered him to leave her alone. As you've discovered, he doesn't always listen to me."

"I don't blame you."

"Well . . . good."

Their conversation faltered, and they stared, a thousand issues swirling between them. He yearned to raise the subject of her being Henrietta, but he wasn't sure how. What subject was she yearning to raise? She was likely trying to devise a method to politely kick him out of her house.

"Could we talk for a minute?" he said.

"Aren't we talking now?"

"Libby . . ." He had to swallow over and over before he could continue. "Fish had me read your box of letters."

She was aghast. "You read them?"

"Yes."

"Clearly, Fish should butt out of my private business."

"Don't be angry about it. I'm glad she showed them to me."

There was a lengthy pause, one that was so protracted it seemed the whole universe was eagerly awaiting her response.

"Why would you be glad about it?" she ultimately asked.

"Because I think they're genuine." It was a tepid remark, and he said, "I should rephrase that. I *know* two of them were penned by your mother. I recognized her handwriting, so your Uncle Harry couldn't have forged them."

She frowned. "You believe I'm Little Henrietta?"

"Yes, I believe you are."

"I guess I'm delighted to hear it. I'm shocked, but delighted."

"That's my feeling too: shocked, but delighted." He reached out and took her hand. "We need to have some extensive discussions about how to go forward."

"Maybe."

"Would you travel to Roland and stay with me for a bit? Please?"

She drew away from him, but what had he been expecting? Had he imagined she'd weep with joy and tumble into his arms?

Yes, actually, he'd imagined exactly that. He was such an idiot!

"I would hate to encounter your sister-in-law again," she said.

"She's no longer at Roland. After she had you and Fish arrested, I sent her home to live with her own relatives instead of mine."

"Good. I didn't like her, and she didn't deserve the spot she occupied in your life."

"Penny and Simon will ride in very soon," he said. "They'll be a pair of annoying newlyweds, and I'm struggling with how I should greet them. They have to understand how upset I am, but I won't cause a rift with them right off the bat. It would be a tremendous benefit to me if you were there when they arrived."

"I'll think about it."

"You tried to tell me you were Henrietta, and I never gave you a chance to speak up. I most humbly apologize for that."

"I was positive that it would be hard for you to swallow. It's hard for *me* to swallow, and I've had months to ponder it. It's why I didn't inform anyone."

"With our stumbling on the truth, we have to develop a plan for the future. I want to publicly claim you so you'll be part of my family. I hope you want that too."

He waited with bated breath for her to gush, *Of course I want that too! Of course I want to be your daughter!*

But her composed expression remained firmly in place. "I can't decide what's best. I have to ask Fish her opinion, then I'll have to engage in some serious reflection."

"If it will help in your deliberations, I've invited Fish to return to Roland too. You're aware of my fondness for her, and it's vexing me that she left. I'd like her to come back. In fact, I begged her to come back."

"Has she agreed?"

"No. She's being entirely stubborn about it."

Libby smirked. "I like that you'll have to work to get back in her good graces."

"Do you suppose I'll succeed?"

"Yes, eventually."

"What about *your* good graces?" he asked. "Will I ever manage it?"

"I can't predict what will occur." She pulled the door open. "I appreciate you stopping by. It was kind of you to make the effort."

He chuckled. "Am I being kicked out?"

"Let's not say you're being *kicked* out." Wasn't that what he'd told her at Roland? "Let's just say you were departing, and I've delayed you."

"Let's just . . ." he murmured, and he sighed. "I'm going to start writing to you. We'll correspond regularly."

"I guess that would be all right."

"And whenever I'm in town, we'll get together."

"That would probably be all right too."

"If you'd like to visit me at Roland, you don't have to contact me first. You can simply show up and tarry for as long as you like. I'll always be glad to see you."

"Thank you."

"Would you call me Charles? I'd request that you call me *Father* as Penny does, but it would sound awkward."

"You correct, so I will contemplate the notion of calling you Charles."

He stepped into the doorway and gave her hand a final squeeze. "Come to Roland, Libby. Bring Fish with you. Make me happy."

"I'll think about it," she said again.

He hovered, craving something more, something different, but she was practically pushing him out. When he'd initially learned that she might be Henrietta, he hadn't known how to react. Now he was claiming her, and *she* didn't know how to react.

Like father, like daughter . . .

The thought flitted in his mind, and he smiled and said, "I'll be watching for you at Roland. Don't disappoint me."

Then he spun away and nearly skipped out to the street. He was that exultant. His carriage was parked around the corner, and he headed for it. At the last second, he glanced back, and she was dawdling on the stoop and studying him intently. He waved, and she waved too, which he took as a sign of progress.

He kept on, curious as to how long it would be before he saw her again. They'd found each other, so how could she bear for them to be apart?

❧

"Was that Charles leaving?"

"Yes."

Libby was in the foyer, and Fish was up on the stairs, dressed only in her robe. Libby snickered with disgust.

"An afternoon romp, Fish? Really? One would deem people your age to have more control over their lusty impulses."

Fish shrugged. "I've never been able to resist him."

"I wish you wouldn't have carnal relations with my father. Or if you feel compelled to have them, that you wouldn't perform them right under my nose."

"You're an adult, Libby, and you weren't raised in the proper way. You won't swoon over a bit of dissipation."

Libby wasn't in any position to lecture Fish on how she should behave. She'd simply like Lord Roland to stay away from them until she could figure out what she sought from the lofty man.

"He believes I'm Henrietta," she said. After how she'd been treated at Roland, she hadn't expected the moment to ever occur, and she was a tad stunned.

"I had him read the letters."

"He's asked us to travel to Roland. What do you think about that?"

"I think we should *think* about it. At least, *I* should think about it. As to you, you should go at once. Let him welcome you into the family. Become his daughter. It's what you've always wanted—to belong somewhere."

"I'd be too afraid."

"You—afraid? Don't be daft. You're Libby Carstairs. You're the Mystery Girl of the Caribbean, and you've never been afraid of anything."

"I'm afraid of the water. I'm afraid of the dark and tight spaces."

"Well, after your ordeal when you were little, that's understandable, but you shouldn't be scared of your father urging you to live with him."

"What if it doesn't turn out as I'm hoping?" Libby absurdly asked.

"Why wouldn't it? The entire kingdom has always loved you and that was before they knew you were Henrietta. Charles Pendleton will eventually love you too. He'll spend the rest of his life proving it, so you're being ridiculous—as usual—and I need to continue with my nap."

Fish spun away and stomped to her bedchamber.

Libby collapsed against the wall, and she stood there for an eternity, struggling to process Lord Roland's comments.

"I have a father," she said to the quiet room. "He wants me to come home."

She smiled, wondering if she'd ever dare.

Luke was irked by what his butler, Mr. Hobbs, had just imparted. Apparently, Miss Fishburn was in his front parlor and anxious to speak with him. He was hurrying down the hall to oblige her, but with each step he took, he worried he was growing deranged.

Ever since he'd crossed paths with Libby Carstairs, he'd acted like an idiot, and he couldn't imagine why Miss Fishburn had arrived. She must intend to tell him a detail about Libby that he shouldn't hear. No doubt Fish planned to drag him back into Libby's world, but he refused to be dragged into it!

He couldn't abide the drama that had arisen since he'd met her. He simply yearned for matters to return to normal. He would marry the appropriate aristocratic debutante, settle down, and be happy. Or if not happy, then somewhat content. He couldn't tolerate more of the insanity Libby stirred, yet here he was, keenly ready to be sucked into the whirlwind that surrounded her.

Fish was over by the window, staring outside, and drinking an alcoholic beverage, whiskey from the looks of it. He walked to the sideboard, poured himself a glass too, and went to stand next to her.

"Hello, Fish," he said. "May I still call you Fish? Or are you too angry with me?"

"I'm not angry with you. Not much anyway, so Fish is fine."

"Thank you. Aren't you a city girl? What brings you to the country?"

"I'm headed to Roland—to stay with Charles."

As a . . . what? he almost asked, but he had no idea how. So instead, he said, "I'm sure you'll have an enjoyable visit."

"Charles demanded I come."

Her use of his Christian name was troubling, but then, Charles had alluded to their being romantically involved. Perhaps they were much closer than Luke had realized.

"Charles *demanded* it?" He tried to keep from sounding overly dubious.

"I debated forever over whether to oblige him, then I decided I might as well. I have no reputation to protect, so I can carry on however I like."

He was never comfortable with women who were so blunt, so he wasn't certain how to reply. Charles could misbehave in a reckless manner. There was no one with the authority to tell him he couldn't, but the neighbors and the servants might have quite a strident opinion about *her* illicit conduct. Had she considered that problem?

She was no fool, so she probably had, but she didn't care. Such disregard for propriety was disturbing in too many ways to count.

He stammered, "Ah . . . I hope it works out as you're expecting."

"It will or it won't. I'm tossing the dice to see what happens."

"Are you a gambler, Fish?"

"Yes, and I usually win too." She switched subjects. "Have you talked to Charles recently?"

"No."

"Then you haven't heard, but I don't suppose he could bear to inform you. Your ego might not survive the news."

"What news?"

With no preamble, she announced, "I'm sorry to be the one to notify you, but Penny has eloped with Simon."

"Simon Falcon?" Luke was so stunned he was surprised his knees didn't buckle.

"Yes, Simon Falcon. It's mad, isn't it? He'd been flirting with her, but we didn't recognize the danger until it was too late."

"Gad, Charles must be beside himself."

"That's putting it mildly."

"Have there been any messages from them?" he asked.

"No, but I figure they'll show up shortly and beg to be welcomed home."

"Will they be? Has Charles said?"

"He'll welcome them. He's always doted on Penny, and he won't start off by bickering with her new husband."

"But Simon Falcon!" Luke couldn't rein in his disparagement. "You're fond of him, so I apologize for being derogatory, but I'm very astonished. Not so much that I lost Penny over it, but that she'd agree to have Simon in the first place. I can't imagine what she was thinking."

"I am fond of him," she said, "but I have no illusions. I know exactly what he's like, but she's young, and he's dashing and gorgeous, so I grasp why she'd be smitten. He's not all bad, so she might have some good years with him."

"I shall pray you're correct."

He meant it sincerely. He had no quarrel with Penny, and in fact, he was feeling as if a huge weight had been lifted from his shoulders. He didn't have to wed her! Whew!

At the same time, he was concerned for Charles, and he would have to jump in and support his friend as he waded through the morass Falcon had created. The boy was a charlatan, and Luke would warn Charles to always be wary.

Fish yanked him out of his miserable reverie. "You won't receive Penny's dowry."

"It appears I won't."

"I'm guessing you'll run to London and begin searching for another heiress."

"I have no idea if I will. I'm flummoxed by what you just shared, and I have to recover from the shock of it."

She snorted at that. "Libby is in London. Charles invited her to come to Roland with me, but she wouldn't."

Don't ask! Don't ask! He asked, "What's she doing in London?"

"She's performing again. With all that's transpired, she's being paid a bloody fortune too. She couldn't resist."

"Yes, I suppose the crowds are flocking to see her."

"Men especially are swirling. Every dandy in town is trying to glom onto her, but Simon and I have abandoned her just when she needed us the most. She's alone and fending them off by herself."

The declaration set a spark to his rampant jealousy. He'd once thought he could have Libby for his own, but she hadn't been interested in binding herself, and he was tired of nagging about it. If the London dandies were chasing her, what was it to him?

"She's never been rich," Fish said, "but she's suddenly an earl's daughter."

Luke frowned. "Is Charles claiming her?"

"Yes. He hasn't publicly confirmed it yet, but there's no doubt she's Little Henrietta."

"My goodness," he murmured. "I hadn't heard."

"He'll be eager to make up for lost time, so I'm betting he'll fund a dowry for her. He'll probably give her some of Penny's—as a punishment for Simon. If he seeks my opinion, it's what I'll suggest when he inquires."

Again, he couldn't deduce the appropriate response, so he said, "Why are you telling me all of this?"

She clucked her tongue as if she was talking to an imbecile. "Will you take some advice from someone who is older and wiser than you, Lord Barrett?"

"Charles says much the same to me. Are you older and wiser, Fish?"

"Yes, and here it is: You don't have to wed for money. Who cares if your manor is a bit bedraggled? It's not about to collapse. It's merely deteriorated, so you could marry for love rather than money. If you attempted that peculiar stunt, you might wind up being happy forever."

"Marry for . . . *love*?" It was the most bizarre notion ever.

"Yes, for love, you arrogant beast. It's what Libby has always wanted—to wed for love. It would be a shame if the only man who could goad her into it was too proud and thick-headed to convince her."

She downed her drink, put the glass on the tray, then marched out. He glowered at her, feeling like a dunce.

"You believe I should propose to Libby?" The question sent a wave of joy coursing through him.

She halted and glanced over her shoulder. "Far be it from me to butt into the middle of such a weighty topic, but it's clear that you are awful at pursuing these kinds of decisions on your own. You can have Charles's daughter—as you always planned. You can get her dowry—as you always planned. It will simply be a different daughter, but why not? What's stopping you?"

She sauntered out, and he stood like a statue, listening to her go. Then he staggered over to a chair and sank down.

Marry Libby Carstairs? Shackle himself to the most stubborn, willful female in the kingdom? Why would he deliberately throw himself into such a quagmire? He'd be emasculated in two seconds flat.

But as that message rang in his mind, a louder, more powerful message was drowning it out.

Libby was alone in London, and scoundrels were circling. She was working at another theater where any sort of cretin could slip backstage to accost her. Cads would be tempting her with gifts, jewels, and wicked promises.

Could Luke ignore what was happening? Hadn't he previously vowed that Libby belonged to him and could never belong to anyone else? Did he still think that? And if he did, what was he prepared to do about it?

Chapter
24

Libby meandered backstage, winding around props and crates. She'd finished her performance for the evening and was eager to change her clothes and head home.

The theater had been packed again, with tickets selling like mad. The manager was happy, as were the other actors. The current play wasn't all that interesting, so the income she was generating would keep them working much longer than they might have otherwise. If she hadn't been the main attraction, the audience might not have been half as large.

She entered her changing room and sat at the dressing table so she could study herself in the mirror. She was attired in the simple sort of costume she wore when she told stories about her sojourn on the island with Caroline and Joanna, so she could remove it on her own easily enough.

Her street garments would be harder to arrange, and Fish had abandoned her. In Fish's absence, an actress was supposed to help her, but the woman was occupied until after the show, so she wouldn't be available for many minutes. Libby wasn't an invalid though, so she could get started without an assistant. She was just being petulant and didn't feel she should have to tend herself.

She swallowed her frustration. She understood why Fish had traveled to Roland to renew her doomed affair with Charles. She understood it, but she didn't like it. She didn't want Fish involved with him. It would only lead to heartbreak in the end, so it would be much more difficult for Libby to establish a bond with Charles.

She was aggrieved too at the notion of Simon being married to Penny. She hadn't heard that the reckless pair was back at Roland. She'd asked Fish to send a note once they arrived, but so far, there hadn't been any message.

She constantly envisioned Fish and Simon loafing at Roland, while Libby was alone in London. Of course she could have accompanied Fish, but she wasn't ready. She couldn't deduce how to become Charles's daughter. So much water had passed under the bridge, and she wasn't an aristocrat's child.

In reality, she was Harry Carstairs's child, a girl he'd molded to earn lots of money so he didn't have to earn any himself. She'd been good at it, and she'd had an enormous amount of fun being Libby. She enjoyed the freedom and independence Harry had provided, and she couldn't imagine carrying on any other way.

Charles was planning to publicly claim her, but then what? An earl's daughter could never be employed in a theater. Would she retire to Roland and dawdle there in quiet isolation until the tedium drove her insane?

Yet she yearned to be part of a family, to be valued and cherished as a member. Shouldn't she glom onto Charles and figure out the rest later on?

Though it was humiliating to admit, she was terrified to proceed. She—who'd never been afraid of anything—was afraid she might wedge herself into a spot by Charles's side, but that she'd never fit there.

She had no idea how to be his daughter or Penny's sister. She'd likely jump in with both feet only to have them acknowledge the mistake they'd made in welcoming her, so she'd tarried in London by herself rather than face her fears. It was stupid and cowardly, but there it was.

The door opened, and for a fleeting instant, she smiled, automatically presuming it would be Fish, but recognition swiftly dawned, and her shoulders slumped. Fish was heedlessly pursuing her ridiculous amour at Roland, and Libby was on her own, but then, hadn't she always been on her own?

A male voice spoke from behind her, and she blanched, then whirled on the stool to glare at her intruder.

"Well, well," Luke said, his tone a tad snotty, "if it isn't Little Libby Carstairs, Mystery Girl of the Caribbean."

"What are you doing here, Lord Barrett?"

"You've begun calling me Lord Barrett instead of Luke. Why is that? Are you pretending we aren't intimately attached?"

"Yes, I'm pretending exactly that." She scoffed. "I'm sure it will be a huge blow to your massive ego, but I'm over you."

"Really? Are you positive?"

"Yes, so you can turn around and head off to entertain yourself however a rude, obnoxious nobleman entertains himself on a Saturday night in London."

"I'm not here to be entertained. I rode to town specifically to see you."

"I can't fathom why you would have, so it was a wasted trip. The last time we chatted, I was very clear as to my opinion about you." She frowned, feigning confusion. "Where did it occur again? Oh, that's right. I was in jail because I'd dared to reveal the identity of my father."

"Why are you so angry with me? When I bailed out your sorry behind, I thought you might be a bit grateful."

"I wasn't."

"I could have sworn you were fond of me."

"I was fond—in the past—but any affection has vanished. It faded the minute you accused me of lying about my being Charles's daughter."

"I was an ass about it, wasn't I?"

She was still seated on the stool, and there was one chair in the small room. He grabbed it and put it directly in front of her, then he plopped down on it, sitting so close that their legs were tangled together.

He looked magnificent as ever, dressed in formal evening clothes, a black velvet jacket and trousers, a white shirt, a pristine cravat sewn from the finest Belgian lace. The space surrounding him was full of delicious masculine odors: horses, tobacco, fresh night air.

He was handsome and dashing, and he simply enticed her as no other man had ever been able to manage. Very much against her will, she could feel herself leaning toward him, anxious to fall into his arms and return to that fantastic period when any conclusion had seemed possible between them.

What was wrong with her? Yes, she was desperately attracted to him, but he couldn't give her what she truly desired, that being a devoted husband, so any continuation of their affair was pointless.

Lucas Watson was a walking, talking scoundrel who'd lured her to misbehave, and she had to buck up, grow a spine, and move on.

"Fish stopped by Barrett the other day," he said.

"She can't stand you anymore than I can. Why would she have?"

"First, she was eager to brag about traipsing off to Roland to disgrace herself with Charles."

"If you're about to scold me over it, please don't. I tried to dissuade her, but no one listens to me on any topic."

"I wasn't planning to lecture you," he said. "I just mention it because she's an intriguing female. It's rare to stumble on a woman who is so blunt about her immoral choices. Men can sin with relish, but women aren't allowed such liberty."

"She's always lived however she liked. She's been lucky."

"I suppose some people might believe that."

"I take it you're not one of them."

"No. You see, I'm quite set in my ways. I think a woman's place is in the home, and she should be meek, modest, and deferential to men in all matters."

She snorted with disgust. "Then I'm certain you'll be very delighted with whatever silly debutante you ultimately wed."

She was being an incredible shrew, but polite conversation was beyond her. He overwhelmed her, and she'd erected plenty of mental barriers to keep him at bay. If she let down her guard for a single second, she'd stagger right back into his life. She couldn't and wouldn't do it!

He scrutinized her as if she were a strange insect he'd never encountered before.

"I need to marry, don't I?" he said. "With my being thirty and having inherited my title, I can't delay a decision."

"Yes, the nursery at Barrett Manor must be calling out for you to get busy and pick a bride so you can begin packing it with little Watsons."

"Have you heard about Penny and Simon?"

"Yes, and don't scold me about them either. I warned Simon to leave her alone, but I've never had the power to make him heed me."

"Penny has been very sheltered, and he seems sophisticated and jaded to me. In my view, they don't have much in common. Do you imagine they'll be happy?"

"Happy enough," she churlishly muttered.

She couldn't predict how it would unfold. Simon was charming and charismatic, but he could also be devious and dishonest. Girls threw themselves at him, and he wasn't in the habit of declining their amorous overtures. The word *monogamy* had never entered his vocabulary.

Would he be faithful? Libby couldn't picture it.

Then again, most of his schemes were implemented because he was broke and trying to quickly fill his purse, and Penny was very rich.

Maybe that money would calm him down and he wouldn't be such a charlatan.

She wouldn't talk about any of it with Lord Barrett though. Her relationship with Simon wasn't any of his business.

"After Fish finished crowing about her fling with Charles," he said, "she pointed out an interesting detail with regard to Penny."

"Penny is my new sister, so don't you dare denigrate her."

"I wasn't about to. I like Penny. She's very nice. Not a good choice to have been my wife probably, but nice all the same."

"You just noticed she wasn't a good choice?"

"She was too young and inexperienced for me."

It was Libby's opinion too, but she swallowed down her agreement. "It sounds as if Simon—by running off with her—ensured you dodged a bullet."

"It appears I have." He studied her carefully, an odd gleam in his eye. "I can't have Penny. She'll always be the one who got away, so I have to start searching for someone else."

"Poor, poor you," she murmured.

She couldn't bear to have him expound on the *next* debutante he'd woo. Was that why he was really in town? Was it because Penny had spurned him, so he had to find an heiress just like her?

The whole notion left her extremely bereft. She nearly slid to the floor, curled into a ball, and wept like a baby.

Why couldn't *she* be the woman he needed? Why wasn't she—beautiful, talented, amazing Libby Carstairs—enough for him? Why had she never been *enough* for anyone?

Her temper sparked. "You're determined to wax on about the situation, but I can't believe you'd have the gall to presume I'd commiserate. And you've overstayed your welcome in this dressing room."

She shifted away from him, marched to the door, and yanked it open. She gestured into the hall, indicating he should depart, but he was a vain oaf, and he didn't move. He grinned as if he were a wolf stalking its prey. There was no doubt about it. She was the prey.

"Shut the door, Libby," he said.

"If the show wasn't still in progress at the front of the theater, I'd shout for help and have the stage hands toss you out."

"I'd like to see them try," he boasted. "Where were we? Oh, yes, we were discussing how I have to select another betrothed."

"I won't listen to you blathering on about it!"

The fight went out of her, and she was on the verge of bursting into tears, but she never cried. Harry had drummed out that sort of emotion, so she never displayed much passionate sentiment.

She was simply sad and hurt, and she wished he'd go away so she could head home to her quiet, empty house and her quiet, empty life with no Simon or Fish for company.

He stood and came over, and he shut the door for her. Then he leaned in and trapped her against the wood. Instantly, her torso was on fire with memories of how thrilling it was to be close to him.

"I can marry whoever I want now," he brazenly said, crushing her a bit more.

"Bully for you. I hope you settle on a flighty ninny who makes you miserable forever."

He was unfazed by her fit of pique. "The prospect worries me. I don't have a parent to advise me in this arena, and it's why I was relying so heavily on Charles to guide me."

"Yes, and Charles thought Penny would be a stellar match for you, so I wouldn't necessarily give him any medals for shrewd assessment."

He snorted. "I'd persuaded myself that—since I lost out on Penny—I should once again seek out the perfect aristocratic girl."

"Who would that be?" she snidely asked. "I can just imagine the type of paragon you'd relish."

She squirmed away and walked to the dresser where there was a bottle of wine. She poured herself a glass and took a hefty drink, not because she was thirsty, but because she had to keep her hands busy so she didn't strangle him with them.

Obviously, he had an issue he was anxious to get off his chest, and he wouldn't leave until he had. He was too big for her to push him out, so there was no option but to hurry him along so he'd speak his piece, then go.

He was still leaned on the door and watching her as if she were a frightened rabbit. He was so annoyingly smug, as if he held all the cards. She'd like to bring him down a peg, but with his being such a haughty cretin, she had no idea how.

"I'm averse to scandal," he said.

"Yes, yes, you've been abundantly clear on that subject."

"My brother was such a wastrel, and I'm working hard to clean up my family's name and reputation."

"You couldn't prove it by me," she said. "You were ready to wed Penny, but have me as your mistress, which is a secret that always leaks out. It doesn't sound to me as if you're strolling down a moral path."

"I heartily agree. It was mad for me to pursue you when I was about to betroth myself. With your notoriety being front and center, I couldn't have concealed an affair."

Yes, it had been mad, but it wounded her to have him admit it. Blithely, she retorted, "You were definitely out of control over me. It's refreshing to see how quickly you've come to your senses."

"I've been loafing at Barrett, feeling sorry for myself and focusing on how I like women who are modest, unassuming, and honorably inclined. I was actually writing lists of the attributes I would demand in the next candidate I courted."

She'd never been modest or unassuming. By her growing up in the public eye, it had been impossible to acquire humble traits. She'd tried, but she'd rarely succeeded.

Her mood plummeted to the lowest level ever. Why didn't he depart? Why continue torturing her? It was needlessly cruel.

"I'm sure a splendid bride is waiting for you out there," she glumly said.

"I'm sure she is too," he cheerily concurred, "but after I wrote those stupid lists, guess what I figured out?"

"What?"

"I don't want a modest, unassuming wife. Are you joking? What would I do with a female like that? Now that I've met you, I'd throw myself off a cliff rather than wed someone so boring."

At the bizarre comment, her jaw dropped in astonishment. "You're not serious."

"I don't want an immature debutante. I don't want an heiress whose only redeeming quality is her fat bank account. I don't want an *ordinary* wife."

He emphasized his point by stepping toward her until he was standing beside her. He yanked the wine glass away from her, downed the contents, then smacked the goblet onto the dresser. Then he trapped her against it.

Before she realized what he intended, he dipped down and kissed her fiercely. She hadn't expected it, but her traitorous anatomy leapt into the fire. They carried on as if they were the last two people who would ever kiss, and the wild interlude sent shivers down her spine. She was instantly and gleefully prepared to debase herself in any mortifying way he requested.

Finally, she mustered the energy to stagger away, but she was so off balance that she had to grab the chair so she didn't fall to the floor in a stunned heap.

"You can't just barge in and kiss me!" she fumed.

"Really?" He was all innocence. "No one told me it wasn't allowed."

"I can't dawdle while you brag about your pending nuptial exploits. You're killing me with your stories about matrimony and the fiancée you're about to pick. Go away! Please! Have mercy on me!"

He smirked with irritation. "You ridiculous creature! You've driven me insane, so I have no idea why I'm fussing with you, but I've decided—if I don't resolve this with you—I might have to be locked in an asylum. You've left me that unhinged."

"My condition isn't any better. Why are you here? Will you spit it out and put me out of my misery?"

"I'm *trying* to inform you, but you keep interrupting. Will you listen for once?"

"I'm listening! I'm listening!"

Suddenly, without warning or preamble, he said, "I want to marry you Libby Carstairs or Henrietta Pendleton or whoever the bloody hell you are. I want to marry you!"

"You do not!" The words were out before she could swallow them down.

"I have to be clear with you, don't I? I'm committed to making numerous personal concessions in order to have you. You're magnificent and bewildering and the complete opposite of everything I told myself I sought in a bride, but after we're wed, *I* will be the man of the family. *I* will wear the trousers. Not you! And you will not tell me what to think!"

She studied him, her penetrating gaze digging deep. He looked aggrieved, but very sincere too, and she stammered, "Are you . . . are you . . . proposing?"

"Yes, you daft shrew. Are your ears plugged? I swear, if you refuse to provide the answer I'm demanding, I can't predict how I'll react."

Her knees gave out, and she lurched over and plopped down on the chair.

"You'd like to marry me," she mumbled. "*You,* Lucas Watson, Lord Barrett, would like to wed *me,* Libby Henrietta Pendleton Carstairs. You're deranged to even consider it."

"I am deranged; I won't deny it. You are flamboyant and alluring and divinely beautiful. You constantly entice men until they become obsessed.

With you as my wife, I figure I will suffer perpetual jealousy and resentment over how everyone dotes on you. Yet I'm willing to bind myself anyway."

"Why would you?" she could only ask.

"Don't you know? You silly fool, I love you. I'm not the brightest oaf in the world though, so I didn't understand what was wrong with me. I thought I was about to perish from an undiagnosed illness."

"You don't love me," she insisted. "Don't pretend."

"Haven't we been through this? You will *not* tell me what to think."

He was furious, and she laughed. "All right, all right, but I simply have to mention that you are behaving like a lunatic. I'm worried you'll wake up tomorrow morning and regret your declaration."

"You're correct. I will probably regret this forever. You will drive me mad with lust and joy and wild living. I will have abandoned every bit of propriety and moral rectitude merely for the chance to wallow in your precious company. I will climb any mountain—I will debase myself, humiliate myself—to have you for my very own. Don't you dare claim that dream won't come true."

He appeared genuinely earnest, and she began to shake uncontrollably.

"You need an heiress," she reminded him, "and I'm poor."

"No, you're not. According to the newspapers, you're Lord Roland's daughter. When Fish visited me at Barrett, she apprised me that Charles will give you a dowry. He's generous that way, and he feels guilty that he didn't watch over you when you were small."

"He will not dower me. That's absurd."

"Fish thinks he'll likely confiscate a pile of it from Penny—as punishment for her running off with Simon."

Libby gasped. "I couldn't take it from Penny! I would never permit that."

"Well, *I* would, and any decision would be between Charles and me."

"What do you mean?"

"You have a father now, Libby. Your *father* will pick your husband, and in my view, it should be me. I simply have to approach him and ask for your hand." He puffed himself up, seeming officious and annoying. "Which is precisely how I will proceed if you don't immediately agree to have me. Just say *yes,* and we can avoid all the drama."

"You can't bother Charles about it!"

"I will—if you don't start obliging me."

"Ooh, you're such a bully."

He grinned. "Yes, and I especially like bullying you. I'm amused by how your glorious blue eyes flash with temper when you're angry with me."

"Don't ply me with compliments. They won't work."

"They won't? Then how about this? Fish and Simon—the two people you care most about—will be residing at Roland. It's next door to Barrett. If you stay in London, won't you miss them?"

"I already miss them, and I can't imagine how I'll stumble forward without them. I've never been on my own before."

"If you were with me at Barrett, you'd be able to see them all the time."

"It's cruel of you to drag Fish and Simon into the discussion. You don't play fair."

"I'm desperate, so I'm prepared to pursue desperate measures."

He walked over to her, and to her consternation, he dropped to a knee and clasped hold of her hand. There was only one reason a man put himself in that position, and her trembling grew even more pronounced.

"Lucas Watson," she scolded, "what are you doing?"

"You know what I'm doing. Now hush."

"Don't do this. Don't force me to refuse you."

He scowled ferociously. "You're not refusing me. Remember: If you don't behave, I'll tattle to your father."

"You're insane."

"Yes, very possibly, but if I've tipped off my rocker, you pushed me off it." He leaned in and kissed her again, just a quick brush of his lips to hers, then he said, "I have loved you from the moment we met."

"You couldn't have. You're a confirmed bachelor. Such a demented notion would never have occurred to you."

"I explained the situation, didn't I? I thought I was dying from a peculiar malady, so the truth didn't dawn on me until much later. How could I have guessed it would turn out to simply be a terrible case of loving Libby Carstairs?"

It was such a pretty comment, and she was flummoxed by it. A few chinks in her armor began to appear. When he was sweet, when he was wonderful, it was so hard to keep her distance.

"I might love you too," she grudgingly confessed, "but with my admitting it, you better not tease me."

"I wouldn't dream of it, so would you be silent and listen to me?"

"I would, but you never get to the point."

"I've fought with myself and pretended you were a passing fancy."

"If I recall correctly, you asked me to be your mistress."

"I will always be deeply ashamed of that lurid proposition." His tone and expression sobered. "I have traveled the globe and honorably served my country. I have resigned my commission and journeyed to England to assume my spot as head of the family. Our name is renowned throughout the kingdom, but it was tarnished by my brother. I'm rebuilding what he squandered."

"I realize that, so I can't fathom why you're suggesting we wed. It's why I'm sure you'll regret it in the morning."

"Hush, Libby! I'm sharing something important."

"What is it?"

"I don't care about my reputation. I don't care about tamping down rumors or living a quiet, dreary life in the country. If that sort of existence means I can't have you too, then I'll give it up without a backward glance."

She laid a hand on his cheek. "I'm notorious, and scandal follows me. People glom onto me—men especially—and won't let go. I'm fascinating and exotic, and I'm very independent. I carry on however I please. How would you stand it?"

He drew her hand from his cheek and kissed the center of her palm. "I will tarry off to the side, watching over you as your most steadfast friend. I will cherish and protect you until my dying day. I'm not claiming I'm much of a catch—"

She cut him off. "Don't denigrate yourself to me. You're a fine man."

"But I offer you what I have: my name, my home, and an exalted role as my countess. Say *yes,* Libby-Henrietta. Be my wife."

"Would you demand I cease my performing?"

Gad, was she actually considering his wild scheme? If she would ask such a question, she must be. Obviously, she was as deranged as he was.

"I would never tell you what you could and couldn't do," he said. "I wouldn't be that foolish. You wouldn't heed me anyway, would you?"

"I'd heed you—if you ever voiced a remark that didn't annoy me."

"You're Little Libby Carstairs. You're the Mystery Girl of the Caribbean, and you'll always be her. Even if you become Lady Barrett, even if you become Mrs. Lucas Watson, you'll always be Little Libby and Little Henrietta. I could never take any of that away from you, and I'm certain your fawning admirers wouldn't permit it."

He was still on his knee, prostrate before her, and gazing at her with such affection.

The few weeks they'd been acquainted, where they'd misbehaved so egregiously, had been the best of her life. If she rejected him, when would she ever again be that content? He would be lost to her forever.

He was offering her what she craved. A devoted husband. A beautiful home. And someone to love. Someone who would love her back.

Why wouldn't she consent? Why wouldn't she reach out and grab Luke Watson? Why wouldn't she keep him for her very own?

He dug into his coat and pulled out a ring. It was a simple gold band with a gorgeous sapphire stone in the middle that exactly matched the color of her eyes. He slipped it onto her finger, and it fit perfectly. As she stared down at it, she decided she would never remove it. Not ever.

"Libby-Henrietta," he said, "will you marry me? Will you be my bride once and for all? Will you make me the happiest man in the world?"

She delayed as long as she dared, until he glowered and squirmed. When he grew too impatient, he clasped her waist and gave her a firm shake.

"Answer me, you tempting vixen. Stop being such a tease."

"Yes, Lucas Watson, Lord Barrett, I will marry you. I will be your bride. I'll try to make you happy, but it's more likely I'll drive you mad on a very regular basis."

He smiled and she smiled too, then he rose and lifted her up too as he asked, "Are you sure?"

"Yes, I'm sure."

"You can't get cold feet later on. I won't allow it."

"Let's don't worry about me," she told him. "You're the bachelor in this crazed duo. If anyone gets cold feet, I'm betting it will be you."

"You figure it will be me? Why would it? I'll have you, Libby Carstairs, as my wife for the rest of my days. I'm predicting I'll never have a dull moment."

'I promise you won't."

"Shall we elope to Scotland like Penny and Simon? I'm afraid if you have an opportunity to reflect on this, you'll change your mind."

She studied him, reveling in how handsome he was, how dashing, how marvelous. "We don't need to hurry off to Scotland. I'll never change my mind."

"Swear."

"I swear," she said.

Then he was kissing her, twirling her in circles until they were crashing into the furniture like a pair of drunken fools. Finally, he released her, and he was grinning, preening.

"I knew I could convince you," he arrogantly said. "I never had any doubt about it."

"I won't argue the point," she replied. "With you, I never stood a chance. Not from the very start."

THE END

About the Author

CHERYL HOLT IS A *New York Times, USA Today,* and Amazon "Top 100" bestselling author who has published over fifty novels.

She's also a lawyer and mom, and at age forty, with two babies at home, she started a new career as a commercial fiction writer. She'd hoped to be a suspense novelist, but couldn't sell any of her manuscripts, so she ended up taking a detour into romance where she was stunned to discover that she has a knack for writing some of the world's greatest love stories.

Her books have been released to wide acclaim, and she has won or been nominated for many national awards. She is considered to be one of the masters of the romance genre. For many years, she was hailed as "The Queen of Erotic Romance," and she's also revered as "The International Queen of Villains." She is particularly proud to have been named "Best Storyteller of the Year" by the trade magazine Romantic Times BOOK Reviews.

She lives and writes in Hollywood, California, and she loves to hear from fans. Visit her website at www.cherylholt.com.

CPSIA information can be obtained
at www.ICGtesting.com
Printed in the USA
LVHW031454241220
675096LV00001B/49